Anya and I would never be free to live as normal human beings. There would always be the Creators to pull my strings, never leaving us alone. Always a new task, a new enemy, a new time and place. But never a time and place for happiness. Not for me. Not for us.

She sensed my soul's exhaustion. Stroking my brow with her cool, smooth fingers, Anya soothed, "Sleep, my darling. Rest and sleep."

I slept. But only for the span of a few heartbeats. For I saw Set's satanic face, his red eyes burning, his sharp teeth gleaming in a devil's version of a smile.

"I told you I would send you a punishment, Orion. The hour has come."

I sat bolt upright, startling Anya.

"What is it?"

There was no need to answer. A terrified shriek split the night. From one of the caves.

I grabbed at the spear lying near the cave's entrance and dashed out onto the narrow ledge of rock that formed a natural stairway down to the canyon floor. Others were spilling out of their caves, screaming, jumping to the rocks below. Kraal's men among them, running and shrieking in absolute terror, stumbling down the rough stone steps, leaping to certain injury or death in their panic to escape....

TOR BOOKS BY BEN BOVA

ORION
IN THE
DYING
TIME

BEN BOVA

A TOM DOHERTY ASSOCIATES BOOK
NEW YORK

ORION IN THE DYING TIME

Copyright © 1990 by Ben Bova

A Tor Book
Published by Tom Doherty Associates, Inc.
49 West 24th Street
New York, NY 10010

Cover art by Boris Vallejo

ISBN: 0-812-51429-7

First edition: August 1990
First mass market printing: August 1991

Printed in the United States of America

0 9 8 7 6 5 4 3 2 1

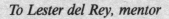

To Lester del Rey, mentor

"An intelligence knowing, at a given instance of time, all forces acting in nature, as well as the momentary position of all things of which the universe consists, would be able to comprehend the motions of the largest bodies of the world and those of the lightest atoms in one single formula, provided his intellect were sufficiently powerful to subject all data to analysis; to him nothing would be uncertain, both past and future would be present in his eyes."

—*Pierre-Simon de Laplace*

What if there were more than one such person?

Prologue

With Anya beside me, I walked out of the ancient temple into the warming sunshine of a new day. All around us a lush green garden grew: flowering shrubs and bountiful fruit trees as far as the eye could see.

Slowly we walked along the bank of the river, the mighty Nile, flowing steadily through all the eons.

"Where in time are we?" I asked.

"The pyramids have not been started yet. The land that will someday be called the Sahara is still a wide grassland teeming with game. Bands of hunting people roam across it freely."

"And this garden? It looks like Eden."

She smiled at me. "Hardly that. It is the home of the creature whose statue stood on the altar."

I glanced back at the little stone temple. It was a simple building, blocks of stone fitted atop one another, with a flat wooden slat roof.

"Someday the Egyptians will worship him as a powerful and dangerous god," Anya told me. "They will call him Set."

"He is one of the Creators?"

"No," she said. "Not one of us. He is an enemy: one of those who seek to twist the continuum to their own purposes."

"As the Golden One does," I said.

She gave me a stern look. "The Golden One, power mad as he is, at least works for the human race."

"He created the human race, he claims."

"He had help," she replied, allowing a small smile to dimple her cheeks.

"But this other creature . . . Set, the one with the lizard's face?"

Her smile vanished. "He comes from a distant world, Orion, and he seeks to eliminate us from the continuum."

"Then why are we here, in this time and place?"

"To find him and destroy him, my love," said Anya. "You and I together, Hunter and Warrior, through all spacetime."

I looked into her glowing eyes and realized that this was my destiny. I am Orion the Hunter. And with this huntress, that warrior goddess, beside me, all the universes were my hunting grounds.

BOOK I

PARADISE

A book of verses underneath the bough
A jug of wine, a loaf of bread—and thou
Beside me singing in the wilderness—
Oh, wilderness were paradise enow!

Chapter 1

Anya pulled off her glittering silvery robe and flung it to the grassy ground. Beneath it she wore a metallic suit of the kind I vaguely remembered from another time, long ages ago. It fit her skintight, from the tops of her silver boots to the high collar that circled her neck. She was a dazzling goddess with long dark hair that tumbled past her shoulders and fathomless gray eyes that held all of time in them.

I wore nothing but the leather kilt and vest from my previous existence in ancient Egypt. The wound that had killed me then had disappeared from my chest. Strapped to my right thigh, beneath the kilt, was the dagger that I had worn in that other time. A pair of rope sandals was my only other possession.

Anya said, "Come, Orion, we must hurry away from this place."

I loved her as eternally and completely as any man has ever worshiped a woman. I had died many deaths for her

sake, and she had defied her fellow Creators to be with me
time and again, in every era to which they had sent me.
Death could not part us. Nor time nor space.

I took her hand in mine and we headed off along a
wide avenue between the heavily laden trees.

For what seemed like hours, Anya and I walked
through the garden, away from the bank of the ageless Nile
flowing patiently through this land that would one day be
called Egypt. The sun rose high but the day remained
deliciously cool, the air clean and crisp as a temperate
springtime afternoon. Cottony clumps of cumulus clouds
dotted the deeply blue sky. A refreshing breeze blew
toward us from what would one day be the pitiless oven of
the Sahara.

Despite her denying it, the garden did remind me of
the legends I had heard of Eden. On both sides of us row
upon row of trees marched as far as the eye could see, yet
no two were the same. Fruits of all kinds hung heavy on
their boughs: figs, olives, plums, pomegranates, even ap-
ples. High above them all swayed stately palms, heavy with
coconuts. Shrubs were set out in carefully planned beds
between the trees, each of them flowering so profusely that
the entire park was ablaze with color.

Yet not another soul was in sight. Between the trees
and shrubbery the grass was clipped to such a uniformly
precise height that it almost seemed artificial. No insects
buzzed. No birds flitted among the greenery.

"Where are we going?" I asked Anya.

"Away from here," she replied, "as quickly as we can."

I reached toward a bush that bore luscious-looking
mangoes. Anya grabbed at my hand.

"No!"

"But I'm hungry."

"It will be better to wait until we are clear of this park.
Otherwise . . ." She glanced back over her shoulder.

"Otherwise an angel will appear with a flaming sword?" I teased.

Anya was totally serious. "Orion, this park is a botanical experimental station for the creature whose statue we saw in the temple."

"The one called Set?"

She nodded. "We are not ready to meet him. We are completely unarmed, unprepared."

"But what harm would it be to eat some of his fruit? We could still hurry along as we ate."

Almost smiling, Anya said, "He is very sensitive about his plants. Somehow he knows when someone touches them."

"And?"

"And he kills them."

"He doesn't drive them into the outer darkness, to earn their bread by the sweat of their brows?" I noticed that even though my tone was bantering, we were walking faster than before.

"No. He kills them. Finally and eternally."

I had died many times, yet the Creators had always revived me to serve them again in another time, another place. Still I feared death, the agony of it, the separation and loss that it brought. And a new tendril of fear flickered along my nerves: Anya was afraid. One of the Creators, a veritable goddess who could move through eons of time as easily as I was walking along this garden path—she was obviously afraid of the reptilian entity whose statue had adorned the temple by the bank of the Nile.

I closed my eyes briefly to picture that statue more clearly. At first I had thought it was a representation of a man wearing a totem mask: the body was human, the face almost like a crocodile's. But now as I scanned my memory of it I saw that this first impression had been overly simple.

The body was humanoid, true enough. It stood on two

legs and had two arms. But the feet were claws with three toes ending in sharply hooked talons. The hands had two long scaly-looking fingers with an opposed thumb for the third digit, all of them clawed. The hips and shoulders connected in nonhuman ways.

And the face. It was the face of a reptile unlike anything I had seen before: a snout filled with serrated teeth for tearing flesh; eyes set forward in the skull for binocular vision; bony projections just above the eyes; a domed cranium that housed a brain large enough to be fully intelligent.

"Now you begin to realize what we are up against," Anya said, reading my thoughts.

"The Golden One sent us here to hunt down this thing called Set and destroy him?" I asked. "Alone? Just the two of us? Without weapons?"

"Not the Golden One, Orion. The entire council of the Creators. The whole assemblage of them."

The ones whom the ancient Greeks had called gods, who lived in their own Olympian world in the distant future of this time.

"The entire assemblage," I repeated. "That means you agreed to the task."

"To be with you," Anya said. "They were going to send you alone, but I insisted that I come with you."

"I am expendable," I said.

"Not to me." And I loved her all the more for it.

"You said this creature called Set—"

"He is not a creature of ours, Orion," Anya swiftly corrected. "The Creators did not bring him into being, as we did the human race. He comes from another world and he seeks to destroy the Creators."

"Destroy . . . even you?"

She smiled at me, and it was if another sun had risen. "Even me, my love."

"You said he can cause final death, without hope of revival."

Anya's smile disappeared. "He and his kind have vast powers. If they can alter the continuum deeply enough to destroy the Creators, then our deaths will be final and irrevocable."

Many times over the eons I had thought that the release of death would be preferable to the suffering toil of a life spent in pain and danger. But each time the thought of Anya, of this goddess whom I loved and who loved me, made me strive for life. Now we were together at last, but the threat of ultimate oblivion hung over us like a cloud blotting out the sun.

We walked on until the lines of trees abruptly ended. Standing in the shade of the last wide-branched chestnut, we looked out on a sea of grass. Wild uncut grass as far as the limestone cliffs that jutted into the bright summer sky, marking the edge of the Nile-cut valley. Windblown waves curled through the waving fronds of grass like green surges of surf rushing toward us.

Silhouetted against the distant cliffs I saw a few dark specks moving slowly. I pointed toward them and Anya followed my outstretched arm with her eyes.

"Humans," she muttered. "A crew of slaves."

"Slaves?"

"Yes. Look at what's guarding them."

Chapter 2

focused my eyes intently on the distant figures. I have always been able to control consciously all the functions of my body, direct my will along the chain of neural synapses instantly to make any part of my body do exactly what I wished it to do.

Now I concentrated on the line of human beings trudging across the grassy landscape. They were being led by something not human.

At first it reminded me of a dinosaur, but I knew that the great reptilians had become extinct millions of years before this time. Or had they? If the Creators could twist time to their whim, and this alien called Set had comparable powers, why not a dinosaur here in the Neolithic era?

It walked on four slim legs and had a long whiplike tail twitching behind it. Its neck was long, too, so that its total length was nearly twenty feet, about the size of a full-grown African bull elephant. But it was much less bulky, slimmer, more graceful. I got the impression that it could run faster than a man.

Its scales were brightly colored in bands of red, blue, yellow, and brown. Horny projections of bone studded its back like rows of buttons. The head at the end of that elongated neck was small, with a short stubby snout and eyes set wide apart on either side of a rounded skull. Its eyes were slitted, unblinking.

It strode up at the front of the little column of humans, and every few moments turned its long neck back to look at the slaves it led.

And they were slaves, that was obvious. Fourteen men and women, wearing nothing but tattered loincloths, emaciated ribs showing clearly even at the distance from which we watched. They seemed exhausted, laboring for breath as they struggled to keep up to the pace set by their reptilian guard. One of the women carried a baby in a sling on her back. Two of the men looked like teenagers to me. There was only one gray head among them. I got the impression they rarely lived long enough to become gray.

Hiding behind the bole of the chestnut tree at the edge of the garden, we watched the pitiful little parade for several silent moments.

Then I asked, "Why slaves?"

Anya whispered, "To tend this garden, of course. And the other desires of Set and his minions."

The woman with the baby stumbled and fell to her knees. The giant reptile instantly wheeled around and trotted up to her, looming over her. Even from this distance I could hear the faint wailing of the baby.

The woman struggled to her feet, or tried to. Not fast enough for the guard. Its slim tail whipped viciously across her back, striking the baby as well. She screamed and the baby shrieked with pain and terror.

Again the tail flicked back and struck at her. She fell facedown on the grass.

I strained forward, but Anya grasped my arm and held me back.

"No," she whispered urgently. "There's nothing you can do."

The huge lizard was standing over the prostrate mother, bending its neck to sniff at her unmoving form. The baby still wailed. The other men and women stood unmoving, mute as statues.

"Why don't they fight?" I seethed.

Anya replied, "With their bare hands against that monster?"

"They could at least run away while its attention is diverted. Scatter—"

"They know better, Orion. They would be hunted down like animals and killed very slowly."

The lizard was squatting on its two rear legs and tail now, nudging the woman's body with one of its clawed forepaws. She did not move.

Then the beast pulled the infant out of the sling and lifted it high, swinging its head upward as it did so. I realized it was going to crunch the baby in its jaws.

Nothing could hold me back now. I bolted out from the protection of the trees and raced pell-mell toward the monster, bellowing loudly as I could while I ran. All my bodily senses went into hyperdrive, as they always do when I face danger. The world around me seemed to slow down, everything moved with an almost dreamlike languor.

I saw the lizard holding the squalling baby aloft, saw its head turning toward me on the end of that long snaky neck, saw its narrow slit eyes register on me, its head bobbing back and forth as if it were saying no. In reality it was merely trying to get a fix with both eyes on what was making the noise.

I saw the baby still clutched in the lizard's claws, its tiny legs churning in the empty air, its blubbering face contorted and red with crying. And the mother, her naked back livid with the welts from the beast's tail, was pushing herself up on one elbow in a futile effort to reach her baby.

The lizard dropped the baby and turned to face me, hissing. Its tongue darted out of its tiny mouth as its head bobbed left and right. The tail flicked as it dropped to all fours.

I had my dagger in my right hand. It seemed pitifully small against the talons on the monster's paws, but it was the only weapon I possessed. As I closed the distance between us I saw the other humans standing behind the lizard. My brain registered that they were totally cowed, unmoving, not even trying to get away or distract the beast in any manner. I would get no help from them.

The lizard took a few trotting steps toward me, then reared up on its hind legs like an enraged bear. It towered over me, advancing on those monstrous clawed hind legs while its neck bent down between its wide-spread forelegs, hissing at me. Its teeth were small and flat, I saw. Not a flesh-eater. Just a killing machine.

Suddenly bright yellow frills snapped open on both sides of its neck, making its head appear twice as large; a trick for frightening enemies, but I knew it for what it was.

I ran straight at the big lizard and saw its long tail whipping toward my left. Like a slow-motion dream I watched its tip swinging toward me. I gauged its speed and jumped over it as it snapped harmlessly beneath my feet. My impetus carried me straight toward the lizard's scaled underside and I sank my dagger blade into its belly with every ounce of my strength.

It screeched like a steam whistle and reached to grab me. I ducked under the clutching claws and plunged my dagger into its hide again.

In the heat of battle I had forgotten about its tail. It caught me this time, knocking me off my feet. I hit the ground with a thud that made me grunt with pain and surprise. The lizard reached for me again, but with my

senses in hyperdrive I could see its every move easily and
rolled away from those clutching claws.

The tail slashed at me again. I stepped inside its arc
and carved a bloody slice down the lizard's thigh. My blade
caught bone and I worked it in deeper, hoping to disable its
knee joint and cripple it. Instead I felt its claws circle
around me, cutting into my midsection as it yanked me
high into the air. The dagger was wrenched from my grasp,
still stuck in its knee.

It carried me up above its head and I saw those narrow
yellow reptilian eyes staring coldly at me, first one and then
the other. Its teeth were not made for rending flesh but
those jaws could crush my body quite easily, I knew. That
was just what the beast was going to do. Its yellow collar
frills relaxed slightly; the monster no longer felt threatened.

I strained to break free of the demon's claws, but I was
just as helpless as the baby had been moments before.

"Orion! Here!"

Anya's voice made me glance down while I struggled
in the lizard's powerful grip. She had come up behind me
and was pulling my knife out of the lizard's knee. Before
the beast understood what was happening, she threw the
dagger as expertly as any assassin. It pierced the soft folds
beneath the lizard's jaw with a satisfying *thunk*.

With its free hand the dragon started to reach for the
steel in its throat. But I was closer and faster. I grabbed the
projecting hilt of the dagger and began working the blade
across the lizard's jawline, back toward the frills that had
snapped fully erect once again. It shrieked and released me,
but I clutched at its neck and swung up behind its head,
pulling the dagger free and jamming it in beneath the base
of the skull.

It collapsed as suddenly as a light being switched off. I
had severed its spinal cord. The two of us came crashing
down to the grassy ground. I felt myself bounce and then
everything went blank.

Chapter 3

I opened my eyes and focused blearily on Anya's beautiful face. She was kneeling over me, deep concern etched across her classic features. Then she smiled.

"Are you all right?" she asked.

I ached in every part of my body. My chest and thighs were slashed from the lizard's claws. But I consciously clamped down on the capillaries to stop the bleeding and closed off the pain centers in my brain. I made myself grin up at her.

"I'm alive."

She helped me to my feet. I saw that only a few moments had passed. The big lizard was now nothing more than a huge mound of brightly colored scales stretched out across the grass.

The crew of slaves, however, was something else. The slaves were terrified. And instead of being grateful, they were angry.

"You have slain one of the guardians!" said a scrawny

bearded man, his eyes wide with terror.

"The masters will blame us!" one of the women wailed.

"We will be punished!"

I felt something close to contempt for them. They had the mentality of true slaves. Instead of thanking me for helping them, they were fearful of their master's wrath. Without a word I went to the dead beast and pulled my dagger from the back of its neck.

Anya said to them, "We could not stand idly and watch the monster kill the baby."

The baby, I saw, was alive. The mother was sitting silently on the grass, holding the child to her emaciated breast, her huge brown eyes staring at me blankly. If she was grateful for what I had done, she was hiding it well. Two long red weals scarred her ribs and back. The baby also had a livid welt across its naked flesh.

But the scrawny man was tugging at his tangled gray beard and moaning, "The masters will descend upon us and kill us all with great pain. They will put us in the fire that never dies. All of us!"

"It would have been better to let the baby die," said another man, equally gaunt, his hair and beard also filthy and matted. "Better that one dies than all of us are tortured to death. We can always make more babies."

"If your masters do not find you, they cannot punish you," I said. "If the two of us can kill one of these overgrown lizards, then all of us can work together to protect ourselves against them."

"Impossible!"

"Where could we hide that they will not find us?"

"They have eyes that see in the night."

"They can fly through the air and even cross the great river."

"Their claws are sharp. And they have the eternal fire."

As they spoke they clustered around Anya and me, as if seeking protection. And they constantly looked up into the sky and scanned the horizon, as if seeking the first sign of avenging dragons. Or worse.

Anya asked them in a gentle voice, "What will happen to you if the two of us go away and leave you alone?"

"The masters will see what has happened here and punish us," said the beard tugger. He seemed to be their leader, perhaps merely by the fact that he was their eldest.

"How will they punish you?" I asked.

He shrugged his bony shoulders. "That is for them to decide."

"They will flay the skin from our bodies," said one of the teenagers, "and then cast us into the eternal fire."

The others shuddered. Their eyes were wide and pleading.

"Suppose we stayed here with you until your masters find us," I asked. "Will they punish you if we tell them that we killed the beast and you had nothing to do with it?"

They gaped at us as if we were stupid children. "Of course they will punish us! They will punish every one of us. That is the law."

I turned to Anya. "Then we've got to get away."

"And bring them with us," she agreed.

I scanned the area where we stood. The Nile had cut a broad, deep valley through the limestone cliffs that rose like jagged walls on either side of the river. Atop the cliffs, according to Anya, was a wide grassy plain. If this region would truly become the Sahara one day, then it must stretch for hundreds of miles southward, thousands of miles to the west. A flat open savannah, with only an occasional hill or river-carved valley to break the plain's flat monotony. Not good country to hide in, especially from creatures that can fly through the air and see in the dark. But better than being penned between the river and the cliffs.

I had no doubt that the slaves were telling the truth about their reptilian masters. The beast Anya and I had just slain was a dinosaur, that seemed certain. Why not winged pterosaurs, then, or other reptiles that can sense heat the way a pit viper does?

"Are there trees nearby?" Anya was asking them. "Not like the garden, but wild trees, a natural forest."

"Oh," said the scrawny elder. "You mean Paradise."

Far to the south, he told us, there were forest and streams and game animals in endless abundance. But the area was forbidden to them. The masters would not let them return there.

"You lived there once?" I asked.

"Long, long ago," he said wistfully. "When I was even younger than Chron here." He pointed at the smaller of the two teenage boys.

"How far away is it?"

"Many suns."

Pointing southward, I said, "Then we head for Paradise."

They made no objection, but it was clear to see that they were terrified. The spirit had been beaten out of them almost totally. Yet even if they did not want to follow my lead, they had no real alternative. Their masters had frightened them so completely that it made no difference to them which way they went; they were certain that they would be caught and punished most horribly.

My first aim was to get away from the carcass of the lizard. It would take a while for whoever was in charge of the garden—Set, I supposed—to realize that one of his trained animals had been killed and a crew of slaves was loose on the landscape. We had perhaps a few hours, and by then it would be nightfall. If we could move quickly enough, we might have a chance to survive.

We climbed the cliff face. It was not as difficult as I had feared; the stone was broken and tiered into what seemed almost like stairways. They puffed and gasped and struggled their way up to the top with me leading them and Anya bringing up the rear.

At the summit I saw that Anya had been right. An endless rolling plain of grass stretched out to the horizon, green and lush and seemingly empty of animal life. A broad treeless savannah that extended all the way across the northern sweep of Africa to the very shore of the Atlantic. To the south, according to the gray-bearded slave, was the forest land he called Paradise.

Pointing with my left hand, I commanded, "Southward."

I set as brisk a pace as I could, and the slaves half trotted behind me, gasping and groaning. They did not complain, perhaps because they did not have the breath to. But each time I glanced back over my shoulder to see if they were keeping up, they were glancing back over their shoulders in fear of the inevitable.

I had hardly worked up a sweat despite the warm sun slanting down on us from near the western horizon. I associated the sun with the Golden One, the Creator who called himself Ormazd in one era and Apollo in another, the half-mad megalomaniac who had created me to hunt down his enemies across the span of the eons.

"You must let them rest," Anya said, jogging easily beside me through the knee-high wild grass. "They are exhausted."

I reluctantly agreed. Up ahead I saw a small hill. Once we reached its base I stopped. All of the slaves immediately sprawled on the ground, wheezing painfully, rivers of sweat cutting grimy streaks through the dirt that crusted their bodies.

I climbed to the hilltop, less than thirty feet high, and scanned the view. Not a tree in sight. Nothing but trackless savannah in every direction. In a way it was thrilling to be in a time and place where no human feet had yet beaten out paths and trails. The sky was turning a blazing vermilion now along the western horizon. Higher up, the blue vault was deepening into a soft violet. There was already a star shining up there, even though we were far from twilight.

A single star, brighter than any I remembered seeing in any era. It did not twinkle at all, but shone with a constant ruddy, almost brownish light, bright and big enough to make me think that I could see a true disk instead of a mere pinpoint of light. The planet Mars? No, it was brighter than Mars had ever been, even in the clear skies of Troy, thousands of years in this era's future. And its color was darker than the bright ruby red of Mars, a brooding brownish red, almost like drying blood. Nor could it be Antares: that great red giant in the Scorpion's heart twinkled like all other true stars.

A shriek of fear startled me out of my astronomical musings.

"Look!"

"He comes!"

"They are searching for us!"

I followed the outstretched emaciated arms of my newfound companions and saw a pair of winged creatures crisscrossing the darkening sky to the northeast of us. Pterosaurs, sure enough. Enormous leathery wings flapping lazily every few heartbeats, then a slow easy glide as their long pointed beaks aimed down toward the ground. They were searching for us, no doubt of it.

"Stay absolutely still," I commanded. "Lie down on the ground and don't move!"

Winged reptiles flying that high depended on their vision above all other senses. My crew of scrawny slaves were as brown as dirt. If they did not attract attention by moving, perhaps the pterosaurs would not recognize them. They hugged the ground, half-hidden even from my view by the long grass.

But I saw the long rays of the setting sun glittering off

Anya's metallic suit. For an instant I wanted to tell her to move into the shadow of the hill. But there was no time, and the motion would have caught the beady eyes of the searching pterosaurs. So I stretched myself out flat on the crest of the little hill and hoped desperately that the winged reptiles were not brainy enough to realize that a metallic glinting was something they should investigate further.

It seemed like hours as the giant fliers soared slowly across the sky, crisscrossing time and again in an obvious hunting pattern. They may have looked ugly and ungainly on the ground, with their long beaks and balancing bony crests extending rearward from their heads, but in the air they were nothing less than magnificent. They flew with hardly any effort at all, soaring along gracefully on the warm air currents rising from the grassy plain.

They passed us by at last and disappeared to the west. Once they were out of sight I got to my feet and started southward again. The slaves followed eagerly, without a grumble. Fear inspired them with new strength.

As the sun touched the green horizon I spotted a clump of trees in the distance. We hurried toward them and saw that a small stream had cut a shallow gorge through the grassland. Its muddy banks were overshadowed by the leafy trees.

"We can camp here for the night," I said. "Under the trees, with plenty of water."

"And what do we eat?" whined the elder.

I looked down at him, more in exasperation than anger. A true slave, waiting for someone to provide him with food rather than trying to get it for himself.

"What is your name?" I asked.

"Noch," he said, his eyes suddenly fearful.

Clasping his thin shoulder in my hand, I said, "Well, Noch, my name is Orion. I am a hunter. Tonight I will find you something to eat. Tomorrow you begin to learn for yourselves how to hunt."

Cutting a small branch from one of the trees, I whittled as sharp a point as I could on one end while the young Chron watched me avidly.

"Do you want to learn how to hunt?" I asked him.

Even in the shadows of dusk I could see his eyes gleam. "Yes!"

"Then come with me."

It could hardly be called hunting. The small game that lived by the stream had never encountered humans before. The animals were so tame that I could walk right up to them and spear one of them as it drank at the water's edge. Its companions scampered away briefly, but soon returned. It took only a few minutes to bag a brace of raccoons and three rabbits.

Chron watched eagerly. Then I let him have the makeshift spear, and after a few clumsy misses, he nailed a ground squirrel, squealing and screeching its last breath.

"That was the enjoyable part," I told him. "Now we must skin our kills and prepare them for cooking."

I did all that work, since we had only the one knife and I had no intention of letting any of the others touch it. As I skinned and gutted our tiny catch, to the avid eyes of the whole little tribe, I worried about a fire. If there were reptiles out there that could sense heat the way a rattlesnake or a cobra does, even a small cooking fire would be like a blazing beacon to them.

But there seemed to be no such reptiles in the area. The pterosaurs had passed us by hours earlier, and I had seen no other reptilians in this open savannah, not even the tiniest of lizards. Nothing but small mammals—and we few humans.

I decided to risk a fire, just large enough for cooking our catch, to be extinguished as soon as the cooking was done.

Anya surprised me by showing she could light a fire with nothing more than a pair of sticks and some sweat.

The others gaped in astonishment as wisps of smoke and then a flicker of flame rose from Anya's rubbing sticks.

Gray-bearded old Noch, kneeling next to her, said in an awed voice, "I remember my father making fire in the same way—before he was killed by the masters and I was taken away from Paradise."

"The masters have the eternal fire," said a woman's voice from out of the flickering shadows.

But none of the others seemed concerned with that now, not with the delicious aroma of roasting meat making them salivate and their stomachs rumble.

After we had eaten and most of the tribe had drifted off into sleep I asked Anya, "Where did you learn to make fire?"

"From you," she answered. Looking into my eyes, she added, "Don't you remember?"

I could feel my brows knitting with concentration. "Cold—I remember the snow and ice, and a small team of men and women. We were wearing uniforms. . . ."

Anya's eyes seemed to glow in the night shadows. "You *do* remember! You can break through the programming and remember earlier existences."

"I don't remember much," I said.

"But the Golden One wiped your memory clean after each existence. Or tried to. Orion, you are growing stronger. Your powers are growing."

I was more concerned with our present problems. "How do the Creators expect us to deal with Set with nothing but our bare hands?"

"They don't, Orion. Now that we have established ourselves in this era we can return to the Creators and bring back whatever we need: tools, weapons, machines, warriors . . . anything."

"Warriors? Like me? Human beings manufactured by the Golden One or the other Creators and sent back in time to do their dirty work?"

With a tolerant sigh, Anya replied, "You can hardly expect them to come themselves and do the fighting. They are not warriors."

"But *you* are here. Fighting. That monster would have killed me if you hadn't been there."

"I am an atavism," she said, almost with pleasure in her voice. "A warrior. A woman foolish enough to fall in love with one of our own creatures."

The fire had long been smothered in mud, and the only light sifting through the trees came from the cold white alabaster of the moon. It was enough for me to see how beautiful Anya was, enough to make me burn with love for her.

"Can we go to the Creators' realm and then return here, to this exact place and time?"

"Yes, of course."

"Even if we spend hours and hours?"

"Orion, in the realm of the Creators there is a splendid temple atop a crag of marble that is my favorite retreat. We could go there and spend hours, or days, or months, if you wish."

"I do wish it!"

She kissed me gently, merely a brushing of lips. "Then we will go there."

Anya put her hand in mine. Reflexively, I closed my eyes. But I felt nothing, and when I opened my eyes, we were still in the miserable little camp by the muddy bank of a Neolithic stream.

"What happened?"

Anya's whole body was stiff with tension. "It didn't work. Something—some*one*—is blocking access to the continuum."

"Blocking access?" I heard my own voice as if a stranger's: high-pitched with sudden fear.

"We're trapped here, Orion!" said Anya, frightened herself. "Trapped!"

Chapter 4

Now I knew something of how the tribe of ex-slaves felt.

It was easy to feel brave and confident when I knew that all the paths of the continuum were open to me. Knew that I could travel through time as easily as stepping through a doorway. Certainly I could feel pity, even contempt, for these cowardly humans who bowed down to the terrifying reptilian masters. I could leave this time and place at will, as long as Anya was with me to lead the way.

But now we were trapped, the way was cut off, and I felt the deep lurking dread of forces and powers far beyond my own control looming over me as balefully as final, implacable death.

We had no choice except to press on southward, hoping to reach the forests of Paradise before Set's scouting pterosaurs located us. Each morning we rose and trekked toward the distant southern horizon. Each night we made camp in the best available protective foliage we could find.

The men were learning to hunt the small game that abounded in this endless grassy veldt, the women gathered fruits and berries.

Each time we saw pterosaurs quartering the skies above us we went to ground and froze like mice faced with a hunting hawk. Then we resumed our march to the south. Toward Paradise. And the horizon remained just as flat, just as far away, as it had been the first day we had started.

Sometimes in the distance we saw herds of grazing animals, big beasts the size of bison or elk. Once we stumbled close enough to them to see a pride of saber-toothed cats stalking the herd's fringes; the females sleek and deadly as they prowled through the long grass, bellies almost on the ground, the males massive with their scimitarlike incisors and shaggy manes. They ignored us, and we steered as far away from them as we could.

Anya troubled me. I had never seen her look frightened before, but frightened she was now. I knew she was trying each night to make contact with the other Creators, those godlike men and women from the distant future who had created the human race. They had created me to be their hunter, and I had served them with growing reluctance over the millennia. Gradually I was remembering other missions, other lives. Other deaths.

Once I had been with another tribe of Neolithic hunter/gatherers, far from this monotonous savannah, in the hilly country near Ararat. In another time I had led a desperate band of abandoned soldiers through the snows of the Ice Age in the aftermath of our slaughter of the Neanderthals.

Anya had always been there with me, often disguised as an ordinary human being of that time and place, always ready to protect me even in the face of the displeasure of the other Creators.

Now we trekked toward a Paradise that may be nothing more than a half-remembered legend, fleeing devilish monsters who had apparently taken total control of this aspect of the continuum. And Anya was as helpless as any of us.

Some nights we made love, coupling as the others did, on the ground in the dark, silently, furtively, not wanting the others to see or hear us, as though what we were doing was shameful. Our passions were brief, spiritless, far from satisfying.

It was several nights before I realized that the mother whom I had saved from the lizard's punishment had taken to sleeping beside me. She and her baby remained several body lengths away the first night, but each evening she moved closer. Anya noticed, too, and spoke gently with her.

"Her name is Reeva," Anya told me as we marched the following morning. "Her husband was beaten to death by the guard lizards for trying to steal extra food for her so she could nurse the baby."

"But why—"

"You protected her. You saved her and her baby. She is very shy, but she is trying to work up the courage to tell you that she will be your number-two woman, if you will have her."

I felt more confusion than surprise. "But I don't want another woman!"

"Shhh," Anya cautioned, even though we were not speaking in the language of these people. "You must not reject her openly. She wants a protector for her child and she is willing to offer her body in return for your protection."

I cast a furtive glance at Reeva. She could not have been more than fourteen or fifteen years old. As thin as a piece of string, caked with days' worth of grime, her long hair matted and filthy. She carried the sleeping baby on one bony hip and walked along in uncomplaining silence with the rest of the tribe.

Anya, who bathed whenever we found enough water and privacy, seemed to be taking the situation lightly. She seemed almost amused.

"Can't you make Reeva understand," I virtually pleaded with her, "that I will do the best I can to protect all of us? I don't need her . . . enticements."

Anya grinned at me and said nothing.

Each night that baleful star looked down at us, like a glowing blot of dried blood, bright enough to cast shadows, brighter even than the full moon. Sunrise did not blot it out; it lingered in the morning sky until it dropped below the horizon. It could not be any planet that I knew of; it could not be an artificial satellite. It simply hung in its place among the other stars, unblinking, menacing, blood-chilling.

One night I asked Anya if she knew what it was.

She gazed at it for long moments, and its dark light made her lovely face seem grim and ashen. Then tears welled up in her eyes and she shook her head.

"I don't know," she answered in a whisper that carried untold misery. "I don't know *anything* anymore!"

She tried to stifle her tears, but she could not. Sobbing, she pressed her face against my shoulder so that the others would not hear her crying. I held her tightly, feeling strange, uncomfortable. I had never seen a goddess cry before.

By my count, it was on the eleventh day when young Chron came dashing back toward me with an ear-to-ear grin on his face.

"Up on the hill! I can see trees! Lots of trees!"

The teenager had taken to scouting slightly ahead of the rest of us. For all our wearying march and the terror that drove us onward, the tribe was actually in better physical condition now than when I had first stumbled across them. They were eating regularly, and a protein-rich diet at that. Skinny little Chron looked better and certainly had more energy than he had shown only ten days earlier. The hollow places between his ribs were beginning to fill in.

I went up to the top of the hillock with him and, sure enough, the distant horizon was no longer a flat expanse of grass. It was an undulating skyline of trees, waving to us, beckoning.

"Paradise!" Noch had come up to stand beside me. His voice trembled with joy and anticipation.

We headed eagerly for the trees, and even though it took the rest of the day, we finally entered their cool shade and threw ourselves exhausted on the mossy ground.

All around us towered broad-spreading oaks and lofty pines, spruce and balsam firs, the lovely slim white boles of young birch punctuating this world of leafy green. Ferns and mosses covered the ground. I saw mushrooms clustered between the roots of a massive old oak tree, and flowers waving daintily in the soft breeze.

An enormous feeling of relief washed over us all, a sense of safety, of being in a place where the terrible fear that had hovered over us was at last dissipated and driven away. Birds were singing in the boughs high above us, as if welcoming us to Paradise.

I sat up and took a deep breath of clean, sweet air redolent of pine and wild roses and cinnamon. Even Anya looked happy. We could hear the splashing of a brook nearby, beyond the bushes and young saplings that stood between the sturdy boles of the grown trees.

A doe stepped daintily out of those bushes and regarded us for a moment with large, liquid brown eyes. Then it turned and dashed off.

"What did I tell you, Orion?" Noch beamed happily. "This is Paradise!"

The men used the rudimentary hunting skills I had taught them to trap and kill a wild pig that evening as it came down to the brook to drink. They showed more enthusiasm than skill, and the pig screeched and squealed and nearly got away before they finally hacked it to death with their makeshift spears. But we feasted long into the night and then went to sleep.

Anya curled into my arms and fell asleep almost immediately. As our fire died slowly into embers I gazed down on her face, smudged and stained with grease from our pork dinner. Her hair was tangled and stubborn ringlets fell over her forehead. Despite her best efforts she was no longer the smoothly groomed goddess from a far superior culture. I remembered vaguely another existence, with that other hunting tribe, where she had become one of them, a fierce priestess who reveled in the blood and excitement of the hunt.

It would not be so bad to stay in this time, I thought. Being cut off from the other Creators had its compensations. We were free of their schemes and machinations. Free of the responsibilities they had loaded upon me. Anya and I could live here in this Paradise quite happily like two normal human beings; no longer goddess and creature, but simply a man and a woman living out normal lives in a simple, primitive time.

To live a normal life, free of the Creators. I smiled to myself in the darkness, and for the first time since we had arrived in this time and place, I let myself fall completely and unguardedly into a deep delicious sleep.

But with sleep came a dream. No, not a dream: a message. A warning.

I saw the statue of Set from that little stone temple back along the bank of the Nile. As I watched, the statue shimmered and came to life. The blank granite eyes turned carnelian, blinked slowly, then focused upon me. The scaly head turned and lowered slightly. A wave of utterly dry heat seemed to bake the strength from my body; it was as if the door to a giant furnace had suddenly swung open. The acrid smell of sulfur burned my lungs. Set's mouth opened in a hissing intake of breath, revealing several rows of sharply pointed teeth.

He was an overpowering presence. He loomed over me, standing on two legs that ended in clawed feet. His long tail flicked back and forth slowly as he regarded me the way a powerful predator might regard a particularly helpless and stupid victim.

"You are Orion."

He did not speak the words; I heard them in my mind. The voice seethed with malevolence, with an evil so deep and complete that my knees went weak.

"I am Set, master of this world. You have been sent to destroy me. Abandon all hope, foolish man. That is manifestly impossible."

I could not speak, could not even move. It had been the same when I had first been created by the Golden One. His presence had also paralyzed me. He had built such a reaction into my brain. Yet even so, I had learned to overcome it, somewhat. Now this monstrous apparition of evil held me in thrall even more completely than the Golden One ever had. I knew, with utter certainty, that Set could still my breath with a glance, could make my heart stop with a blink of his burning red eyes.

"Your Creators fear me, and justly so. I will destroy them and all their works utterly, beginning with you."

I struggled to move, to say something back to him, but I could not control any part of my body.

"You think you have struck a blow against me by killing one of my creatures and stealing a miserable band of slaves from my garden."

The terror that Set struck in me went beyond reason, beyond sanity. I realized that I was gazing upon the human race's primal fear, the image that would one day be called Satan.

"You think that you are safe from my punishment now that you have reached your so-called Paradise," Set went on, his words burning themselves into my mind.

He was incapable of laughter, but I felt acid-hot amusement in his tone as he said, "I will send you a punishment that will make those pitiful wretches beg for death and the eternal fire. Even in your Paradise I will send you a punishment that will seek you out in the darkest night and make you scream for mercy. Not this night. Perhaps not for many nights to come. But soon enough."

I was already screaming with the effort of trying to break free of his mental grasp. But my screams were silent, I did not have the power to voice them. I could not even sweat, despite bending every gram of my strength to battle against his hold over me.

"Do not bother to fight against me, human. Enjoy what little shreds of life you have remaining to you. I will destroy you all, including the woman you love, the self-styled goddess. She will die the most painful death of all."

And suddenly I *was* screaming, roaring my lungs out. Sitting up on the mossy ground beneath the trees of Paradise as the sun rose on a new day, bellowing with terror and horror and the self-hate that comes from weakness.

Chapter 5

The others clustered around me, eyes wide, questioning.

"What is it, Orion?"

"Nothing," I said. "A bad dream, nothing more." But I was soaked with cold sweat, and had to consciously control my nerves to keep from trembling.

They asked me to relate the dream to them so they might interpret it. I told them I could not remember any of it and eventually they left me in peace.

But they were clearly unsettled. And Anya regarded me with probing eyes. She knew that it would take something much more than an ordinary nightmare to make me scream.

"Come on," I said to them all. "We must move deeper into these woods, away from the grassland." As far away from Set as possible, I meant, even though I did not say the words aloud.

Anya walked beside me. "Was it the Golden One?" she

asked. "Or one of the other Creators?"

With a shake of my head I answered with one word: "Set."

The color drained from her face.

For several days more we traveled through the forest, following the brook as it led to a wider stream that seemed to flow southward. The men all had spears now, and I was teaching them to fire-harden their points. I wanted to find a place where there was flint and quartz so we could begin making stone tools and weapons.

Birds flitted through the trees, bright flashes of color in the greenery. Insects buzzed a constant background hum. Squirrels and other furry little mammals scampered up tree trunks at our approach and then stopped, tails twitching, watching until we hiked past them. My sense of danger eased, my fear of Set's lurking presence slowly diminished, as we moved deeper into this cool peaceful friendly forest.

It was peaceful and friendly by day. Night was a different matter. The world was different in the dark. Even with a sizable campfire to warm and light us the forest took on a menacing, ominous aspect in the darkness. Shadows flickered like living things. Hoots and moans floated through the misty gloom. Even the tree trunks themselves became black twisted forms reaching out to ensnare. Cold tendrils of fog hovered like ghosts just beyond the warmth of our fire, creeping closer as the flames weakened and died.

Our little band endured the dark frightening nights, sleeping fitfully, bothered by restless dreams and fears of things lurking in the shadows beyond our sight. We marched in the light of day when the forest was cheerful with the calls of birds and bright with mottled sunshine filtering through the tall trees. At night we huddled in fear of the unseeable.

At last we came to a line of high rugged cliffs where the

stream—a fair-sized river now—had cut through solid stone. Following the narrow trail between the water's edge and the cliff, we found a hollowed-out area, as if a huge semicircular chunk of stone had been scooped out of the cliff by a giant's powerful hand.

I left Anya and the others by the river's edge while I went in to explore this towering bowl of stone. Its curving walls rose high above me, layered in tiers of ocher, yellow, and the gray of granite. Pinnacles of rock rose like citadels on either side of the bowl, standing straight and high against the bright blue sky.

Through the screen of brush and young trees that covered the boulder-strewn floor of the little canyon I saw the dark eyes of caves up along the bowl's curving wall. Water and woods near at hand, a good defensive location with a clear view of any approaching enemy.

"We will make this our camp," I called back to the others, who were resting by the river's edge.

". . . this our camp," came an echo rebounding from the bowl of rock.

They leaped to their feet, startled. Before I could go down to them they came rushing up to where I stood.

"We heard your voice twice," said Noch, fearfully.

"It is an echo," I said. "Listen." Raising my voice, I called out my own name.

"Orion!" came the echo floating back to our ears.

"A god is in the rock!" Reeva said, her knees trembling.

"No, no," I tried to assure them. "You try it. Shout out your name, Reeva."

She clamped her lips tight. Staring down at her crusted toes, she shook her head in frightened refusal.

Anya called out. And then young Chron.

"It *is* a god," said Noch. "Or maybe an evil demon."

"It is neither," I insisted. "Nothing but a natural echo.

The sound bounces off the rock and returns to our ears."

They could not accept a natural explanation, it was clear.

Finally I said, "Well, if it is a god, then it's a friendly one who will help to protect us. No one will be able to move through this canyon without our hearing it."

Reluctantly, they accepted my estimate of the situation. As we walked along the narrow trail that wound through the jutting boulders and trees toward the caves it was obvious that they were wary of this strange, spooky bowl of rock. Instead of being exasperated with their superstitious fears I felt almost glad that at last they were showing some spirit, some thinking of their own. They were doing as I told them, true enough, but they did not like it. They were no longer docile sheep following without question. They still followed, but at least they were asking questions.

Noch insisted on building a cairn at the base of the hollow to propitiate "the god who speaks." I thought it was superstitious nonsense, but helped them pile up the little mound of stones nevertheless.

"You are testing us, Orion, aren't you?" Noch said, puffing, as he lifted a stone to the top of the chest-high mound.

"Testing you?"

The other men were gathered around, watching, now that we had completed the primitive monument.

"You are a god yourself. Our god."

I shook my head. "No. I am only a man."

"No man could have slain the dragon that guarded us," said Vorn, one of the older men. His dark beard showed streaks of silver, his head was balding.

"The dragon almost killed me. I needed Anya's help, or it would have."

"You are a full-grown man, yet you grow no beard," Noch said, as if proving his point.

I shrugged. "My beard grows very slowly. That doesn't make me a god, believe me."

"You have brought us back to Paradise. Only a—"

"I am not a god," I said firmly. "And you—all of you—brought yourselves back to Paradise. You walked here, just as I did. Nothing godly about that."

"Still," Noch insisted, "there *are* gods."

I had no answer for that. I knew that there were men and women in the distant future who had godlike powers. And the corrupted egomania that accompanies such powers.

They were all staring at me, waiting for my reply. Finally I said, "There are many things that we don't understand. But I am only a man, and the voice that comes from the rock is only noise."

Noch glanced around at the others, a knowing smile on his lips. Eight ragged, dirty Neolithic men—including Chron and the other beardless teenager. They knew a god when they saw one, no matter what I said.

If they feared me as a god, or feared the echo that they called "the god who speaks," after a few days their fears vanished in the glow of well-being. The caves were large and dry. Game was abundant and easy to catch. Life became very pleasant for them. The men hunted and fished in the stream. The women gathered fruits and tubers and nuts.

Anya even began to show them how to pick cereal grains, spread the grain on a flat rock, and pound it with stones, then toss the crushed mass into the air to let the breeze winnow away the chaff. By the end of the week the women were baking a rough sort of flat bread and I was showing the men how to make bows and arrows.

Chron and his fellow teenagers became quite adept at snaring fowl in nets made from vines. We used the birds' feathers for our arrows after feasting on their flesh.

One night, as Anya and I lay together in a cave apart

from the others, I praised her for her domestic skills. She laughed. "I learned them a few lifetimes ago, just before the flood at Ararat. Don't you remember?"

A vague recollection flitted through my mind. A hunting tribe much like this one. A flood caused by a darkly dangerous enemy. I felt the agony of drowning in the lava-hot floodwaters.

"Ahriman," I said, more to myself than Anya.

"You remember more and more!"

The cave was dark; we had no fire. Yet even with nothing but starlight I saw that Anya was suddenly filled with a new hope.

Propping herself up on one elbow, she asked urgently, "Orion, have you tried to make contact with the Creators?"

"No. If you can't, then how can I?"

"Your powers have grown since you were first created," she said, her words coming fast, excited. "Set is blocking me, but perhaps you can get through!"

"I don't see how—"

"Try! I'll work with you. Together we might be able to overcome whatever force he's using to block me."

I nodded and rolled onto my back. The stone floor of the cave was still warm from the day's sunlight. Just like the rest of the tribe, we had constructed a bed of boughs and moss in a corner of the cave. I had covered it with the skin of a deer I had killed, the largest animal we had caught in this abundant forest. There were wolves out there, I knew; we had heard their howling in the night. But they had not come anywhere near our caves, high up the steep rock face and protected by fire.

"Will you try?" Anya pleaded.

"Yes. Of course." But something within me was hesitant. I *liked* this place, this time, this life with Anya. I felt a real aversion to reestablishing contact with the Creators. They would force us to resume the tasks they wanted us to carry out, their endless schemes to control the continuum, their petty arguments among themselves that resulted in slaughters such as Troy and Jericho. Our pleasant existence in Paradise would end the moment we reached them.

Then I remembered the implacable evil of Set. I saw his devil's face and burning eyes. I heard his seething words: *I will destroy you all, including the woman you love, the self-styled goddess. She will die the most painful death of all.*

I grasped Anya's hand and closed my eyes. Side by side, we concentrated together and strained to touch the minds of the Creators.

I saw a glow, and for an instant thought we had broken through. But instead of the golden aura of the Creators' distant spacetime, this radiance was sullen red like the dark flames of hell, like the unblinking baleful eye of the blood red star that hung above us each night.

The glow contracted, pulled itself together like an image in a telescope coming into focus. Set's remorseless hateful face glowered at me.

"Soon, Orion. Very soon now. I know where you are. I will send you the punishment I promised. Your doom will be slow and painful, wretched ape."

I bolted up to a sitting position.

"What is it?" Anya asked, startled, sitting up beside me. "What did you see?"

"Set. He knows where we are. I think we revealed ourselves to him by trying to make mental contact with the Creators. We've stepped into his trap."

Chapter 6

All that night Anya and I discussed what we should do. Our options were pitifully few. We could stay where we were, even though Set knew our location now. We could try to escape deeper into the forest and hope that he could not find us. If we tried to contact the Creators, the mental energy we expended would signal Set like the bright beam of a laser cutting through the dark. If we could not contact the Creators, we were practically helpless against this reptilian demon and the enormous powers he possessed.

We came to no conclusion, no decision. Whichever direction we looked in, nothing but bleak disaster appeared. Finally, as the first rays of the new day began to brighten the sky, Anya stretched out on the deer hide and closed her eyes in troubled, exhausted sleep.

I sat at the cave's entrance, my back against the stubborn stone, my eyes scanning the wooded, rock-strewn floor of the canyon. I could see out to the smooth-flowing river and a little beyond it. Any enemy approaching us could be easily spotted from up here. Any noise was amplified and echoed by the natural sounding board of the hollowed rock cliff.

The lurid brownish red star hung in the morning sky despite the sun's radiance. Somehow it made my blood run cold; the star did not belong there. It was intrusion in the heavens, a signal that things were not as they should be.

I saw Noch and the others stirring. Noch was actually getting muscular. His arms and chest had thickened. He held his chin high. Even scrawny Reeva had filled out enough to begin looking somewhat attractive. The welts on her back were fading blue-black bruises now.

Scrambling down the steep rocky slope to the canyon floor, I caught up with Noch on his way to the stream. His head barely reached my shoulder's height, and he had to squint up into the morning sunlight to speak to me. But the old servility had disappeared.

Side by side we went to the stream and urinated into its muddy bank. Equals in that, at least.

"Do we hunt again today?" Noch asked.

I replied, "What do you think? Should we go out?"

"There's still a fair amount of meat from the goat we caught yesterday," he said, tugging at his unkempt beard, "but on the way back home I saw the tracks of a big animal in the mud by the bank of the stream. Tracks like we've never seen before."

He showed me. They were the prints of a bear, a large one, and I told him I thought it would be wise to keep away from such a beast. From the size of the prints, it was a cave bear that stood more than seven feet tall on its hind legs. The massive paws that made those prints could break a man's back with a single swipe. I described what a bear looks like, how ferocious it could be, how dangerous it was to tangle with one.

To my surprise, my words only excited Noch. He became eager to track down the bear.

"We could kill it!" he said. "All of us men, working together. We could track it down and kill it."

"But why?" I asked. "Why risk the danger?"

Noch pulled at his beard again, struggling to find the words he wanted. I thought I knew what was going through his mind: he wanted to kill the bear to prove to himself—and to the women—that he was a mighty hunter. The king of the forest.

But what he said was, "If this beast is as dangerous as you say, Orion, might it not come to our caves in the night and attack us? It could be more of a danger *not* to kill it than to hunt it down."

I grinned at him as we stood by the stream's muddy bank. He was thinking for himself, his slavish docility replaced now by the spirit of a hunter. Perhaps he could even become a leader of men.

Then a new thought struck me. Could this bear be a weapon sent against us by Set? A huge cave bear could kill half our little band or more if it struck suddenly in the night.

"You're right," I said. "Round up all the men and we'll track the beast down."

The eight males of the little band came with me, each of them carrying a couple of rough spears. I had a bow slung across my shoulders and a half-dozen arrows tied in a sheaf on my back. Several of the men had crude flint knives, nothing more than sickle-shaped chunks of flint sized to fit in the palm, one edge sharpened. Anya had wanted to come with us, but I begged her to stay with the women and not upset the precarious division of labor that we had so recently established.

"Very well," she said, with an unhappy toss of her head. "I will stay here with the women while you have all the fun."

"Keep a sharp lookout," I warned. "This bear might be merely a diversion sent by Set to draw the men away from the caves."

It was a long, punishingly hard day, and I was constantly on the alert. Perhaps there was more than a cave bear in these woods. Certainly there should be more than a solitary bear. Where there was one there should be others. Yet no matter how diligently we searched, that one set of tracks was all we could find.

The tracks followed the river's course, and we trailed along its bank beneath the overhanging trees. Colorful birds chirped and called to us and insects danced before our eyes like frantic sunbeams in the heat of the afternoon.

Chron clambered up a tall slanting pine and called down, "The river makes a big bend to the right, and then grows very wide. It looks like . . . *yaa!*"

His sudden scream startled us. The youngster was frantically swatting at the air around his head with one hand and trying to climb down from his perch at the same time. Looking closer, I saw that he was enveloped in a cloud of angry, stinging bees.

I raced toward the tree. Chron slipped and lost his grip, plummeting toward the ground, crashing through the lower branches of the tree. I dived the last few feet and reached out for him, caught him briefly in my arms, and then we both hit the ground with an undignified *thump*. The air was knocked out of me and my arms felt as if they'd been pulled from their shoulder sockets.

The bees came right after him, an angry buzzing swarm.

"Into the river!" I commanded. All nine of us ran as if chased by demons and splashed without a shred of dignity into the cool water while the furious bees filled the air like a menacing cloud of pain. None of the men could swim, but they followed me as I ducked my head beneath the water's surface and literally crawled farther away from the bank.

Nine spouting, spraying heads popped up from the water, hair dripping in our eyes, hands raised to ward off our tiny tormentors. We were far enough from the riverbank; the cloud of bees was several yards away, still buzzingly proclaiming their rights, but no longer pursuing us.

For several minutes we stood there with our feet in the mud and our faces barely showing above the water level. The bees grudgingly returned to their hive high up in the tree.

I picked the soggy stem of a water lily from my nose. "Still think I'm a god?" I asked Noch.

The men burst into laughter. Noch guffawed and pointed at Chron. His face was lumpy and fire red with stings. It was not truly a laughing matter, but we all roared hysterically. All but poor Chron.

We waded many yards downstream before dragging ourselves out of the river. Chron was in obvious pain. I made him sit on a log while I focused my eyes finely enough to see the tiny barbs embedded in his swollen face and shoulders and pulled them out with nothing more than my fingernails. He yelped and flinched at each one, but at last I had them all. Then I plastered his face with mud.

"How does it feel now?" I asked him.

"Better," he said unhappily. "The mud feels cool."

Noch and the others were still giggling. Chron's face was caked so thickly with mud that only his eyes and mouth showed through.

The sun was low in the west. I doubted that we would have enough daylight remaining to find our bear, let alone try to kill it. But I was curious about Chron's description of the river up ahead.

So we cut through the woods, away from the riverbank's bend. It was tough going; the undergrowth was thick and tangled here. Nettles and thorns scratched at our bare skin. After about half an hour of forcing our way through the brush we saw the water again, but now it was so wide that it looked to me like a sizable lake.

And hunched down on the grassy edge of the water sat our bear, intently peering into the quietly lapping little waves. We froze, hardly even breathing, in the cover of thick blackberry bushes. The breeze was blowing in from the broad lake, carrying our scent away from the bear's sensitive nostrils. It had no idea that we were close.

It was a huge beast, the size and reddish brown color of a Kodiak. If we stood Chron on Noch's shoulders, the bear would still have been taller, rearing on its hind legs. I could feel the cold hand of reality clamping down on my eager hunters. I heard someone behind me swallowing hard.

I had been killed by such a bear once, in another millennium. The sudden memory of it made me shudder.

The bear, oblivious to us, got up on all fours and walked slowly, deliberately, out into the lake a half-dozen strides. It stood stock still, its eyes staring into the water. For long moments it did not move. Then it flicked one paw in the water and a big silvery fish came spiraling up, sunlight sparkling off its glittering scales and the droplets of water spraying around it, until it plopped down on the grass, tail thumping and gills gasping desperately.

"Do you still want the bear?" I whispered into Noch's ear.

He was biting his lower lip, and his eyes looked fearful, but he bobbed his head up and down. We had come too far to turn back now with nothing to show for our efforts except the bee stings on Chron's mud-caked face.

With hand signals I directed my band of hunters into a rough half circle and made them crouch in the thick bushes. Slowly, while the bear was still engrossed in his fishing, I slipped the bow from my shoulder and untied the crudely fledged arrows. Signaling the others to stay where they were, I crept on my belly slowly, cautiously forward, more like a slithering snake than a mighty hunter.

I knew the arrows would not be accurate enough to hit even a target as big as the cave bear unless I was almost on top of it. I crawled through the scratching burrs and thorns while the birds called overhead and a squirrel or chipmunk chittered scoldingly from its perch on a tree trunk's rough bark.

The bear looked up and around once, and I flattened myself into the ground. Then it returned to its fishing. Another flick of its paw, and another fine trout came flashing out of the water in a great shining arc, to land almost touching the first one.

I rose slowly to one knee, braced myself, and pulled the bow to its utmost. The bear loomed so large, so close, that I knew I could not miss. I let the arrow fly. It thunked into the cave bear's ribs with the solid sound of hardened wood striking meat.

The bear huffed, more annoyed than hurt, and turned around. I got to my feet and put another arrow to the bowstring. The bear growled at me and lurched to its hind legs, rearing almost twice my height. I aimed for its throat, but the arrow curved slightly and struck the bear's shoulder. It must have hit bone, for it fell off like a bullet bouncing off armor plate.

Now the beast was truly enraged. Bellowing loud enough to shake the ground, it dropped to all fours and charged at me. I turned and ran, hoping that my hunters were brave enough to stand their ground and attack the beast from each side as it hurtled past.

They were. The bear came crashing into the bushes after me and eight frightened, exultant, screaming men rammed their spears into its flanks. The animal roared again and turned around to face its new tormentors.

It was not pretty. Spears snapped in showers of splinters. Blood spurted. Men and bear roared in pain and anger. We hacked at the poor beast until it was nothing more than a bloody pile of fur shuddering and moaning in the reddened slippery bushes. I gave it the coup de grace with my dagger and the cave bear finally collapsed and went still.

For several moments we all simply slumped to the ground, trembling with exhaustion and the aftermath of adrenaline overdose. We, too, were covered with blood, but it seemed to be only the blood of our victim. We had suffered just one injury; the man called Pirk had a broken forearm. I pulled it straight for him while he shrieked with pain, then tied a splint cut from saplings and bound the arm into a sling improvised from vines.

"Anya can make healing poultices," I told Pirk. "Your arm will be all right in time."

He nodded, his face drained white from the pain, his lips a thin bloodless line.

The others fell to skinning the bear. Noch wanted its skull and pelt to bring back to the women, to show that we had been successful.

"No beast will dare to threaten us once we mount this ferocious skull before our caves," he said.

Twilight was falling when I sensed that we were not alone. The men were half-finished with their skinning. Chron and I had gathered wood and started a fire. Deep in the shadows around us other presences had gathered, I realized. Not animals. Men.

I got to my feet and moved slightly away from the fire to peer into the shadows flickering among the thick foliage. Without conscious thought I reached down and drew my dagger from its sheath on my thigh.

Chron was watching me. "What is it, Orion?"

I silenced him with a finger to my lips. The other seven men looked up at me, then uneasily out toward the shadows.

A man stepped out from the foliage and regarded us solemnly, our firelight making his bearded face seem ruddy, his eyes aglow. He wore a rough tunic of hide and carried a long spear in one hand, which he butted on the ground. In height he was no taller than Noch or any of the others, although he seemed more solid in build and much more assured of himself. Broad in the shoulders. Older too: his long hair and beard were grizzled gray. His eyes took in every detail of our makeshift camp at a glance.

"Who are you?" I asked.

"Who are *you?*" he countered. "And why have you killed our bear?"

"Your bear?"

He raised his free hand and swept it around in a half circle. "All this land around the lake is our territory. Our fathers have hunted here, and so have their fathers and their fathers before them."

A dozen more men stepped out of the shadows, each of them armed with spears. Several dogs were with them, silent, ears laid back, wolflike green eyes staring at us menacingly.

"We are newcomers here," I said. "We did not know any other men hunted in this area."

"Why did you kill our bear? It was doing you no harm."

"We tracked it from our home, far up the river. We feared it might attack us in the night, as we slept."

The man made a heavy sigh, almost a snort. This was as new a situation for him, I realized, as it was for us. What to do? Fight or flee? Or something else?

"My name is Orion," I told him.

"I am called Kraal."

"Our home is up the river a day's walk, in the vale of the god who speaks."

His brow wrinkled at that.

Before he had time to ask a question I went on, "We have come to this place only recently, a few days ago. We are fleeing the slave masters from the garden."

"Fleeing from the dragons?" Kraal blurted.

"And the seekers who fly in the air," Noch added.

"Orion killed one of the dragons," said Chron, proudly. "And set us free of the masters."

Kraal's whole body seemed to relax. The others behind him stirred, too. Even the dogs seemed to ease their tension.

"Many times I have seen men taken by the slave masters to serve their dragons. Never have I heard of any man escaping from them. Or killing a dragon! You must tell us of this."

They all stepped closer to our fire, lay down their spears, and sat among us to hear our story.

Chapter 7

I spoke hardly a word. Noch, Chron, and even broken-armed Pirk related a wondrous tale of how I had single-handedly slain the dragon guarding them and brought them to freedom in Paradise. As the night wore on we shared the dried scraps of meat and nuts that each man had carried with him and the stories continued.

We talked as we ate, sharing stories of bravery and danger. The dogs that accompanied Kraal's band went off by themselves for a good part of the night, but eventually they returned to the fire and the men still gathered around it, still talking.

Kraal told of how his own daughter and her husband had been abducted by dragons who had raided their village by the lakeshore many years earlier in search of slaves.

"They left me for dead," he said, pulling up his tunic to show a long brutal scar carved across his ribs. In the firelight it looked livid and still painful. "My wife they did kill."

One by one the men told their tales, and I learned that Set's "dragons" periodically raided into these forests of Paradise and carried off men and women to work as slaves in the garden by the Nile. And undoubtedly elsewhere, as well.

My first notion about Set's garden had been almost totally wrong. It was not the Garden of Eden. It was this thick forest that was truly the Paradise of humankind, where men were free to roam the woods and hunt the teeming animals in it. But the people were being driven out of the forest by Set's devilish reptilian monsters, away from the free life of Neolithic hunters and into the forced labor of farming—and god knew what else.

The legends of Eden that men would repeat to one another over the generations to come would get the facts scrambled: humans were driven out of Paradise *into* the garden, and not by angels but by devils.

Obviously the reptilian masters allowed their slaves to breed in captivity. Reeva's baby had been born in slavery. I learned that night that Chron and most of the other men of my band had also been born while their parents toiled in the garden. Noch, I knew, had been taken out of Paradise in early childhood. So had the remaining others.

"We hunt the beasts of field and forest," said Kraal, his voice sleepy as the moon's cold light filtered through the trees, "and the dragons hunt us."

"We must fight the dragons," I said.

Kraal shook his head wearily. "No, Orion, that is impossible. They are too big, too swift. Their claws slice flesh from the bone. Their jaws crush the life from a man."

"They can be killed," I insisted.

"Not by the likes of us. There are some things that men cannot do. We must accept things as they are, not dream idle dreams of what cannot be."

"But Orion killed a dragon," Chron reminded him.

"Maybe so," Kraal replied with the air of a man who had heard tall tales before. "It's time for sleeping now. No more talk of dragons. It's enough we'll have to fight each other when the sun comes up."

He said it matter-of-factly, with neither regret nor anticipation in his tone.

"Fight each other?" I echoed.

Kraal was settling himself down comfortably between the roots of a tree. "Yes. It's a shame. I really enjoyed listening to your stories. And I'd like to see this place of your talking god. But tomorrow we fight."

I glanced around at the other men: their dozen, our nine, including me.

"Why must we fight?"

As if explaining to a backward child, Kraal said patiently, "This is our territory, Orion. You killed our bear. If we let you go away without fighting you, others will come here and kill our animals. Then where would we be?"

I stood over him as he turned on his unscarred side and mumbled, "Get some sleep, Orion. Tomorrow we fight."

Chron came up beside me and stood on tiptoes to whisper in my ear, "Tomorrow they'll see what a fighter you are. With you leading us, we'll kill them all and take this land for ourselves."

Smiling in the moonlit shadows, he trotted off to a level spot next to a boulder and lay down to sleep.

One by one they all dropped to sleep until I stood alone among their snoring bodies. At least they did not fear treachery. None of them thought that someone might slit the throats of sleeping men.

I walked down to the shore of the lake and listened to the lapping of the water. An owl hooted from the trees, the sacred symbol of Athena. Anya was the inspiration for the legends of Athena, I knew, just as the Golden One, mad as he is, inspired the legends of Apollo.

And me? The so-called gods who created me in their distant future called me Orion and set me the task of hunting down their enemies through the vast reaches of time. In ancient Egypt I would be called Osiris, he who dies and is reborn. In the barren snowfields of the Ice Age my name would be Prometheus, for I would show the earliest freezing, starving band of humans how to make fire, how to survive even in the desolation of mile-thick glaciers that covered half the world.

Who am I now, in this time and place? I looked up at the stars scattered across the velvety-dark sky and once again saw that baleful dark red eye staring down at me, brighter than the moon, bright enough to cast my shadow across the ground. A star that had never been in any sky I had seen before. A star that somehow seemed linked with Set and his dragons and his enslavement of these Neolithic people.

For a moment I was tempted to try once more to make contact with the Creators. But the fear of alerting Set again made me hesitate. I stood on the shore of the broad lake, listening to the night breeze making the trees sigh, and wished with all my might that the Creators would attempt to contact us.

But nothing happened. The owl hooted again; it sounded like bitter laughter.

I stayed by the lake side rather than returning to the makeshift camp where the men sprawled asleep. Kraal insisted that we had to fight, and I felt certain he did not mean any bloodless ritual. With the dawn we would battle each other with wooden spears and flint knives.

Unless I could think of something better.

I spent the long hours of the sinister menacing night thinking. A cold gray fog rose from the lake, slowly wrapping the trees in its embrace until I could not make out their tops nor see the stars. The moon made the fog glow all silver and the world became a chill dank featureless bowl of cold gray moonlight, broken only by an occasional owl's hoot or the distant eerie howl of a wolf. Kraal's dogs bayed back at the wolves, proclaiming their own territory.

The fog was lifting and the sky beginning to turn a soft delicate pink when I sensed a man walking slowly through the mist-shrouded trees toward me at the water's edge. It was Kraal. He came up beside me without the slightest bit of fear or hesitation and looked out across the lake. The fog was thinning, dissolving like the fears of darkness dispelled by the growing light of day.

He pointed toward the growing brightness on the horizon where the Sun would soon come up. "The Light-Stealer comes closer."

I followed his outstretched arm and saw the dull reddish star glowing sullenly in the brightening sky.

"And the Punisher is almost too faint to see," Kraal added.

"The Punisher?"

"Can't you see it? Just beside the Light-Stealer, very faint . . ."

For the first time I realized that there was a second point of light close to the red star that Kraal called the Light-Stealer. A dim pinpoint barely on the edge of visibility.

"What do those names mean?" I asked.

He gave me a surprised look. "You don't know about the Light-Stealer and his Punisher?"

"I come from far away," I said. "Much farther than Noch and his band."

Kraal's expression turned thoughtful. He explained the legend of the Light-Stealer. The gods—which include the Sun-god, mightiest of them all—had no care for human beings. They saw humans struggling to exist, weaker than the wolves and bears, cold and hungry always, and turned their backs to us. The Light-Stealer, a lesser god, took pity on humankind and decided to give us the gift of fire.

My breath caught in my throat. The Prometheus legend. It was I who gave the earliest humans the gift of fire, deep in the eternal cold and snow of the Ice Age. Kraal told the story strangely, but his tale caught the cruel indifference of the so-called gods almost perfectly.

The Light-Stealer knew that the only way to bring fire to the human race was to steal it from the Sun. So every year the dull red star robs the Sun of some of its light. Instead of remaining in the night sky, as all the other stars do, it gradually encroaches on the daytime domain of the Sun, getting closer and closer each day. Finally it reaches the Sun and steals some of its fire. Then it runs away to return to the night, where it gives light to men in the dark hours, light that is brighter than the moon's.

The legend of Prometheus thrown against the background of the stars. What Kraal was telling me could make sense only if the Sun were accompanied by another star, a dim brownish red dwarf that orbited far out in the deeper distances of the solar system. Yet the Sun was a single star, accompanied by a retinue of planets, not by a companion star. Through all of my journeys across the spacetime continuum the Sun had always been a solitary star.

Until now.

"And what of the Punisher?" I heard myself ask.

"The Sun and the other gods become angry when the Stealer robs fire from the Sun," Kraal went on. "The Punisher tears at the Light-Giver, rips into its guts again and again, all year long, forever."

The companion star has a planet of its own orbiting around it, I translated mentally. From the Earth they can see it bobbing back and forth, disappearing behind the star and reappearing on its other side. A Punisher ripping into the Light-Stealer's innards, like the vulture that eats out Prometheus' liver once the gods have chained him to the rock.

"That is how fire was given to us, Orion," said Kraal. "It happened a long time ago, long before my grandfather's grandfather hunted around this lake. The stars show us what happened, to remind us of our debt to the gods."

"But from what you say," I replied, "the gods are not friendly to us."

"All the more reason to respect and fear them, Orion." With that he walked away from me, back toward the camp, with the air of a man who had made an unarguable point.

By now the Sun was fully risen over the lake's farther shore and the men were up, stretching and muttering, relieving themselves against a couple of trees. They shared the food they had remaining, Kraal's men and my own, and washed it down with water from the lake, which Chron and one-armed Pirk brought up to our makeshift camp in animal bladders.

"Now for our fight," said Kraal, picking his long spear up from the ground. His men arrayed themselves behind him, each of them gripping spears, while my band came together behind me. The dogs lay sleepily on their bellies, tongues lolling. But their eyes took in every move.

"You are twelve, we are only nine," I said.

He shrugged. "You should have brought more men."

"We don't have any more."

Kraal made a gesture with his free hand that said, *That's your problem, not mine.*

"Instead of all of us fighting," I suggested, "why not an individual combat: one against one."

Kraal's brow furrowed. "What good would that do?"

"If your side wins, my men will go back to their home and never come here again."

"And if my side loses?"

"We can both hunt in this area, in peace. There's

plenty of game for us both."

"No, Orion. It will be better to kill you all and be finished with it. Then we can take your women, too. And any other tribes who come by here will know that this is *our* territory, and they must not hunt here."

"How will they know that?"

He seemed genuinely surprised by such a stupid question. "Why, we will mount your heads on poles, of course."

"Suppose," I countered, "we kill all of you? What then?"

"Nine of you? Two of them lads and one of the men with a bad arm?" Kraal laughed.

"One of us has killed a dragon," I said, making my voice hard.

"So you claim."

"He did! He did!" my men shouted.

I silenced them with a wave of my hand, not wanting a fight to break out over my claims of prowess. An idea was forming itself in my brain. I asked Chron to bring me my bow and arrows.

"Do you know what this is?" I held them up before Kraal.

"Certainly. Not much good against a spear, though. The bow is a weapon of ambush, not face-to-face fighting."

Handing the bow and arrows to him, I said, "Before we start the fighting, why don't you shoot me with this."

Kraal looked surprised, then suspicious. "What do you mean?"

Walking toward a stately old elm, I explained, "Fire an arrow at me. I'll stand here."

"I don't understand."

"You don't believe I killed a dragon. Well, there are no dragons about this morning for me to show you how I did it, so I'll have to give you a different kind of proof. Shoot me!"

Puzzled, wary, Kraal nocked an arrow and pulled the bowstring back. My men edged away from me; Kraal's seemed to lean in closer, eager to see the show. I noticed that Kraal pulled the string only back to his chest instead of his cheek.

I willed my body to go into hyperdrive, and saw the world around me slow down. The pupils of Kraal's eyes contracted slightly as he aimed. A bird flapped languidly from one bough to another, its red-feathered wings beating the air with dreamlike strokes.

Standing ten paces before me, Kraal let the arrow fly. I saw it wobbling toward me; it was a crude piece of work. I easily reached out with one hand and knocked it aside.

The men gasped.

"Now," I said, "watch this."

Striding up to one of Kraal's men, I instructed him to hold his spear in both hands, level with the ground. He looked at his leader first, and when Kraal nodded, he reluctantly did as I asked. Swinging my arm overhand and yelling ferociously, I snapped the rough spear in two with the edge of my hand.

Before they could say or do anything, I spun around and grabbed Kraal around the waist. Lifting him high over my head, I held him there, squirming and bellowing, with one hand.

"Do you still want to fight us, Kraal?" I asked, laughing. "Do you want us to take your women?"

"Put me down!" he was shouting. "This isn't the proper way to fight!"

I set him down gently on his feet and looked into his eyes. He was angry. And fearful.

"Kraal, if we fight, I will be forced to kill you and your men."

He said nothing. His chest was heaving, sweat trickling down his cheeks and into his grizzled beard.

"I have a better idea," I went on. "Would you allow my

men to join your tribe? Under your leadership?"

Noch yelped, "But you are our leader, Orion!"

"I am a stranger here, and my true home is far away. Kraal is a fine leader and a good hunter."

"But . . ."

They both had plenty of objections. But at least they were talking, not fighting. Kraal's face went from fear-driven anger to a more thoughtful expression. His eyes narrowed, became crafty. He was thinking hard about this new opportunity. I invited him to come and see the place where the god speaks, and as we walked back toward the echo canyon we continued to talk about merging the two bands.

The idea that had entered my mind was far greater than these two ragged gangs of Stone Age hunters. I reasoned that there were far more humans in these forests of Paradise than reptiles. If I could weld the tribes together into a coherent force, we would outnumber Set and his dragons. I knew that Set had a far superior technology at his command than my Neolithics did, but with numbers—and time—we might be able to begin fighting him on a more equal basis.

The first step was to see if I could merge Noch's band of ex-slaves with Kraal's tribe. It would not be easy, I knew. But the first step never is.

Chapter 8

Kraal was impressed with the echo—the god who speaks. But he tried to hide it.

"The god only repeats what you say."

"Most of the time," I replied, a new idea forming in my mind. "But sometimes the god speaks its own words to us."

He grunted, trying to keep up an air of skepticism.

He was also impressed with Anya, who greeted him courteously, seriously, as befits a man of importance. Kraal had never seen a metallic fabric such as Anya wore: it was practically impervious to wear, of course, and literally repelled dirt with a surface electrical charge. She seemed to glow like a goddess.

He had never seen a woman so beautiful, either, and his bearded face plainly showed the confusion of awe, longing, and outright lust that percolated through him. He was an experienced leader who seemed to grasp the advantages of merging Noch's band into his own. But it had never been done before, and Kraal was not the type to agree easily to any innovation.

We feasted that night together on the rocky canyon floor, our whole band plus Kraal's dozen men clustered around a roaring fire while we roasted rabbits, possums, raccoons, and smaller rodents on sticks. The women provided bread, something Kraal and his men had never seen before, as well as mounds of nuts, carrots, berries, and an overpowering root that would one day be called horse-radish.

Earlier, I had spoken at length to Anya about my idea, and she had actually laughed with the delight of it.

"Are you sure you can do it?" I had asked.

"Yes. Of course. Never fear."

It was wonderful to see her smile, to see the delight and hope lighting her gray eyes.

After our eating was finished the women went back to the caves and the men sat around the dying embers of our big fire, belching and telling tales.

Finally I asked Kraal, "Have you thought about merging our two groups?"

He shook his head, as if disappointed. "It can't be done, Orion."

"Why not?"

All the other men stopped their talk and watched us. Kraal answered unhappily, "You have your tribe and I have my tribe. We have no people in common: no brothers or brides or even cousins. There are no bonds between the two tribes, Orion."

"We could create such bonds," I suggested. "Several of our women have no husbands. I'm sure many of your men have no wives."

I saw nods among his men. But Kraal shook his head once more. "It's never been done, Orion. It's not possible."

I pulled myself to my feet. "Let's see what the god has to say."

He looked up at me. "The god will repeat whatever you say."

"Maybe. Maybe not."

Raising my hands above my head, I called into the night, "O god who speaks, tell us what we should do!"

My voice echoed off the bowl of rock, ". . . tell us what we should do!"

For several heartbeats there was nothing to hear except the chirping of crickets in the grass. Then a low guttural whisper floated through the darkness: "I am the god who speaks. Ask and you shall receive wisdom."

All the men, mine included, jumped as if a live electrical wire had touched their bare flesh. Kraal's eyes went so wide that even in the dying firelight I could see white all around the pupils. None of them recognized Anya's voice; none of them could even tell that the rasping whisper they heard came from a woman.

I turned to Kraal. "Ask the god."

His mouth opened, but no sound came out. Most of the other men had gotten to their feet, staring toward the looming shadow of the hollowed rock. I felt some shame, tricking them this way. I realized that an unscrupulous person could easily make the "god" say whatever he or she wanted it to say. One day oracles and seers would use such tricks to sway their believers. I would have much to answer for.

But at this particular instant in time I needed Kraal to accept the idea of merging our two tribes.

To my surprise, it was Noch who spoke up. His voice quavering slightly with nervousness, he shouted toward the rock wall, "O god who speaks, would it be a good thing for our tribe to merge with Kraal's tribe?"

". . . merge with Kraal's tribe?"

Again silence. Not even the wind stirred. The crickets had gone quiet.

Then the whispered answer: "Are two men stronger than one? Are twenty men stronger than ten? It is wise to make yourselves stronger."

"Then we should merge our two bands together?" Noch wanted a definite answer, not godly metaphors.

"Yesss." A long drawn-out single syllable.

Kraal found his voice. "Under whose leadership?"

". . . whose leadership?"

"The leader of the larger of your two tribes should be the leader of the whole. Kraal the Hunter shall be known from this night onward as Kraal the Leader."

The man's chest visibly swelled. He broke into a broad, gap-toothed grin and turned toward the other men, nodding approval at the wisdom the god displayed.

"But what about Orion?" Noch insisted.

". . . Orion?" the echo repeated.

"Orion will remain among you for only a little while," came the answer. "He has other tasks to undertake, other deeds to accomplish."

My satisfaction at having conned Kraal and the others melted away. Anya was speaking the truth. We could not remain here much longer. We had other tasks ahead of us.

I watched Kraal and Noch embrace each other, watched the relieved looks on all the men's faces when they realized they would not have to fight each other. How the women would take to embracing strange men, I did not know. Nor did I particularly care. Not at that moment. I had forced these people on the first step of resistance against Set and the reptilian masters. But it was only the first step, and the immensity of the task that lay before me weighed on my shoulders like the burdens of all the world.

I made my way back to the cave I shared with Anya, achingly weary. As the moon set, that blood red star rose above the treetops, glaring balefully down at me, depressing me even further.

Anya was eager with excitement as I crawled into the cave and dropped down onto our pallet of boughs and hides.

"It worked, didn't it! I saw them embracing one another."

"You did a fine job," I told her. "You have real worshipers now—although I'm not certain how they would react if they knew they were obeying a goddess instead of a god."

Kneeling beside me, Anya said smugly, "I've had worshipers before. Phidias sculpted a marvelous statue of me for all of Athens to worship."

I nodded wearily and closed my eyes. I felt drained, demoralized, and all I wanted was to sleep. Anya and I would never be free to live as normal human beings. There would always be the Creators to pull my strings, never leaving us alone. Always a new task, a new enemy, a new time and place. But never a time and place for happiness. Not for me. Not for us.

She sensed my soul's exhaustion. Stroking my brow with her cool, smooth fingers, Anya soothed, "Sleep, my darling. Rest and sleep."

I slept. But only for the span of a few heartbeats. For I saw Set's satanic face, his red eyes burning, his sharp teeth gleaming in a devil's version of a smile.

"I told you I would send you a punishment, Orion. The hour has come."

I sat bolt upright, startling Anya.

"What is it?"

There was no need to answer. A terrified shriek split the night. From one of the caves.

I grabbed at the spear lying near the cave's entrance and dashed out onto the narrow ledge of rock that formed a natural stairway down to the canyon floor. Others were spilling out of their caves, screaming, jumping to the rocks below. Kraal's men among them, running and shrieking in absolute terror, stumbling down the rough stone steps, leaping to certain injury or death in their panic to escape . . .

Escape from what?

"Stay behind me," I muttered to Anya as I started climbing up the steep stairway of rock.

Reeva came screaming toward me, nearly knocking me over the edge in her wild-eyed terror. She was empty-handed. Her baby was still in the cave up above.

I clambered up the uneven stones, sensing Anya right behind me, also armed with a spear. The dreadful gloomy light of the strange star bathed the rock face with the color of dried blood, making everything look ghastly.

The cave Reeva shared with several other women looked empty, abandoned. Below us I could still hear shrieks and screams, not merely fright now, but cries of pain, of agony. Men and women running, thrashing wildly, as if trying to beat off some invisible attacker.

It was darker than hell inside the cave, but my eyes adjusted to the minuscule light level almost instantly. I saw Reeva's baby—disappearing into the distended jaws of a huge snake.

Before I could even think I flung myself at the serpent and slashed at its head with my dagger. It coiled around my arm, but I had it at its most vulnerable, with a half-swallowed meal between its teeth. I hacked at the snake, just behind its skull. It was as thick as my leg at the thigh, and so long that its body twined almost the full circumference of the cave and still could wrap half a dozen coils around my flailing arm.

Anya rammed her spear into its writhing body again and again while I sawed through its spinal cord and finally cut off its head. Dropping my dagger I pried at its jaws and worked the baby free of its fangs. The baby was quite dead, already cold, its skin blue gray in the dim starlight.

"It's poisonous," I said to Anya. "Look at those fangs."

"There are others," she said.

They were still screaming outside. I rose to my feet, burning hot fury seething within me. Set's punishment, I knew. Snakes. Huge venomous snakes that come slithering silently in the darkness of night to do their work of killing. Death and terror, those were the hallmarks of our adversary.

I strode to the lip of the cave. "Up here!" I bellowed, and the rock amplified my voice into the thunder of a god. "Come up here where we can see them! Get away from the floor of the canyon."

Some obeyed. Only a few. Already I could see dead bodies stretched out on the grass, twisted among the boulders and brush that formed natural hiding places for the snakes. Up here on the rocks, at least we would be able to see them. What we could see, we could fight.

Most of the people had fled terrified into the night, their only thought to get away from the sudden silent death that struck in the shadows. A woman lay down among the stones on the floor of the canyon, broken by her panicked leap away from the caves. I could see a long writhing ghastly white snake gliding toward her, jaws spread wide, fangs glittering. She screamed and tried to scrabble away from the snake. Anya threw her spear at it and missed. The snake sank its deadly fangs into her flesh and the woman's screams rose to a hideous crescendo, then died away in a gurgling, strangling agony.

The others were stumbling, staggering up toward me, clambering up the steep stone steps to the narrow ledge where Anya and I stood. And the snakes came slithering after them, long thick bodies of deathly gray white, yellow eyes glittering, forked tongues flicking, their fangs filled with venom, their bodies gliding silently over the rocks in pursuit of their prey.

I gathered our little band on the ledge, men armed with spears and knives on the perimeter, women inside the cave. All except Anya, who stood at my shoulder, a fresh jabbing spear in one hand, a flint hand knife in the other, panting with excitement and exertion, eyes aflame with battle lust.

The snakes attacked us. Wriggling up the stone steps, they dodged this way and that to avoid our spears, coiled up just beyond our reach, struck at us with lightning speed. We too dodged, hopping back and forth, trying to keep our bare legs from their fangs.

We fought back. We jabbed at them with our wooden spears, we turned the shafts into clubs and hammered at them. One snake began coiling around the spear Anya held, slithering up its length to get at her, driven by an intelligent sense of purpose that no serpent's brain could originate.

I shouted a warning as Anya calmly ripped the snake open with her flint knife. It reared back. I grabbed it around its bleeding throat and Anya hacked its head off. We threw the bloody remains off the ledge, down to the canyon floor below.

The fight seemed to go on for hours. Two of our men were struck and died shrieking, their limbs twisting in horrifying pain. Another was jostled off the ledge and fell screaming to the ground below. He was badly injured, and in minutes several snakes gathered around him. We heard his wailing screeches, and then he went silent forever.

Abruptly, there were no more snakes. No more live ones, at any rate. Nearly a dozen lifeless bodies twitching in their own blood at our feet. I blinked at the shambles of our battlefield. The sun had risen; its bright golden rays were shining through the trees.

Below us lay eight dead bodies, their limbs twisted,

their faces horribly constricted. We went down, still warily searching for more snakes as we gathered up the bodies of the slain. Broken-armed Pirk was among them. And three of Kraal's men. And gray-bearded Noch; his return to Paradise had been brief and bitter.

All that day we scoured the canyon floor for bodies. To my surprised relief we found only two others. About noontime Kraal and three of his men came to me.

He shook his head at the bodies of the slain. "I told you, Orion," he said sadly, choking back tears of frustrated hate. "There is nothing we can do against the masters. They hunt us for their sport. They make slaves of our people. All we can do is bow down and accept."

Anya heard him. She had been kneeling among the dead bodies, not of the humans but of the snakes, dissecting one of them to search for its poison glands.

Angrily she sprang to her feet and flung the flayed body of the twenty-foot snake at Kraal. Its weight staggered him.

"All we can do is bow down?" Anya raged at him. "Timid man, we can *kill* our enemies. As they would kill us!"

Kraal goggled at her. No woman had ever spoken so harshly to him before. I doubt that any man had.

Seething like the enraged goddess she was, Anya advanced on Kraal, flint knife in hand. He backed away from her.

"The god called you Kraal the Leader," Anya taunted. "But this morning you look more like Kraal the Coward! Is that the name you want?"

"No . . . of course not . . ."

"Then stop crying like a woman and start acting like a leader. Gather *all* the bands of people together and, together, we will fight the masters and kill them all!"

Kraal's knees actually buckled. "All the tribes . . . ?"

Several of the other men had gathered around us by

now. One of them said, "We must ask the god who speaks about this."

"Yes," I agreed swiftly. "Tonight. The god only speaks after the sun goes down."

Anya's lips twitched in a barely suppressed grin. We both knew what the god would say.

Chapter 9

Thus we began uniting the tribes of Paradise.

Once Kraal got over the shock of the snakes' attack and heard Anya's god-voice telling him that it was his destiny to resist the masters in all their forms and might, he actually began to develop into Kraal the Leader. And our people began to learn how to defend themselves.

Months passed, marked by the rhythmically changing face of the moon. We left the place of the god-who-speaks and moved even deeper into the forest that seemed to stretch all the way across Africa from the Red Sea to the Atlantic. It extended southward, according to the tales we heard, evolving gradually into the tropical rain forest that covered much of the rest of the continent.

Each time we met another tribe we tried to convince them that they should work with us to resist the masters. Most tribal leaders resisted, instead, the idea of doing anything new, anything that would incur the terrible wrath of the fearsome dragons who raided their homes from time to time.

We showed them the skulls of the snakes we had slain. We told stories about my fight against the dragon. Anya developed into a real priestess, falling into trances whenever it was necessary to speak with the voice of a god. She also showed the women how to gather grains and bake bread, how to make medicines from the juices of leaves and roots. I showed the men how to make better tools and weapons.

I found, stored in my memory, the knowledge of cold-working soft metals such as copper and gold. Gold, as always, was extremely rare, although we found one tribe where the chief's women hung nuggets of gold from their earlobes for adornment. I showed them how to beat the soft shining metal into crescents and circles, the best I could do with the primitive stone hammers available. Yet it pleased the women very much. I became an admired man, which helped us to convince the chief to join our movement.

In several scattered places we found lumps of copper lying on the ground, partially buried in grass and dirt. These I cold-worked into slim blades and arrowheads, sharp but brittle. I taught the hunters how to anneal their copper implements by heating them and then quenching them in cold water. That made them less brittle without sacrificing their sharpness.

As the months wore on we developed stone molds for shaping arrowheads and axes, knives and spear points, awls and scrapers. When I recognized layers of rock bearing copper ore, I taught them how to build a forge of stones and make the fire hotter with a bellows made from a goat's bladder. Then we could smelt the metal out of the rock and go on to make more and better tools. And weapons. Instead of Orion the Hunter I was filling the role of Hephaestus, blacksmith of the gods. But it was during those months that human tools and weapons gleamed for the first time with metal edges.

While most of the tribal elders we met were just as stubborn as Kraal had been, many of the younger men eagerly took up our challenge to resist the devilish masters. We won their loyalty with appeals to their courage, with new metal-edged weapons, and with the oldest commodity of all—women.

Every tribe had young women who needed husbands and young men who wanted wives. Often the unmarried men formed raiding parties to steal women from neighboring tribes. This usually started blood feuds that could last for generations.

Under Anya's tutelage we created a veritable marriage bureau, bringing news of available mates from one tribe to another. Primitive though these men and women were in technology and social organization, they were no fools. They soon recognized that an arranged marriage, where both families willingly gave their consent, was preferable to raiding and stealing—and the constant threat of retaliation.

Despite the fearsome stories some men like to tell about human savagery and lust, despite the cynical boasts of the Golden One about how he built ferocity into his creation of Homo sapiens, human beings have always chosen cooperation over competition when they had the choice. By giving the tribes the chance to extend ties of kinship we extended ties of loyalty.

Even shy Reeva found herself a new mate: Kraal himself. Since her baby had been killed by the snakes Reeva had seemed to become even more withdrawn, quieter, brooding, almost morose. Then one bright morning Kraal told me that Reeva had agreed to be his wife. His gap-toothed grin was a joy to see.

Yet I felt uneasy. I asked Anya about it, and she shrugged.

"Reeva seeks protection," she told me. "If she can't have it from you, she'll get it from the next most powerful male available."

"Protection?" I wondered. "Or power?"

Anya looked at me thoughtfully. "Power? I hadn't considered that."

It was a happy time for Anya and me. Despite the lurking threat of Set and his monsters we lived together joyfully in Paradise. Each day was fresh and new, each night was a pleasure of loving passion. We felt that we were accomplishing something important, helping these struggling tribes to defend themselves against true evil. Time became meaningless for us. We had our cause, we had our work, and we had each other. What more could we ask of Paradise?

After seven months of constant travel through the forest of Paradise, we had built up a loose alliance of several dozen tribes under the nominal leadership of Kraal. Most of the people of those tribes went on living exactly as they had before we met them—except that they now had new tools, new foods, new mates, new ideas stirring them. Only a few young men or women from any single tribe actually traveled with us.

Had we done enough?

I knew that we had not. All through those long months we did not see a dreaded giant snake or dragon. Each time I looked up through the leafy trees I saw only the sky, empty except for clouds. No pterosaurs seeking us. Yet I felt deep within me that Set knew exactly where we were, day by day. Knew precisely what we were doing. With the absolute certainty of inbuilt instinct I realized that Set was preparing to smash us.

How and when I did not know. It dawned on me that I had better find out.

That night Kraal's wandering band camped in a parklike glade beneath lofty pine trees. Their trunks rose straight and tall as the pillars of a cathedral. The ground beneath them was bare of grass but covered with a thick, soft, scented layer of pine needles. We spread our hides and robes and prepared for sleep.

There were about forty of us who roamed the forest of Paradise under Kraal's nominal leadership, offering metal tools and medicines, knowledge and marriageable young men and women in exchange for loyalty and the promise to resist the reptilian masters when next they raided.

A massive gray boulder sat at one end of the glade, gray and imperturbable in the last golden rays of the setting sun. I glanced at Anya, then turned and asked Kraal to follow us up to its top.

We scrabbled up from one rock to another until we stood atop the big boulder, looking down on the others as they huddled in small groups around their cooking fires.

"If the dragons come again to steal slaves for Set," I asked, "how will we be able to bring all the tribes together to fight against them?"

Kraal made a sighing, grunting sound, his way of showing that he was thinking hard. Anya remained silent.

"When we hunt deer or goats," I mused, "we send men out into the brush to search for the game we seek. But what can we do when the dragons come hunting for us?"

Kraal swiftly saw where I was leading. "We could pick men to go to the edge of Paradise and watch for the dragons' approach!"

Anya nodded encouragement to him.

"That would take many men," I said. "And we would need fast runners to carry the news from one group to another."

Thus we created the idea of scouts and messengers, and began training men and women for such duties. We wanted youngsters who were fleet of foot, but not so foolhardy that they would try to attack a dragon by themselves—or so flighty that they would report dragons when they saw nothing more than clouds on the horizon.

After a few weeks of training I myself took the first group of scouts northward, toward the edge of Paradise, where the forest merged with the broad treeless savannah that would eventually become the Sahara.

Anya wanted to come with me but I convinced her that she was needed more at Kraal's side, helping him to win more tribes over to our cause, teaching the women the arts of healing and baking.

"I don't want to leave Kraal entirely alone," I said, "without either one of us close by him."

Anya's eyes widened slightly. "You don't trust him?"

It was the first time that I realized so. "It's not a matter of trust, exactly. What we're doing is new to Kraal—new to all of them. One of us should be at his side at all times. Just in case."

"I'd rather be sticking a spear into a lizard's ribs," she said.

I laughed. "There'll be plenty of chances for that, my love. I have the feeling that Set knows exactly what we're doing and he's merely biding his time to strike us when and where he chooses."

Anya reached up to touch my cheek. "Be very careful, Orion. If you are killed by Set . . . it will be the end. Forever."

There had been times when I longed for eternal death, for the final release from the agony of living. But not now. Now with Anya here in Paradise with me.

I kissed her, long and deep and hard. And then we parted.

Young Chron had become something of an acolyte to me, at my elbow practically every moment of the day. Naturally he volunteered for this first scouting mission. I had to admit that he possessed exactly the qualities we needed in a scout: courage tempered by good sense, keen eyes, and young legs.

There were five of us, and we spent more than a week moving northward through the forest. We headed for the bowl of rock where we had first camped, months earlier. From there, we knew, it was little more than a day's trek to the edge of the grassland.

"Will the god speak to us, Orion?" Chron asked as we tramped through the woods. I had spread our group out in tactical formation: two up ahead, spaced apart the distance that a shout would carry, then the two of us, and finally a one-man rear guard trailing behind us.

"I don't think so," I replied absently. "We won't stay long enough for that."

My attention was on the birds and insects that called and chirped and hummed all around us. As long as they made their usual noises we were probably safe. Silence meant danger in this forest.

A pair of blackbirds seemed to be following us, flapping from tree to tree, cawing noisily from high above us. Looking past them, I saw that the sky was darkening. There would be rain soon.

The clouds burst near sundown and we made a miserable, drenched camp without fire that night. The rain poured down so hard it seemed like solid sheets of water pelting us. We sat beneath a spreading oak, huddled together and hunched over like a quintet of pathetic apes while the rain sluiced over us and chilled us to the bone. We dined on crickets that we found in the grass, silent and inert in the cold. They crunched in my mouth and tasted oddly sweet.

Finally the downpour stopped and the forest came alive once more with the droning of insects and the drip, drip, dripping of rainwater from countless thousands of leaves. A fog rose up, gray and cold, wrapping its ghostly tendrils around us, making our soaked, chilled bodies even more wretched.

My brave scouts were obviously frightened. "The mist," Chron said, shuddering, "it's like the breath of a ghost." The others nodded and muttered, hunched over, wide-eyed, trembling.

I smiled at them. Knowing that reptiles became torpid in the cold, I said, "This mist is a gift from the gods. No snakes or lizards can move through such a mist. The mist protects us."

The morning sun burned away the mist and we marched northward again. Until we came to the end of the lake where Kraal's village had stood.

The birds circling overhead should have been a warning to us. At first we thought they were pterosaurs, so we stayed in the protective shadows of the trees as we approached the village. The birds wheeled and circled in deathly silence.

No more than a handful of Kraal's people had decided to accompany him on his god-inspired journeying. The others had remained where they were, in their huts of boughs and mud by the southern shore of the lake.

The dragons had paid them a visit.

Our noses told us something was wrong long before we reached the remains of the village. The putrid stench of decay was so strong that we were gagging and almost retching by the time we pushed aside the last thorny bushes and stepped out onto the sandy clearing where the village had been built.

The ground was black with ashes. Every hut had been burned to the ground. Tall stakes had been driven into the ground at the water's edge and a dozen men and women had been impaled on them; their rotting remains were what we had smelled. A kind of gibbet had also been built from sturdy logs. Two bodies hung from it by their heels, the flesh ripped so completely from their bones that we could not tell if they had been men or women.

One of my scouts had come from this village. He stared, goggle-eyed, unable to speak, until at last his legs gave way and he collapsed in a blubbering, sobbing heap onto the burned sand.

The others, including Chron, were stunned at first. But gradually, as we slowly walked through the charred remains of huts and human bones, Chron's face went red with rage, even though the others remained pale with shock.

I pointed to immense tracks of three-clawed feet in the ashes and sand. Dragons.

Chron shook his spear in the air. "Let's find them and kill them!"

One of the others looked at him as if he were insane. "We could never kill such as these!"

Glaring at him, Chron said, "Then let's throw ourselves into the lake and be finished with life! Either we avenge these murders or we're not worth the air we breathe!"

I stilled him with a hand on his shoulder. "We will kill the dragons," I said calmly, softly. "But we won't go crashing through the forest following their trail. That is exactly what they want us to do."

As if in confirmation of my suspicion, a pterosaur came gliding into view high above the placid lake. It soared for several moments, wings outstretched, then folded its leathery wings and dove into the lake with barely a splash. An instant later it came up with a fish wriggling in its long beak.

"It's fishing, not searching for us," said Chron.

I lifted an eyebrow. "Even a scout needs to eat."

The pterosaur spread its great wings again and took

off, flapping hard and running on the water's surface with its webbed feet, then wobbled into the air and headed away from us, to the north.

"Come on," I said. "The dragons were here two or three days ago. If we're clever enough, maybe we can trap them while they're waiting to trap us."

Chapter 10

The dragons had left a clearly visible trail through the forest, trampling down bushes and even young trees as they headed back toward the savannah to the north. I saw that their immense three-clawed footprints headed *only* in the northerly direction. They had come down to the village more stealthily, along the riverbank or perhaps wading in the stream itself.

Yes, they were making it easy for us to follow them. I knew that they were waiting up ahead somewhere, waiting to spring their trap on us.

I made my tiny band of scouts stay well away from their trail. We moved through the deep forest as silently as wraiths, slipping through the dense foliage and thickly clustered trees, barely leaving a footprint.

We struck for the high ground, the rocky hills that paralleled the river's course. We clambered up the bare rocks, and once at the top we could easily see the broad trail that the dragons had pounded out down among the trees.

Keeping down below the skyline on the far slope of the ridge, we soon found ourselves above the bowl of rock where we had made our camp months earlier.

And the dragons were there, an even dozen of them, eating.

The five of us flattened ourselves on the rim of the rock bowl and looked down at the giant lizards that had wiped out Kraal's village.

These monsters were considerably different from the beast I had slain so many months earlier. They were slightly bigger, bulkier, more than twenty feet from snout to tail. They walked on their two hind legs only, so that their fearsome heads could rise as much as fifteen feet above the ground. The forelegs were short and relatively slim, used for grasping. Their necks were short and thick, supporting massive heads that seemed to be almost entirely made of teeth the size and shape—and sharpness—of steak knives. Their tails were also shorter and much thicker than I had seen before.

Their colors varied from light dun brown to a mottled green, almost like camouflage. Then, as I watched them I realized that their coloration *was* camouflage; it changed like the coloring of a chameleon as the giant beasts moved slowly from one place on the canyon floor to another.

I recognized the stench wafting toward us; it was from the food they were eating. It took several moments for Chron and the others to understand. I felt his body go rigid beside me. I clamped my hand over his mouth, tightly. The others stirred but did not speak.

The dragons were eating dead human bodies. They must have carried the corpses with them from the village. As we watched in horrified silence I saw that they used the vicious claws on their forelegs to hold their prey and tore off huge chunks of meat with those serrated butcher's knives they had for teeth.

Despite their bulk I thought that they could run quite fast, faster than a human. Those short, thick tails might be useful for clubbing a victim at close quarters, and with those grasping talons and ripping teeth they were fearsomely armed.

At my signal we slithered backward down below the ridge line and crawled, then walked in utter silence for nearly half an hour before any of us said a word. Our copper-edged spears and knives seemed pitifully puny compared to the dragons' teeth and claws.

Even Chron seemed cowed. "How can the five of us kill those monsters?"

"Even if we had all the men from all the tribes, we wouldn't dare to attack them," said one of the others.

"They are fearsome beasts, true enough," I said. "But we have a weapon that they don't."

"Spears won't stop them."

"Their claws are bigger than our knives."

"The weapon we have is not held in our hands," I said. "It's up here." I tapped at my temple.

Coming down off the hillside, we made a wide circle northward and crossed the river at a shallow point where it frothed and babbled noisily white among broken rocks and flat-topped boulders. I kept a wary eye on the sky, but saw no pterosaurs.

Once under the trees on the far bank, I squatted on the sandy ground and drew a map with my finger. "Here is the bowl of the god who speaks, where the dragons are waiting for us, expecting us to walk into their trap. Here is the river. And here we are."

I explained what I wanted them to do. They were doubtful at first, but after a couple of repetitions they saw that my plan could work. If everything went off just the way I wanted it to.

We had another weapon that the dragons did not: fire. The dragons had used the cooking fires of the huts to help destroy the village by the lake. Now I intended to use fire and the element of surprise to destroy them.

We worked all night gathering dry brush for tinder. The floor of the canyon was strewn with bushes and clumps of trees that would burn nicely once ignited. The dragons would either be asleep or torpid, I reasoned, during the cool of the night. Reptiles become sluggish when the thermometer goes down. The time to strike would be just before dawn, the lowest temperature of the night.

My one fear was that they might have some sort of sentries. Perhaps heat-sensitive snakes such as the ones who had attacked us in our caves. My hope was that Set was arrogant enough to think that a band of five little humans would camp for the night and resume their journey only after the sun came up.

We made dozens of trips across the slippery wet rocks, carrying armloads of brush and dead branches from windfalls. The moon rose, a slim crescent that barely shed light, and close enough almost to touch its edge, that glowering red star rose with it. Swiftly, silently, we began to carry our cache of tinder toward the canyon.

I saw the looming dark shadow of a dragon at the canyon's mouth. It was sitting on its hind legs and thick tail, not moving. But I saw the ruddy light of the strange star glint off its eyes. It was awake.

A guard. A sentry. Devilish Set was not so arrogant after all.

I stopped the men behind me with an outstretched arm. They dropped their bundles and gasped at the monster looming in the night. It slowly swung its massive head in our direction. We backed away, hugging the wall of rock and its protective shadows.

The giant lizard did not come after us. To me it

seemed half-asleep, languid.

"We can't get past it!" Chron whispered urgently.

"We'll have to kill it," I said. "And quietly, so that it doesn't rouse the others."

"How can—"

I silenced him with a finger raised to my lips. Then I commanded, "Wait here. Absolutely silent. Don't speak, don't move. But if you hear that monster roar, then run for your lives and don't look back for me."

I could sense the questions he wanted to ask, but there was no time for explanations or discussion. Without another word, I reached up for handholds on the steep cliff face and began climbing straight up.

The rock was crumbly, and more than once I thought I would plunge back to the bottom and break my neck. But after many sweaty minutes I found a ledge that ran roughly parallel to the ground. It was narrow, barely enough for me to edge along, one bare foot after the other. Flattened along the cliff, the rock still warm from the day's sunlight, I made my way slowly, stealthily, to a spot just above the dragon.

The soft hoot of an owl floated through the darkness. Crickets played their eternal scratchy melody while frogs from the riverbank peeped higher notes. Nothing in the forest realized that death was about to strike.

I nearly lost my footing and tumbled off as I turned myself around and pressed my back against the bare rock. Silently I drew my dagger from its sheath on my thigh. I would have one chance and one chance only to kill this monster. If I missed, I would be its next meal.

Taking only enough time to draw in a deep breath and gauge the distance to the dragon's back, I stepped off the ledge and into the empty air.

I dropped onto the monster's back with a thud that almost knocked the wind out of me. Before the dragon realized what had happened I rammed my dagger's blade into the base of his skull. I felt bone, or thick cartilage.

With every ounce of strength in me I pushed the blade in deeper.

I felt the beast die. One instant it was tense, vital, its monstrous head turning, jaws agape. The next it was collapsing like a pricked balloon, as inert as a stone. It fell face-first into the dirt, landing with a jarring crash that sounded to me like the result of an elephant falling off a cliff.

I lay clinging to the dragon's dead hide. For a few heartbeats the noises of the night ceased. Then the crickets and frogs took up their harmony again. Something canine bayed at the rising moon. And none of the other dragons seemed to stir.

I made my way back to the waiting men. Even in the darkness I could see their wide grins. Without wasting a moment, we began piling up our brushwood across the mouth of the canyon.

The sky was beginning to turn gray as we finished the last piece of it. The barrier we had erected looked pitifully thin. Still, it was the best we could do.

Chron and I crawled the length of the brushwood barrier. Through the tangle dry branches I could see the dragons sitting as stolid as huge statues near the cliff wall, tall enough for their snouts to reach the lowest of the caves in the rock face. Their eyes seemed to be open, but they were not moving at all, except for the slow rhythmic pulsing of their flanks as they breathed the deep, regular breath of sleep.

It took several moments for Chron to start a fire from a pair of dry sticks. But at last a tendril of smoke rose from his busy hands and then a flicker of flame broke out. I touched a stick to the flame as Chron plunged his burning brand into the brush. Then we scrambled to our feet and raced back along the length of the barrier, starting new fires every few yards.

The others had their own fire going nicely by the time

we reached them. The whole barrier was in flames, the dry brush crackling nicely, bright tongues of hot fire leaping into the air.

Still the dragons did not stir. I feared that our fire would go out before it could ignite the bushes and trees of the canyon, so I got up and grabbed a burning branch. With this improvised torch I lit several clumps of bush and started a small batch of trees alight. Then the grass caught. Smoke and flames rose high and the wind carried them both deeper into the canyon.

The dragons began to stir. First one of them awoke and seemed to shake itself. It rose on its hind legs, tail held straight out above the ground, head tilting high, nose in the air. A second dragon came to life and hissed loudly enough for us to hear it over the crackle of the flames. Then all the others seemed to awaken at once, shaking and bobbing up and down on their two legs, hissing wildly.

I had thought that they would be sluggish, torpid, in the cool of early dawn. I was wrong. They were quickly alert, pacing nervously along the hollow bowl of the rock wall as the flames rose before them and the wind carried the fire toward them.

For several minutes they merely milled around, hissing, snarling, their hides turning livid red with fear and anger. They were too big to climb the curving wall of rock and escape the way a man would have. They were trapped against the rocky bowl, the trees and grass and bushes in front of them turning into a sea of flame and thickly billowing smoke. I could feel the heat curling the hair on my arms, singeing my face.

We backed away. The dragons, as if in mental contact with one another, all seemed to make the same decision at the same instant. They charged into the crackling flames.

In a ragged column of twos the dragons plunged into the holocaust we had made for them. Hissing and whistling like giant steam engines, they waded into the sea of fire, tossing their immense heads to keep them above the flames and smoke. Those in front crashed through the fiery brush and stands of trees, flattening them out for those behind. One of them went down, screaming terribly. Then another. But the others came rushing forward, trampling over the roasting carcasses of their brethren.

Six of them died in the flames, deliberately giving their lives so that the others could get through. I watched stunned, astounded at this display of intelligence and sacrifice. Reptiles, dinosaurs, could *not* have that level of intelligence. Their brains were too small; their heads were mostly bone.

Something intelligent was directing them. I had no time to puzzle out the mystery, though, because the five remaining monsters were breaking through our fiery barrier.

And bearing down on us.

I could see steaming swaths of raw meat where they had been burned on their legs and flanks. And they could see the five of us, huddled against the cliff face with our copper-tipped spears in our hands.

"Run!" someone screamed.

"No," I yelled. "Face them. . . ."

But it was too late. They broke and ran from the fearsome hissing monsters. All but young Chron. He stayed at my side as three of the giant beasts bore down on us and the remaining pair chased after my fleeing men.

I cursed myself for not having thought to prepare an avenue of retreat. Now we were trapped with the enraged monsters pinning Chron and me against the cliff wall.

The dragons were terribly burned, screeching furiously. We planted our backs against the rock wall and gripped our spears with both hands.

The world slowed down as my body went into hyperdrive. I saw the first of the dragons looming before me, jaws wide, arms reaching for me. Those taloned claws could have ripped a rhinoceros apart.

I ducked beneath its outstretched arms and jammed my spear into its belly, tearing the lizard open from breastbone to crotch. It screamed like all the devils of hell and tottered a few steps sideways, then went down. Turning, I saw Chron with his spear butted against the rock, desperately trying to stave off the dragon that was clawing at him.

Pulling my bloody spear from the beast's gut, I clambered over its whitening body and rammed the metal spear point into the dragon's thigh. It stumbled, turned toward me. Again I rammed my spear into the undefended belly of the beast while Chron stabbed higher, nearer the heart.

Before the dragon could fall, the third of the monsters was on me. My spear was jammed inside the second beast. As I tried to work it loose, to the screams and shrieks of the dying monster, its partner slashed at me with a three-taloned hand. I saw it coming in slow motion and started to duck beneath the blow, but my foot slipped in the thick stream of blood covering the ground and I fell sideways.

I felt the dragon's sharp claws slice through the flesh of my left arm and side. Before the pain could reach my conscious mind I clamped down on the blood vessels and shut off the nerve signals that would carry their message of agony to my brain.

Looking up, I saw Chron ramming his spear into the dragon's throat. It reared up with a screaming roar, tearing the spear out of the teenager's hands. I got to one knee and reached with my good arm for the spear still embedded in the second dragon's hide.

Chron was flattened against the face of the rock, his eyes wide with terror, ducking and dodging as the wounded dragon slashed at him with pain-driven fury. It ignored the spear hanging from its throat in its fury to kill its tormentor. Its claws scored screeching gouges in the solid rock. It bent over to snap at Chron with its frightening teeth, and even I felt its breath, hot and stinking of half-digested flesh.

I reached the spear and worked it free of the dying carcass as Chron desperately twisted away from the dragon's furious slashing and snapping. The lad was faster than the lizard, but not by much. It was merely a question of who would tire first, the defenseless human or the wounded, burned reptile.

Getting shakily to my feet, I rammed the spear into the dragon's flank with all of my remaining strength, felt the copper point scrape against a rib and then penetrate upward, into the lungs.

The dragon shrieked like a thousand demons and swung its thick, blunt tail at me. I couldn't get completely out of the way, and it knocked me sprawling.

The next thing I knew Chron was kneeling over me, tears in his eyes.

"You're alive!" he gasped.

"Almost," I croaked back at him. My back felt numb, there were deep slashes in my left arm and side.

With Chron's help I got to my feet once more. He was unwounded except for a few scrapes and bruises. The three huge dragons lay around us, enormous mounds of deathly gray scaly flesh. Even flat on the ground, their carcasses were taller than my height.

"We killed all three of them." Chron's voice was awed, astonished.

"The others," I said. My throat felt raw, my voice rasped.

Chron picked up our spears and we staggered off in the direction our three comrades had fled. We did not have to go far. Their bloody bodies, sliced to shreds, lay sprawled only a few minutes' walk away.

Chron leaned on the spears, breathing heavily, trying to control his emotions. The dead men were a gruesome sight. Already ants and flies were crawling over their bone-deep wounds.

Then the youngster looked up, his eyes narrowing. "Where are the dragons? Do you think—"

"They've run away," I told him.

"They could come back."

I shook my woozy head. "I don't think so. Look at their tracks. Look at the distance between the prints. They were running. They stopped long enough to slaughter our friends, then headed northward again. They won't be back. Not today, at least."

We started back toward the south. Chron caught our dinner that evening, and with food and a night's rest I felt considerably better.

"Your wounds are healing," he told me in the morning's light. "Even the bruise on your back is smaller than it was last night."

"I heal quickly," I said. Thanks to the Creator who made me.

By the time we returned to the village deep in the forest of Paradise where we had left Anya and Kraal and the others, my strength was almost back to normal. The slashes in my arm were little more than fading scars.

I was eager to see Anya again. And Chron was bubbling with the anticipation of telling the villagers all our news.

"We killed ten dragons, Orion. Ten of them! Wait until they hear about that!"

I gave him a grin, but I wondered how Kraal and his people would take the news of their village being massacred.

Before I could tell him, though, Kraal had his own heavy news to tell me.

"Your woman is gone," he said. "The dragons took her."

Chapter 11

"A nya gone?" I was staggered. "The dragons took her?"

The village was nothing but mud huts beneath spreading oaks and elms. We stood on the bare ground of the central meeting area, the warm sunlight of midday shining through the trees. All the villagers were grouped around Chron and me, staring at us with troubled, frightened eyes.

"We killed dragons!" Chron blurted. "Ten of them!"

I looked straight into Kraal's shaggy-browed shifting eyes. He avoided my gaze, uneasily shuffling from one foot to the other like a guilty little boy. Reeva stood behind him, strangely decked with necklaces of animals' teeth.

There was no sign of a battle in this village. No sign even of a struggle. None of the men were wounded. As far as I could tell, all the people who had been there when I had left were still there.

"Tell me what happened," I said to Kraal.

His face twisted into a miserably unhappy grimace.

"It was her or us," Reeva snapped. "If we did not give her to them, they would kill us all."

"Tell me what happened," I repeated, anger simmering in my blood.

"The dragons came," Kraal said, almost mumbling in his shame and regret. "And their masters. They said they wanted you and the woman. If we gave the two of you to them, they would leave us alone."

"And you did what they asked?"

"Anya did not fight against it," Reeva said, her tone almost angry. "She saw the wisdom of it."

"And you let them take her without a fight?"

"They were *dragons,* Orion," Kraal whined. "Big ones. Six of them. And masters riding them."

Reeva pushed past him to confront me. "I am the priestess now. Anya's power has passed to me."

I wanted to grab her by her scrawny throat and crush her. This was the reward for all that Anya had taught her. My suspicions about little Reeva had been right. She had not been seeking protection; she had sought power.

Looking past her to Kraal, I said, "And you think the dragons will leave you alone now?"

He nodded dumbly.

"Of course they will," Reeva said triumphantly. "Because we will provide them slaves. We will not be harmed. The masters will reward us!"

My anger collapsed into a sense of total defeat. All that Anya and I had taught these people would be used against other humans. Instead of building up an alliance against Set, they had caved in at the first sign of danger and agreed to collaborate with the devils.

"Where did they take Anya?"

"To the north," Kraal answered.

The bitterness I felt was like acid burning inside me. "Then I'll head north. You won't see me again."

"I'll go with you," Chron said.

Reeva's dark eyes flashed. "You will go north, Orion. That is certain."

From behind the row of mud huts strode two reptilian masters. The crowd parted silently to let them advance toward me.

They looked like smaller replicas of Set. Almost human in form. Almost. Clawed feet. Three-fingered taloned hands. Their naked bodies were covered with light red scales that glittered in the mottled sunlight filtering through the tall trees. Slim tails that almost reached the ground, twitching constantly. Reptile faces with narrow slashes for mouths and red eyes with vertical black slits for pupils. No discernable ears and only a pair of breathing holes below the eyes instead of noses.

I whipped the dagger from its sheath on my thigh and Chron leveled his spear at the two reptiles.

"No," I said to the youngster. "Stay out of this."

Then I saw two dozen spear points leveled at me. Most of the men in the village were staring at me grimly, their weapons in their hands.

"Please, Orion," said Kraal in a strangled, agonized voice. "If you fight, they will destroy us all."

The treachery was complete. I realized that Reeva had convinced Kraal to go along with the enemy. He was the tribe's leader, but she was now its priestess and she could twist Kraal to her whims.

Then I heard the crunching sound of heavy footsteps through foliage. From beyond the miserable little huts reared the heads of two dragons, meat-eaters, fighters.

The pair of masters stepped past Kraal and Reeva to confront me. They were my own height, which put them a full head above the tallest villager. Their scaly reptilian faces showed no emotion whatever, yet their glittering serpent's eyes stirred deep hatred within me.

Silently the one on my right extended a three-fingered

hand. Reluctantly I handed him my dagger. I had won it on the plain of Ilios, before the beetling walls of Troy, a gift from Odysseus himself for battle prowess. It was useless to me now, in this time and place. Still, parting with it was painful.

The master made a hissing noise, almost a sigh, and handed my dagger to Kraal. He took it, shamefaced.

The other master turned toward the approaching dragons and raised one hand. They stopped short of the huts, their breath whooshing in and out like spurts of flame in a furnace. The monsters would have wrecked several huts if they had tried to come all the way to this meeting ground in the center of the village. Their masters were keeping their word: no harm would come to the village as long as Kraal's people cooperated.

"You can't let them take him!" Chron shouted at the villagers. There were tears in his eyes and his voice cracked with frustrated rage.

I made myself smile at him. "There's nothing you can do, Chron. Accept the unavoidable." Then I swung my gaze to Kraal and Reeva. "I'll be back."

Kraal looked down at his bare crusted feet but Reeva glared defiantly at me.

"I'll be back," I repeated.

The masters walked me past the huts. With soft whistles they got the big dragons to crouch down and we climbed up on their backs, me behind the one who had taken my dagger. If he—or she, I had no way of telling—was worried that I would grab him around the throat and strangle him, he gave no sign of it.

The dragons lumbered off past the village. I turned for one last look at it, over my shoulder. The villagers were still clustered in the central meeting ground, standing stock still, as if frozen. Chron raised his spear above his head in defiance. It was a pretty gesture, the only thing he could do.

The entire village had been cowed, all except that one teenage boy. I wondered how long he could survive if Reeva decided he was dangerous to her.

Then the trees blotted out the village and I saw it no more. The dragons jounced along at a good pace, jogging on their two legs between the trees, flattening the foliage on the ground. There was no saddle, no reins. I clung to the dragon's hide with both arms and legs, clutching hard to hang on. We rode behind their massive heads, so there was no worry about being knocked off by tree branches. If the dragon could get through, we could easily enough.

The humanoid masters were clad only in their scaly skins, without even a belt or pouch in which to hold things. They seemed to have no tools at all, no weapons except their formidable claws and teeth. And the fearsome dragons we were riding, of course.

I began to wonder if they had language, then wondered even more deeply how a race could be intelligent without language. Clearly Set had communicated with me telepathically. Did these silent replicas of him use telepathy instead of speech?

I tried speaking to them, to no avail. No matter what I said, it made absolutely no impression on the reptilian sitting four inches in front of me. As far as I could tell he was stone deaf.

Yet they controlled the dragons without any trouble at all. It had to be some form of telepathy, I concluded. I remembered the Neanderthals, who also communicated with a form of telepathy, although they could make the sounds of speech if they had to.

We pounded through the forest without stop. Night fell but we barely slowed our pace. If the dragons had a need for sleep, they did not show it, and for all I knew, the masters riding them might have been sound asleep; I had no way of telling. Did they know that I can go without sleep for weeks at a time, if necessary? Or did they conclude that

I could sleep without falling off the back of this gallumphing latter-day dinosaur?

I decided to find out.

I let myself slide off the dragon's back. Hitting the ground on the balls of my feet, I jumped out of the way of the beast pounding along behind me and dashed into the thick brush.

The dragons immediately stopped and reared up. I could hear their snuffling panting in the darkness of the night, like giant steam engines puffing. It was cloudy, threatening rain, so dark that I could not see them at all.

No sound came from the masters riding atop the giant beasts. But I heard the dragons crunching through the underbrush, sniffing like immense bloodhounds. I edged deeper into the bushes, scuttling like a beetle while trying to keep quiet. The forest had gone silent: not an insect chirped.

In the hushed darkness a picture formed itself in my mind. The village I had just left was being trampled by dozens of dragons. Men and women were being torn apart, crushed in the pitiless jaws of the beasts. I saw Chron ripped from throat to groin by a dragon's monstrous claws.

Someone was sending me a powerful message. Whether it was the masters whom I was trying to escape or Set himself in contact with me despite the distance separating us, the message was perfectly clear: either I surrender myself or Chron and all the villagers will be painfully, mercilessly slaughtered.

I rose to my feet. It was still utterly dark. Not even a breeze stirred the air. Within a few minutes, though, I heard the hissing breath and ponderous footfalls of one of the dragons. I stepped out into a slightly clearer space between the trees and saw the burning-red glittering eyes of a master staring down at me from his perch on the dragon's back.

"I fell asleep and slipped off," I lied.

It did not matter. The master watched, wordlessly, as his dragon crouched down enough for me to clamber up onto its back once again. And then we resumed our journey toward the north.

It began to rain at dawn and I hung on to the beast's back, angry, wet, frustrated, and—beneath it all—terrified of what Set was doing to Anya. We had failed, the two of us. Our few moments in Paradise had cost us our lives.

Then a new thought struck me. The masters had actually made a deal with Kraal's tribe. Despicable though it was on Kraal's part, it seemed to me to be a small sign of weakness on the part of Set. The masters had no need of collaborators before I had met Kraal. Our idea of welding all the human tribes into an alliance to resist the masters must have forced Set to make this new accommodation.

The masters *were* vulnerable. At least to a small degree. After all, we had killed some of their most fearsome dragons with the most primitive of weapons. We had been rousing the human tribes to fight back.

But a voice in my head kept asking, What is he doing to Anya?

Probably everything we had accomplished had been wiped away by Set's masterful use of terror. The old hostage maneuver: do as I say or I will kill those you love. Kraal had given in to it, with Reeva's urging. Set would never have stooped to bargaining with humans, even if the bargain was nothing more than threatening hostages, if he had not felt that we were starting to cause damage to him.

But what was he doing to Anya?

Set's hostage ploy has worked to perfection, my inner voice admitted. He has Anya in his grasp, and soon enough he will have you. And all you've accomplished with Kraal is to teach him how to round up fresh slaves for the diabolical masters.

And what is Set doing to Anya?

It was in this turmoil of conflicting fears and regrets

that I rode on the back of the galloping dragon all that long, miserable, rainy day. Wet, cold, and dispirited, I lay my head on the beast's hide and tried to sleep. If the rain bothered the reptilians, they gave no indication of it. The water spattered off the scales of their hides; the chill dankness of the air seemed to have no effect on them at all.

I closed my eyes and willed my body to hang on to the dragon's wet, slippery back. I wanted to sleep, to be as rested as possible for the coming confrontation with Set. I also hoped, desperately, that in sleep the Creators might contact me as they had so often in other lives, other times.

My last waking thought was of Anya. Was she still alive? Was she suffering the tortures that Set told me he would inflict upon her?

I made myself sleep. Without dreams, without messages. Any other time I would have been happy for a few hours of restful oblivion. But when I awoke, I felt disappointed, abandoned, hopeless.

Blinking the sleep away, I saw that it was nearly nightfall again. We had broken clear of the forest and were riding now across the broad sea of grass toward the garden by the Nile. The moon was just rising above the flat horizon and with it that blood red star shone down on me, the same color as the baleful eyes of Set.

Chapter 12

The sun was high in a sky so blue it almost hurt my eyes to look at it. We were riding through the garden by the Nile now, the two dragons pacing less urgently down a long wide avenue of trees. The ground beneath us was grassless bare pebbles, raked smooth by unseen hands.

No slaves were in sight. No other dragons or masters. The garden seemed totally empty except for us.

Then up ahead I saw a structure, a building, or rather a high smooth curved wall. In the shadowless glare of the high sun it seemed the color of eggshell, almost white, and as smooth as the shell of an egg. It slanted inward, sloping a discernable few degrees toward the top. No battlements, no crenellations, no windows. Only a smoothly curving, sloping wall of featureless material that was neither stone nor wood.

Our dragons slowed their pace even further as we approached the wall, then began to trot around its base. It was more than three stories high, I judged, and so wide in

extent that it must have covered more ground than Troy
and Jericho combined.

We rode around the wall's vast curving base for several
minutes before I saw a section slide open to reveal a high,
wide door. The dragons trotted through it.

Now the beasts slowed to a walk as we went down a
long, broad tunnel. Their clawed feet crunched on bare
pebbles. Their heads almost grazed the ceiling, which was
made of the same smooth plastic material as the outer wall.
Finally we stepped out into sunshine again.

We were in a huge circular courtyard, busy with
reptilians of all descriptions and scampering, sweating
half-naked human slaves. The inner wall towered above
me, slanting inward, utterly smooth and impossible to
climb.

There was a corral of sorts built on the far side of the
courtyard, where the four-footed herbivorous dragons that
served as slave guards were penned in. Some of them were
eating, their long necks bent down to troughs piled high
with greens. Others stood placidly, tails swinging slowly,
eyes calmly surveying the courtyard, heads bobbing up and
down. At their full height they reached more than halfway
up the enclosing circular wall.

Exactly opposite the corral were sturdier pens where
several of the fiercer meat-eating dragons paced nervously,
hissing and snapping, their enormous teeth flashing like
sabers in the sunlight.

A terrace jutted out from one section of the curving
wall, more than fifteen feet above the ground. Dozens of
pterosaurs squatted there as if sleeping, their big leathery
wings folded, their long beaks hanging down, eyes closed. I
saw no droppings on the beams that supported the terrace
or the ground below. Either the flying lizards were well
trained or the slaves cleaned up after them.

I counted eight of the humanoid masters in that wide
courtyard, striding across the yard or sitting on benches or

bent over some piece of work. None of them conversed with another. They remained far separated, aloof, as if they had no use for their own kind.

Human slaves scurried to fill the feeding troughs, toting big wicker baskets bulging with leafy vegetation. A quartet of slaves trudged out of a low doorway, leaning heavily into rope harnesses as they dragged a wooden pallet piled high with raw red meat for the carnosaurs. Others dashed here and there on tasks that were not apparent to me, but obviously important to someone from the way they were scampering. Two slaves ran up to us, standing with heads bowed as the masters slid off our mounts and beckoned me to do the same.

It was like a scene from a medieval castle or an oriental bazaar: the dragons in brilliant splashes of colors; the masters' scaly hides in pale coral red, almost pink; the looming walls; the outlandish pterosaurs; the scurrying slaves. Yet there were two things about it that seemed uncannily strange to me. There were no fires anywhere, no smoke, no cooking, no one warming themselves beside crackling flames. And there was virtually no noise.

All this was going on in almost total silence. Not a voice could be heard. Only the occasional hiss of a dragon or buzz of an insect broke the quiet. The slaves' unshod feet were inaudible on the dusty bare ground of the courtyard. The masters themselves made no sound, and their human slaves apparently dared not speak.

I slid to the ground and stared at the two slaves standing mutely before us. One was a young woman, bare to the waist like her male companion. Without a word they motioned to the dragons, which followed them to the pens on the opposite side of the courtyard from the herbivores' corral.

One of my captors touched my shoulder with a cold clawed hand and pointed in the direction of a narrow doorway set into the wall's curving face. I would have sworn the wall had been perfectly smooth a moment earlier.

With one master ahead of me and the second behind, I entered the cool shadows of a corridor that seemed to curve along the wall's inner circumference. We came to a ramp that led down and began a long, silent, spiraling descent. It was dark inside, especially after the brightness of the afternoon sun. The downward-ramped corridor had no lights at all; I could barely make out the back of the reptilian walking a few feet in front of me, his tail swinging slightly from side to side.

Finally we stopped at what seemed to be a blank wall. A portion of it slid aside. My escorts gestured me through.

I stepped into a dimly lit chamber and the door slid shut behind me. I knew I was not alone, however. I could sense the presence of another living entity.

Even though my eyes can adjust to very low light levels almost immediately, the chamber remained shrouded in gloomy shadows. Almost complete inky blackness. Then a beam of dark red light, like the angry glower of the blood star in the night, bathed the part of the chamber in front of me.

Set reclined on a low, wide backless couch. A throne of blackest ebony, raised three feet above the floor on which I stood. On either side of him stood several statues, some of wood, some of stone, one of them seemed to be carved from ivory. No two were the same size; they had been apparently carved by many different hands. Some were outright crude. The ivory statue was truly a beautiful masterwork.

They were all of the same subject: the hellish creature who was called Set.

His red slitted eyes radiated implacable hatred. His horned face, crimson-scaled body, long twitching tail *were* the devil incarnate. Thousands of generations of human beings would fear his image. His was the face of nightmares, of terror beyond reason, of an eternal enmity that knew no bounds, no restraints, no mercy.

I felt that burning hatred in my soul. My knees went weak with the seething dread and horror of standing face-to-face with the remorseless enemy of humankind.

"You are Orion." The words formed themselves in my mind.

Aloud I replied, "You are Set."

"Pitiful monkey. Are you the best your Creators could send against me?"

"Where is Anya?" I asked.

Set's mouth opened slightly. In a human face it might have been a cruel smile. Rows of pointed teeth, like a shark's, glittered in the sullen red light.

"The weakness of the mammal is that it is attached to other mammals. At first literally, physically. Then emotionally, all its life."

"Where is Anya?" I repeated.

He raised a clawed hand and part of the wall to his right became a window, a display screen. I saw dozens of humans packed into a dank airless chamber. Some were sitting, some were grubbing colorless globs of food from a bin with their bare hands and stuffing it into their mouths. A man and a woman were coupling off in a corner, ignoring the others and ignored by them.

"Monkeys," Set said in my mind.

I searched the scene but could not see Anya. Then I realized that this was the first example of real technology that I had seen from Set or any of the reptiles.

He raised one talon and I began to hear the hum and chatter of human speech, shouting, conversing, even laughing. A baby cried. An old man's cracked voice complained bitterly about someone who had called him a fool. A trio of women sat huddled together on the grimy floor, heads bent toward one another, whispering urgently among themselves.

"Chattering stupid monkeys," Set repeated. "Always talking. Always gibbering. What do they find to talk about?"

The human voices sounded warm and reassuring to me.

Set's words in my mind became sardonic. "Humans that see each other every hour of every day still make their mouth noises at each other constantly. This will be a better world when the last of them are eliminated."

"Eliminated?"

"Ah, that roused your simian curiosity, did it not?"

"You expect to wipe out the entire human race?"

"I will erase you, all of you, from the face of this world." Even though he projected the thought mentally, I seemed to hear a sibilant hissing in his words.

My mind was racing. He couldn't wipe out the entire human race. I knew that the Creators existed in the far future, which meant that humanity survived.

Then I heard Set's equivalent of laughter, an eerie blood-chilling high-pitched shrill, like the scrape of a claw against a chalkboard.

"The Creators will not exist once I have finished my task. I will bend the continuum to *my* will, Orion, and your pitiful band of self-styled gods will disappear like smoke from a candle that has been snuffed out."

The display on the wall went dark.

"Anya . . ."

"You wish to see the woman. Come with me." He got to his feet, looming over me like a fearsome dark shadow of death. "You will see her. And share her fate."

We went through another hidden door and into a corridor so dimly lit I could barely see his powerful form in front of me. He and his kind must be able to see far into the infrared, I reasoned. Does that mean they cannot see the higher-energy parts of the spectrum, the blues and violets? I mentally filed that conjecture for future consideration.

The corridor became a spiraling ramp that led down, down, deeper into the earth. The walls glowed a feeble dull red, barely enough for me to guide my steps. Still we descended. Set was nearly a foot taller than I, so tall that the scales of his head nearly scraped the tunnel's ceiling. He was powerfully built, yet his body did not bulge with muscle; it had a fluid grace to it, like the silent deadly litheness of a boa constrictor.

His skull was ridged, I saw, with two bony crests that ran down the back of his neck and merged with his spine. From the front those ridges looked like small horns just above his slitted snake's eyes. From the rear I saw that his spine was knobby with vestigial spikes, projections that may have been plates of bony armor in eons past. There was a small knob at the end of his tail, also, that might once have been a defensive club.

The tunnel was getting narrower, steeper. And hotter. I was perspiring. The floor was uncomfortably warm against my bare feet.

"How far down are we going?" I asked, my voice echoing off the smooth walls.

His voice answered in my mind, "Your Creators draw their energy from their sun, the golden light of the bigger star. I draw mine from the depths of the planet, from the ocean of molten iron that surges halfway between this world's outer crust and its absolute center."

"The earth's liquid core," I muttered.

"A sea of energy," Set continued, "heated by radioactivity and gravity, seething with electrical currents and magnetic fields, so hot that iron and all other metals are molten and flow like water."

He was describing hell. He drew his energy from hell.

Down and still further down we walked. I began to wonder why Set had not constructed an elevator. We walked on in silence, in the eerie dull red light, for what seemed like hours. It was like walking through an oven.

He's holding Anya down here, I told myself. What can he have down at this depth? Why so deep underground? Is he afraid of being seen? Does he have other enemies, in addition to the Creators? Perhaps some of his own kind are at odds with him?

My thoughts circled endlessly, but always came back to the same fearful question: What is he doing to Anya?

Gradually I became aware of a presence in my mind, another intelligence, probing so gently I could hardly feel it. At first I thought it might have been Anya. But this presence was alien, hostile. Then I realized why we were spending so much time walking toward Anya's prison. Set was probing my mind, interrogating me so subtly that I had not even realized it, searching my memories for—for what?

He sensed my awareness of his probe.

"You are just as stubborn as the woman. I shall have to use more forceful methods on you, just as I have had to do with her."

Hot fury driven by fear raged through me. I wanted to leap on his back and snap his neck. But I knew that he could overpower me. I could feel his evil amusement at my thoughts.

"She is in great pain, Orion. Her agony will become even greater before I allow her to die."

Chapter 13

The steep spiraling tunnel ended finally at another blank door. Set did nothing that I could see, but the door slid open to reveal what seemed, at first glance, to be an elaborate laboratory.

Anya was nowhere in sight. The chamber we stepped into hummed with electrical power. Row upon row of buzzing throbbing consoles stood along two of the four walls of the cramped little room. Behind us was a long table cluttered with strange objects and a backless chair, almost like an ornate bench, for a tailed two-legged creature to sit upon. The fourth wall was absolutely blank.

Set clicked the talons of his right hand and that featureless wall slid up, revealing a much larger room, also packed with arcane equipment.

And Anya.

She was imprisoned in a glass cylinder standing atop a raised platform. Totally naked, she stood motionless, eyes closed, hands flat at her sides. Blue flickers of electricity played up and down every inch of her body.

"She appears quite serene," said Set's hissing voice in my mind.

She seemed to be in frozen stasis. Or dead. On the four corners of the raised platform, outside the glass cylinder holding Anya, stood four rudely carved statues of Set. The largest was as high as my chest and made of wood.

"Look here," he commanded.

I turned and followed his outstretched claw to see a row of display screens against the wall.

"They show her brain-wave patterns."

Jagged spikes, red with agony, jittering up and down in rhythm to the sparks of electricity crawling over her body.

With a wave of Set's hand the blue flickers intensified, became brighter, raced across Anya's skin. Her naked body seemed to cringe, shudder. Her eyelids squeezed shut tighter. Tears crawled out from behind them. From the corner of my eye I saw the spikes of the display screens turn sharper, steeper, racing across the screens like tongues of flame burning themselves into my brain.

This monster was torturing Anya. Torturing her as heartlessly and efficiently as a swarm of army ants stripping the flesh from any living thing that stood in its path.

"Stop it!" I screamed. "Stop it!"

"Open your mind to me, Orion. Let me see what I want to see."

"And then?"

"And then I will allow you both to die."

I stared into his glittering reptilian eyes. There was no triumph there, no joy, not even sadistic pleasure. Nothing but pure hate. Hatred for the human race, hatred for the Creators, for Anya, for me. Set was remorselessly doing what he had to do to reach his goal.

I, too, burned with hatred. But, powerless, I let my shoulders slump and my head droop.

"Stop her pain and you can do what you want with me," I said.

"I will ease her pain," Set replied. "It will not stop until I have learned what I must know from you. Then you can both die."

The blue flickers crawling across Anya's skin turned paler, moved more slowly. The display screens showed her pain lessened.

And Set's powerful, merciless mind drove into mine like a spike of red-hot iron, ruthlessly seeking the knowledge he wanted. I felt frozen, totally immobile, unable to twitch a finger as he ransacked my brain for its memory storage.

I saw, I heard, I felt things from my pasts. The insane Golden One sneering at me, telling me that he will destroy all the other Creators and be worshiped by the human race as its one true god. The barbaric splendor of Karakorum and Ogatai, the Mongols' high khan, my friend, the man I assassinated. The piercing wet cold of Cornwall on that darkest day of the Dark Age, when Arthur's knights slaughtered each other by the score.

Set was rampaging through my mind, touching on memories, thoughts, lifetimes that had been erased from my consciousness, seeking, seeking, greedily ripping across the eons I have lived to find what he sought.

Yet while he tore through my defenseless mind he exposed his own to me. The link between us, agonizing as it was, went in both directions. I could not see much of his thoughts, nor could I create an active probe to seek out his memory bank as he was doing to me. But Set could not ravage my mind without exposing at least some of his thoughts to me.

I was in the laboratory where the Golden One created me. I was on a becalmed sea beneath a brazen sky of hammered copper, dying of thirst. I was on a world that circled the star Sirius. I died with Anya in my arms as a great starship exploded.

At last I was standing in this alien fiendish torture chamber with Anya suffering within her glass prison and Set's hateful red eyes glowering at me.

"Pah! This is pointless. You know less about it than I do." For the first time his words, burning in my mind, seemed edged with frustration and anger.

My body came alive again. I felt it tingle as Set's control over me relaxed.

He turned his reptilian gaze toward Anya once more. "She knows. I will have to tear it out of her."

"No!" I bellowed as he raised his hand toward the instruments on the wall.

He turned to the wall of instruments once again, ignoring me for just a fraction of a second. Enough.

I grabbed the nearest of the four carved wooden statues and smashed him across his ridged back with it. Down he went, smashing into the dials and display screens lining the wall. Raising the carving over my head, I swung it with all my might at the tube of glass enclosing Anya. It shattered into a spray of fragments and the electrical flames that slithered over her naked flesh winked out.

I reached for her wrist and pulled her down off that pedestal of pain.

"Wh—what . . . ?" Her eyes opened, bloodshot from pain.

"This way!" I snapped, pulling her along with me.

Set was on one knee, pulling himself to his feet. "Stop!" his voice roared in my head. And something within me wanted to obey him.

But something even stronger drove me on, overriding his mental command. I yanked Anya through the doorway and into the small outer chamber, then out into the corridor as Set barked out commands telepathically.

The corridor did not truly end where we had stopped.

That much I had seen in Set's mind. A section of its wall slid away smoothly and Anya and I plunged into this new branch of the long spiraling tunnel.

Heading down.

"Orion—he captured you, too?"

"Reeva and Kraal made a deal with him: his price was both of us."

We were pounding along the dim tunnel as it sloped sharply downward, our bare feet slapping against the smooth flooring. It felt hot. The feeble light emanating from the narrow walls cast no shadows.

"Are you all right?" I asked, her wrist still firmly in my grasp.

She gasped as we ran, "The pain . . . it was in my mind."

"You're all right?"

"Physically . . . but . . . I remember . . . Orion, he's a heartless fiend."

"I'll kill him."

"Where are we heading? Why are we descending?"

"Energy," I said. "His energy source is below, down deep in the earth."

What I had seen in Set's mind had been a confused tangle of impressions. He could manipulate spacetime as the Creators did, and the source of the titanic energies he needed for that was deeply buried beneath us.

"We can't get away," Anya said as we raced breathlessly down the tunnel, "by going down."

"We can't get away by heading up. Set's cohorts are there. Dozens of dragons up at the surface, and I don't know how many so-called masters he has with him."

"They'll be coming after us."

I nodded grimly.

Set had been seeking in my mind a knowledge that the Creators apparently had and he did not. Something about a nexus in the spacetime continuum, a crisis that had occurred millions of years earlier that he was trying to change, undo, reverse.

Suddenly I saw his face in my mind, seething fury. "You cannot escape my wrath, pathetic ape. Excruciating pain and utter despair are all that you can look forward to."

Anya saw him, too. Her eyes widened momentarily. Then she snapped, "He's afraid, Orion. You've made him fear us."

"FEAR ME!" Set's voice boomed in our minds.

I said nothing and we plunged onward, down the spiraling dim tunnel, heading away from the sun and freedom. I knew that dozens of Set's humanoid underlings were racing down the tunnel after us, cutting off any hope of returning to the surface and the world of warmth and light.

Not that it was cold in the tunnel as we sped down its steeply sloped spiral. The floor was now blistering hot, the walls glowed red. It was if we were heading for the entrance to hell.

I realized that I still grasped the statue of Set in my left hand, my fingers wrapped tightly around its neck. It was the only thing even close to a weapon that we possessed and I hung on to it, despite its hefty weight. It had served me well once and I was certain I would be wielding it again before long.

The tunnel finally widened into a broad circular chamber filled with more instruments and equipment of Set's alien technology. This womb of rock was lit more brightly than the tunnel, though its ceiling was low, claustrophobic. In its center was a circular railing. We went to it and peered down a long featureless tube so deep that its end was lost from sight. Pulses of heat surged up through it, and I thought I could hear a rumbling low throbbing sound, like the slow pulsing of a gigantic heart at the core of an incalculably immense beast.

"A core tap," Anya said, peering down that endless shaft.

"Core tap?"

"The energy source for Set's attempt to warp the continuum. It must extend down to the molten core of the earth itself."

I knew she was correct but the realization still made me blink with astonishment. Set was tapping the seething energies of the earth's molten core. For the purpose of altering spacetime. But why? To what end? That I did not know.

This chamber was the end of the corridor. There was no exit except the way we had just come, and I sensed that dozens, scores of Set's humanoid reptilians were racing down the corridor toward us.

Anya was totally absorbed in scanning the banks of instruments and display panels lining the chamber's circular wall. We had only a few minutes before every reptilian master in Set's domain came clawing at us, but she concentrated entirely on the hardware surrounding us. She was focused so completely on the machinery that the pain of Set's torture was forgotten, her nudity ignored.

Not by me. She was the most beautiful woman in the world, slim and tall and lithe as a warrior goddess should be, lustrous black hair tumbling past her bare shoulders, luminous gray eyes intently studying the alien technology before her.

"The spacetime warp is building up at the bottom of the shaft, on the edge of the core. The energies down there are enough to distort the continuum completely, if focused properly."

From the way she muttered the words it seemed that she was speaking more to herself than to me.

Then she turned. "Orion, we've got to destroy these instruments. Smash them! Quickly."

"With pleasure," I said, raising the wooden statue.

You are only increasing the agonies that I will inflict upon you, Set warned inside my head.

"Ignore him," said Anya.

I swung the statue at the nearest bank of instruments. It crashed through the light plastic casing easily. Sparks showered, cold blue and white. A thin hiss of smoke seeped out of its battered face.

Methodically I went from one console to the next, smashing, breaking, destroying. I pictured Set's face in place of the lifeless instruments. I enjoyed crushing it in.

I was only a quarter of the way around the wide circle when Anya warned, "They're coming!"

I dashed to the circular chamber's only entrance and heard the clatter of dozens of clawed feet scraping down the sloping ramp toward us.

"Hold them off for as long as you can," Anya commanded.

I had only a brief instant to glance at her. She attacked the next set of consoles with her bare hands, ripping off the lightweight paneling and tearing at their innards, her fingers bloodied, the flash of electrical sparks throwing blue-white glare across the utterly determined features of her beautiful face.

Then the reptilians were on me. The doorway was not as narrow as I would have liked. More than one of the humanoid masters could confront me, sometimes as many as three at once. I used the statue of their lord and ruler as a weapon, striking at them with all the accumulated fury and hatred that had been building in me for these many months.

I killed them. By the pairs, by the threesomes, by the dozens and scores. I stood in that doorway and smashed and swung and clubbed with a might and bloodlust that I had never known before. The wooden statue became an instrument of death, crushing bones, smashing skulls, spurting the blood of these inhuman enemies until the doorway was clogged with their scaly bodies, the floor slick with gore.

They had no weapons except those that nature had given them. They slashed with their wicked claws, ripping my flesh again and again. My own blood flowed with theirs, but it did not matter to me. I was a killing machine, as mindless as a flame or an avalanche.

Then Anya was beside me, a long sharp strip of metal torn from the consoles in her hand, wielding it like a sword of vengeance. She shrieked a primal battle cry, I roared with rage born of desperation, the reptiles hissed and clawed at us both.

Slowly, inexorably, we were driven back from the doorway, back into the big circular chamber. They tried to get around us, surround us, swarm us under. We stood back-to-back, swinging, cutting, smashing at them with all the fury that human blood and sinew could generate.

Not enough. For every reptilian that fell another took its place. Two more. Ten more.

Without a word passing between us, Anya and I cut a swath through the monsters and made it to the railing around the core shaft. We used it to protect our backs as we fought on, all hope gone, just fought for the sake of killing as many of them as we could before they inevitably wore us down.

One of the humanoids clambered over the railing behind us, across the wide gap of the core shaft, and tried to leap across it to land on our backs. He could not span the width of the shaft and fell screeching wildly into its yawning abyss.

I had long since clamped down on the nerve impulses signaling pain and fatigue to my brain, but my arm felt heavier with each stroke, slower. A reptilian's claws raked my chest, another tore at my face. It was the end.

Almost.

In the midst of the blood and battle I finally realized

that they were not trying to kill us. They were dying by the dozens to obey Set's implacable command. He wanted us alive. Quick death was not his plan for us.

I would not let him get his vicious hands on Anya again. With the last painful gasp of my ebbing strength I grasped Anya around the waist and pushed the two of us over the top of the railing and into the yawning, gaping mouth of the red-hot pit that ended in the surging molten fury of the earth's seething core.

Down and down we plummeted. Down toward the molten, surging heart of the earth.

And death.

BOOK II

PURGATORY

Lo! Death has reared himself a throne
In a strange city lying alone
Far down within the dim West,
Where the good and the bad and the worst and the best
Have gone to their eternal rest.

Chapter 14

Down and down and down we plunged.

Lit by the sullen red glower from deep below us, Anya and I were weightless, in free-fall, like parachutists or astronauts in zero gravity. We seemed to be hanging in mid-air, floating eerily on nothingness, slowly roasting in the blistering heat welling up from below. A fiery wind like the blast from a bellowing rocket engine howled past us. We could not breathe, could not speak.

I willed my body to draw oxygen from the vacuoles within its cells: a temporary expedient, but it was better than drawing in a breath of burning air that would sear my lungs. I hoped Anya could do the same.

The brief glimpse into Set's mind that I had obtained told me that this seemingly endless tube we were falling through reached down toward the earth's core, where the raging heat powered a warping device that might fling us into another spacetime.

That was our only chance to escape Set and the slow

death he had planned for us. That, or death itself in the searing embrace of molten iron that was rushing up toward us.

I gripped Anya tightly to me and she wrapped her arms around my neck. There were no words. Our embrace said everything we needed to say. I thought that Set and his reptilian minions could never know this kind of closeness, this sharing of body contact, flesh to flesh, that is uniquely mammalian.

Squeezing my eyes shut, I tried to recall the sensations of previous passages through spacetime warps. With all my strength I tried to make contact with the Creators, to will the two of us into the safety of their domain in the far future. But it was useless. We continued to plummet toward the earth's core, clinging to each other in our free-fall weightlessness as the heat boiling up from below began to cook our flesh.

Energy. It takes the titanic energy of a planet's fiery core or the churning radiant surface of a star to distort the flow of spacetime and create a warp in the continuum. The closer we got to the molten iron at the bottom of Set's core tap, the closer we got to the energy needed for the warp. Yet that same energy was killing us, driving the breath from our bodies, charring our flesh.

We had no choice. I forced my body to drain every drop of moisture it could generate to cover my body with sweat, desperately hoping that the thin film of moisture would absorb the heat blasting at me and save me from being broiled alive, at least for a few moments longer.

Anya's face, so close to my own, began to shimmer in the burning heat. I thought my eyes were melting away, but then I *felt* her fading into nothingness in my arms. Her body seemed to waver and grow transparent.

Her lovely face was set in a bitterly tragic expression, half apology, half desperation. It rippled and flickered before my streaming eyes, blurring, dimming, waning into a transparent ghostly shadow.

There in my arms, Anya changed her form. She began to glow, her solid body dissolving away into nothingness, transforming herself into a radiant sphere of silvery light tinged ruddy by the glow from beneath us.

I realized that she truly was a goddess, as advanced beyond my human form as I am beyond the form of the algae. The human body that she had worn, that she had suffered in, was a sacrifice she made because she loved me. Now, faced with searing death, she reverted to her true form, a globe of pure energy that pulsated and dwindled even as I watched it.

"Farewell," I heard in my mind. "Farewell, my darling."

The silvery globe disappeared and I was left alone, abandoned, plunging toward hell itself.

My first thought was, At least she'll be safe. She can escape, perhaps even get back to the other Creators, I told myself. But I could not hide the bitterness that surged through me, the black sorrowing anguish that filled every atom of my being. She had abandoned me, left me to face my fate alone. I knew she was right to do it, yet a gulf of endless grief swallowed me up, deeper and darker than the pit I was falling through.

I roared out a wordless, mindless scream of rage: fury at Set and his satanic power, at the Creators who had made me to do their bidding, at the goddess who had abandoned me.

Anya had abandoned me. There was a limit to how much a goddess would face for love of a mortal. I had been a fool even to dream it could be otherwise. Pain and death were only for the miserable creatures who served the Creators, not for the self-styled gods and goddesses themselves.

Then a wave of absolute cold swept through me, like the breath of the angel of death, like being plunged into the heart of an ancient glacier or the remotest depths of intergalactic space. Darkness and cold so complete that it seemed every molecule in me was instantly frozen.

I wanted to scream. But I had no body. There was no space, no dimension. I existed, but without form, without life, in a nullity where there was neither light nor warmth nor time itself.

In the nonmaterial essence that was my mind I saw a globe, a planet, a world spinning slowly before me. I knew it was Earth, yet it was an Earth such as I had never known before. It was a sea world, covered with a global ocean, blue and sparkling in the sun. Long parades of purest whitest clouds drifted across the azure sea. The world ocean was unblemished by any islands large enough for me to see, unbroken by any landmass. The poles were free of ice and covered with deep blue water just as the rest of the planet was.

The Earth turned slowly, majestically, and at last I saw land. A single continent, brown and green and immense: Asia and Africa, Europe and the Americas, Australia and Antarctica and Greenland, all linked together in one gigantic landmass. Even so, much of the land was covered with shallow inland seas, lakes the size of India, rivers longer than the eternal Nile, broader than the mighty Amazon.

As I watched, disembodied, floating in emptiness, the vast landmass began to break apart. In my mind I could hear the titanic groaning of continent-sized slabs of basalt and granite, see the shuddering of earthquakes, watch whole chains of mountains thrusting upward out of the tortured ground. A line of volcanoes glowered fiercely red and the land split apart, the ocean came rushing in, steaming, frothing, to fill the chasm created by the separating continents.

I felt myself falling once again, speeding toward that spinning globe even as its continents heaved and buckled and pulled apart from one another. I felt my senses returning, my body becoming substantial, real.

Then utter darkness.

My eyes focused on a flickering glow. A soft radiance that came and went, came and went, in a gentle relaxed rhythm. I was lying on my back, something spongy and yielding beneath me. I was alive and back in the world again.

With an effort I focused on this world around me. The glow was simply sunlight shining through the swaying fronds of gigantic ferns that bowed gracefully in the passing hot breeze. I started to pull myself up to a sitting position and found that I was too weak to accomplish it. Dehydrated, exhausted, even my blood pressure was dangerously low from sapping so much liquid to protect my skin from being roasted.

Above me I saw these immense ferns swaying. Beyond them a sky of pearl gray featureless clouds. The air felt hot and clammy, the ground soft and wet like the spongy moss of a swamp. I could hear insects droning loudly, but no other sounds.

I tried to at least lift my head and look around, but even that was too much for me.

Almost, I laughed. To save myself from the fiery pit of hell only to die of starvation because I no longer had the strength to get off my back—the situation had a certain pathetic irony to it.

Then Anya bent over me, smiling.

"You're awake," she said, her voice soft and warm as sunshine after a rain.

A flood of wonder and joy and fathomless inexpressible gratitude hit me so hard that I would have wept if there had been enough moisture in me to form tears. She had not abandoned me! She had not left me to die. Anya was here beside me, in human form, still with me.

She was clad in a softly draped thigh-length robe the

color of pale sand, fastened on one shoulder by a silver
clasp. Her hair was perfect, her skin unblemished by the
roasting heat and slashing claws we had faced.

I tried to speak, but all that escaped my parched throat
was a strangled rasping.

She leaned over me and kissed me gently on my
cracked lips, then propped up my head and put a gourd full
of water to my lips. It was green and crawling with swamp
life, but it tasted as cool and refreshing as ambrosia to me.

"I had to metamorphose, my love," she told me,
almost apologetically. "It was the only way we could
survive that terrible heat."

I still could not speak. Which was just as well. I could
not bear the idea of confessing to her that I had thought she
had abandoned me.

"In my true—" She hesitated, started over again: "In
that other form I could absorb energy coming from the core
tap and use it to protect us."

Finally finding my voice, I replied in a frog's croak,
"Then you didn't . . . cause the jump. . . ."

Anya shook her head slightly. "I didn't direct the
spacetime transition, no. Wherever and whenever we are
now, it is the time and place that Set's warping device was
aimed at."

Still flat on my back, with my head in her lap, I rasped,
"The Cretaceous Period."

Anya did not reply, but her perceptive gray eyes
seemed to look far beyond this time and place.

I took another long draft of water from the gourd she
held.

A few more swallows and I could speak almost normally. "The little I gleaned from Set's mind when he was
probing me included the fact that something is happening,
or has happened, or maybe will happen here in this
time—sixty to seventy million years in the past from the
Neolithic."

"The Time of Great Dying," Anya murmured.

"When the dinosaurs were wiped out."

"And thousands of other species along with them, plant as well as animal. An incredible disaster struck the earth."

"What was it?" I asked.

She shrugged her lovely shoulders. "We don't know. Not yet."

I pushed myself up on one elbow and looked directly into her divinely beautiful gray eyes. "Do you mean that the Creators—the Golden One and all the others—don't know what took place at one of the most critical points in the planet's entire history?"

Anya smiled at me. "We have never had to consider it, my love. So take that accusative frown off your face. Our concern has been with the human race, your kind, Orion, the creatures we created. . . ."

"The creatures who evolved into you," I said.

She bobbed her head once in acknowledgment. "So, up until now we have had no need to investigate events of sixty-five million years previous to our own era."

My strength was returning. My flesh was still seared red and slashed here and there by the claws of Set's reptilians. But I felt almost strong enough to get to my feet.

"This point in time is crucial to Set," I said. "We've got to find out why."

Anya agreed. "Yes. But not just this moment. You lie there and let me find us something to eat."

I saw that she was bare-handed, without tools or weapons of any kind.

She sensed my realization. "I was not able to return to the Creators' domain, my love. Set has still blocked us off from any contact there. The best I could do was to ride along the preset vector of his warping device." She glanced down at herself, then added with a modest smile, "And use some of its energy to clothe myself."

"It's better than roasting to death," I replied. "And your costume is charming."

More seriously, Anya said, "We're alone here, cut off from any chance of help, and only Set knows where and when we are."

"He'll come looking for us."

"Perhaps not," Anya said. "Perhaps he feels we're safely out of his way."

Painfully I raised myself to a sitting position. "No. He will seek us out and try to destroy us completely. He'll leave nothing to chance. Besides, this is a critical nexus in spacetime for him. He won't want us free to tamper with his plans—whatever they are."

Scrambling to her feet, Anya said, "First things first. Food, then shelter. And then—"

Her words were cut off by the sounds of splashing, close enough to startle us both.

For the first time I took detailed note of where we were. It looked like a swampy forest filled with enormous ferns and the gnarled thick trunks of mangrove trees. Heavy underbrush of grotesque-looking spiky cattails pressed in on us. The very air was sodden, oppressive, steaming hot. No more than ten yards away the spongy ground on which we rested gave way to muddy swamp water flowing sluggishly through stands of reeds and the tangled mangrove roots. The kind of place that harbored crocodiles. And snakes.

Anya was already on her feet, staring into the tangled foliage that choked the water and cut off our view a scant few feet before us. I forced myself up, tottering weakly, and gestured for Anya to climb up the nearest tree.

"What about you?" she whispered.

"I'll try," I breathed back.

Several of the tree trunks leaned steeply and were wrapped with parasitic vines that made it almost easy for me to climb up, even as weak as I was. Anya helped me and we crept out onto a broad branch and stretched ourselves flat on its warm, rough bark. I felt insects crawling over my skin and saw a blue-glinting fly or bee or *something* the size of a sparrow buzz past my eyes with an angry whizzing of wings.

The splashing sounds were coming closer. Set's troops, already searching for us? I held my breath.

It looked as if a hillside had come loose from the ground and was plodding through the swamp. Mottled mud brown, olive green, and gray, a fifteen-foot-high mass of living scale-covered flesh pushed through the dense foliage and into the clear area of the swamp where the green-scummed water flowed sluggishly.

And I almost laughed. It had a broad flat snout, like a duck's bill. The curvature of its mouth gave it a silly-looking grin permanently built into its face, like an idiotic cartoon character.

No matter the expression on its face, though, the dinosaur was cautiously looking around before it came further out into the open. It reared up on its hind legs, taller than the branch on which we hid, and looked around, sniffing like the huffing of a steam locomotive. Its feet were more like hooves than clawed fighting weapons. Its yellow-eyed gaze swept past the tree where Anya and I were clinging.

With a snort like the air brakes of a diesel bus, the duckbill dropped down to all fours and emerged fully into the lethargic stream. It was some thirty feet long from its snout to the tip of its tail. And it was not alone.

There was a whole procession of duckbilled dinosaurs, a parade of forty-two of them by my count. With massive dignity they plodded along the swampy stream, sinking knee deep in the muddy water with each ponderous step.

We watched, fascinated, as the dinosaurs marched down the stream and slowly disappeared into the tangled foliage of the swamp.

"Dinosaurs," Anya said, once they were out of sight and the forest's insects had resumed their chirruping. There was wonder in her voice, and not a little awe.

"We're in the Cretaceous," I told her. "Dinosaurs rule the world here."

"Where do you think they were heading? It looked like a purposeful migration—"

Again she stopped short, held her breath. All the sounds of the forest had stopped once again.

I was still lying prone on the broad tree branch. Anya flattened out once again behind me. We could hear nothing; somehow that bothered me more than the splashing sounds the duckbills had made.

The foliage parted not more than thirty yards from where we were hiding and the most hideous creature I have ever seen emerged from the greenery. An enormous massive head, almost five feet long from snout to base, most of it a gaping mouth armed with teeth the size of sabers. Angry little eyes that somehow looked almost intelligent, like the eyes of a hunting tiger or a killer whale.

It pushed slowly, cautiously into the sluggish stream that the duckbills had used as a highway only a minute earlier.

Tyrannosaurus rex. No doubt of it. Tremendous size, dwarfing Set's fighting carnosaurs that we had seen in Paradise. Withered vestigial forelegs hanging uselessly on its chest. It reared up to its full height, taller than all but the biggest trees, and seemed to peer in the direction that the duckbills had gone. Then it stepped out into the muddy stream on two powerful hind legs, its heavy tail held straight out as if to balance the enormous weight of that fearsome head.

I could feel the terrified tension in Anya's body, pressing against mine. I myself was as rigid as a frightened mouse confronted by a lion. The tyrannosaur loomed over us, its scales striped jungle green and dark gray. Its feet bore claws bigger and sharper than reapers' scythes.

Slowly, stealthily, it moved upstream in the tracks of the duckbills. Just when I was about to breathe again, a second tyrannosaur pushed through the foliage as silently and carefully as the first. And then a third.

Anya nudged me with an elbow and, turning my head slightly, I saw two more of the enormous brutes emerging from the tangled trees on the other side of us.

They were hunting in a team. Stalking the duckbills with the care and coordination of a pack of wolves.

They passed us by. If they saw us or sensed us in any way, they gave no indication of it. I had always pictured the tyrannosaurus as a brainless ravening killing machine, snapping at any piece of meat it came across, regardless of its size, regardless of whether the tyrant was hungry or not.

Obviously that was not the case. These brutes possessed some intelligence, enough to work cooperatively in tracking down the duckbills.

"Let's follow them," Anya said eagerly after the last of them had disappeared into the reeds and giant swaying ferns that closed off our view of the waterway.

I must have looked at her as if she were crazy.

"We can stay a good distance away," she added, her lips curving slightly at the expression on my face.

"I have the impression," I replied slowly, "that they can run a good deal faster than we can. And I don't see a tree for us to climb that's tall enough to get away from them."

"But they're after the duckbills, not us. They wouldn't even recognize us as meat."

I shook my head. Brave I may be, but not foolhardy. Anya was as eager as a huntress on the trail of her prey, avid to follow the tyrannosaurs as closely as possible. I feared those monstrous brutes, feared that they would swiftly make us the hunted instead of the hunters.

"We have no weapons, nothing to defend ourselves

with," I said. Then I added, "Besides, I'm still weak from . . ."

Her face went from smug superiority to regretful apology in the flash of instant. "I forgot! Oh, Orion, I'm such a fool . . . forgive me . . . I should have remembered. . . ."

I stopped her babbling with a kiss. She smiled and, still looking shamefaced, told me to wait for her while she found something for us to eat. Then she scampered down the tree trunk and headed off across the mossy muddy swampland.

I lay on my back as the sun filtered down through the leaves. A tiny gray furred thing raced across a branch slightly above me, ran down the tree's trunk to the branch where I lay, and stared at me for half a moment, beady eyes black and shining, long hairless tail twitching nervously. It made no sound at all.

I said to it, "Greetings, fellow mammal. For all I know, you are the grandfather to us all."

It dashed back up the trunk and disappeared in the leafy branches above me.

Clasping my hands behind my head, I waited for Anya to return. She had escaped the core-tap pit by reverting to her true form of pure energy, absorbing the heat that had been roasting our flesh, using Set's own warping device to fling us into this time and place. And reconstructing herself back into human form, unscratched and even newly clothed in the bargain.

An ancient aphorism came unbidden to my mind: Rank hath its privileges. A goddess, a highly advanced creature evolved from human stock but so far beyond humanity that she had no need of a physical body—that kind of creature could happily go thrashing through a Cretaceous landscape after a pack of tyrannosaurs. Death meant nothing to her.

It was different for me. I have died and been returned

to life many times. But only when the Creators willed it. I am their creature, they created me. I am fully human, fully mortal. I have no way of knowing if my death will be final or not, no way of assuring myself that I will be rescued from permanent oblivion and brought to life once more.

The Buddhists would teach, millions of years ahead, that all living creatures are bound up on the great wheel of life, dying and being reincarnated over and over again. The only way out of this constant cycle of pain is to achieve nirvana, total oblivion, escape from the world as complete and final as falling into a black hole and disappearing from the universe forever.

I did not want nirvana. I had not given up all my desires. I loved a goddess and I desperately wanted her to love me. She said she did, but in those awful timeless moments when she left me falling down that endless burning pit, I realized all over again that she is not human, not the way I am, despite her outward appearance.

I feared that I would lose her. Or worse yet, that she would grow tired of my human limitations and leave me forever.

Chapter 15

For three days we remained in the steaming swamp while I recuperated and regained my strength. I felt certain that Anya and I were the only human beings on the whole earth in this time—although she was actually more than merely human.

The swamp was miserably hot and damp. The ground squelched when we walked; every step we took was a struggle through thick ferns and enormous broad leaves bigger than any elephant's ear that clung wetly to our bodies when we tried to push through them. Vines looped everywhere, choking whole trees, spreading across the spongy ground to trip us.

And it stank. The stench of decay was all around us; the swamp smelled of death. The constant heat was oppressive, the drenching humidity sapped my strength.

I felt trapped, imprisoned, in a glistening world of sodden green. The jungle pressed in on us like a living entity, squeezing the breath from our lungs, hiding the world from our view. We could not see more than a few yards ahead in any direction unless we waded out into the oozing mud of midstream, and even then the jungle greenery closed off our view so quickly that a herd of brontosaurs could have been passing by without our seeing them.

There was little to eat. The plants were all strange to us; hardly any of them seemed to bear anything that looked edible. The only fish I could see in the dark water were tiny flitting glints of silver, too small and fast for us to catch. We subsisted on frogs and wriggling furry insect grubs, nauseating but nourishing enough. Barely.

It rained every evening, huge torrents of downpour from the gray towering clouds that built up during the sopping heat of the afternoons. My skin felt wet all the time, as if it were crawling, puckering, in the unremitting humidity. After three days and nights of being soaked and steamed, even Anya began to look bedraggled and unhappy.

The sky was gray almost all the time. The one night it cleared enough to see the stars, I wished it had not. Peering through the tangled foliage while Anya slept, I tried to find the familiar patterns of recognizable constellations. All that I saw was that dismal red star hanging high in the dark sky, as if spying down on us.

I searched for Orion, my namesake among the stars, and could not find the constellation. Then I saw the Big Bear, and my heart sank. It was different, changed from the Dipper I had known in other eras. Its big square "bowl" was slim and sharp-angled, more like a gravy pitcher than a ladle. Its curving handle was sharply bent.

We were so many millions of years removed from any period I had known that even the eternal stars had changed. I stared at the mutated Dipper, desolate, downcast, filled with a dreadful melancholy such as I had never known before.

Other than an occasional shrewlike gray furry creature that seemed to live high in the trees, we did not even see another mammal. Reptiles, though, were everywhere.

One morning Anya was filling a gourd at the edge of the muddy stream when suddenly a gigantic crocodile erupted from the water where it had been lurking, its massive green scaly body hidden perfectly among the reeds and cattails with nothing but its horn-topped eyes and nostrils showing above the surface. Anya had to run as fast as she could and clamber up the nearest tree to escape the crocodile's rush; despite its spraddling short legs, it nearly caught her.

There were turtles in the swamp and long-tailed lizards the size of pigs and plenty of snakes gliding through the water and slithering up the trees.

This world of the Cretaceous, however, was truly ruled by dinosaurs. Not all of them were giants. The second day Anya, using a thick broken branch for a club, tried to kill a two-legged dinosaur that was only as big as an overgrown chicken. It scampered away from her, whistling like a teakettle. Accustomed to dodging its larger cousins, it easily escaped Anya's attempts to catch it.

From our tree perch I saw one afternoon a waddling reptile plated with bony armor like an armadillo, although it was almost the size of a pony. It dragged a short tail armed with evil-looking spikes.

Insects buzzed and crawled around us all the time but, oddly, none seemed to bother us. I thought this strange at first, until I realized that there were so few mammals in this landscape that hardly any insects had developed an interest in sucking warm blood.

The third night I told Anya that I felt strong enough to travel.

"Are you sure?"

"Yes. It's time we left this soggy hellhole."

"And go where?" she asked.

I shrugged. The evening cloudburst had just ended. We sat huddled on a high branch beneath a rude makeshift shelter of giant leaves that I had put together. It had not been much help; the torrents of rain had wormed through the leaves and wet us anyway. The last remnants of the rain dripped from a thousand leaves and turned our green world into a glittering, dewy symphony of pattering little splashes. Anya's once-sparkling robe was sodden and gray. My leather vest and kilt clung to me like clammy, smelly rags.

"Anywhere would be better than this," I replied.

She agreed with a nod.

"And probably as far away from this location as we can get," I added.

"You're worried about Set?"

"Aren't you?"

"I suppose I should be. I can't help thinking, though, that he won't bother with us. We're trapped here, why spend the effort to seek us out and kill us? We're going to die here, my love, in this forsaken miserable time, and no one will save us."

In the shadows of dusk her lovely face seemed somber, her voice low with dejection. I had been content to live a normal human lifetime with Anya in the Neolithic, but the cool forest of Paradise was very different from this rotting fetid jungle. Even though the people there had turned traitor against us, there were human beings in Paradise. Here we were totally alone, with no human companionship except each other.

"We're not dead yet," I said. "And I don't intend to give Set any help in killing us."

"Why would he bother?"

"Because this is a crucial nexus for him," I told her. "He knows where his spacetime warp was set, he knows we're here. As soon as he has the device operating again he'll come looking for us, to make certain that we don't upset whatever it is he's planning for this point in the continuum."

Anya saw the logic of it, but still she seemed reluctant to take action.

"We'll be better off out of this damned swamp," I added. "This is no place to be. Let's start out tomorrow morning, first light. We'll head upland, to where it's cooler and dryer."

In the deepening shadows I saw her eyes sparkle with sudden delight. "We can follow the path that the duckbills took. They were heading toward higher ground, I'm certain."

"With the tyrannosaurs after them," I muttered.

"Yes," Anya said, some of her old enthusiasm back in her voice. "I'm curious to see if they caught up with the duckbills."

"There are times," I said, "when you seem absolutely bloodthirsty."

"Violence is part of human makeup, Orion. I am still human enough to feel the excitement of the hunt. Aren't you?"

"Only when I'm the hunter, not the hunted."

"You are my hunter," she said.

"And I've found what I was searching for." I pulled her to me.

"Being the prey isn't all that terrible," Anya whispered in my ear. "Sometimes."

Chapter 16

The next morning we started our trek out of the swamplands and up toward the cooler, cleaner hills. Subconsciously I expected to find a more familiar world, a landscape of flowering plants and grass, of dogs and rabbits and wild boars. I knew there would be no other humans, but my mind was seeking familiar life-forms nonetheless.

Instead we found ourselves in a world of dinosaurs and very little else. Giant winged pterosaurs glided effortlessly through the cloudy skies. Tiny four-legged dinosaurs scurried through the brush. Their larger cousins loomed here and there like small mountains, gently cropping the ferns and soft-leafed bushes that abounded everywhere.

There were no flowers anywhere in that Cretaceous landscape, at least none that I could recognize. Some of the barrel-shaped bushes bore clumps of colored leaves beneath the feathery fronds at their tops. Otherwise the plants we saw looked nasty, repulsive, armed with spikes and suckers, soft and pulpy and altogether alien.

Not even the trees were familiar to me, except for occasional stands of tall straight cypresses and the mangroves that clustered by the edge of every pond and stream, their gnarled tangled roots gripping the soggy earth like hundreds of sturdy wooden fingers. And palm trees, some of them huge, their trunks bare and scaly, their feathery leaves catching the moist warm breezes high above us. There was neither grass nor grains to be seen, only wavering fronds of reeds and ugly cattails that sometimes covered ponds and watercourses so thickly they looked like solid ground. Until we stepped into it and squelched through to water up to the knees or deeper.

We climbed trees for the nights, although as far as I could tell the dinosaurs slept the dark hours away just as we did. Still, unarmed against the ferocious likes of tyrannosaurs, we had no alternatives except running and hiding.

We saw no more of the tyrannosaurs during our first few days' march, although their deep three-toed footprints were plentiful. Anya insisted that we follow their tracks, which moved right along with the even deeper hoofprints of the duckbilled dinosaurs. There were places where the tyrants' claws had stepped precisely into the duckbills' prints.

There were other meat-eaters about, however. Swift two-legged predators taller than I who ran with their tails straight out and their forearms clutching avidly at smaller dinosaurs, who bleated and whistled like a steamboat in distress when the carnosaurs' claws and teeth ripped into their flesh.

Anya and I went to ground whenever a meat-eater was in sight. Armed with nothing but our senses and our wits, we flattened ourselves on the mossy ground and lay unmoving the instant we saw one of the hunters. None of them bothered with us. Whether that was because they did not see us or because they did not recognize us as meat, I could not say. Nor did I want to find out, particularly.

Once we saw a half-dozen triceratops drinking warily at a stream's edge, each of them bigger than a quartet of rhino, with three long spikes projecting from their heads and a heavy shield of bone at the base of the skull. Their flanks were spotted with rosettes of color: shades of red and yellow and brown. They looked awkward and ungainly and extremely nervous. Sure enough, a pair of two-legged carnosaurs splashed into the stream from the other side; not tyrannosaurs, but big and toothy and mean looking.

The triceratops looked across the stream and then pulled themselves together in a rough shoulder-to-shoulder formation, heads lowered and those long spikes pointing at the meat-eaters like a line of pikes or a gigantic hedgehog. The carnosaurs huffed and snorted, jinked up and down on their hind legs, looked the situation over. Then they turned and dashed away.

I almost felt disappointed. Not that I especially wanted to watch the violence and gore of a dinosaur battle. I simply felt that no matter who won the fight, there would most likely be plenty of meat for us to scavenge. We had been eating little else but the small dinosaurs and furry shrewlike mammals we could catch with our crude nets and clubs. A thick slab of meat would have been welcome.

The second night of our trek I awoke in pitch blackness to a sense of danger. Anya and I were half sitting in the crotch of a tree, as high above the ground as we could find branches to support us.

We were not alone. I felt the menacing presence of someone—something—else. I could see nothing in the utter darkness. The night was quiet except for the background drone of insects. There were no wolves howling in this Cretaceous time, no lions roaring. Only the forefathers of field mice and tree squirrels were awake and active in the darkness, and they made as little sound as possible.

The clouds parted overhead. The moon was down, but the ruddy star that I had first seen in the Neolithic glowered down at me. In its blood red light I caught the glint of a pair of evil eyes watching me, unblinking.

Without consciously willing it, my body went into hyperdrive. Just in time, as the huge snake struck at me, jaws extended, poisonous fangs ready to sink into my flesh.

I saw the snake coiled around our tree branch, saw its mouth gaping wide and the fangs already dripping venom, saw its head rear back and then lunge forward at me. All as if in slow motion. Those lidless slitted eyes glared hatefully at me.

My right hand darted out and caught the snake in midstrike. It was so big that my fingers could barely reach around half its width to clutch it. The momentum of its long muscular body nearly knocked me off the branch into a long fall to the shadows far below. But I gripped the branch with my legs and free hand as my back slammed against the tree trunk with a force that made me grunt.

Pressing my thumb against the snake's lower jaw, I held its head at arm's length away from me. It writhed and coiled and tried to shake loose. Anya awoke, took in the situation immediately, and reached for her club.

I struggled to one knee, fearful of being knocked off the branch by the snake's bucking and writhing.

"Lie down flat!" I commanded Anya.

As she did I let my hand slide partway down the snake's body and swung it as mightily as I could against the tree trunk. Its head hit the wood with a loud, satisfying *thunk.* Again I bashed it against the tree, and again. It stopped writhing, stopped moving at all. The head hung limp in my grasp. I threw the serpent away, heard it crash among the lower branches and finally hit the ground.

Anya raised her head. "From Set?" she asked, her voice little more than a whisper.

I made a shrug that she could not see in the shadows.

"Who knows? There are plenty of snakes here. They probably prey on the little nocturnal mammals that live in these trees. We may simply have picked the wrong tree."

Anya moved close to me. I could feel her shuddering. From that night onward we always slept in shifts.

And I realized why all human beings have acquired three instinctive fears: fear of the dark, fear of heights, and fear of snakes.

Chapter 17

Gradually, as we walked the rising land, Anya and I began to fashion a few primitive tools. I could not find flint anywhere, but I did pick up a stone that fit nicely into the palm of my hand and worked each night scraping one side of it against other stones to make a reasonably sharp edge. Anya looked for fairly straight branches among the windfalls from the trees we passed and used our nightly fire to harden their ends into effective spear points.

I worried about making a fire each night. We needed it to cook what little food we could find, of course. In another age I would have wanted it to help ward off predators while we slept. But here in this world of dinosaurs and snakes, this world ruled by reptiles instead of mammals, I wondered if a fire might not attract heat-seeking predators instead of frightening them away.

Besides, there was still Set to consider. Certainly no one except Anya and I would light a fire each night in this

Cretaceous landscape. It would stand out like a beacon to anyone with the technology to scan wide areas of the globe.

Yet we needed a nightly fire, not merely for cooking or safety but for the psychological comfort that it provided. Night after night we huddled close together and stared into the warm dancing flames, knowing that it would be more than sixty million years before any other humans would create a campfire.

The skies were clearer in the uplands, away from the deep swamp. But the stars were still unfamiliar to me. Night after night I searched for Orion, in vain.

I began to show Anya my prowess as a hunter. Using the spears she made, I started to bag bird-sized dinosaurs and, occasionally, even bigger game such as four-legged grazers the size of sheep.

One night I asked Anya a question that had been nagging at me ever since we had come to this time of dinosaurs. "When you changed your form . . . metamorphosed into a sphere of energy"—the idea of that being her true self still bothered me—"where did you go? What did you do?"

The firelight cast flickering shadows across her face, almost the way she had shimmered and glittered when she had left my arms as we fell down the well of Set's core tap.

"I tried to return to the other Creators," she said, her voice low, almost sad. "But the way was blocked. I tried to move us both to a different time and place, anywhere in the continuum except where we were. But Set's device was preset for this spacetime and it had too much energy driving it for me to break through and direct us elsewhere."

"You're conscious and aware of what you're doing when you—change form?"

"Yes."

"Could you do it now?"

"No," she admitted somberly. Gesturing toward our

little campfire and the scraps of dinosaur bones on the ground, she said, "There isn't enough energy available. We barely have energy input to keep our human forms going."

Her voice smiled when she said that, but there was an underlying sadness to it. Perhaps even fear.

"Then you're trapped in this human form," I said.

"I *chose* this human form, Orion. So that I could be with you."

She meant it as a sign of love. But it made me feel awful to know that because of me she was just as trapped and vulnerable as I was.

Within a week we were up in the hilly country where the air was at least drier, if not much cooler, than it had been in the swamps below.

Night after night I found myself searching the skies, seeking my namesake constellation and trying to avoid the feeling that the baleful red star was watching me like the eye of some angry god—or devil.

Anya always woke near midnight to take the watch and let me sleep. One night she asked, "What do you expect to see in the stars, my love?"

I felt almost embarrassed. "I was looking for myself."

She pointed. "There."

It was not Orion. Not the familiar constellation of the Hunter that I had known. Rigel did not yet exist. Brilliant red Betelgeuse was nowhere to be seen. Instead of the three stars of the belt and the sword hanging from it, I saw only a faint, misty glow.

My blood ran cold. Not even Orion existed in this lonely place and time. We had no business being here, so far from everything that we had known. We were aliens here, outcasts, abandoned by the gods, hunted by forces that we could not even begin to fight against, doomed to be extinguished forever.

An intense brooding misery filled my soul. I felt completely helpless, useless. I knew that it was merely a matter of time until Set tracked us down and made an end of us.

No matter how hard I tried, I could not shake this depression. I had never felt such anguish before, such despair. I tried to hide it from Anya, but I saw from the anxious glances she gave me that she knew full well how empty and lifeless I felt.

And then we came across the duckbills' nesting ground.

It was the broad, fairly flat top of a gently sloped hill. There were so many duckbill tracks marching up the hillside that their heavy hooves had worn an actual trail into the bare dusty ground.

"The creatures must come up here every year," Anya said as we climbed the trail toward the top of the hill.

I did not reply. I could not work up the enthusiastic curiosity that was apparently driving Anya. I was still locked in gloom.

We should have been warned by the noisy whistling and hissing of dozens of pterosaurs flapping their leathery wings up above the summit of the hill, swooping in for landings. As Anya and I climbed up the easy slope of the hill we heard their long bony bills clacking as if they were fighting among themselves.

A faint half memory tugged at me. The way the pterosaurs were behaving reminded me of something, but I could not recall what it was. It became clear to me the instant we reached the crest of the hill.

It was a boneyard.

Up on the bare ground of the hilltop there were hundreds of nests where the duckbills had been laying their eggs for uncounted generations.

But the tyrannosaurs had been there.

A gust of breeze brought the stench of rotting flesh to our nostrils. The pterosaurs flapped and hissed at us, tiny claws on the front edges of their wings quite conspicuous. I realized that they were behaving like vultures, picking the bones of the dead. I swatted at the nearest of the winged lizards with the spear I carried and they all flapped off, hissing angrily, hovering above us on their wide leathery wings as if waiting for us to leave so they could resume their feast.

I thought Anya would break into tears. Nothing but bones and scraps of rotting flesh, the rib cages of the massive animals standing like the bleached timbers of wrecked ships, taller than my head. Leg bones my own body length. Massive flat skulls, thick with bone.

"Look!" Anya cried. "Eggs!"

The nests were shallow pits pawed into the ground where oblong eggs the length of my arm lay in circular patterns. Most of them had been smashed in.

"Well," I said, pointing to a pair of unbroken eggs that lay side by side on the bare ground, "here's dinner, at least."

"You couldn't!" Anya seemed shocked.

I cast an eye at the pterosaurs still flapping and gliding above us.

"It's either our dinner or theirs."

She still looked distressed.

"These eggs will never hatch now," I told her. "And even if they did, the baby duckbills would be easy prey to anything that comes along without their mothers to protect them."

Reluctantly Anya agreed. I went down the hill to gather brushwood for a fire while she stayed at the nests to protect our dinner against the pterosaurs.

It struck me, as I picked dead branches from the ground and pulled twigs from bushes, that the tyrannosaurs had been unusually efficient in their assault on the duckbills. As far as I could see they had killed every one of the herbivores. That did not seem natural to me. Predators usually kill what they can eat and allow the rest of their prey to go their way. Were the tyrannosaurs nothing but killing machines after all? Or were they being *directed* by someone—such as Set or his like?

Had they followed the migrating herd we had seen so that they could find the duckbills' nesting ground and kill *all* the dinosaurs nesting there? Obviously the hilltop was being used by more than the forty-some duckbills we had seen in the swamp. There were more than a hundred nests up there. But they had all been slaughtered by the tyrannosaurs.

When I returned to the hilltop with an armload of firewood, Anya showed me the answer to my question.

"Look here," she said, pointing to the edge of one of the nests.

I dropped the tinder near the nest where our prospective dinner waited and went to where she stood.

Footprints. Three-clawed toes, but much too small to be a tyrannosaur's. Human-sized. Or humanoid, rather.

"One of Set's troops?"

"There are more," Anya said, gesturing toward the other nests. "I think they deliberately smashed the eggs that weren't broken when the tyrannosaurs attacked."

"That means Set—or someone like him—is here, in this time and place."

"Attacking the duckbills? Why?"

"More important," I said, "whoever it is, he's probably searching for us."

Anya raised her eyes and scanned the horizon, as if she could see Set or his people heading toward us. I looked, too. The land was flat and depressingly green, nothing but the same tone of green as far as the eye could see. Not a flower, not a sign of color. Even the streams meandering through the area looked a sickly, weed-choked green. Mangroves lined the waterways and giant ferns clustered thickly, waving in the warm wind. Whole armies could be hidden in that monotonous flat bayou country and we could not have seen them.

It struck me all over again how helpless we were, how useless in the Creators' struggle to overthrow Set and his kind. Two people alone in a world of dinosaurs. I shook my head as if to clear it of cobwebs but I could not shake this feeling of depression.

Anya showed no signs of dismay, however. "We've got to find their camp or headquarters," she said. "We've got to find out what they are doing in this era, what their goals are."

I heaved a big hungry sigh. "First," I countered, "we've got to have dinner."

Returning to the two unbroken eggs, I started to build a small fire, knowing now that there were eyes out there in the distance that could detect it and locate us. Yet we had to eat, and neither of us was ready to face raw eggs or uncooked meat. Using a duckbill's pointed scapula, I scraped out a pit in the soft dirt so that the meager flames could not be seen above the crest of the hill by anyone watching from below. Yet I knew that even primitive heat detectors could probably spot our fire from its thermal signature against the cooler air of the late afternoon.

"Orion! Quickly!"

I turned from my blossoming fire, grabbing for the nearest bone to use as a weapon, and saw Anya staring tensely at our eggs. One of them was cracked. No, cracking. As we watched, it split apart and a miniature duckbilled dinosaur no more than two feet long crawled out of the shell on four stubby legs.

Anya dropped to her knees in front of it.

The baby dinosaur gave a weak piping whistle, like the toot a child might make on a tin flute.

"Look, it has an egg tooth," Anya said.

"It's probably hungry," I thought aloud.

Anya dashed over to my tiny fire and pulled out a couple of twigs that still had some pulpy leaves on them.

Stripping the leaves off, she hand-fed them to the little duckbill, which munched on them without hesitation.

"She's eating them!" Anya seemed overjoyed.

I was less thrilled. "How do you know it's a female?"

She ignored my question. Eating the other egg was out of the question now, even though it never opened that evening and was still not open the following morning. Our dinner consisted of a single rat-sized reptile that I managed to run down before darkness fell, and a clutch of melons that I picked from a bush, the first recognizable fruit I had seen.

In the morning Anya made it clear that she had no intention of leaving our baby duckbill behind.

"We'll have to feed it," I complained.

"It eats plants," she countered. "It's not like a mammal that needs its mother's milk."

I was anxious to get away from this hilltop massacre site and leave it to the scavenging pterosaurs. Our best defense against whoever had directed the attack on the duckbills was to keep moving. Anya agreed, but our pace that morning was terribly slow because the little duckbill could not trot along with any real speed. It seemed to show no curiosity about the world around it, as a puppy would. It merely followed Anya the way ducklings fixate on the first moving object they see, believing it to be their mother.

Anya seemed quite content with motherhood. She picked soft pulpy leaves for her baby and even chewed some of them herself before feeding the little beast.

I had brought something quite different from the duckbill boneyard: a forearm bone that fit my hand nicely and had the proper size and heft to be an effective club. We had to make tools and weapons if we were to survive.

Why we had to survive, what our goal might be beyond mere physical survival, was a total blank to me. Oh, I knew we were supposed to be battling against Set and whatever plans he had for this period in time. But how the two of us, alone and practically defenseless, were supposed to over-come Set and his people—that was beyond my reckoning.

Despite my misgivings, Anya set us out on the tracks of the tyrannosaurs.

"The humanoids went with them," she said, pointing at the smaller tracks set in between the giant prints of the tyrants.

"Some distance behind them," I guessed.

"I suppose so. We must find those humanoids, Orion, and learn from them what Set is doing."

"That won't be easy."

She smiled at me. "If it were easy, it would have already been done. You and I are not meant for easy tasks, Orion."

I could not make myself smile back at her. "If they can truly control the tyrannosaurs, we haven't a chance in hell."

Anya's smile wilted.

We quickly saw that the tyrannosaur tracks led back toward the swamps we had quit only a few days earlier. I felt miserably disheartened to be returning to that fetid, humid, steaming gloom. I wanted to run as far away from there as possible. For the first time in my lives I was feeling real fear, a terror that was dangerously close to panic.

Anya overlooked my brooding silence. "It makes sense that Set's headquarters here would be very close to the place where we entered this spacetime. Maybe we can use his warping device in reverse and return to the Neolithic when we're finished here."

"Return to his fortress?"

She ignored my question. "Orion, do you realize that the tyrannosaurs left their usual habitat there in the lowlands, marched up to the duckbills' nesting area to slaughter them, and then returned immediately back to the swamps? They *must* have been under Set's control."

I agreed that it did not seem likely that the giant

carnivores would trek all the way to the nesting site and back without some form of outside stimulus.

We camped that evening by a large, placid lake, on a long curving beach of clean white sand so fine it almost felt like powder beneath our feet. The beach was some twenty to thirty yards wide, then gave way to a line of gnarled, twisted cypresses festooned with hanging moss and, behind them, tall coconut palms and feathery fringe-leafed ferns that rose like gigantic swaying fans.

The sand was far from smooth, though. It was crosscrossed with the prints of innumerable dinosaurs: blunt deep hooves of massive sauropods, birdlike claws of smaller reptiles, and the powerful talons of carnosaurs. They all came to this shore to drink—and, some of them, to kill.

As the sun dropped toward the horizon, turning sky and water both into lovely pastel pinks and blue greens, I saw a streak of brilliant red and orange drop out of the sky and plunge into the lake. In half a moment it popped to the surface with a fish flapping in its toothy jaws.

The thing looked more like a lizard than a bird, with its long, toothed snout and longer tail. But it was feathered, and its forelimbs were definitely wings. Instead of taking off again, though, it paddled to the water's edge and waddled up onto the shore, then turned to face the setting sun and spread its wings wide, as if in worship.

"It can't fly again until it dries its wings," Anya surmised.

"I wonder how it tastes," I muttered back to her.

If the lizard-bird heard our voices or felt threatened by them, it gave no indication. It simply stood there on the shore of the gently lapping wavelets, drying its feathers and digesting its fish dinner.

Suddenly I realized that we could do the same. "How would you like to eat fish tonight?" I asked Anya.

She was sitting by a clump of bushes, feeding the little

duckbill again. It seemed to eat all day long.

Without waiting for her to reply, I waded out into the shallow calm water, turning hot pink in the last rays of the dying sun. The lizard-bird clacked its beak at me and waddled a few paces away. It took only a few minutes to spear two fish. I felt happy with the change in our diet.

Anya had spent the time gathering more shrubs for our baby duckbill to nibble. And a handful of berries. The dinosaur ate them with seeming relish.

"If they don't hurt him, perhaps we can eat them, too," she said as I started the fire.

"Maybe," I acknowledged. "I'll sample one and see how it affects—"

The duckbill suddenly emitted a high-pitched whistle and scooted to Anya's side. I scrambled to my feet and stared into the gathering darkness of the woods that lined the lakeshore. Sure enough, I heard a crashing, crunching sound.

"Something heading our way," I whispered urgently to Anya. "Something big."

There was no time to douse the fire. We were too far from the edge of the trees to get to them safely. Besides, that was where the danger seemed to be coming from.

"Into the water," I said, starting for the lake.

Anya stopped to pick up the duckbill. It was as motionless as a statue, yet still a heavy armful. I grabbed it from her and, tucking its inert body under one arm, led Anya out splashing into the lake.

We dove into the water as soon as we could, me holding the duckbill up so it could breathe. It wiggled slightly, but apparently had no fear of the water. Or perhaps it was more terrified of whatever was heading our way from the woods. The lake water was tepid, too warm to be refreshing, almost like swimming in lukewarm bouillon.

We went out deep enough so that only our heads showed above the surface. The duckbill crawled onto my shoulder with only a little coaxing and I held him there with one arm, treading water with Anya beside me, close enough to grasp if I had to.

The woods were deeply shadowed now. The trees seemed to part like a curtain and a towering, terrifying tyrannosaur stepped out, his scaly hide a lurid red in the waning sunset.

The tyrant took a few ponderous steps toward our campfire, seemed to look around, then gazed out onto the water of the lake. I realized with a sinking heart that if it saw us and wanted to reach us, it had merely to wade out and grab us in those monstrous serrated teeth. The water that was deep enough for us to swim in would hardly come up to its hocks.

Sure enough, the tyrannosaur marched straight to the water's edge. Then it hesitated, looking ridiculously like a wrinkled old lady afraid of getting her feet wet.

I held my breath. The tyrannosaur seemed to look straight at me. The trembling package of frightened duckbill on my shoulder made no sound. The world seemed to stand still for an eternally long moment. Not even the lapping waves seemed to make a noise.

Then the tyrannosaur gave an enormous huffing sigh, like a blast from a blacksmith's forge, and turned away from the lake. It stamped back into the woods and disappeared.

Almost overcome with relief, we swam shoreward and then staggered out of the water and threw ourselves onto the sandy ground.

Only to hear an eerie hooting whistle coming out of the twilight on the lake.

Looking around, I saw the enormous snaky neck of an aquatic dinosaur rising, rising up from the depths of the lake, higher and higher like an enormous escalator of living flesh silhouetted against the glowing pastel sunset. Our duckbill wriggled free of my arms and ran to worm his body as close to Anya as he could.

"The Loch Ness Monster," I whispered.

"What?"

Suddenly it all became clear to me. The damned tyrannosaur would have waded into the lake after us, except that the lake was inhabited by even bigger dinosaurs who had made it their territory. As far as the tyrannosaur was concerned, anything in the water was meat for the beastie who lived in the lake. That was why it had left us alone.

The lake dinosaur hooted again, then ducked its long neck back beneath the waves.

I rolled onto my back and laughed uncontrollably, like a madman or a soldier who becomes hysterical after facing certain unavoidable death and living through it. We had literally been between the devil and the deep blue sea without even knowing it.

Chapter 18

My laughter subsided quickly enough. We were truly trapped and I knew it.

"I don't see anything funny," Anya said in the purpling shadows of the twilight.

"It isn't funny," I agreed. "But what else can we do except laugh? One or more tyrannosaurs are patrolling through the woods, one or more even bigger monsters prowling through the lake, and we're caught in between. It's beyond funny. It's cosmic. If the Creators could see us now, they'd be splitting their sides laughing at the stupid blind ridiculousness of it all."

"We can get past the tyrannosaur," she said, a hint of cold disapproval, almost anger, in her voice. I noticed that she assumed there was only the one monster lurking in the woods, waiting for us.

"You think so?" I felt bitterly cynical.

"Once it's fully night we can slip through the woods—"

"And go where? All we'll be accomplishing is to make Set's game a little more interesting."

"Do you have a better idea?"

"Yes," I said. "Transform yourself into your true form and leave me here alone."

She gasped as if I had slapped her. "Orion—you . . . you're angry with me?"

I said nothing. My blood seethed with frustration and fury. I raged silently at the Creators for putting us here. I railed inwardly at myself for being so helpless.

Anya was saying, "You know that I can't metamorphose unless there's sufficient energy for the transformation. And I won't leave you no matter what happens."

"There is a way for you to escape," I said, my anger cooling. "I'll go into the woods first and lead the tyrannosaurs away from you. Then you can get through safely. We can meet back at the duckbill nests—"

"No." She said it flatly, with finality. Even in the gathering darkness I could sense the toss of her ebony hair as she shook her head.

"We can't—"

"Whatever we do," Anya said firmly, "we do together."

"Don't you understand?" I begged her. "We're trapped here. It's hopeless. Get away while you can."

Anya stepped close to me and touched my cheek with her cool, soft hand. Her gray eyes looked deeply into mine. I felt the tension that had been cramping my neck and back muscles easing, dissolving.

"This is unlike you, Orion. You've never given up before, no matter what we faced."

"We've never been in a situation like this." But even as I said it, I felt calmer, less depressed.

"As you said a few days ago, my love, we still live. And while we live we must fight against Set and his monstrous designs, whatever they are."

She was right and I knew it. I also knew that there was no way for me to resist her. She was one of the Creators, and I was one of her creatures.

"And whatever we do, my unhappy love," Anya said, her voice dropping lower, "we will do together. To the death, if necessary."

My voice choked with a tangle of emotions. She was a goddess, yet she would never abandon me. Never.

We stood facing each other for a few moments more, then decided to start walking around the edge of the lake, for lack of any better plan. The duckbill trotted after us, silently following Anya.

How can two human beings fight a thirty-ton tyrannosaur with little more than their bare hands? I knew the answer: They can't. Something deep in my mind recalled that I had killed Set's carnosaurs in the Neolithic with not much more than bare hands. Yet somehow the tyrannosaurs seemed far beyond that challenge. I felt hopeless, powerless; not afraid, I was so depressed I was beyond fear.

So we walked through the deepening night, the glistening froth of the gently breaking waves on our right, the sighing trees of the woods on our left. The moon rose, a crescent slim as a scimitar, and later that blood red star raised its eerie eye above the lake's flat horizon.

Anya was thinking out loud, in a half whisper: "If we can find one of Set's people, capture him and learn from him where Set's camp is and what he's trying to achieve here, then we could form a plan of action."

I made a grunting noise rather than saying out loud how naive I thought she was being.

"They must have tools, weapons. Perhaps we could capture some. Then we'd be better prepared. . . ."

It was on the tip of my tongue to tell her what I really thought of her daydreaming.

"I haven't seen any weapons or tools of any kind on them," I muttered.

"Set has a technology as powerful as our own," she said. I knew that by "our own" she meant the Creators.

"Yes, but his troops go empty-handed—except for their claws." Then I realized: "And the reptiles they control."

Anya stopped in her tracks. "The tyrannosaurs."

"And the dragons, back in Paradise."

"They use the animals the way we use tools," she said.

Our baby duckbill snuffled slightly, just to let us know that it was there in the darkness, I think. Anya dropped to one knee and picked it up.

My mind was racing. I recalled another kind of intelligent creature who controlled animals with their minds. The Neanderthals and their leader, Ahriman. My memory filled with half-forgotten images of the suicidal duel he and I had fought over a span of fifty thousand years. I squeezed my eyes shut and stood stock still, straining every cell of my brain to recall, remember.

"I think," I said shakily, "I might be able to control an animal the same way that the humanoids do."

Anya stepped closer to me. "No, Orion. That ability was never built into you. Not even the Golden One knows how to accomplish that."

"I've looked deeply into the mind of Ahriman," I told her. "Many times. I lived with the Neanderthals. I think I can do it."

"If only you could!"

"Let me try—on your little friend here."

We both sat cross-legged on the sand, Anya with the sleepy duckbill in her lap. It curled up immediately, tail wrapping over its snout, and closed its eyes.

I closed mine.

It was a simple mind, yet not so primitive that it did not have a sense of self-preservation. In the cool of the evening it sought Anya's body warmth and the sleep it needed to prepare itself for the coming day. I saw nothing, but a symphony of olfactory stimuli flooded through me: the warm musky scent of Anya's body, the tang of the lake's sun-heated water, the drifting odor of leaves and bark. My own mind felt surprise that there were no flowers to add their fragrances to the night air, but then I realized that true flowering plants did not yet exist here.

I opened the duckbill baby's eyes and saw its world, murky and indistinct, blurred with the need to sleep. An overwhelming reluctance to get up and leave the protection of Anya's mothering body welled through me, but I rose shakily to all fours and slithered off Anya's warm lap. I half trotted to the lapping edge of the water, sniffed at it and found no danger in it, then waded in until my tiny hooves barely touched the muddy bottom. Then I turned around and made my way gladly back to the motherly lap.

"She's all wet!" Anya complained, laughing.

"And sound asleep," I said.

For many minutes we sat facing each other, Anya with the little dinosaur sighing rhythmically in her lap.

"You were right," she whispered. "You can control it."

"It's only a baby," I said. "Controlling something bigger will be much more difficult."

"But you can do it," Anya said. "I know you can."

I replied, "You were right, too. Our little friend is a female."

"I knew it!"

Looking toward the darkened woods, I let my awareness sift in through the trees and mammoth ferns, swaying and whispering in the night wind. There were tyrannosaurs out there, all right. Several of them. They were asleep now, lightly. Perhaps we could make our way past them. It was worth a try.

"Are their masters with them?" Anya asked when I suggested we try to get away.

"I don't sense them," I said. "That doesn't mean they aren't there."

We waited while I sensed the tyrannosaurs drifting deeper into sleep. Crickets chirped in the woods, the slim crescent moon rose higher, followed by the baleful red star.

"When can we start?" Anya asked, absently stroking the baby dinosaur on her lap.

I rose slowly to my feet. "Soon. In a few—"

That eerie hooting echoed through the night. Turning toward the lake, I saw the long snaky neck of the enormous aquatic dinosaur silhouetted against the stars and the filmy white haze that would one day be the constellation of Orion. From far away came an answering call floating through the darkness.

A cool breeze wafted in from the lake. It seemed to clear my mind like a wind blows away a fog.

I helped Anya to her feet. The baby duckbill hardly stirred in her arms.

"Do you think," I asked her, "that Set could influence my mind the way his people control the dinosaurs?"

"He probed your mind there in his castle," she said.

"Could that have caused me to feel so"—I hesitated to use the word—"so depressed?"

She nodded solemnly. "He uses despair like a weapon, to undermine your strength, to lead you to destruction."

I began to understand the whole of it. "And once you realized it, you counteracted it."

Anya replied, "No, Orion, *you* counteracted it. You did it yourself."

Did I? Anya was kind to say so, perhaps. But I wondered how large a role she played in my mental revival.

With the blink of an eye I dismissed the matter. I did not care who did what. I felt strong again, and that terrible despair had lifted from me.

"The tyrannosaurs are sleeping soundly," I told Anya. "We can get past them if we're careful."

As I put a hand to her shoulder I heard a frothing, bubbling, surging sound from out in the lake. Turning, I expected to see one or more of the huge dinosaurs splashing out there.

Instead, the waters seemed to be parting far out in the lake, splitting asunder to make way for something dark and massive and so enormous that even the big dinosaurs were dwarfed by it.

A building, a structure, an edifice that rose and rose, dripping, from the depths of the lake. Towers and turrets and overhanging tiers so wide and massive that they blotted out the sky. Balconies and high-flung walkways spanning between slim minarets. Tiny red lights winked on as we watched level upon level still rising up out of the water, mammoth and awesome.

Anya and I gaped dumbfounded at the titanic structure rising from the lake like the palace of some sea god, grotesque yet beautiful, dreadful yet majestic. The water surged into knee-high waves that spread across the lake and broke at our feet, then raced back as if eager to gather themselves at the base of the looming silent castle of darkness.

I saw that one tower rose higher than all the others, pointing straight upward into the night sky. And directly above it, like a beacon or lodestone, rode the blood red star at zenith.

"What fools we've been!" Anya whispered in the shadows.

I glanced at her. Her eyes were wide and eager.

"We thought that Set's main base was back in the Neolithic, beside the Nile. That was merely one of his camps!"

I understood.

"This is his headquarters," I said. "Here, in this era. He's inside that huge fortress waiting for us."

Chapter 19

There was no thought of running away. Set was in that brooding, dripping castle. So was the core tap that reached down to the earth's molten heart to provide the energy for Set and all his works. We needed that energy if we were to accomplish anything, even if it was merely to escape from this time of dinosaurs.

More than mere escape was on my mind, though. I wanted to meet Set again, confront him, hunt him down and kill him the way he had tried to hunt us down and kill us. He had enslaved my fellow humans, tortured the woman I love, drained me of the will to fight, to live. Now I burned with a yearning to wrap my fingers around his scaled neck and choke the life out of him.

I was Orion the Hunter once again, strong and unafraid.

In the back of my mind a voice questioned my newfound courage. Was I being manipulated by Anya? Or was I merely reacting the way I had been created to react?

The Golden One had often boasted to me that he had built these instincts for violence and revenge into me and my kind. Certainly the human race has suffered over the millennia for having such drives. We were made for murder, and the fine facade of civilization that we have learned to erect is merely a lacquered veneer covering the violence that simmers behind the mask.

What of it? I challenged the voice in my mind. Despite it all the human race has survived, has endured all that the gods of the continuum have forced upon us. Now I must face the devil incarnate, and those human instincts will be my only protection. Once more I must use the skills of the hunter: cunning, strength, stealth, and above all, patience.

"We've got to get inside," Anya said, still staring wide-eyed at the castle of darkness.

I agreed with a nod. "First, though, we've got to find out what Set is trying to do here, and why."

Which meant that we must hide and observe: see without being seen. Anya recognized the sense of that, although she was impatient with such a strategy. She wanted to plunge boldly into that fortress, just the two of us. She knew that was a hopeless fantasy and agreed that we must bide our time. Yet her agreement was reluctant.

I took the baby duckbill from her arms and led us back into the trees, keeping wide of the tyrannosaurs sleeping there in well-separated locations. The little dinosaur seemed heavier than it had been earlier. Either I was tired or it was gaining weight very rapidly.

We pushed our way through the thick underbrush as quietly as possible. The duckbill remained asleep—as did the tyrannosaurs lurking nearby.

"This baby of yours is going to be a problem," I whispered to Anya, following behind me as I pushed leafy branches and ferns aside with my free hand.

"Not at all," she whispered back. "If you show me

how to control her, she can be a scout for us. What is more natural in this world than a baby dinosaur poking around in the brush?"

I had to admit that she was at least partially right. I wondered, though, if the duckbills were ever seen alone. They seemed to be herd animals, like so many other herbivores that found safety in numbers.

We stopped at a spot where a heavy palm tree had toppled over and fallen onto a boulder as tall as my shoulders. Thick bushes grew behind the fallen bole and heavy tussocks of reeds in front of it. With our spears Anya and I scratched a shallow dugout into the sand, just long enough for us to stretch out flat on the ground. With the heavy log above us, the boulder to one side, and the bushes screening our rear, it was almost cozy. We could peer through the reeds and tufts of ferns to see the beach and the lake beyond it.

"No fire as long as we're camped here," I said.

Anya smiled contentedly. "We'll eat raw fish and try the berries and fruits from the different bushes."

Thus we began what became many weeks of watching the castle in the lake. Each morning it submerged, the entire titanic structure sinking slowly into the frothing water as if afraid of being seen by the rising sun. Each night it rose up again, dripping and dark like a brooding, malevolent giant.

We hunted and fished while the castle was submerged. We avoided the tyrannosaurs prowling through the woods and the more open flat land beyond. In all truth they did not seem to be particularly searching for us. Just the opposite. We were being ignored.

I began to teach Anya how to control our duckbill, which was rapidly growing out of its babyhood. She had named the little beast Juno, and when I asked her why, she laughed mysteriously.

"A joke, Orion, that only the Creators would appreciate."

I knew that the Creators sometimes assumed the names of ancient gods. The Golden One referred to himself as Ormazd sometimes, at other times he had called himself Apollo, or Yawveh. Anya herself was worshiped as Athena by the Achaians and Trojans alike. Apparently there was a Juno among the Creators, and it amused Anya to name our heavy-footed round-backed duckbill after her.

After many days I began to realize that the castle was rising out of the water a bit later each night and lingering a few minutes longer into the dawn each morning. This puzzled me at first, but I was more interested in the comings and goings from the castle than its risings and submergings. In the dawn's early light we could see more clearly what was happening, and why.

Each time the castle rose out of the water a long narrow ramp slid out from a gate set into its wall like a snake's probing tongue and reached to the shore of the lake, almost a quarter of the way around its roughly circular circumference from the beach where Anya and I lay watching. Invariably, a dozen or so of the humanoid servants of Set, red-scaled and naked as they had been in the Neolithic, marched down that narrow ramp, across the sandy beach, and into the trees.

Tyrannosaurs waited for them there, gathered to this lake by forces unknown to us. In the dark of night or the glimmering gray of dawn, the humanoids selected a dozen or so of the monstrous brutes and headed off, away from the lake.

It did not take us long to realize that each reptilian humanoid controlled a single tyrannosaur. Each team of humanoids created a pack of tyrannosaurs and took them off on some mission. After many days a team would return with its pack. The humanoids would go back into the waiting castle; the tyrannosaurs would inevitably head for the swamplands that seemed to be their natural environment.

"They're calling the tyrannosaurs here and then using them for some purpose," Anya concluded one bright morning after the castle had sunk beneath the lake's surface once again.

We were making our way back from the beach to our dugout, each of us carrying our spears, the duckbill—almost as tall as my hips now—sniffing and whistling beside us. I had a string of three fish thrown over one shoulder: our breakfast.

"There can only be one purpose for using the tyrannosaurs," I said to Anya, recalling the slaughter at the duckbills' nesting ground. "But it doesn't make any sense."

Anya had the same thought, the same question.

At least I had settled the question of why the castle's emergence from the lake was taking place a few minutes later each day. It surfaced only when the red star was high in the sky. And it submerged when the red star sank toward the horizon.

When I told Anya, she looked at me questioningly. "Are you sure?"

"The star is so bright that it will be visible in midday," I replied. "Then the castle will emerge in daylight. I'm certain of it."

"So Set is not trying to hide from anyone," she mused.

"Who is there for him to hide from? Us?"

"Then why does the castle sink back into the water? Why not have it out in the open all the time?"

"I don't know," I said. "But there's a bigger question for us to answer: Why does it rise only when that bloody star is in sight?"

Anya's mouth dropped open. She stopped where she stood, in the heavy foliage near our nest. Turning, she peered out between the leaves toward the western horizon.

The red star was almost touching the flat line of the lake, tracing a shimmering narrow red line across the water, aimed like a stiletto blade toward us.

For two more nights we watched and saw that the castle rose up from the water only once the red star was riding high in the sky, near zenith. It stayed above the water well into daylight now, and only sank back again once the star began to dip close to the horizon.

"You're right," Anya said. "It seeks that star."

"Why?" I wanted to know.

"Set must come from the world that circles that star," Anya realized. "That must be his home."

Our other big question, what the humanoid-tyrannosaur teams were doing, could only be answered by following one of the packs and watching them. I could not decide whether we should both go together to observe a tyrannosaur pack, or if I should go alone and leave Anya at the lake to continue watching the castle.

She was all for coming with me, and in the end I agreed that it would be best if she did. I feared leaving her alone, for there was no way for us to communicate with one another once we were separated. If either of us needed help, the other would never know it.

So, one bright hot morning, we took our spears in our hands and headed out after a team of nine humanoids who walked a discreet distance behind nine huge grotesque tyrannosaurs. We let them get over the horizon before leaving the shelter of the woods. I did not want them to see us following them. There was no fear of them eluding us; even a myopic infant could follow the monstrous tracks of the tyrants in the soft claylike ground.

Across the Cretaceous landscape we trekked for three days. It rained half the time, gray cold rain from a grayer sky covered by clouds so low I thought I could put a hand up and touch them. The ground turned to mud; the world shrank to the distance we could see through the driving rain. The wind sliced through us.

Little Juno seemed totally unperturbed by the foul weather. She munched on shrubs battered nearly flat by the rain and wind, then trotted on after us, a dark brown mound of rapidly growing dinosaur with a permanent silly grin built into its heavy-boned duck's bill and a thickening flattish tail dragging behind it.

Our progress slowed almost to a crawl through the rainstorm, and stopped altogether when it became too dark to move further. We made a miserable soaked camp on a little rocky hummock that projected a few feet above the sea of mud. Once the sun came out again, the land literally steamed with moisture boiled up out of the drenched ground. We saw that the tyrannosaurs had continued to slough along through the mud almost as fast as they had gone before. They apparently stopped to sleep each night, as we did—shivering cold and wet, without fire, hungry.

The tyrannosaurs should have been hungry, too, I thought. It must take a constant input of food to keep twenty tons of dinosaur moving as fast as they were going. But we saw no signs that they had slackened their pace, no bones or scavenging pterosaurs in the air to mark the site of a kill.

"How long can they go without eating?" Anya asked as the hot sun baked away the moisture from the rain. The earth was steaming in chill mist rising up from the ground. I was glad of it; the fog hid us from any eyes that might be watching.

"They're reptiles," I mused aloud. "They don't need to keep their bodies at a constant internal temperature the way we do. They can probably go a good deal longer without food than a mammal the same size."

"Obviously," said Anya. She looked tired. And hungry.

We caught a couple of dog-sized dinosaurs. They were basking in the morning sun, sluggish until the heat could sink into them. They seemed completely unafraid of humans, never having seen any before. They would never see any again.

Even though we tried to light a small fire, the shrubs and scrubby growth was so wet from the previous day's rain that we finally ate the meat raw. It took a lot of chewing, but at least there was plenty of water to wash it down with from the ponds and puddles that laced through the area.

We used Juno as a taster, as far as vegetable matter was concerned. If the duckbill nibbled at a plant and then spat it out, we stayed away from it. If she chomped on it happily, we tried it ourselves. As far as we knew, we created the first salads on Earth—out of pulpy, soft-leafed plants that would be wiped out and become as extinct as the dinosaurs that fed on them when the Cretaceous ended.

The ground we traveled was rising, becoming browner, drier than the marshy flatlands we had traversed. Still the deep tracks of the tyrannosaurs led us on, but now we began to see the tracks and hoofprints of other dinosaurs pounded into the hard bare ground by countless numbers of animals.

"This must be a migration trail," Anya said, mounting excitement in her voice.

I had my eyes on the hills rising before us. "We don't want to go too fast here. We might blunder into a pack of meat-eaters."

At my insistence we kept well to one side of the broad worn trail that marked the dinosaurs' migration route. Still we saw the clawed tracks of carnosaurs, most of them considerably smaller than tyrants, although there were plenty of tyrannosaur tracks as well.

Apparently the duckbills and other herbivores trekked this way each year as the seasons slowly changed. I had detected no noticeable change in the weather, although the rainstorm we had suffered through had lasted longer than anything previous to it, and the mornings *did* seem slightly chillier than before.

It was the pterosaurs again that showed us where to look. Vast clouds of them were wheeling high in the sky, circling somewhere beyond the ridge line of the hills we were approaching. With reckless anticipation Anya began loping toward the ridge, impatient to see what was happening there. I ran after her and left little Juno gallumphing behind.

We heard bleating, whistling, hooting shrieks and knew that they could not be coming from the winged lizards hovering so high above. These were the sounds of terror and death.

Anya reached the crest of the ridge and stopped, aghast. I pulled up beside her and looked down at the long narrow valley below us.

It was a battle.

Chapter 20

Thousands of herbivores were under attack by hundreds of tyrannosaurs. The battle stretched over miles of dry bare rocky ground, already red and slick with blood.

A running battle in the long narrow valley below us, with the duckbills and triceratops and smaller four-footed herbivores desperately trying to get through the rocky neck of the gorge and into the more open territory beyond while the tyrannosaurs ravaged through them like destroying monsters, crunching backbones in those terrible teeth, tearing bodies apart with their slashing scimitar claws.

It was like a naval battle in the days of sail, with powerful deadly dreadnoughts ripping through the line of clumsy galleons. Like fierce speedy brigades of mounted warriors slicing apart a fat caravan.

The screams and hoots of the dying herbivores echoed weirdly off the rocky walls of the valley. Our own Juno bleated pitifully and trembled at Anya's side.

There were no humanoids to be seen. None of Set's troops were visible. But I knew they were there, hidden in the rocks or watching from the valley crests as we were, directing their tyrannosaurs to slaughter the migrating herds.

The battle was not entirely one-sided. Here a trio of triceratops charged a tyrant, knocked it to the ground, and gored it again and again with their long sharp horns. There a small dinosaur, covered with armor plate like an armadillo, waddled out of the dust and blood and escaped into the open country beyond the end of the valley.

But the tyrannosaurs killed and killed and killed again. Duckbills and horned triceratops and countless others were slashed apart by those ferocious claws and teeth.

Anya said, quite clinically, "The humanoids must have brought the tyrannosaurs here to wait in ambush for the migration."

I felt anger, hot rage at the senseless slaughter taking place below us.

"Let's find some of those humanoids," I said, stalking off along the ridge line, my spear gripped tightly in my right hand.

Anya trotted along behind me, with Juno following her but clearly not liking the direction in which we were heading. The baby dinosaur made sounds remarkably like whining.

"Orion, what are you thinking of . . . ?"

Grimly I replied, "One thing I've learned in the lives I've led—hurt your enemy whenever and however you can. Set wants to kill these dinosaurs? Then I'm going to do my best to stop the slaughter."

She followed me in silence as we climbed higher along the rocky crest line, but Juno kept whimpering.

"Stay here with her," I told Anya. "She's terrified, and her mewling will warn the humanoids."

"We'll follow you from below the ridge line," Anya said. "If she can't see the slaughter, perhaps she'll settle down."

She and the duckbill scrambled down the rocky slope a hundred yards or so. I could see them paralleling my path as I made my way toward the area where I thought the humanoids would be. I hunched over so deeply that my left hand was knuckling the ground like a gorilla.

I saw one of Set's minions within a few minutes, lying belly down on the sun-warmed rocks, watching intently the screaming, screeching battle going on below. I gave him no warning, drove my spear into his back so hard that it splintered on the rock underneath him. He made a hissing sound and thrashed for a moment like a fish. Then he went still.

I felt for a pulse and found none. Brownish red blood seeped from under him. I flattened out on the rock beside his corpse and peered down into the valley. It was difficult to make out details now because of the billows of dust wafting up, but I saw one tyrannosaur standing upright, blinking its hideous red eyes. It had stopped killing. As I watched, it bent over the gory body of a triceratops and began feeding, tearing great chunks of meat from its heavy body.

The other tyrants were still ravaging through the herbivores, still under mental control of Set's troops. I got to my feet and moved onward.

My spear was blunted and split. Anya clambered up to me and gave me hers. I hesitated, then took it. She kept mine. She could use it as a club if she had to.

Two more humanoids were sitting in a cleft between boulders, their attention focused on the carnage below. It must take all their concentration to control the tyrannosaurs in the midst of such frenzy, I realized. They were virtually deaf and blind to the world around them.

Still I approached them cautiously, coming up from

behind. I dashed the last few yards and rammed my spear
straight through one of them. He shrieked like a steam
whistle as he died. The other leaped to his feet and turned
to meet me, but far too slowly as my senses went into
hyperdrive.

I saw him turning, saw his red slitted eyes glittering,
his mouth opening in what might have been anger or
surprise or sudden fear. His clawed hands were empty,
weaponless. With all my weight and strength I planted a
kick on his chest that crushed bones. He went over
backward, tumbling down the steep rocky wall and landing
almost at the feet of a suddenly befuddled tyrannosaur.

The great beast, released from its mental control,
snatched at its former master and tore the humanoid's
body in two with one crunch of its deadly teeth.

I squatted on my haunches and looked for the tyrant
that the other humanoid had been controlling. That one,
there, blinking with confusion at the mayhem surrounding
it. I closed my eyes briefly. When I opened them, I was
standing more than thirty feet above the blood-soaked
valley floor, blinking at the dust swirling around me.
Bloodlust blazed through me, overpowering the dull ache
of hunger that gnawed at my innards.

I was Tyrannosaurus rex, king of the tyrant lizards, the
most ferocious carnivorous animal ever to stride the earth.
I gloried in the strength and power I felt surging through
me.

Hooting a piercing whistling screech, I plunged into
the maelstrom of violence whirling all around me. I did not
seek out the weakling unarmed duckbills nor even the
dangerous triceratops. I strode through the carnage toward
the other tyrannosaurs, the ones still under the murderous
control of Set's humanoids.

They were killing but not eating. Rip open the throat
of a duckbill and let it fall to the dust, all that rich hot
blood steaming and wasting, all that meat dying without

sinking your teeth into it. Kill and then go on to another to kill again.

I pushed myself through a mound of dead and dying herbivores to reach one of my fellow tyrants. It paid me no attention, snapping after a bleating, screeching duckbill desperately trying to find a path through the blood to safety.

Just as the tyrannosaur was about to bite at the duckbill's soft neck I crunched its own spine between my mighty teeth and felt blood and bone and warm flesh in my mouth. The tyrant screeched once, then its heavy head collapsed onto the vestigial forearms against its chest, its powerful jaws closed forever.

I dropped the dead beast and charged toward another. It took no notice of me, and I ripped its throat out with a single quick bite. Now I saw two other tyrants; they had stopped their pursuit of the herbivores and turned their glittering eyes on me.

Without hesitation I ran straight at them, slashing and clawing. The three of us tumbled to the ground hard enough to make the earth shake.

Very far away I heard a tiny voice warning, "Orion, look out!"

But I was fighting the battle of my life against the two tyrannosaurs. And winning! Already one of them was staggering, half its flank ripped open and gushing rich red blood. I was bleeding, too, but I felt no pain, only the exultant joy of battle. I backed away slightly, saw my other opponent stalking toward me, jaws agape, tiny useless forearms twitching.

Behind it other tyrannosaurs were gathering, all focused on me. I backed up until my tail brushed against the rock of the valley wall.

"Orion!" I heard it again. This time a scream, more urgent, more demanding.

And then everything went black.

Somehow I realized that I had been knocked unconscious. I was in darkness, cut off from all sensory input, but
this was not the disembodied utter cold of the void
between spacetimes. I had not left the continuum. Someone had come up behind me while I was directing the
tyrannosaur and knocked me senseless. Despite Anya's
warnings.

I had been a fool. Now I would pay the price.

Once I realized what had happened I quickly made my
body recover. Shut off the pain signals from my aching
head and send an enriched flow of blood to the bruise on
my scalp. Open all the sensory channels. But I kept my eyes
shut and did not stir. I wanted to learn what the situation
was without letting anyone know I was conscious once
more.

My wrists were tightly bound behind me and more
vines or ropes or whatever were wound around my arms
and chest. I was lying facedown on the warm rocky ground,
several pebbles and sharper small stones poking uncomfortably into me.

The only sound I heard was the snuffling half whistle
of Juno. No voices, not even Anya's. With my mind I
probed the area around me. Anya was near, I could sense
her presence. And half a dozen others whose minds were as
cold and closed to me as a corpse frozen in ice.

"Let me see to him," I heard Anya at last. "He might
be dead—or dying."

No response. Not a sound. In the distance I could hear
the wind gusting, but no more screeching and hooting of
the dinosaurs. The battle had ended.

There was no more than I could learn with my eyes
shut, so I opened them and half rolled onto one side.

Anya was on her knees, her arms pulled tightly behind
her and ropes of vines cinched around her torso below her
breasts. Juno lay flat on her belly, silly duckbilled face
between her front hooves, like a puppy.

Six red-scaled humanoids stood impassively staring down at me, their tails hanging to slightly below their knees. Their crotches were wrinkled but otherwise feature-less; like most reptiles, their sexual organs were hidden.

They spoke no words. I doubted that they could make any sounds of speech even if they wanted to. Nor did they project any mental images. Either they were incapable of communicating with us mentally or they refused to do so. Obviously they communicated with one another and had the mental power to control the tyrannosaurs.

Two of them yanked me roughly to my feet. My head swam momentarily, but I swiftly adjusted the blood-pressure levels and the giddy feeling subsided. Another of the humanoids grabbed Anya by the hair and pulled her up from her knees. She screamed. I pulled away from the pair near me and karate-kicked the scaly demon under his pointed chin. His head snapped back so hard I heard vertebrae cracking. He fell over backward and lay still.

I turned to face the others, my hands tightly tied behind my back. Anya stood grim-faced, pale, with Juno trembling at her feet.

One of the humanoids went over to its felled compan-ion, knelt over the body, and briefly examined it. Then it looked up at me. I had no way of reading what was going through the mind behind that expressionless lizard's face. Its red eyes stared at me unblinking for a long moment, then it rose and pointed down the slope of the rocky ground in the general direction of the lake where the castle waited.

We began walking. Two of the humanoids took up the van, ahead of us; the other three followed behind. None of them touched either of us again.

"How do they communicate?" Anya wondered aloud.

"Some form of telepathy, obviously," I replied. Then: "Do you think they can understand what we say?"

She tried to shrug despite her bonds. "I'm not certain

that they can even hear us. I don't think their senses are the same as ours."

"They see deeper into the red end of the spectrum than we do," I recalled from our time inside Set's dimly lit fortress in the Neolithic.

"Some reptiles can't hear anything at all."

I glanced over my shoulder at the trio pacing along behind us. "I have the feeling that they understand us very well. They seemed to grasp the idea that I would fight to protect you from harm."

"You made that quite clear!"

"Yes, I know, but the important thing is that they understood that I would *not* try to fight them if they did not hurt you."

We marched along in silence for a while. Then I remembered to ask, "What happened in the valley after they knocked me out?"

"Most of the dinosaurs that were still alive got away," Anya said, her lips sketching a bittersweet smile. "The humanoids had to give up their control of the tyrannosaurs to deal with you. . . ."

I felt my face redden. "And I was easy prey for them, concentrating on the tyrannosaur I was controlling."

"But all the other tyrannosaurs stopped attacking and started eating the instant they let up their controls."

I thought about the overwhelming exhilaration I had felt while I controlled the tyrannosaur. I wasn't merely directing the beast from afar, I *was* the tyrant lizard, powerful, terrifying, glorying in my strength and bloodlust. The seduction of the senses had been overpowering. If ever I had to take control of such a monster again, I would have to be on my guard: it was too easy to become the monster and forget everything else.

The humanoids marched us back the way we had come until night had fallen and the world was completely dark. Heavy clouds had been building up through the late afternoon and evening, and there were no stars to be seen. The dark wind was chill, and I could smell rain coming.

We stopped on the hummocky ground between two shallow ponds. The humanoids helped Anya and me to sitting positions, but did not loosen our bonds in the slightest. The five of them squatted in a semicircle facing us. Juno, who had been nibbling on just about anything green all day long, wormed her growing body between Anya and me and promptly went to sleep.

"We're hungry," I said to the blank-faced humanoids.

"And cold," said Anya.

No reaction from them at all. They were not hungry, that was clear. No telling how long they could go without food. Either they never stopped to consider that we mammals needed meals more frequently, or—more likely—they didn't care. Or—more likely still—they realized that hunger weakened us and reduced the chances of our trying to fight them or escape.

The rain held off until just after dawn. We slogged through ankle-deep mud, slipping and falling continuously, unable to stop our falls with our hands tied behind our backs. The humanoids always helped us to our feet, not gently, but not roughly either. Two of them always helped Anya while the other three stood between me and them.

It rained off and on all the time we trekked back to the castle in the lake. We finally arrived on a steaming afternoon, wet, hungry and exhausted.

The castle stood glistening in the afternoon sun, its massive walls and high-flung towers wetly gleaming. High overhead, so bright it was easily visible in the washed-blue sky, the bloodred star glowered down at us.

Chapter 21

We were led up the long narrow ramp toward the single gate in the castle's wide high walls. The gate was barely wide enough for two of the slim humanoids to pass through side by side, but it was tall, at least twenty feet high. Sharp spikes ran all around its sides and arched top, like pointed teeth made of gleaming metal.

As we stepped out of the hot sunshine into the dimly lit shadows of the castle I felt the subtle vibrating hum of powerful machinery. The air inside the castle was even warmer than the steaming afternoon outside, an intense heat that flowed over me like a stifling wave, squeezing perspiration from every pore, drenching us with soul-draining fatigue.

Our quintet of captors turned us over to four other humanoids, slightly larger but otherwise so identical to the others that I could not tell them apart. They might have been cloned from the same original cell, they looked so much alike.

These new guards undid our bonds, and for the first time in days we could move our stiffened arms, flex our cramped fingers. Ordinary humans might have been permanently paralyzed, their arms atrophied, their hands gangrenous from lack of blood circulation. I had been able to force blood past the painfully tight ropes by consciously redirecting the flow to deeper arteries. Anya had done the same. Still, it would be a long time before the marks of our bonds left our flesh.

The first thing Anya did after flexing her numbed fingers was to pet little Juno, who hissed with pleasure at her attention. I almost felt jealous.

We were put in a cell the size of a dormitory room, all three of us. It was absolutely bare, not even a bit of straw to cover the hard seamless floor. The entire castle seemed to be made of some sort of plastic, just as Set's fortress in the Neolithic had been.

The walls looked absolutely seamless to me, yet a panel slid back abruptly to reveal a tray of food: meat steaming from the spit, cooked vegetables, flagons of water, and even a pile of greens for Juno.

We ate greedily, although I couldn't help thinking of the last meal a condemned man is given.

"What do we do now?" I asked Anya, wiping scraps of roasted meat from my chin with the back of my hand.

She glanced around at our bleak prison cell. "Can you feel that energy vibrating?"

I nodded. "Set must power everything here with the core tap."

"That's what we must reach," Anya said firmly. "And destroy."

"Easier said than done."

She regarded me with her grave, gray eyes. "It must be done, Orion. The existence of the human race, the whole continuum, depends on it being done."

"Then the first step," I said, with a sigh of resignation, "is to get out of this cell. Any ideas?"

As if in answer, the metal door slid back to reveal another pair of humanoid guards. Or perhaps two from the quartet that had ushered us into the cell in the first place, I could not tell.

They beckoned to us with taloned fingers and we went meekly out into the corridor, Juno clumping warily behind us.

The corridor was hot and dim, the overhead lights so deeply red that I felt certain most of their energy was emitted in the infrared, invisible to my eyes but apparently clear and bright to the reptiles. I closed my eyes and sought to make contact with Juno as we walked. Sure enough, through the duckbill's vision the corridor was brilliantly lit, and the temperature was wonderfully comfortable.

The corridor slanted downward. Not steeply, but a definite downward slope. As I walked along, seeing our surroundings through Juno's eyes, I realized that the walls were not blank at all. They were decorated with lively mosaics showing scenes of these graceful humanoid reptiles in beautiful glades and parks, in lovingly cultivated gardens, standing at the sea's frothing edge or atop rugged mountains.

I studied the artworks as we marched down the corridor. There was never more than one humanoid in any picture, although many of the scenes showed other reptiles, some bipedal but most of them four-legged. None of the humanoids wore any kind of clothing or carried anything resembling a tool or a weapon. Not even a belt or a pouch of any sort.

Then, with a sudden startling chill, I realized that every picture showed a sun in the sky that was deep red, not yellow, and so big that it often covered a quarter of the sky. There were even a few scenes in which a second sun appeared, small and yellow and distant.

These were pictures of a world that was not Earth. The red star they showed was the darkly crimson star that I had seen night after night, the evil-looking blood red star that was so bright I could see it in broad daylight, the star that was hovering above the castle even at this very moment.

I was about to tell Anya, but our guards stopped us at an ornately carved door, so huge that a dozen men could have marched through it at once. I reached out to touch it. It looked like dark wood, ebony perhaps, but it felt like cold lifeless plastic. Strange, I thought, that it can feel cold in such an overheated atmosphere.

The door split in two and swung open silently, smoothly. Without being told or prodded, Anya and I automatically stepped into an immense high-vaulted chamber. Juno trotted between us.

Using my own vision once more, I could barely see the top of the ribbed, steeply arched ceiling. The lighting was dim, the air oppressively hot, like standing in front of an open oven on a midsummer's afternoon.

Set reclined on a backless couch atop a platform raised three high steps above the floor. There were no statues of him here, no human slaves to worship him and try to placate him. Instead, rows of dully burning torches flanked Set's throne on either side, their flames licking slowly against the gloom, seeming to shed darkness rather than light.

We walked slowly toward that jet black throne and the devilish figure sitting upon it. Anya's face was grim, her lips pressed into a tight bloodless line, her fists clenched at her sides. The welts of the ropes that had bound her showed angry purple against her alabaster skin.

Once again I felt the fury and implacable hatred that cascaded from Set like molten lava pouring down the cone of an erupting volcano. And once again I felt the answering fury and hatred in my own soul, burning inside me, rising to a crescendo as we approached his throne. Here was evil incarnate, the eternal enemy, and my unalterable task was to strike him down and kill him.

And once again I felt Set take control of my body, force me to stop a half-dozen paces before his dais, paralyze my limbs so that I could not leap upon him and tear the heart from his chest.

Anya stood beside me as tensely as I. She felt Set's smothering mental embrace, too, and was struggling to break through it. Perhaps the two of us, working in unison, could overcome his fiendish power. Perhaps I could distract him in some way. Even if only momentarily, a moment might be enough.

"You are more resourceful than I had thought," his voice seethed in my mind.

"And more knowledgeable," I snapped.

His slitted red eyes glittered at me. "More knowledgeable? How so?"

"I know that you are not of this Earth. You come from the world that circles the red star, the planet that Kraal called the Punisher."

His pointed chin dropped a centimeter toward his massive scaled chest. It might have been a nod of acknowledgment, or merely an unconscious gesture as he thought over my words.

"The star is called Sheol," he replied mentally. "And my world is its only planet, Shaydan."

"In my original time," I said, "there is only one sun in the sky, and your star does not exist."

Now Set did nod. "I know, my apish enemy. But your original time, your entire continuum, will be destroyed soon enough. You and your kind will disappear. Sheol and Shaydan will be saved."

Anya spoke. "They have already been destroyed. What you hope to achieve is beyond hope. You have been defeated, you simply don't understand it yet."

Set's lipless mouth pulled back to reveal his pointed teeth. "Don't try to play your games with me, Creatress. I know full well that the continuums are not linear. There is a nexus here at this point in spacetime. I am here to see that you and your kind are swept away."

"Reptiles replacing human beings?" I challenged. "That can never be."

His amusement turned to acid. "So certain of your superiority, are you? Babbling mammal, the continuum in which you reign supreme on this planet is so weak that your Creators must constantly struggle to preserve it. Mammals are not strong enough to dominate spacetime for long, they are always swept away by truly superior creatures."

"Such as yourself?" I tried to say it with a sneer and only half succeeded.

"Such as myself," Set replied. "Frenetic mammals, running in circles, chattering and babbling always, your hot blood is your undoing. You must eat so much that you destroy the beasts and fields that feed you. You breed so furiously that you infest the world with your kind, ruining not merely the land but the seas and the very air you breathe as well. You are vermin, and the world is well rid of you."

"And you are better?"

"We have no need to keep our blood heated. We do not need to slaughter whole species of beasts for our stomachs. We do not overbreed. And we do not constantly make those noises that you call intelligent communication! That is why we are better, stronger, more fit to survive than you over-specialized jabbering apes. That is why we will survive and you will not."

"You'll survive by killing the dinosaurs and planting your own seed here?" I asked.

I sensed amusement from him. "So . . ." he answered

slowly, "the hairless ape is not so knowledgeable after all."

Sensing my confusion, Set went on: "The dinosaurs are mine to do with as I please. I created them. I brought my—seed, as you put it—to this planet nearly two hundred million of your years ago, when there was nothing on this land but a few toads and salamanders, fugitives from the seas."

Set's voice rose in my mind, took on a depth and power I had not experienced before. "I scrubbed this miserable planet clean to make room for *my* creations, the only kind of animal that could survive completely on dry land. I wiped out species by the thousands to prepare this world for *my* offspring."

"You created the dinosaurs?" I heard an astonished voice pipe weakly. My own.

"They are the consequences of my work from two hundred million years before this time. The fruits of my genius."

"But you went too far," Anya said. "The dinosaurs have been too successful."

He shifted his slitted gaze toward her. "They have done well. But now their time is at an end. This planet must be prepared for my true offspring."

"The humanoids," I said.

"The children of Shaydan. I have prepared this world for them."

"Killer!" Anya spat. "Destroyer! Blunderer!"

I could feel his contempt for her. And a cold amusement at her words. "I kill to prepare the way for my own kind. I destroy life on a planetwide scale to make room for my own life. I do not blunder."

"You do!" Anya accused. "You blundered two hundred million years ago. Now you must destroy your own creations because they have done too well. You blundered sixty-five million years from now, because the human race will rise up against you and your kind. You will be their symbol of unrelenting evil. They will be against you forever."

"They will cease to exist," Set replied calmly, "once my work here is finished. And you will cease to exist much sooner than that."

All through this conversation, with Anya and I speaking and Set answering in silent mental projections, I strained to break through his control of my body. I knew Anya was doing the same. But no matter how hard we tried, we could not move our limbs. Even Juno, cowering by Anya's feet, seemed unable to move.

"You'll never be able to wipe out the dinosaurs," I said. "We foiled your attempt to slaughter the duckbills and—"

He actually hissed at me. I sensed it was a form of laughter. "What did you accomplish, oversized monkey? On one particular day you helped a few hundred dinosaurs escape the death I had planned for them. They will meet that death on another day, perhaps next week, perhaps ten thousand years from now. I have all of time to work in, yammering ape. I created the dinosaurs and I will destroy them—at my leisure."

With that, he beckoned to Juno. Our little duckbill seemed reluctant to go toward him, yet helpless to resist. Grudgingly, as if being pulled by an invisible leash, Juno plodded to the dais and lumbered up its three steps to the clawed feet of Set.

Anya flared: "Don't!"

I strained with every atom of my being to break free of Set's mental bonds. As I struggled I watched with horrified eyes as Set picked up Juno like a weightless toy. The baby duckbill squirmed, frightened, but could no more escape Set's grasp than I could break free.

"Don't!" Anya screamed again.

Set lifted Juno's head up and sank his teeth into her soft unprotected throat. Blood gushed over him. The baby dinosaur gave a single piercing, whistling shriek that ended in a bubbling of blood. Its yellow eyes faded, its clumsy legs went limp.

I sensed Set's smirking, smug feeling of triumph and power. He let Juno's dead body, still twitching, fall to his feet and laughed mentally at Anya's anguish.

And dropped his guard just a fraction. Enough for me to burst loose and hurl myself up the dais, my fingers reaching for Set's red-scaled throat.

He swatted me with a backhand slap as easily as I might swat a fly. I was knocked sideways, tumbled down the dais, landing flat on my back, stunned and almost unconscious.

Chapter 22

Through a blood red haze I saw Set still on his throne. He had barely moved to deal with me.

"You think that I keep you paralyzed out of fear that you might attack me?" His voice in my buzzing brain was mocking. "Puny ape, I could crush your bones with ease. Fear me! For I am far mightier than you."

Forcing the pain away, pumping extra blood to my head to drive away the wooziness, I pulled myself up to a sitting position, then got slowly, warily to my feet.

"You are not convinced?"

Anya was still locked into immobility, but the look on her face was awful: a mixture of loathing and helpless terror. Juno's dead body lay sprawled clumsily at the foot of the dais in a welling pool of blood.

I could move. I took a step toward that throne and the monster sitting upon it.

Set rose to his full height and stepped down to the floor. He towered over me, several heads taller, a shoulder-span wider, his red scales glittering in the torchlight, his eyes burning with an amused contempt that overlay eternal hatred.

My senses went into hyperdrive and everything around me slowed. I saw the veins in Set's skull pulsing, saw transparent eyelids flicking back and forth across the red slits of his pupils. I could see the muscles in Anya's arms and legs tensing, straining to break free of Set's mental control. In vain.

I went into a defensive crouch, hands up in front of my face, backing away from Set. He advanced toward me in total confidence, arms by his sides, the talons of his feet clicking on the smooth bare floor like a metronome counting off time.

I dove at his knees in a rolling block. Knock him down and his size advantage is lessened, I thought. But fast as I was, his reflexes were even faster. He caught me in the ribs with a kick that sent me sailing. I hit the floor painfully hard. With an effort I climbed to my feet. He was still advancing on me, hissing softly in his reptilian equivalent to laughter.

I feinted left, then drove my right fist toward his groin with all the strength in me. He blocked the blow with one huge hand and grabbed me by the throat with the other. Lifting me off my feet, he raised my head to his own level. We were face-to-face, me with my feet dangling a yard or more off the floor, the breath slowly being squeezed out of me.

Set's face was in front of me, so close that I could smell the rancid hot breath hissing from his sharp-toothed mouth, see the glistening blood of Juno drying on his pointed chin. He was choking me to death and enjoying it.

With the last of my strength I jabbed both my thumbs at his eyes. He blocked my right with his free hand but my left found its mark. Set screeched in unexpected pain and threw me against the wall like an angry child tossing away a toy that displeased him.

I blacked out. My last conscious thought was a satisfied thrill that I had hurt the monster. Small consolation, but better than none at all.

How long I was unconscious I have no way of reckoning. I lay in darkness, huddled on the floor of Set's throne chamber. Dimly I felt the sensation of being lifted up and carried somewhere. But I could see nothing, hear nothing. Then I was dumped onto a hard floor again and left alone.

From far, far away I heard a sound. A faint voice, calling. It was so distant, so indistinct, that I knew it had nothing to do with me.

Yet it kept calling, time and again, as constant as waves rolling up onto a beach, as insistent as an automated beacon that will repeat itself endlessly until someone turns it off.

Somehow its call began to sound familiar. From repetition, a part of my mind suggested dreamily. Hear the same noise long enough and it will become familiar to it. Pay no attention. Rest. Ignore the sound and it will fade away.

Yet it did not fade. It got louder, clearer.

"Orion," it called.

"Orion."

I don't know how many times I heard it before I realized that it was calling my name, calling for me.

"Orion."

I was still unconscious, I knew that. Yet my mind was alert and functioning even though my body was inert, insensate, comatose.

"Who is calling me?" my mind asked.

"We have met before," answered the voice. "You called me Zeus."

I remembered. In another time, a different life. He was one of the Creators, like Anya, like the power-mad Golden One who let the ancient Greeks call him Apollo.

Zeus. I remembered him among the Creators. Like all of them his physical appearance was flawless, godlike. Perfect physique, perfect skin, grave dark eyes, and darker hair. His beard was neatly trimmed, slightly flecked with touches of gray. I realized that all that was an illusion, an appearance put on for my sake. I knew that if I saw Zeus in his true form, he would be a radiant sphere of energy, like Anya, like all the other Creators.

I thought of him as Zeus not because he was the leader of the Creators. They had no true leader, nor any of the common relationships that mortal humans experience. Yet to me he seemed wiser, more solemn, more circumspect in his views and his actions than the other Creators. Where they seemed swept by their private jealousies or passions for power, he seemed to be gravely striving to keep events under control, to protect the flow of the continuum, to prevent disasters that could erase all of humankind—and the Creators themselves. Of all the Creators, only he and Anya seemed to me to be worthy of my loyalty.

"Orion, can you hear me?"

"Yes."

"Set has shielded himself against us quite effectively. We can't get through to you and Anya."

"He is holding us prisoner. . . ."

"I know. Everything you have experienced, I know."

"We need help."

Silence.

"We need help!" I repeated.

"There is no way we can get help to you, Orion. Even this feeble communications link is draining more energy than we can afford."

"Set will kill her."

"There is nothing we can do. We'll be fortunate to escape with our own lives."

I knew what he meant. I was expendable; there was no sense risking themselves for their creature. Anya was a regrettable loss. But she had brought it on herself, daring to assume human form to consort with a creature. She had always been an atavism, risking her own being instead of letting creatures such as Orion take the risks that they had been created to face.

The other Creators—including this so-called Zeus— were ready to flee. In their true forms, they could scatter through the universe and live on the radiated energy of the stars for uncountable eons.

"Yes," Zeus admitted to me reluctantly, "that is our final option."

"You'll let her die?" I knew that my life counted little to them. But Anya was one of them. Had they no loyalty? No courage?

"You think in human terms, Orion. Survival is our goal, sacrifice is your lot. Anya is clever, perhaps she will surprise you and Set both."

I sensed the blind link between us fading. His voice grew fainter.

"If there were something I could do to help you, Orion, truly I would do it."

"But not at the risk of your own survival," I snapped.

The thought surprised him, I could sense it. Risk the survival of a Creator over one of their creatures? Risk the survival of all the remaining Creators over the plight of one of their number? Never.

They were not cowards. Godlike beings that they were, they were beyond cowardice. They were supreme realists. If they could not defeat Set, they would run from his wrath. What did it matter to them that the entire human race would be expunged from the continuum forever?

"Orion," called Zeus's voice, even fainter. "We deal with forces beyond your understanding. Universes upon universes. We must face the ultimate crisis out there among the stars and whirling plasma clouds that pinwheel through the galaxy. Perhaps the human race has played its part in evolving us, and now has no further role to play."

I snarled mentally, "Perhaps Set will seize such firm control of the continuum that he will track you down, each and every last one of you, no matter where you flee, no matter where you hide. Abandon the human race and you give Set the power to seek you through all of spacetime and destroy you utterly."

"No," came Zeus's reply, so weak it was nothing more than a ghostly whisper. "That cannot be. It cannot. . . ."

But there was doubt in his voice as it trailed off into nothingness. Doubt and fear.

My eyes opened. I was in a bare little cell, hardly bigger than a coffin stood on end, huddled into it like a folded, crumpled sack of grain. My head was resting on my knees, my arms hung limply at my sides, pressing against the cool smooth back wall of the cell on one side and the cool smooth door on the other.

The only light was from a dim dull red fluorescence emanating from the cell walls. The only sound was my own breathing.

Abandoned. The Creators were going to abandon Anya and me to final destruction. They were going to abandon the entire human race and flee to the depths of interstellar space.

And there was nothing I could do about it.

I almost wept, hunched over in that cramped claustrophobic cubicle. Orion the mighty hunter, created by the gods to track down their enemies and destroy them, defender of the continuum. How laughable! Instead of crying, I howled with maniacal glee. Orion, tool of the Creators, locked helpless and alone in a dungeon deep within the ultimate enemy's castle while the goddess I love is probably being tortured to death for the amusement of that fiend.

I could hardly move, the cell was so narrow. Somehow I slithered to my feet. Almost. The cubicle was too low for me to stand erect. My head bowed, my shoulders, arms, back, and legs pressed against the cool smooth flat surfaces of the cell. It made my blood run cold. The walls and door felt, not slimy, but slick, like rubbery plastic. It made me shudder.

I pushed as hard as I could against the door. It did not even creak. I strained every gram of strength in me, yet the door did not budge at all.

Defeated, exhausted, I let myself slide back down to the floor, knees in my face, muscles aching from frustrated exertion.

A mocking voice surged up from my memory. "You were created to act, Orion, not think. I will do the thinking. You carry out my orders."

The voice of the Golden One, the self-styled god who claimed to have created me.

"The intelligence I built into you is adequate for hunting and killing," I heard him saying to me, in his mocking deprecating way. "Never delude yourself into thinking that you have the brains to do more than that."

I had been furious with his sneering taunts. I had worked against him, challenged him, and finally driven him into a paroxysm of egomaniacal madness. The other Creators had to protect him against my anger and his own hysterical ravings.

I can think, I told myself. If I can't use my physical strength, then all that's left to me is my mental power.

"Set uses despair like a weapon." I recalled Anya's words.

He had tried to manipulate me, control me, through my emotions. Tried and failed. What was he trying to do to me now, penning me in this soul-punishing cell?

He comes from another world, the planet that circles the sun's companion star, Sheol. Why has he come here? From what era did he originate? What is his grievance against the human race?

He claims that he created the dinosaurs some two hundred millions years earlier than this era. He claims that he will extinguish the dinosaurs to make room on Earth for his own kind.

A thrill of understanding raced through my blood as I recalled Set's own words, heard again in my mind his sneering, hate-filled voice: *You breed so furiously that you infest the world with your kind, ruining not merely the land but the seas and the very air you breathe as well. You are vermin, and the world is well rid of you.*

And again: *We do not overbreed.*

Then why is he here on Earth? Why is he not content with his own world, Shaydan, where his kind live in harmony with their environment? I had seen the idyllic pictures of that world in the wall mosaics of this castle. Why leave that happy existence to seed the earth with reptilian life?

I could think of three possibilities:

First, Set had lied to me. The mosaics were idealizations. Shaydan *was* overcrowded and Set's people needed more living room.

Alternatively, Set had been driven off Shaydan, exiled from his native world, for reasons that I had no way of knowing.

Or, even more harrowing, the planet Shaydan was threatened by some disaster so vast that its was imperative to transfer the population to a safer world.

Which could it be? Possibly a combination of such reasons, or others that I had not an inkling of.

How to find out? Probing Set's mind was impossible, I knew. Even in the same room with him I could no more penetrate his formidable mental defenses than I could muscle my way out of this miserable dungeon.

Could Anya probe his mind?

I closed my eyes there in the dimness of my cell and reached mentally for Anya's mind. I had no way of knowing where in the castle she was, or even if she was still in the castle at all. Or even if she still lived, I realized with a cold shudder.

But I called to her, mentally.

"Anya, my love. Can you hear me?"

No response.

I concentrated harder. I brought up a mental picture of Anya, her beautiful face, her expressive lips, her strong cheekbones and narrow straight nose, her midnight black hair, her large gray eyes shining and luminous, regarding me gravely with depths of love in them that no mortal had a right to hope for.

"Anya, my beloved," I projected mentally. "Hear me. Answer my plea."

I heard nothing, no reply whatever.

Maybe she's already dead, I thought bleakly. Maybe Set has raked her flesh with his vicious talons, torn her apart with his hideous teeth.

Then I sensed the tiniest of flickers, a distant spark, a silver glint against the all-encompassing darkness of my soul. I focused every neuron of my mind on it, every synapse of my being.

It was Anya, I knew. That infinitesimal spark of silver led me like a guiding star.

I felt almost the way I had when I had entered Juno's simple mind. But now I was projecting my consciousness into a mind infinitely more complex. It was like falling down an endlessly spiraling chute, like stepping from subterranean darkness into blinding sunlight, like entering an overpoweringly vast universe. I knew how Theseus felt in the palace of Knossus, trying to thread his way through a bewildering maze.

Anya said nothing to me, gave no indication even that she knew I had entered her mind. I thought I understood why. If she gave any hint at all that she recognized my presence, Set would immediately know that I was awake and active—at least mentally. The only way to keep me hidden was not to make any response to me at all.

Swiftly, wordlessly, I gave her the details of my contact with Zeus. No reaction from her, none at all. She was guarding her mind from Set with every defensive barrier she could maintain. I wondered if she really knew I was there, so completely did she ignore me.

Set was still lounging on his throne, horned face staring at Anya, tail twitching unconsciously behind him. Poor Juno's body had been removed and the bloodstains cleaned away. I wondered how long it had been since he had smashed me into senselessness. Perhaps only minutes had passed. Perhaps days.

Anya was not in pain. Set was not torturing her or even threatening her. They were speaking together, almost as equals. Even the deadliest of foes have reasons to communicate peacefully, at times.

"You are prepared, then, to leave this planet forever?" I heard Set's voice in Anya's mind.

"If there is no alternative," she replied, also without speaking.

"What guarantee do I have that you will keep the agreement?"

"Agreement?" I asked Anya, but still there was no response from her. It was as if I did not exist, as far as she was concerned.

"You have won. Your power is too great, too firmly entrenched here, for us to dislodge you. If you permit us to escape with our lives and agree not to pursue us further, the planet Earth is yours forever."

"Yes, but how do I know I can trust you? In a thousand years or a thousand million, how can I be certain that you will not return to battle against my descendants?"

Anya shrugged mentally. "You will have destroyed the human race. We will have no means of fighting you then."

"You could create more humans, just as you created

the one called Orion."

"No. That was an experiment that failed. Orion has been of no use to us against you."

I burned with shame at Anya's words. They were true, and it hurt me to admit it.

"Then you have no intention of trying to bring him with you when you leave the earth?"

"How could he accompany us?" Anya replied. "He is nothing more than a human. He cannot change his form. He cannot exist in the depths of interstellar space, where we will make our new homes."

A shuddering horror filled me. Anya and all the Creators were indeed fleeing from Earth and abandoning the human race to extinction at Set's hands. Abandoning the entire human race. Abandoning me.

"Then you leave this creature Orion to me?" Set's words were half request, half demand.

"Of course," Anya replied carelessly. "He is of no further value to us."

Deep in my underground cell I screamed a shriek of agony like a wild animal howling with pain and fright and the utter furious agony of betrayal.

BOOK III

HELL

I fled, and cri'd out *Death*;
Hell trembl'd at the hideous Name, and sigh'd
From all her Caves, and back resounded *Death*.

Chapter 23

I did not withdraw from Anya's mind. I was driven out of it, repelled like an invading bacterium, thrown out like an unwanted guest.

For hours I howled like a chained beast in my dark coffin of a cell, unable to move, to stand, unable even to pound the walls until my fists became bloody pulps. I huddled there in a fetal position, wailing and bellowing to a blindly uncaring universe. Betrayed. Abandoned by the only person in the continuum whom I could love, left to my fate as callously as if I were nothing more to her than the husk of a melon she had tasted and then thrown away.

Anya and the other Creators were fleeing for their lives, reverting to their true physical forms, globes of pure energy that can live among the stars for all eternity. They were abandoning the human race, their own creations, to be methodically wiped out by Set and his reptilian brethren.

What did it matter? I wept bitterly, thinking of how

foolish I had been ever to believe that a goddess, one of the Creators, could love a man enough to risk her life for his sake. Anya had been all fire and courage and adventure when she had known that she could escape whatever danger we faced. Once she realized that Set had the power to truly end her existence, her game of playing human ended swiftly.

She had chosen life for herself and her kind, and left me to die.

I lost track of time, languishing and lamenting in my cell. I must have slept. I must have eaten. But my conscious mind had room for nothing but the enormity of Anya's betrayal and the certainty of approaching death.

Let it come, I told myself. The final release. The ultimate end of it all. I was ready to die. I had nothing to live for.

I don't consciously recall how or when it happened, but I found myself on my feet once more, standing in Set's audience chamber again, facing him on his elevated throne.

Blinking stupidly in the dull flickering ruddy light of the torches flanking his throne, I realized that I could move my arms and legs. I was not fettered by Set's mental control.

His enormous bulk loomed before me. "No, there are no chains of any kind holding you," his words formed in my mind. "We have no need of them now. You understand that I can crush you whenever I choose to."

"I understand," I replied woodenly.

"For an ape you show promising intelligence," his mocking voice echoed within me. "I see that you have pieced together the fact that I intend to bring my people to this world and make Earth our new home."

"Yes," I said, while my mind wondered why.

"Most of my kind are content to accept their fate upon

Shaydan. They realize that Sheol is an unstable star and will soon explode. Soon, that is, in terms of the universe's time scale. A few million years from now. Soon enough."

"You are not content to accept your fate upon a doomed planet," I said to him.

"Not at all," Set replied. "I have spent most of my life shaping this planet Earth to my purposes, fashioning its life-forms into a fitting environment for my people."

"You travel through time, just like the Creators."

"Better than your puny Creators, little ape," he answered. "Their pitiful powers were based on the tiny slice of energy that they could obtain from your yellow sun. They allowed most of the sun's energy to waft off into space! Unused. Wasted. A foolish mistake. A *fatal* mistake."

He hissed with pleasure as he continued, "My own people have depended on the wavering energy from dying Sheol. I alone understood how much energy can be tapped from the molten core of a planet as large as Earth. Taken in its totality, a star's energy output is millions of times stronger. But no one uses the total output of a star, only the miserable fraction that their planet intercepts."

"But a core tap . . ." I muttered.

"Tapping the planet's molten core gives me more energy, enormously concentrated energy, constant and powerful enough to leap across the eons of spacetime as easily as you can hop across a puddle. That is why I have won this planet for myself and your Creators are running for their lives, scattering out among the distant stars."

I said nothing. There was nothing for me to say. My only question was when Set would put me to death, and how long it would take.

"I have no intention of killing you soon," he said in my mind, knowing my thoughts without my speaking them. "You are my prize of victory over your Creators, my trophy. I will exhibit you all across Shaydan."

I looked up into his red snake's eyes and realized what he had in mind. Most of his kind did not believe that they could be saved by migrating to Earth. Set intended to show me to them, to prove that he was master of the planet, that there would be no resistance to their relocation.

"Good again, thinking ape! You perceive my motives and my intentions. I will be the savior of my kind! The conqueror of an entire world and the savior of my people! That is my accomplishment and my glory."

"A glorious accomplishment indeed," I heard myself answer. "Exceeded only by your vanity."

"You grow bolder, knowing that I do not intend to kill you immediately." I could sense anger in his words. "Be assured that you will die, in a manner and at a time that will not merely please me, but will convince all of Shaydan that I am to be obeyed by one and all. Obeyed and adored."

"Adored?" I felt shock at his words. "Like a god?"

"Why not? Your bumbling Creators allowed themselves to be worshiped by their human spawn, did they not? Why should not my own people adore me for saving our race? I alone have conquered the Earth. I alone have opened the gates to Shaydan's salvation."

"By killing off billions of Earth's creatures."

Set shrugged his massive shoulders. "I created most of them, they are mine to do with as I please."

"You didn't create humankind!"

He hissed laughter. "No, I did not. Those who did are fleeing to the farthest reaches of the galaxy. The human race has lost its reason for existence, Orion. Why should they be allowed to last beyond their usefulness, any more than the dinosaurs or the trilobites or the ammonites?"

I will not be allowed to outlive my usefulness, either, I thought. Once I ceased being useful to the Creators they abandoned me. Once I cease being useful to Set he will kill me.

"Before you die, overgrown monkey," Set went on tauntingly, "I will allow you to satisfy your apish curiosity and see the world of Shaydan. It will be the final satisfaction of your existence."

Chapter 24

S et lumbered off his throne and led me down long dim
corridors that sloped downward, always downward.
The light was so deeply red, so dim to my eyes, that I
might as well have been blind. The walls seemed blank,
although I felt certain they were decorated with mosaics
the way the upper corridors had been. I simply could not
perceive them.

Set's massive form marched in front of me, the scales
of his broad heavily muscled back glinting in the gloomy
light, his tail swinging left and right in time to the strides of
his clawed feet. Those talons clicked on the hard floor.
Absurdly, his swinging tail and clicking claws made me
think of a metronome. A metronome counting off the final
moments of my life.

We passed through laboratories and workrooms filled
with strange equipment. And still we went on, downward,
deeper. I tried to see these interminable corridors through
Set's eyes, but his mind was completely shielded from me. I

could not penetrate it at all.

He felt my attempt, though.

"You find the light too dim?" he asked in my mind.

"I am nearly blind," I said aloud.

"No matter. Follow me."

"Why must we walk?" I asked. "You have the ability to leap across spacetime, yet you walk from one end of your castle to another? No elevators, no moving beltways?"

"Jabbering monkey, we of Shaydan use technology to help us do those things we could not do unaided. Unlike your kind, however, we do not have a simian fascination with toys. What we can accomplish with our unaided bodies we do for ourselves. In that way we help to maintain a balance with our environment."

"And waste hours of time and energy," I grumbled.

I sensed a genuine amusement from him. "What matter a few hours to one who can travel through spacetime at will? What matter a bit of exertion to one who is assured of feeding?"

I realized that it had been too long since my last meal. My stomach felt empty.

"One of your mammalian shortcomings," Set told me, sensing my thought. "You have this absurd need to feed every few hours merely to maintain your body temperature. We are much more in harmony with our environment, two-footed monkey. Our need for food is modest compared to yours."

"Regardless of the environmental fitness of my kind," I said, "I am hungry."

"You will eat on Shaydan," Set answered in my mind. "We will both feast on Shaydan."

At last we entered a large circular chamber exactly like the one at the heart of his fortress in the Neolithic. Perhaps the same one, for all I could tell, although now it showed no signs of the battle Anya and I had put up there.

At the thought of Anya, even the mere mention of her name, my entire body tensed and a flame of anger flared through me. More than anger. Pain. The bitter, racking anguish of love that had been scorned, of trust that had been shattered by deceit.

I tried to put her out of my mind. I studied the chamber around me. Its circular walls were lined with row after row of dials and gauges and consoles, machines that controlled and monitored the titanic upwelling energy rising from the core tap. In the center of the chamber was a large circular hole, domed over with transparent shatter-proof plastic, I saw, not merely the metal railing that had been there in the Neolithic fortress.

The chamber pulsated with energy. Set's entire castle was hot, far hotter than any human being would feel comfortable in. But this chamber was hotter still; some of the heat from the earth's molten core leaked through all the machines and safety devices and shields to make this chamber the anteroom of hell.

Set reveled in it. He strode to the plastic dome and peered down into the depths of the core tap, its molten energy throwing fiery red highlights across the horns and flaring cheekbones of his red-scaled face. Like a sunbather stretching out on a beach, Set spread his powerful arms around that scarlet-tinged dome in a sort of embrace, soaking up the heat that penetrated through it.

I stood as far from it as I could. It was too hot for my comfort. Despite my efforts to control the temperature of my body, I still had to allow my sweat glands to do their work, and within seconds I was bathed in a sheen of perspiration from head to toe.

After several moments Set whirled back toward me and pointed to a low platform on the other side of the circular chamber. Its square base was lined by a series of black tubular objects, rather like spotlights or the projectors used to cast pictures against screens. Above the platform the low ceiling was covered with similar devices.

Wordlessly we stepped onto the platform. Set stood slightly behind me and to one side. He clamped a taloned hand on my shoulder; a clear sign of possession for any species that has hands. I gritted my teeth, knowing that I was no match for him either physically or mentally. Not by myself. A human being without tools is not a noble savage, I realized; he is a helpless naked ape, soon to be dead.

Halfway across the room I could see our reflection in the plastic dome that topped the core tap. Distorted weirdly on its curving surface, my own grim face looked pale and weak with Set's powerful shoulders and expressionless reptilian head rising above me. And his claws clamped on my shoulder.

Suddenly we were falling, dropping in utter darkness as if the world had disappeared from beneath our feet. I felt a bitter cryogenic cold as I whirled in nothingness, disembodied yet freezing, falling, frightened.

"Forgive me."

Anya's voice reached my awareness. A faint, plaintive call, almost sobbing. Just once. Only those two words. From somewhere in the interstices between spacetimes, from deep in the quantized fabric of the continuum, she had reached out with that pitifully fleeting message for me.

Or was it my imagination? My own self-pitying ego that refused to believe she could willingly abandon me? Forgive her? Those were not the words of a goddess, I reasoned. That was a message fashioned by my own emotions, my own unconscious mind trying to build a fortress around my pain and grief, trying to erect a castle to replace the desolation at the core of my soul.

The instant of cold and darkness passed. My body took on dimensions and form once more. Once again I stood on solid ground, with Set's claws pressing on my left shoulder.

We were on the planet Shaydan.

I was lost in murk. The sky was dark, covered with sick-looking low clouds the gray-brown color of death. A hot dry wind moaned, lashing my skin with fine particles of dust. Squinting against the blowing grit, I looked down at my feet. We were standing on a platform, but beyond its edge the ground was sandy and covered with small rocks and pebbles. A bit of scrawny bush trembled in the wind. A desiccated gray tangle of weeds rolled past.

It was *hot*. Like an oven, like the baking dry heat of a pottery kiln. I could feel the heat soaking into me, sapping my strength, almost singeing the hairs on my bare arms and legs. I felt heavy, sluggish, as if loaded down with invisible chains. The gravity here is stronger than on Earth, I realized. No wonder Set's muscles were so powerful; Earth must seem puny to him.

I could not see more than a few feet in any direction. The very air was thick with a yellow-gray haze of wind-blown dust. It was difficult for me to breathe, like sucking the blistering sulfurous fumes of a fire pit into my lungs. I wondered how long I could survive in this atmosphere.

"Long enough to accomplish my goal," Set answered my thought.

I tried to speak, but the gagging air caught in my throat and I coughed instead.

"You find Shaydan less than beautiful, chattering monkey?" He radiated amused contempt. "Perhaps you would feel differently if you could see it through my eyes."

I blinked my tearing eyes and suddenly I *was* seeing this world through Set's eyes. He allowed me into his mind. Allowed? He forced me, plucked my consciousness as easily as picking fruit from a tree. He kidnapped my awareness.

And I saw Shaydan as he did.

The mosaics I had seen in his castle immediately made sense to me. Through the eyes of this reptilian, born in this environment, I saw that we were standing in the middle of an idyllic scene.

What had been haze and mist to me was perfectly transparent to Set. We were standing at the summit of a little knoll, looking out over a broad valley. A city stood off near the horizon, its buildings low and hugging the ground, colored as the ground itself was in shades of green and brown. A single road led from the city to the knoll where we stood. The road was lined with low trees, so small and wind-tangled that I wondered if they were truly trees or merely large bushes.

What had seemed like a scorching, searing wind that drove stinging particles of dust now felt like a gentle caressing breeze. I knew that my own skin was being sandpapered by the flying dust, but to Set it was nothing more than the long-remembered embrace of his home world.

I saw that we stood on a platform exactly like the one in Set's castle back on Earth. Perhaps it was the very same one: it may have been translated through spacetime with us. The same black tubular projectors lined its four sides, except for the place where steps allowed one to mount or descend.

Looking up, I saw other projectors overhead, mounted on tall slim poles spaced evenly around the platform.

Beyond them was Sheol, so close that it covered more than a quarter of the sky, so huge that it seemed to be pressing down on me, hanging over me like some enormous massive doom that was squeezing the breath out of my parched lungs.

The star was so close that I could see mottled swirls of hot gases bubbling on its surface, each of them larger than a whole world. Sickly dark blotches writhed here and there, tendrils of flame snaked across the surface of the star. Its color was so deeply red that it almost seemed to be projecting darkness rather than light. It seemed to be pulsating, to be breathing in and out irregularly, gasping with an enormous shuddering vibration that racked its whole wide expanse.

This was a dying star. And because it was dying, the planet Shaydan was doomed also.

"Enough."

With that one word Set pushed me out of his mind. I stood half-blind, cringing at the stinging whips of the scorching, cutting wind, alone on the world of my enemies.

But Set had not cut the mental link between us fast enough for me to be ejected from his mind empty-handed. While I had gazed upon the face of Sheol through his eyes, I had learned what he knew of the star and the other worlds that formed our solar system.

The sun had been born with this companion, a double-star system. While the sun was a healthy bright yellow star with long eons of stable life ahead of it, its smaller companion was a sickly dull reddish dwarf, barely massive enough to keep its inner fusion fires going, unstable and doomed to extinction.

Huddled close to the sun were four worlds of rock: the closest named after the messenger of the gods because it sped back and forth in the sky so swiftly; the next named for the goddess of love because of its beauty; the third was Earth itself, and the fourth, rust red in appearance, received the name of a war god.

More than twice as far from the sun as the red planet lay the orbit of the feeble dwarf star that Set and his kind called Sheol. A single planet orbited around Sheol, Set's world of Shaydan. Doomed world of a doomed star.

Unwilling to accept the death of his kind, Set had spent millenia examining the other worlds of the solar system. Using the seething energy of his planet's core, Set learned how to travel through spacetime, how to move himself through the vastness between the worlds, and through the even greater gulfs between the years.

He found that beyond Sheol lay the giant worlds, planets of gas so cold they were liquified, gelid, too far from the sun to be abodes for his kind.

Of the four rocky worlds orbiting close to the warm yellow star, the first was nothing but barren rock pitilessly blasted by the heat and hard radiation of the nearby sun. The next was beautiful to gaze upon from afar, but below its dazzling clouds was a hellish world of choking poisonous gases and ground so hot it melted metal. The red planet was cold and bare, its air too thin to breathe, the life that had once flourished upon its surface long since died away. Worse yet, it was too small to have a molten core; there was no energy to tap on the red planet.

That left only the third planet from the yellow sun. From earliest times it had been the abode of life, a safe harbor where liquid water—the elixir of life—flowed in streams and lakes and seas, fell out of the sky, thundered across planet-girdling oceans. And this watery world was massive enough to hold a molten core of metal at its heart, energy enough to warp spacetime again and again, energy enough to bend the continuum in response to Set's will.

The earth harbored life of its own, but Set saw this as a challenge rather than an obstacle. With enough energy and a central driving purpose, he could accomplish anything. Far back into the earliest time of the planet's existence he traveled, sampling the millennia and the eons, studying, watching, learning. While the others of his kind watched Sheol shuddering and writhing in the beginnings of its death throes, Set pondered carefully and drew his plans.

Reaching far back in time, to the point where life was just beginning to emerge from the waters and stake its claim on dry land, Set scrubbed the earth clean of almost every one of its life-forms and seeded the planet with reptilian stock. Long eons passed and those reptiles took command of the ground, the seas, and the air. They changed the planet's entire ecosystem, even altered the composition of its atmosphere.

Now they were marked for destruction. The time had come for the descendants of Set's seed, the dinosaurs, to give way to Set's own people, the inhabitants of Shaydan. Set began the elimination of the dinosaurs and thousands of other species, cleansing the Earth once again to prepare it for his own kind.

A problem arose. From the distant future of the time where Set worked, the descendants of chattering inquisitive monkeys had evolved into powerful creatures who could also manipulate spacetime. Like monkeys, they busied themselves altering the continuum to suit themselves, even creating a breed of warriors to be sent to various points in spacetime to shape the continuum to their liking.

I realized that I was one of those warriors. The Creators had sent me to deal with Set, underestimating his abilities so tragically that now they were scattering out to the stars, abandoning the Earth and all its life to Set's merciless hand.

Set had won a cosmic victory. The Earth was his. The human race was to be exterminated completely. I was to be exhibited around the planet Shaydan as proof of Set's triumph and then ceremonially destroyed.

I knew that there was no way I could avoid my fate. With Anya gone, her back turned to me, I hardly had the will to keep on living.

I had died many times, but always the Creators had resurrected me to continue doing their bidding. I knew the pain that death brings, and the fear that comes with it every time, no matter how often. Is this the final destruction? Is the end of *me?* Will I be erased forever from the book of life?

Always in the past the Creators had restored me. But now they themselves were fleeing across the stars in fear of their lives.

I marveled that Set, as thorough and merciless as he was, would allow them to continue living.

Chapter 25

The ability to manipulate spacetime gives you control of the clock that counts out the hours, days, seasons, years. The ability to control time removes the frantic hurry from existence, teaches patience and prudence, allows the leisure to examine each step in life from every possible angle before proceeding further.

Set had traveled across millennia, across eons, to prepare his plans for the migration of his people to Earth. He felt no need for haste, no urge to speed.

Now he moved in a calm, deliberate manner to show me to his people even while Sheol seethed and writhed in the sky above.

Most of the time I was as good as blind in the murky atmosphere of Shaydan. The planet was slightly more massive than Earth; its more powerful gravity pulled on me, dragged my feet, made me feel tired and strained all the time. The merciless wind whipped at me and drove stinging particles of grit against my flesh. I was constantly exhausted, half-starved, my skin red and raw as if I were being lashed every hour of the day.

On rare occasions Set would allow me to see the world through the eyes of his people, and once again I saw a calm and beautiful desert world, severe but entrancing with its bold wind-sculpted rock mountains and bright yellow sky.

Set never allowed me into his own mind again. Did he realize that I had learned from him things that he would rather I did not know?

Slowly, as we traveled across the breadth of Shaydan, going from city to city in a seemingly endless round of visits and conferences, I began to understand the true nature of the people of Shaydan.

The fact that reptiles could evolve intelligence had puzzled me since I had first stepped out into the Neolithic garden along the Nile. Obviously Set and his kind had developed large complex brains, as mammals had done on Earth. Yet intelligence is more than a matter of brain size. If size were all that mattered, elephants and whales would be the intellectual equals of humankind, rather than the mental equals of dogs or pigs.

I had always thought that no matter what the size of their brains, reptiles who lay eggs the way the dinosaurs did and leave them to hatch on their own could never achieve the kind of parent-child communication necessary for the development of true intelligence. Yet obviously Set and his people had somehow overcome this obstacle.

Intelligence, I was convinced, depended on *communication.* Apes learn by watching their elders. Human babies learn at first by watching, then later through speech and finally reading. Set continually complained about the human race's constant monkeylike chattering. He derided our need to speak to one another, no matter whether the information being conveyed was monumental or trivial.

The people of Shaydan did not speak. They communicated with one another in silence, mentally, just as Set communicated with me. That I understood. But how did this telepathic ability arise in the first place?

I tried to ferret out the answer to this puzzle as Set exhibited me across the length and breadth of Shaydan. I watched as best as I could in the dimness of my captivity. Listening did me no good at all because the reptilians did not speak. But whenever Set allowed me to view his world through the eyes of one of his people, I tried to pluck out as much information about them as I could.

Our visits reminded me of a medieval king with his royal entourage touring his domain. We traveled on the backs of four-legged reptiles, not unlike compact versions of the sauropods of Earth. The civilization of Shaydan was apparently arranged into many distinct communities, each of them centered on a modest-sized city built of stone, baked clay, and other nonorganic materials. I saw no metals, or wood, in any of the buildings.

We traveled from city to city in a procession, with Set at its head flanked by two of his people on their own mounts. I rode behind Set, and trailing me came a dozen more riders and pack animals carrying food and water for our journey. Each trip took nearly a week, as near as I could calculate in the murky, dust-filled air. For the planet kept its face always turned to its star, Sheol, and all the cities of this world were on the daylit side of Shaydan.

Every moment of that endless day the remorseless grit-laden wind flayed my flesh, half-blinded my squinting reddened eyes. Set and his people had scales to protect their flesh and transparent lids to cover their eyes; he pointed this out to me as another proof of reptilian superiority over mammals. I had neither the strength nor the will to argue.

There was no magnificent panoply, no gorgeous robes and billowing silks, no gleaming gold or silver among his entourage. The reptilians wore nothing except their scaly hides: Set deep carmine, his minions lighter shades of red. Our mounts were dusty dull tones of brown. I still dressed in my ancient leather kilt and vest; I had nothing else.

Water was not abundant on Shaydan. It was a desert world, with meager streams and rare lakes. Nothing as large as a sea or an ocean. The food they gave me to eat consisted of raw leafy vegetables and occasional chunks of meat.

"We keep herds of meat animals," Set replied to my unspoken question. "We harvest them carefully and keep their numbers in balance with the environment. When the time comes to slay them, we put them to sleep mentally and then stop their hearts."

"Very humane," I said, wondering if he would understand my wordplay. If he did he gave no indication of it.

The cities we entered were not walled. From the weathered looks of their sturdy, domelike buildings, the cities were very old. Even in the wind-whipped dusty atmosphere of this hellish world it must have taken millennia to wear down such solid stone structures to the smooth rounded shapes they now presented. I saw no new buildings at all; everything seemed to be of the same age, and extremely ancient.

No blaring trumpets announced our approach to a new city, and no noble retinue came out to greet us. Still, crowds gathered at each city as we approached, lining the road to the city and the streets within it to bow solemnly as we passed and then stare wordlessly at us. More throngs clustered in the main city square where we invariably were met by the local leaders.

All in total silence. It was eerie. The people of Shaydan neither spoke nor made noise of any kind. No applause, not even the snapping of fingers or the clicking of claws. They would watch in complete silence as we stopped in the main square and dismounted. Sometimes a reptilian would point at me. Once or twice I thought I heard a hiss—

laughter? Otherwise it was in total silence that we would be led into the largest building on the square. No sound at all except the eternal keening of the stinging wind. In silence a quartet of guards would march behind me as I stumbled, drag-footed and exhausted, behind Set and the city officials who would come out to greet him.

All of these people, Set's entourage and the people of each city, looked to me like smaller copies of Set himself. Squinting in the gloomy dusty haze that passed for broad daylight among them, I began to notice minor variations from one city to another. Their scales were lime green here, shades of violet there. I even saw a whole city full of reptilians whose scales were patterned almost like a highlander's tartan.

In each city, however, *all* the people were the same color. It was as if they all wore the same uniform, except that this coloration was the natural pigment of their scales. There were some variations in tone; the smaller a reptilian, the lighter the tone of its coloring, I found. Were size and color indicators of an individual's age? I wondered. Or did they show an individual's rank?

I received no answer from Set to my unspoken questions.

Regardless of the local color, in every city, once we dismounted, we were led into the largest building on the main square. The rounded domes of the city structures were only a small part of their true extent. Most of the cities were underground, their buildings interconnected by broad tunnels and buried arcades.

We were always brought to a large oblong room where a reptilian of Set's own size sat on a raised dais at the far end. Obviously the local patriarch. The audience chamber would then be filled with smaller citizens of the city, lighter in color, lesser in rank. So I supposed.

Set would stand before the patriarch with me at his side, feeling puny and tired in the heavy gravity. More than once I slumped to the floor; Set would ignore it and allow me to lie there, and I felt grateful for the chance to rest. To Set, of course, it was a perfect exhibition of the weakness of the native life-forms on Earth, an obvious proof that his plan was achievable.

The chambers were as dimly lit as every other room I had been in; artificial light so deeply into the red end of the spectrum that it seemed to radiate darkness. And the heat. These reptilians basked in heat that made me almost giddy despite my efforts to keep my internal temperature under control.

Now and then Set would allow me to see the chamber through the eyes of one of his entourage. I waited eagerly for such moments. Then I would see a splendid audience hall, its majestic walls ablaze with mosaics showing the ancient history and lineage of the patriarch sitting before us. And while my borrowed vision drank in the scene all around me, I busily delved into the mind of my temporary host, trying to learn as much as I could without alarming either him or his master, Set.

Sometimes our audience took only a few minutes. More often Set stood before the patriarch's dais for hours on end, silently conversing, hardly moving a muscle or twitching his tail. I knew he was exhibiting me as proof that the people of Shaydan could emigrate to Earth with impunity. I did not find out, however, what success he was meeting with. Did the brief interviews indicate quick agreement or adamant refusal? Did the long hours of mute discourse mean that Set and his host were arguing bitterly or that they were happily discussing every detail of the plan to colonize Earth?

Gradually, as we trekked from city to city across the broad desiccated face of Shaydan, as I was granted glimpses into the minds of Set's followers, I began to piece together a rudimentary understanding of these people and their civilization.

Despite my physical weakness my mind was still active. In fact, I had little else to do except try to fathom as much as I could glean about my captor and his world. It helped me to forget my constant hunger and the pain of that remorseless lashing wind. My body was under Set's control, but my mind was not. I probed whenever I could. I watched and studied. I learned.

The beginning point, of course, was that they are reptiles. Or the Shaydanian equivalent of terrestrial reptiles. They do not actively control their body temperature as mammals do, although they maintain their body heat rather well and can be active and alert even during the chill of night.

They reproduced by laying eggs, originally. Like the reptiles of Earth, virtually all of the species of Shaydan left their nests once the eggs were laid and never returned to see their young.

What came out of those eggs were miniature versions of adult reptiles, fully equipped with teeth and claws and all the instincts of their parents. The hatchlings possessed everything their parents had except size. Successful offspring who made it into adulthood grew to great size, and the older the individual, the larger he grew and the deeper the color of his scales. The only limitations imposed on a Shaydanian's size were the ultimate physical limits of bone and muscle's ability to support increasing weight.

This meant that Set and the other patriarchs that we met at each city must have been considerably older than the others around them. How old was Set? I began to wonder. Centuries, at least. Perhaps millennia.

Newly hatched Shaydanians inherited *all* the physical characteristics of their parents—including not merely brain structure, but the ability to communicate telepathically. Eons earlier, this trait must have arisen as a mutation, and then was passed on to the following generations. Telepathic individuals lived longer and produced more offspring, who were also telepathic. As the generations went by, the telepaths drove their less-talented brethren into extinction. Perhaps they did it by violence, just as the Creators once drove the Neanderthals into oblivion, almost.

Telepathic communication led the way to intelligence. While laying her eggs, a Shaydanian mother imprinted her unformed offspring with all the experiences of her life. Each generation of telepathic reptile imparted *all* the knowledge of *every* previous generation to its young. Once a new hatchling could learn, in the egg, all the experiences that every generation of its ancestors had lived through, it was armed mentally as well as physically to deal with the world around it.

The civilization that these intelligent reptilians built on Shaydan had existed for millions of terrestrial years. Each community was led by its eldest member. Their ages ran to thousands of years. To creatures who could open their minds completely to one another, distrust was unknown. Disagreements between individuals were decided by the patriarch—indeed, that seemed to be his main reason for existence.

Each community worked with the tireless self-effacing efficiency of an ant's nest or a beehive. There were no wars because each community lived within the bounds of its environment. The children of Shaydan lived in harmony.

Until they realized that their star, Sheol, would one day destroy them.

The patriarchs consulted among themselves about how to face this dreadful certainty. Most of them felt that doom was inevitable and the only thing that could be done was to accept the fact. A few even recommended suicide, insisting it was better to die with dignity at one's own choosing rather than wait for the cataclysm to strike them down.

Yet the urge to live was strong among them. They

began to dig in, to extend their cities and dwellings underground in the hope that the bulk of their planet would help to protect them from the worst of the radiation that Sheol would one day rain upon the surface of Shaydan. Even so, they knew that the lethal radiation would be merely the first stage of Sheol's death throes. Ultimately the star would explode and destroy their world along with itself.

Of all the patriarchs of Shaydan, only Set stood against the counsels of passivity and acceptance. He alone searched for a path to avert the doom that faced Shaydan. He alone determined to find a way to save himself, his people, his entire race. The other patriarchs thought him mad, at first, or supremely foolish to spend his remaining centuries trying to escape the inevitable. Set ignored them all.

Now, more than a century after he first started out to do it, he was exhibiting me to his fellow patriarchs as proof that they could migrate to Earth and begin life anew beneath the warmth of the stable life-giving yellow Sun.

I had no way of calculating how long we spent traveling from city to city. There was no way to count days, and there did not seem to be any noticeable seasons on Shaydan. Whenever I was permitted a glimpse into one of the reptilians' minds and tried to ferret out such information, I could not understand how they reckoned time.

It occurred to me that the telepathic abilities of the Shaydanians must have a limited range. Otherwise why would Set go to the trouble and time of our planet-girdling travels? Why not remain comfortably in his own city and converse with the other patriarchs telepathically? Alternatively, if he found it necessary to exhibit me physically to each of the patriarchs, that meant that telepathic communication could not perform such a function. They had to see me in person.

Either way, it meant that there were limits even to

Set's formidable mental powers. I stored that hope away for future use; there was little other hope for me to cling to.

Now and then on our travels I thought I felt the ground tremble. More than once I heard a low rumbling reverberation like the growl of distant thunder. Neither Set nor his servants appeared to take any note of it, although our mounts seemed to hesitate and sniff the air worriedly.

In the middle of one of our audiences the ground did shake. The stone floor beneath me heaved, knocking me to my knees. A crack zigzagged in the wall behind the patriarch's dais. He clutched the arms of his wide chair, hissing in a sibilant note I had never heard before. Even Set staggered slightly, and as I looked around I saw that the onlookers gathered on either side of the long chamber were clinging to one another and glancing around fearfully.

For the first time I heard the telepathic voices of many Shaydanians, clear and unshielded.

"The ground quakes again!"

"Our time grows short."

"Sheol reaches out to seize us!"

Like a thunderbolt it struck me that the violent upheavals churning deep in the heart of the star Sheol were causing pulsations within the core of its planet Shaydan.

Our time grows short, one of the reptilians had gasped. But if Set and the patriarch felt that way, they gave no outward sign of it. Once the dust raised by the brief tremblor had settled, Set unceremoniously yanked me to my feet and resumed his silent conversation with the olive-scaled patriarch seated before him.

Not before I finally learned what a truly horrible monster Set was. With so many minds open to me simultaneously, even if only for a few seconds, I learned that Set and his fellow patriarchs ruled their smaller fellows with a despicable iron despotism, a remorseless tyranny woven inextricably into the very genes of their people.

I realized in that horrifying flash of mental communication that almost everything Set had told me had been a distortion, a perversion of the truth. He **was** the prince of lies.

I had long wondered why not one of the people in any of the cities we had visited were anywhere near the size of Set and the other patriarchs. At first I had thought that this meant none of them were of patriarchal age. But why not? There should have been just as many reptilians hatched in his generation as these later ones. What had happened to Set's generation? Were they all dead?

In that brief glimpse into the minds of so many Shaydanians inspired by the quake, I saw the sickening answer to my question. Set and his fellow patriarchs were the winners of a devastating war that had nearly destroyed all of Shaydan a thousand years before they learned that Sheol would explode. For Set himself had discovered the way to clone his cells, to make copies of himself, to do away with the need for breeding, for laying eggs, to do away with the female of his species completely.

Even worse, he had learned how to configure his cloned replicas to suit his own desires: how to limit their intelligence so that they would never challenge him, how to limit their life spans so they would never grow to his age and experience.

Swiftly, with cold ruthlessness, Set gathered about himself a merciless cadre of males his own age, offering them domination of their entire world for all the millenia of their lives. They led a remorseless war of extinction against their own kind, especially against their females, cloning warriors as they needed them, slaughtering all who opposed them. For two centuries the genocidal war raged across the face of Shaydan. When it ended, Set and the patriarchs ruled over a world of submissive clones. All males. Every mother and daughter had been methodically butchered. Every unhatched egg had been found and smashed.

It took centuries for them to repair the ecological damage they had done to their world. But time meant little to them. They knew that they would rule for millenia to come. And leave their power, when the time eventually came, to exact copies of themselves. With telepathy it might even be possible to transfer their personalities to cloned bodies and continue to exist forever.

Of course their society ran as efficiently as an ant colony. Of course warfare was now unknown to them. Set and his fellow patriarchs ruled a world of clones incapable of doing more than obeying. But Set wanted still more. He wanted to be adored.

Then, like a punishment for their sins, came the certain knowledge that Sheol would explode and destroy their entire world.

Cosmic justice. Or at least cosmic irony. It made me smile inwardly to know that Set, for all his moralistic cant about reptilian fitness and their care for their environment, was at heart a ruthless mass murderer. A genocidal slaughterer of his own kind who had chosen power and death over nature and life.

I should have known I could not have kept my new knowledge from him.

"You think I am hypocritical, hairless ape?" he asked one murky day as we rode through a stinging windstorm. He was up ahead of me, as usual, his broad back to me.

"I think you are mercilessly evil, at the very least," I replied. It did not matter if he heard my words or not. He could sense the thoughts forming in my brain.

"I saved Shaydan from the kind of excesses that mammals would have created. Without firm control, the people would have eventually destroyed their environment."

"So you destroyed the people."

"They would have destroyed themselves and their whole environment, had I not intervened."

"That's nothing but a rationalization. You took total power for yourselves, you and your fellow patriarchs. You rule without love."

"Love?" He seemed genuinely surprised. "You mean sex."

"I mean love, caring for your own kind. Friendship so deep that you'd be willing to lay down your life to protect—" The words gagged in my throat. I thought of Anya and the memory of her betrayal burned inside me like bitter bile. I wanted to vomit.

Amused contempt radiated from his mind. "Loyalty and self-sacrifice. Mammalian concepts. Signs of your weakness. Just as your ideas of so-called love are. Love is an apish invention, to justify your obsession with breeding. Sex was never as important to my species as it is to yours, hot-blooded monkey."

I found the strength to retort, "No, it's power that's your obsession, isn't it?"

"I cleansed this world so that I could bring new life to it, a better form of life."

"Artificially created. Maimed in mind and body so that your creatures have no choice but to obey you."

In my mind I heard the hiss of his laughter. "Just as you are, Orion. An overspecialized monkey created by your superior beings, maimed in mind and body to serve them without choice."

Hot anger flared within me. Because he was right.

"Naturally you hate me and what I have done." Set's cool amusement washed over me like glacier melt. "You realize that it is exactly what the Creators have done to you, and you hate them for it."

Chapter 26

Finally, after months or perhaps even years of travel, we returned to Set's own city.

It was much like all the others. Above ground a group of ancient low stone buildings weathered by millennia of wind and rasping dust. Below ground a honeycomb of passageways and galleries, level after level, deeper and deeper.

All the Shaydanians here were scaled in tones of red. The entire population came out into the main thoroughfare leading into the city to welcome their master home in silent obedient reptilian fashion.

A trio of salmon pink guards led me deep underground to a hot, bare little cell, so dark that I had to grope along its nearly scalding walls to make out its dimensions. It was roughly square, so small that I could almost touch opposing walls by standing in its center and stretching out my arms. No windows, of course. No light at all. And insufferable heat, as if I were being slowly roasted by microwaves.

Wherever I touched the walls or floor, it scorched my skin. From some dim memory I recalled that on Earth bears had been trained to "dance" by forcing them onto a heated floor so that they rose to their hind legs and hopped around in a pitiful effort to avoid being burned. Likewise I tried to stay on my feet, on my toes, for as long as I could. But eventually exhaustion and that overburdening heavy gravity got the better of me and I collapsed to the hot stone floor.

For the first time since I had arrived on Shaydan I dreamed. I was with Anya once again in the forests of Paradise, living simply and happily, so much in love that wherever we walked, flowers sprang up from the ground. But when I put my arms out to embrace her, Anya changed, transformed herself. For a moment she was a shimmering sphere of silvery light, too bright for me to look at. I staggered back away from her, one arm thrown across my face to shield my eyes from her radiance.

From far, far away I heard the mocking voice of the Golden One, the godlike being who had created me.

"Orion, you reach too far. Can you expect a goddess to love a worm, a slug, a paramecium?"

All the so-called gods materialized before me: the dark-bearded, solemn-eyed one I thought of as Zeus; the lean-faced grinning Hermes; the cruelly beautiful Hera; broad-shouldered, redheaded Ares; dozens of others. All of them splendidly robed, magnificent in gleaming jewels and flawless, perfect features.

They laughed at me. I was naked and they pointed at my emaciated body, covered with raw sores and red welts from the pelting wind of Shaydan. They howled with laughter at me. Anya—Athena—was not among them, but I sensed her distant presence like cold sifting flakes of snow chilling my soul.

The gods and goddesses roared with amusement at me as I stood dumbfounded, unable to move, unable even to speak. The forests of Paradise wavered and bowed as snow fell, covering the trees, blanketing the ground. Even the laughter of the gods was smothered by the silent smooth white snow. They faded into nothingness and I was left alone in a world of glittering white.

The soft whiteness of the snow transformed into a glittering silvery metallic sheen. Then the silver light took on a ruddy glow. It became fiery red and seemed to pull in on itself, taking a shape once again. This time it was the massive looming form of Set who stood before me, hissing laughter at my pain and loss.

I realized that I had not dreamed during all the long months of our travels because he had not allowed me to dream. And now that our journey was finished, he was amusing himself by invading my dreams and perverting them to his own enjoyment.

I seethed with hate all the time I spent in that dark scorchingly hot cell. Set's servants fed me only enough to keep me barely alive: a thin warm liquid that tasted rancid, pulpy rotting leaves, nothing more. I was out of that stinging, lashing wind, but the heat down in this deep underground chamber baked the strength out of me, blistered my skin, and seared my lungs.

Every night I dreamed of Anya and the other Creators, knowing that Set was watching, digging into memories I never knew I had. The dreams turned into nightmares as night after night I tried to warn Anya and the others while before my sleeping eyes I saw the Creators being sliced to bloody ribbons, bodies slashed open spurting blood, faces torn apart, limbs hacked from their torsos.

By me.

Horrified, I was their executioner. I burned them alive. I tore out their eyes. I drank their blood. Zeus's. Hera's. Even Anya's.

Night after night the nightmares were the same. I would visit the Creators in their golden sanctuary. They would scorn me. Mock me. I would reach for Anya, begging her to help me, to understand the message of terror and death that I was carrying. But she would run away or transform herself into some form unobtainable.

Then the killing would start. I always began with the Golden One, tearing at him like a ferocious wolf, ripping the smirking smile from his face, rending his perfect body with claws of razor-sharp steel.

Night after night, the same dream. The same horror. And each night it became more real. I awoke bathed in sweat, shaking like a man possessed, hardly daring to look down at my trembling hands for fear that I would find them reeking with blood.

Behind each nightmare I sensed Set's lurking, menacing presence. He was clawing ruthlessly through my mind, dredging into memories that the Golden One or whoever created me had long since sealed off from my conscious recall. I relived life after life, hurtling from the very origins of the human race to such distant futures that humankind itself had evolved into shapes and powers beyond recognition. Yet each dream inevitably, inexorably came down to the same horrifying scene.

I confronted the Creators. I tried to tell them what was going to happen, tried to warn them. They laughed at me. I begged them to listen to me, pleaded with them to save their own lives. They thought it was uproariously funny.

Then I killed them. Slashed them while they laughed, tore out their entrails while their faces still smirked and grinned at me. I killed them all. I tried to spare Anya. I screamed at her to run away, to transform herself so that I could not reach her. Sometimes she did. Sometimes she became that glowing silvery sphere that was forever beyond my touch. But when she did not, I killed her as mercilessly as I butchered all the others. I tore her throat out. I disemboweled her. I crushed her beautiful face in my clawed hands.

And woke up whimpering. I had not the strength for screaming. I awoke in that oven-hot lightless cell blind and terribly weak, my body wasting and my mind being pillaged.

The worst of it was that I knew what Set was doing. He was exploring my mind, using the memories that had been sealed away from me to learn everything he could about the Creators. Most of all he wanted to find out how he could send me back through spacetime to the Creators' own domain, that golden paradise of theirs far in the future of this time.

I could feel his cold cruel presence in my mind, searching, rampaging through my memories like a conquering army looting a helpless village, looking for the key that would allow him to project me into the Creators' realm.

He wanted to send me to a point in the continuum *before* the Creators had become aware of his own existence. He wanted to plant me among them when their defenses were down, when they were not expecting to be attacked, especially by their own creature.

Set would accompany me on this trip through spacetime. His mind and will would ride within my brain. He would see with my eyes. He would strike with my hands.

The hell of it was that there truly was hatred for the Creators inside me. He found that vein of anger, of bitter resentment, that seethed through me. He hissed with pleasure when he realized how I hated the Golden One, the very person who had created me. He saw how I had defied him and tried to kill him, how I hated the other Creators for shielding him from my wrath.

And he found the blistering-hot fury deep within me that etched my soul like acid eating steel whenever I thought of Anya. Love turned to hate. No, worse, for I still loved her yet hated her, too. She had chained me to a rack that was pulling me apart, worse torture than anything Set could inflict upon my body.

But the devil knew how to use the torment in my mind, how to employ that hatred for his own purposes.

"You are being very helpful to me, Orion," I heard him in my mind as I writhed in that utterly black cell.

I knew it was true. I loathed myself for it, but I knew that there was enough rage and hatred within me to serve as a murderous weapon for Set's malevolence.

The nightmares returned whenever I slept. No matter how hard I fought against it, inevitably my eyes would close and my starved, exhausted body would drift into slumber. And the nightmare would begin anew.

Each time more real. Each time I saw a little more detail, heard my own words and those of the Creators with better clarity, felt the solidity of their flesh in my ravening hands, smelled the hot sweetness of their blood as it spurted from the wounds I slashed into them.

There would come, inexorably, one final dream. I knew that one of these times the reality would be perfect, that I would actually be among my Creators, that I would kill them all for Set, my master. And then all dreams would cease. My pain and longing would be at an end. The crushing, forsaken sense of abandonment that filled my heart with despair would at last be wiped away.

All I had to do was surrender to the will of Set. I realized now that it was only my own foolish, stubborn resistance that stood in the way of final peace. A few moments of blood and anguish and everything would be finished. Forever.

I had to stop fighting against Set and admit to myself that he was my master. I had to allow him to send Orion the Hunter on this final stalk, and then he would allow me peace. I almost smiled to myself there in the blind darkness of that searingly hot cell. How ironic that Orion's final hunt would be to track down his very Creators and kill them all.

"I am ready," I called out. My voice was cracked, rasping. My throat and lungs parched.

In response I heard a vast hissing sigh that seemed to echo through all the underground chambers of Set's magnificent palace of darkness.

It seemed like an eternity before anything happened. I lay on the stone floor of my cell in total darkness and absolute quiet except for my own ragged, labored breathing. Perhaps the floor became somewhat cooler. Perhaps the air became a little moister. Perhaps it was only my imagination.

I was too weak to stand, and I wondered how I might do my master's bidding in such an exhausted condition.

"Have no fear, Orion," Set's voice echoed in my mind. "You will be strong enough when the moment comes. *My* strength will fill your body. I will be within you at every moment. You will not be alone."

So his magnanimity in allowing the Creators to flee the Earth had been nothing more than a ruse. He intended to strike at them, to destroy them, at a time when they were completely unprepared to meet his attack. And I would be his weapon.

With the Creators permanently obliterated, all of the continuum was Set's. He could colonize the Earth with his own species and destroy the human race at his leisure. Or enslave humankind, as he had been doing in the Neolithic.

There were depths here that I could not fathom. I remembered being told, more than once, that spacetime was not linear.

"Pathetic creature," I heard the Golden One's scornful voice in my memory, "you think of time as a river, flowing constantly from past to future. Time is an ocean, Orion, a great boundless sea on which I can sail in any direction I choose."

"I don't understand," I had replied.

"How could you?" he had taunted. "I did not build

such understanding into you. You are my hunter, not my equal. You exist to serve my purposes, not to discuss the universes with me."

I am maimed in mind and body, I told myself. I was created that way. Set had spoken the truth.

And now I was going to be sent back to my Creators to end their existence. And my own.

Chapter 27

Lying in the blind darkness of my cell, waiting for Set to send me on my mission of murder, it seemed as if the heated stones beneath me were slowly cooling. The very air I breathed seemed not as hot as it had been moments before, as if my physical torment was being eased in reward for my capitulating to Set's will.

I did not feel him in my mind, yet I knew he must be there, watching, waiting, ready to control my body.

I felt a hollow sinking sensation within my chest, my belly. The floor seemed to be descending, very slowly at first, then faster and faster. Like an elevator plunging out of control. I sensed myself falling through the inky blackness, the stones beneath me growing colder as I descended.

Then came that wrenching moment of absolute cold, of nothingness, when all the dimensions of time and space seem to disappear. I hung suspended in nowhere, without form or feeling, in a limbo where time itself did not exist. A billion years could have passed, or a billionth of a second.

Brilliant golden radiance lanced through me like spears of molten metal. I squeezed my eyes shut and threw my hands over my face. Tears spurted down my cheeks.

I still could not see; first I had been blind from lack of light, now I was blinded by too much of it. I lay curled in a fetal position, head tucked down, arms across my face. Nothing stirred. Not a breeze, not a bird or a cricket or a rustling leaf. I listened to my own heart pulsing feebly in my ears. I began counting. Fifty beats. A hundred. A hundred fifty . . .

"Orion? Can it be you?"

Weakly I raised my head. The golden light was still blindingly bright. Squinting against the overpowering radiance, I saw the lean form of a man standing over me.

"Help me," I pleaded in a hoarse whisper. "Help me."

He hunkered down on his haunches beside me. Either my eyes began to adjust to the light or it somehow dimmed. My eyes stopped tearing. The world began to come into unblurred focus for me.

"How did you get here? And in such condition!"

Danger, I wanted to say. Every instinct in me wanted to scream out an alarm that would alert him and the other Creators. But my voice froze in my throat.

"Help me," was all I could croak.

The man crouching beside me was the one I thought of as Hermes. Greyhound lean in body and limbs, his face was a set of narrow *V*'s: pointed chin, slanting cheekbones, pointed hairline above a smooth forehead.

"Stay where you are," he told me. "I'll bring help."

He vanished. As if he had been nothing more than an image on a screen, he simply disappeared from my sight.

Weakly I pushed myself up to a sitting position. I remembered this place from other existences. An expanse of unguessable extent, the ground covered with softly billowing mist, the sky above me a calm clear blue darkening at zenith enough to show a few scattered stars. Or were they stars? They did not twinkle at all in this silent, motionless world.

I had met the Golden One here many times. And Anya too. That is why Set had returned me to this spot. As I looked around now, it seemed artificial to me, like a stage setting or an elaborately constructed shrine meant to overawe ignorant visitors. A bogus representation of the Christian heaven, a bourgeois Valhalla. The kind of setting that the Assassins of old Persia would have used to convince their drug-dazed recruits that paradise awaited them—except that the old Assassins would have stocked the place with graceful dancing girls and beautiful houris.

I realized that I was seeing this place of the Creators through Set's cynical mind. He was within me as truly as my own blood and brain. He had prevented me from crying out a warning to Hermes.

The air seemed to glow again, and I squeezed my eyes shut once more.

"Orion."

Opening my eyes, I saw Hermes and two others with him: the grave, dark-bearded one I called Zeus, and a slender breathtakingly beautiful blonde woman of such sweetness and grace that she could only be Aphrodite. All three of the Creators were physically perfect, each in their own way. The men were in glittering metallic suits that fit their forms like second skins, from polished boot tops to high collars. Aphrodite wore a softly pleated robe of apricot pink, fastened at one shoulder by a golden clasp. Her arms and legs were bare, her skin flawless, glowing.

"Anya should be here," she said.

"She is coming," replied Zeus.

No! I wanted to shout. But I could not.

"The Golden One is on his way, also," said Hermes.

Zeus nodded gravely.

"He's in a bad way," Aphrodite said. "Look at how emaciated he is! His skin seems burned, too."

They stood solemnly inspecting me, their creature. They did not touch me. They did not try to help me to my feet or offer me food or even a cup of water.

A sphere of golden light appeared to one side of them, so bright that even the Creators stepped back slightly and shielded their eyes with upraised hands. The sphere hovered above the misty ground for a moment, shimmering, pulsating, then contracted and took on the form of a man.

The Golden One. I had served him as Ormazd, the god of light, in the long struggle against Ahriman and the Neanderthals. I had fought against him as Apollo, the champion of ancient Troy.

He was my creator. He had made me and, through me, the rest of the human race. And the human race, evolving through the millennia, had ultimately produced these godlike offspring who called themselves the Creators. They created us; we created them. The cycle was complete.

Except that now I was a weapon to be used against them. I would kill the Creators, and begin the destruction of the entire human race, through all spacetime, through all the universes, expunging my own kind from the continuum forever.

My creator stood before me, proud and imperious as ever. Golden radiance seemed to glow from within him. He was tall and wide of shoulder, dressed in a robe of dancing winking lights, as if clothed in fireflies. His unbearded face was broad and strong, eyes the tawny color of a lion, a rich mane of golden hair falling thickly to his shoulders.

I hated him. I adored him. I had served him through the ages. I had tried to kill him once.

"You were not summoned here, Orion." His voice was the same rich tenor I remembered, a voice that could thrill a concert audience or a mob of fanatics, a voice tinged with taunting mockery.

"I . . . need help."

"Obviously." His tone was scornful, but I saw something more serious in his eyes.

"He seems to be injured," said Aphrodite.

"How did he get here if you didn't summon him?" asked Hermes.

Zeus's eyes narrowed. "You did not give him the power to translate through the continuum at will, did you?"

"Of course not," the Golden One answered, irritated. Turning back to me, he demanded, "How did you get here, Orion? Where have you come from?"

Instantly I wanted to obey him. With instincts he himself had built within me, I wanted nothing more than to tell him everything I knew. Set. The Cretaceous. I spoke the words within my mind, but my tongue refused to form them. Set's command over me was too strong. I simply stared at the Creators like a stupid ox, like a dog begging its master to show some love even if it failed to follow his commands.

"Something is definitely wrong here," Zeus said.

The Golden One nodded. "Come with me, Orion."

I tried, but could not get to my feet. I floundered there on that ridiculous cloud-covered surface like a baby too weak to stand erect.

Aphrodite said, "Well, help him!" Without taking a step toward me.

The Golden One snorted disdainfully. "You *are* in a bad way, my Hunter. I thought I had built you better than this."

He made a slight movement of one hand and I felt myself being buoyed up, lifted as if by invisible hands, and held in a half-reclining position in midair.

"Follow me," said the Golden One, turning his back on me. The three other Creators winked out like candles snuffed by a sudden gust of wind.

I hung in midair, helpless as a child, with the Golden One's swirling cloak of lights before me. He began walking, yet it seemed to me that we did not truly move—the view

around us shifted and shimmered and changed. I felt no
sense of motion at all. It was as if we were on a treadmill
and the scenery on all sides was rolling past us.

We descended from the cloud-covered area as if we
were going down a mountain slope. But still there was no
real sense of motion. I simply sat on my invisible sedan
chair and watched the world flow past me. Down a long
trail we went and out onto the grassy floor of a broad
valley. Tall spreading shade trees followed the meandering
course of a river. The water gleamed in the light of the high
sun, shining warmly yellow in the blissfully blue sky. A few
chubby clumps of cumulus cloud floated serenely overhead, throwing dappled shadows across the tranquil green
valley.

I searched that peaceful blue sky for a dark red point
of light, the color of dried blood. Sheol. I could not find it.
Did it exist in this time? Or was it merely below the
horizon?

In the distance I saw a shimmering golden dome, and
as we neared it I realized that it was gauzily transparent,
like looking through a fine mesh screen of gold. Under its
beautifully elegant curve there was a city, but a city such as
I had never seen before. Tall slender spires stretching
heavenward, magnificent colonnaded temples, steep
ziggurats with stairs carved into their stone sides, wide
plazas flanked by gracefully curved arcades, broad avenues
decorated by statuary and triumphal arches.

My breath caught in my throat as I recognized one of
the magnificent buildings: the Taj Mahal, set in its splendid
garden. And a giant statue that had to be the Colossus of
Rhodes. Facing it, the green-patinaed Liberty. Further on,
the main temple of Angkor Wat gleaming in the sunlight as
if newly built.

All empty. Unpopulated. As I rode my invisible chair
of energy through the immaculate city with the Golden
One striding unceremoniously ahead of me, I could not see

a single person. Not a bird or cat or any sign of habitation whatever. Not a scrap of paper or even a leaf drifting across the streets on the gently wafting breeze.

At the farther end of the city stood towers of gleaming chrome and glass, straight-edged blocks and slabs that rose tall enough to look down on all the other buildings.

Into the tallest of these the Golden One led me, through a wide atrium of polished marble and onto a gleaming steel disk that began ascending slowly the instant he stepped onto it. Faster and faster it rose, whistling through the open atrium toward the glassed-in roof. The atrium was ringed with balconies whizzing past us at dizzying speed until all of a sudden we stopped, without a jerk or bump, without any feeling of deceleration at all.

The disk drifted to a semicircular niche in the balcony that girdled this level and nestled up to it. The Golden One stepped onto the balcony without a word, and I followed as if carried by invisible slaves.

He led me to a door, opened it, and stepped inside. As I followed him through the doorway a tingle of memory flickered through me. The room looked like a laboratory. It was crowded with vaguely familiar machines, bulky shapes of metal and plastic that I half remembered. In its center was a surgical table. The invisible hands that held me lifted me to its surface and laid me out upon it.

Whether I was too weak to move or held down by those invisible hands of energy, I could not tell.

"Sleep, Orion," commanded the Golden One in an annoyed tone.

My eyes closed immediately. My breathing slowed to the deep regular rhythm of slumber. But I did not fall asleep. I resisted his command and remained alert, wondering if I was doing this of my own volition or if Set was controlling me.

It seemed like hours that I lay there unmoving, unseeing. I heard the faint hum of electrical equipment now and then, little more. No footsteps. No sounds of breathing except my own. Was the Golden One still in human guise, or had he reverted to his true form while his machines examined me?

I felt nothing during all that time except the solidity of the table beneath me. Whatever probes were being put to my body were not physical. The Golden One was scanning me, examining me remotely atom by atom, the way an orbiting spacecraft might examine the planet turning beneath it.

As far as I could tell he stayed out of my mind. I felt no mental probes. I remained awake and aware. My memories were not being stimulated. The Golden One was staying away from my brain.

Why?

"He *is* here!"

Anya's voice! Concerned, angry almost.

"I can't be disturbed now," snapped the Golden One.

"He returned of his own volition and you tried to keep me from seeing him," Anya said accusingly.

"Don't you understand?" the Golden One retorted. "He is unable to return by himself. Someone has *sent* him here."

"Let me see . . . oh! Look at him! He's dying!"

Anya's voice quivered with emotion. She cares about me! I exulted to myself. Immediately a voice answered, As she would care about a pet cat or a wounded deer.

"He's weak," the Golden One said. "But he won't die."

"What have you put him through?" she demanded.

At first he did not reply. Finally, though, he admitted, "I don't know. I don't know where he's come from or how he got here."

"You've questioned him?"

"Briefly. But he made no reply."

"He's been tortured. Look at what they've done to his poor body."

"Never mind that! We have a serious problem here. When I tried to probe his mind, I got nothing but a blank."

"His memories are completely erased?"

"I don't think so. It was more like hitting a barrier. His mind has been shielded, somehow."

"Shielded? By whom?"

Exasperated, the Golden One snapped, "I don't know! And I can't find out unless I can break through the shielding."

"Do you think you can?"

I could sense him nodding. "With enough power I can do anything. The problem is that if I have to use too much power, it might destroy his mind totally."

"You mustn't do that!"

"I don't want to. Whatever is stored inside his skull, I've got to recover it."

"You don't care about him," Anya said. "He's merely a tool that you use."

"Exactly. But now he's a tool that someone else might be using. I've got to find out who. And why."

Deep within me, raging torrents of conflict were tearing at my guts. Anya wanted to protect me while the Golden One wanted only what was locked within my mind. I wanted to kill him. I wanted to love her and have her love me. Yet smothering those emotions, burying them in layers of molten iron, was Set's unrelenting control over me. I saw a vision of my nightmare again. Horrified, I knew that I would kill them all.

Chapter 28

L et me have him," Anya said.

A long pause, then the Golden One answered, "You are emotionally attached to this creature. It wouldn't be wise to let you—"

"How can you let jealousy cloud your judgment at a time like this?"

"Jealousy!" The Golden One sounded astonished. "Is the eagle jealous of the butterfly? Is the sun jealous of its planets?"

Anya laughed, like the cool tinkling of a silver bell. "Let me take care of him, bring him back to his strength. Then perhaps he can tell us what has happened to him."

"No. I have the equipment here—"

"To destroy his mind with your brute-force methods. I will bring him back to health. Then we can question him."

"There isn't time."

Her tone became taunting. "Not time? For the Golden

One, who claims he can travel across the continuum as if it were an ocean? No time for the one who tells us he understands the currents of the universes better than a mariner understands the sea?"

I heard him puff out a heavy sigh, almost a snort. "I will compromise with you. I can restore his physical health much more quickly with my methods than you can by spoon-feeding him. Once he is strong enough to walk and talk, you can begin his interrogation."

"Agreed."

"But if you don't get him to tell us how he got here within a few days," the Golden One warned, "then I will revert to my methods."

More reluctantly Anya repeated, "Agreed."

I heard her leave, then felt myself being lifted on cushions of energy again and carried off the surgical table. I tried to open my eyes a little, just to peep out at where I was being taken, but found I had no control over my eyelids. I could not move my fingers, either, or even wiggle my toes. Either the Golden One or Set was controlling my voluntary muscular system. Perhaps both of them, working inadvertently together for the moment.

I sensed my body being slid into a horizontal vat of some sort, a cylindrical tube that felt cool to my bare scorched skin. The hum of energy. The soft gurgling of liquids. I fell truly asleep, my mind drifting into a deep darkness, more relaxed than it had been in ages. It was like returning to the womb, and my last conscious thought was that perhaps this cylinder of metal and plastic had actually been my womb. I knew I had not been born of woman, any more than Set's minions had been hatched from natural eggs.

I slept, unimaginably grateful that I did not dream.

The patient gentle cadence of surf washing up on a beach awakened me. I opened my eyes. I was sitting in a reclining chair, soft yet gently supportive, on a high balco-

ny overlooking a wide turquoise sea that stretched out
beyond the horizon. A formation of graceful white birds
soared through the cloudless blue sky. The sleek gray forms
of dolphins glided effortlessly through the waves far below
me, their curved fins slicing the surface briefly and then
disappearing, only to reappear moments later.

I took a deep breath of sweet clean air. The sunshine
felt good, warm, while the breeze coming off the sea was
refreshingly cool. I felt strong again. Looking down at
myself, I saw that I was clothed in a sleeveless white
knee-length robe and a pair of shorts.

For several moments I simply lay back in the recliner,
rejoicing in my returned strength. My skin was healthily
tanned, all the old scorches and sores had disappeared. My
arms and legs had filled out once more.

I got to my feet slowly, found that my legs were firm,
and stepped to the balcony's railing. Peering far down, I
scanned the wide expanse of golden sand below. No one.
Not a soul. The curving beach was fringed with stately
palm trees. The building I was in seemed to rise from the
midst of the trees.

The surf drummed softly against the sand. The dolphins plied their way among the waves. One of the birds
made a long, folded-wing dive into the water, splashed in,
and bobbed up again, gulping a fish down its gullet.

"Hello."

I whirled around. Anya was standing at the doorway
that led inside from the balcony. Her robe was gleaming
white silk woven with threads of silver that sparkled in the
sunlight. Shining dark hair pulled back off her face. Classic
features that inspired the sculptors of ancient Greece with
the vision of ideal beauty. The goddess Athena come to
warm, breathing life before me.

Instantly I felt Set's iron-cruel control clamp itself on
my emotions. Love and hate, fear and desire, all buried

beneath his glacial grip.

"Anya," was all I could say.

"How do you feel?" she asked, stepping toward me.

"Normal. Much better than . . . before."

She gazed deeply into my eyes, and I could see that her own silver-gray eyes were troubled, searching.

"What time is it?" I asked.

With a slight smile she replied, "Morning."

"No. I mean—what year? What era are we in?"

"This is the era in which you were created, Orion."

"By the Golden One."

"His true name is Aten."

"That's what the Egyptians call their sun god."

She arched a brow. "He does not lack for ego, you know."

"I was created," I said slowly, "to hunt down Ahriman."

"Yes. Originally. Aten found you useful for other tasks, too."

"He's insane, you know. The Golden One. Aten."

Anya's smile faded. "There is no such thing as insanity among us, Orion. We have evolved far beyond that."

"You're not really human, are you?"

"We are what humans have become. We are the descendants of humankind."

"But this body you show me . . . it's an illusion, isn't it?"

She took the final step that closed the distance between us and reached up to touch my cheek with her hand. It felt vibrantly alive.

"This body is composed of atoms and molecules just as yours is, Orion. Blood courses through my veins. And hormones too. The same as any human female."

"There are humans here? Actual men and women still exist in this time?"

"Yes, of course. There are even a few still living here on Earth."

"Tell me!" I gasped with an urgency forced upon me by the will of Set, lurking within my own mind. With my voice, but his words, I begged, "I want to know everything there is to know about you."

Over the next few weeks Anya told me.

We sailed across that wide sea in a bubble of energy that skimmed across the wave tops. I saw dolphins by the hundreds frolicking among the swells, and heard huge stately whales singing their eerily beautiful songs of the deeps. Through deep cool forests we rode like wraiths wafting along in the breeze. Deer stepped daintily through the woods, so tame that we could pet them. Across mountains and fertile grasslands we glided, wrapped in a sphere of energy that was invisible yet all-protective. When we were hungry, meals appeared out of thin air, steaming and delicious.

I saw small villages where the tiled rooftops glittered with solar panels and ordinary-looking human beings tended fields and flocks. There were no roads between them and no vehicles that I could see. Most of the world was uninhabited, green and flowering, the sky pristine blue.

There were even swamplands teeming with crocodiles and turtles and frogs. I saw the enormous terrifying bulk of a tyrannosaur loom up above the cypresses, but Anya calmed my instinctive fear.

"The entire area is fenced in by an energy screen. Not even a fly can get out."

Once again I was living with the woman I had loved, night and day. But we never touched, never even kissed. We were not alone. I knew Set dwelled within me, and I got the feeling that she sensed it, too.

Yet Anya showed me the world as it existed in the time

of the Creators. The planet Earth, more beautiful than I had ever thought it could be, an abode for all kinds of life, a haven of peace and plenty, a balanced ecology that maintained itself on the energy of the sun and the control of humankind's descendants: the Creators. It was a perfect world, too perfect for me. Nothing was out of place. The weather was always mild and sunny. It rained only at night and even then our energy shell protected us. Not even insects bothered us. I got the feeling that we were riding through a vast park where all the plants were artificial and all the animals were machines under the control of the Creators.

"No, this is all real and natural," Anya told me one night as we lay side by side looking up at the stars. Orion was in his rightful place up there; the Dipper and all the other constellations looked familiar. We were not so far in the future that they had become distorted beyond recognition.

Glowering ruddy Sheol was not in that sky, though. I felt Set's unease and enjoyed it.

The turning point in human history, Anya explained to me, had come some fifty thousand years before this era. Human scientists learned how to control the genetic material buried deep within the cells of all living things. After billions of years of natural selection, humankind took purposeful control not only of its own genetic heritage, but of the genetic development of every plant and animal on Earth. And beyond.

Loud and bitter were the battles against such genetic engineering. There were mistakes, of course, and disasters. For almost a century the planet was racked by the Biowars.

"But the step had been taken, for good or ill," Anya told me. "Once our ancestors learned how to control and alter genes, the knowledge could not be erased."

Blind natural evolution gave way to deliberate, con-

trolled evolution. Where nature took a million years to
make a change, humans changed themselves in a generation.

Human life spans increased by quantum jumps. Two
centuries. Five centuries. Thousands of years. Virtual
immortality.

The human race exploded into space, first expanding
throughout the inner solar system, then leapfrogging the
outer gas-giant planets and riding out to the stars in giant
habitats that housed whole communities, thousands of
men, women, and children who would spend generations
searching for new Earths.

"Some altered their forms so that they could live on
worlds that would kill ordinary human beings," Anya said.
"Others decided to remain aboard their habitats and make
them their permanent abodes."

Yet no matter which path they chose, each group of
star-seekers faced the same ultimate questions: Are we still
human? Do we want to remain human? The hard radiation
of deep space and the strange environments of alien worlds
were sources of mutations beyond their control.

They needed a baseline, a "standard model" Earth-
normal human genotype against which they could compare
themselves and make their decisions. They needed a link
with Earth.

On Earth, meanwhile, generation after generation of
dogged researchers were probing deeply into the ultimate
nature of life. Seeking nothing less than true immortality,
they seized the reins of their own evolution and began a
series of mutations that ultimately led to beings who could
interchange matter and energy at will, transform their own
bodies into globes of pure energy that lived on the radiation of sunlight.

"The Creators," I said.

Anya nodded gravely but said, "Not yet Creators,
Orion, for we had created nothing. We were merely the

ultimate result of a quest that had begun, I suppose, when the earliest hominids first realized that they had no way to avoid death."

They had not become truly immortal. They could be killed. I got the feeling that they had even committed murder among themselves, long ages past. Yet they were immortal enough. They could live indefinitely, as long as they had a source of energy. To such creatures time is meaningless. But to immortal creatures descended from curious apes, with all of eternity at their disposal, time is a challenge.

"We learned to manipulate time, to translate ourselves back and forth almost as easily as we walk across a meadow."

And found, to their horror, that theirs is not the only universe in the continuum of spacetime.

"The universes seem infinite, constantly branching, constantly impinging on one another," Anya said. "Aten— the Golden One—discovered that there was a universe in which the Neanderthals became the dominant species of Earth and our own type of human never came into being."

"The Neanderthals were beautifully adapted to their environment," I recalled. "They had no need to develop high technology or science."

"That universe encroached on our own," Anya said, her silver-gray eyes looking back to those days. "The overlap was so severe that Aten feared our universe would ultimately be engulfed and we would be doomed to nonexistence."

For creatures who had only newly achieved immortality, this discovery raised panic and terror. What good to be immortal if your entire universe will be snuffed out in the cosmic workings of quantized spacetime?

"That is when we became Creators," said Anya.

"The Golden One created me."

"And five hundred others."

"To exterminate the Neanderthals," I remembered.

"To make this universe safe for our own kind," Anya corrected gently.

The Golden One, puffed up by his (my) success over the Neanderthals, began to examine other nexuses in spacetime where he felt he could change the natural order of the continuum to the benefit of his own inflated ego. Using me as his tool, he began to tamper with the continuum, time and again.

He found, to his shock and the anger of the other Creators, that once you have tampered with the fabric of spacetime myriads of geodesic world lines begin unraveling. The more you try to knit everything up into a neat package, the more the continuum warps and alters. You have no choice but to continue to try to manipulate the continuum to your own purposes; you can never allow the fabric of spacetime to unfold along its natural lines again.

Yes, I heard Set hissing within me, the pompous ape rushes to and fro, scattering his energies, distracted as easily as a chattering monkey. I will end his dilemma. Forever.

I strained to tell Anya that there were others who could manipulate spacetime. But not even that much could get past Set's control over me. I felt perspiration breaking out across my forehead, my upper lip beading, so hard was I trying. But Anya did not seem to notice.

"So now we live on this world," she said as we sat in the energy bubble, speeding high above a deep blue ocean striated with long straight combers that were traveling from one side of the earth to the other in almost perfect uniformity.

"And manipulate the continuum," I commented.

"We've been forced to," she admitted. "There's no way we can stop without having the whole fabric of spacetime come crashing down on us."

"And that would mean . . .?"

"Oblivion. Extinction. We'd be erased from existence, along with the whole human race."

"But they've spread throughout interstellar space, you said."

"Yes, but their origin is here. Their world line begins on Earth and then spreads throughout the galaxy. Still, it's all the same. Expunge one part of that geodesic and it all unravels."

Our invisible craft was winging toward the night side of the planet. We reclined in utter physical comfort while racing higher and faster than any bird could fly across the breadth of Earth's widest ocean.

"Do you maintain contact with the other humans, the ones who went out to the stars?"

"Yes," Anya replied. "They still send their representatives back here to check the genetic drift of their populations. We have established a baseline in the Neolithic, just prior to the development of agriculture. That is our 'normal' human genotype, against which all others are measured."

I thought of the slaves I had met in Set's garden, of crippled Pirk and scheming Reeva and the pliable, cowardly Kraal. And I heard Set's hissing laughter. Normal human beings, indeed.

I fell silent and so did Anya. We were returning to the city; as far as I could tell it was the only populated city remaining on Earth. We had glided over the mute, abandoned ruins of ancient cities, each of them protected from the ravages of time by a glowing bubble of energy. Some of them had already been thoroughly destroyed by war. Others were simply empty, as if their entire population had decided one day to leave. Or die.

More than one sprawling city had been inundated by the rising seas. Our energy sphere carried us through watery avenues and broad plazas where fish and squid darted in the hazy sunlight that filtered down from the surface.

As our journey ended and we approached the only living city on Earth, the vast museum-cum-laboratory where the Golden One and the other Creators labored to hold their universe together, I tried to work up the courage to ask Anya the question that was most important to me.

"You . . . that is, we . . ." I stuttered.

She turned those lustrous gray eyes to me and smiled. "I know, Orion. We have loved each other."

"Do you . . . love me now?"

"Of course I do. Didn't you know?"

"Then why did you betray me?"

The words blurted out of my mouth before Set could stop them, before I even knew I was going to say them.

"What?" Anya looked shocked. "Betray you? When? How?"

My entire body spasmed with red-hot pain. It was as if every nerve in me was being roasted in flame. I could not speak, could not even move.

"Orion!" Anya gasped. "What's happened to you?"

To all outward appearances I was in a catatonic state, rigid and mute as a granite statue. Inwardly I was in fiery agony, yet I could not scream, could not even weep.

Anya touched my cheek and flinched away, as if she could sense the fires burning within me. Then she slowly, deliberately, put her fingers to my face once again. Her hand felt cool and soothing, as if it were draining away all the agony within my body.

"I do love you, Orion," she said, in a voice so low it was nearly a whisper. "I have taken human form to be with you because I love you. I love your strength and your courage and your endurance. You were created to be a hunter, a killer, yet you have risen beyond the limits that Aten placed on your mind."

Set's broiling anger seethed through me, but the pain was dying away, easing, as he spent his energies shielding his presence from Anya's probing eyes.

"We have lived many lives together, my darling," Anya said to me. "I have faced final destruction for your sake, just as you have suffered death for mine. I have never betrayed you and I never will."

But you did! I screamed in silence. You will! Just as I will betray you and kill you all.

Chapter 29

He's catatonic," sneered the Golden One.

"He is under someone's control," Anya replied. She had brought me not to the Golden One's laboratory but to the tower-top apartment where I had been quartered before Anya and I had begun our trip around the world.

I could walk. I could stand. I suppose I could have eaten and drunk. I could not speak, however. My body felt wooden, numb, as I stood like an automaton in the middle of the spacious living room, arms at my sides, eyes staring straight into a mirrored wall that showed me my own blank face and rigid posture.

The Golden One was wearing a knee-length tunic of glowing fabric that clung to his finely muscled body. He planted his fists on his hips and snorted with disgust.

"You wanted to treat him with tender loving kindness and you bring him back to me catatonic."

Anya had changed into a sleeveless chemise of pure white, cinched at the waist by a silver belt.

"His mind is being controlled by whoever had tortured his body," she said, brittle tension in her tone.

"How did he get here?" the Golden One wondered, strutting around me like a man inspecting a prize animal. "Did he escape from his torturers or was he sent here?"

"Sent, I would think," said Anya.

"Yes, I agree. But why?"

"Call the others," I heard myself say. It was a strangled groan.

The Golden One looked sharply at me.

"Call the others." My voice became clearer, stronger. Set's voice, actually, not under my own control.

"The other Creators?" Anya asked. "All of them?"

I felt my head bob up and down once, twice. "Bring them here. All of them." Then I added, "Please."

"Why?" the Golden One demanded.

"What I have to tell you," Set answered through me, "must be told to all the Creators at once."

He looked at me suspiciously.

"They must be in human form," Set made me say. "I cannot speak to globes of energy. I must see human faces, human bodies."

The Golden One's tawny eyes narrowed. But Anya nodded to him. I remained silent, locked in Set's powerful control, unable to move or to say more.

"It will be uncomfortable to have us all in here, jostling and perspiring," he said, some of his old scornful tone returning.

"The main square," Anya suggested. "Plenty of room for all of us there."

He nodded. "The main square then."

There were only twenty of them. Twenty majestic men and women who had taken on the burdens of manipulating spacetime to suit themselves. Twenty immortals who found themselves laboring forever to keep the continuum from caving in on them.

They were splendid. The human forms in which they presented themselves were truly godlike. The men were handsome, strong, some bearded but most clean shaven, eyes clear, limbs straight and smoothly muscled. The women were exquisite, graceful the way a panther or cheetah is, with coiled power just beneath the surface. Their skin was flawless, glowing, their hair lustrous, their eyes more beautiful than gemstones.

They wore a variety of costumes: glittering uniforms of metallic fibers, softly draped chitons, long swirling cloaks, even suits of filigreed armor. I felt shabby in a simple short-sleeved tunic and briefs.

The square on which we assembled was a harmonious oblong laid out in the Pythagorean dimension. Marble pillars and steles of imperishable gold rose at its corners. One of the square's long sides was taken up by a Greek temple, so similar to the Parthenon in its original splendor that I wondered if the Creators had copied it or translated it through spacetime from the Acropolis to place it here. On the other side was a splendidly ornate Buddhist temple, with a gold seated Buddha staring serenely across the square at marble Athena standing with spear and shield. The two short ends of the square bore a steeply rising Sumerian ziggurat at one end and an equally precipitous Mayan pyramid at the other, so similar to each another that I knew they must both have originated in the mind of a single person.

Above the square the sky was a perfect blue, shimmering ever so slightly from the dome of energy that covered the entire city.

A sphinx carved from black basalt rested in the middle of the square's smooth marble pavement, its shoulders slightly higher than my head, its female face hauntingly, disturbingly familiar. Yet I could not place it. It was not the face of any of the women among the twenty Creators who gathered around me.

I stood with my back to the sphinx, penned inside a cylinder of cool blue-flickering energy. The Golden One was taking no chances with me, he thought. He suspected that I had been sent here by an enemy. The energy screen was to keep me safely confined.

Set was amused by his precaution. "Foolish ape," he said within me. "How he overestimates his own powers."

The Creators were curious about why they had been summoned here, and not entirely pleased. They clustered in little groups of two and three, talking to each other in low tones, apparently waiting for others to appear. They *are* like monkeys, I realized. Chattering constantly, huddling together for emotional support. Even in their apotheosis they remained true to their simian origins.

Then a gleaming globe of pure white drifted over the roof of the Parthenon and settled slowly as the assembled Creators edged back to make room for it. When it touched the marble pavement of the square, it shimmered briefly and seemed to contract in on itself to produce the grave, dignified, bearded figure of the one I called Zeus.

The other Creators grouped themselves around him as he faced the Golden One and Anya. Clearly, Zeus was their spokesman, if not their leader.

"Why have you called us here, Aten?"

"And demanded that we assume human form?" red-haired Ares grumbled.

Aten, the Golden One, replied, "Most of you know my creature Orion. He has apparently been sent here by someone to deliver a message to all of us."

Zeus turned to me. "What is your message, Orion?"

Every instinct in me screamed at me to warn them, to tell them to flee because I had been sent here to destroy them and all their works. Yet I wanted to break free of the force field that surrounded me and smash in their faces, tear their flesh, rend them limb from limb. Agonized, my mind filling with horror, I stood there mutely as the battle raged inside me between my inbuilt reflex to serve the Creators and the burning hatred for them that was as much my own as Set's.

"Orion!" commanded the Golden One sharply. "Tell us what you have to say. Now!"

He himself had built the instinct to obey him into my mind, burned that obligatory response through my synapses, hard-wired my brain for obedience. Yet I felt Set's overpowering presence counterbalancing that instinct, driving me toward murder. My body was a battlefield where they raged and fought for control, leaving me unable to choose between them, unable to move, unable even to speak.

Zeus made a sardonic smile. "Your toy is out of order, Aten. You've called us here for nothing."

They all laughed. The sneering, self-important, callous, heartless, overbearing would-be gods and goddesses laughed, completely unaware that death was inches away from them, totally uncaring and insensitive to the agony I was going through. I was suffering the pains of hell. For what? For them!

Annoyed, the Golden One grumbled, "There's always been something wrong with this one. I suppose I'll have to dispose of it and make a better one."

Anya looked dismayed but said nothing. The Creators began to turn their backs on me and walk away, many of them still laughing. I hated them all.

"I bring you a message," I said, with Set's powerful booming voice.

They stopped and turned back to stare at me.

"I bring you a message of *death.*"

The sky began to darken. No clouds; the open sky overhead swiftly changed from summer blue to deep violet and finally to impermeable black. I realized that Set had tapped into the generators that powered the dome shield over the city and perverted all the energy that fed it into turning the dome opaque. At a stroke he had trapped the Creators in their own city and cut them off from the energy they required to change their form from human back into glowing spheres of pure energy.

The square was bathed in an eerie red glow; the absolute blackness of the dome seemed to be tightening, drawing closer like the net of a snare or a hangman's noose.

"You are trapped here," Set's voice bellowed from my lips. "Meet your death!"

The flickering blue force field around me winked off, the energy drawn into my own body. It felt like hot knives carving me for an instant, but then I was stronger than ever. And I was free—free to slaughter them all.

I stepped out from the spot where I had been imprisoned, stepped directly toward the Golden One, my hands twitching like the claws of a predatory reptile. He seemed totally unafraid of me, one brow cocked slightly in that smug, sneering manner of his.

"Stop, Orion. I *command* you to stop."

As if I had been plunged into a smothering, suffocating pool of quicksand, my steps slowed, faltered. It was like trying to move through wet concrete. Then I felt a new surge of strength boil up within me like the hot wind of hell rising from the depths of the earth. I lunged through the invisible barrier grinning as I saw the Golden One's face go from smug superiority to sudden astonished fright.

Everything slowed down around me as my senses shifted into hyperdrive. I saw beads of sweat breaking out on the broad smooth brow of the Golden One, saw Zeus's eyes wide and round with unaccustomed fear, powerful Ares stumbling backward away from me, Aphrodite and Hera turning to run away from me, their beautiful robes billowing, the other Creators gaping, desperate, unable to change shape and escape me.

My hands reached out, clawlike, for the Golden One's throat.

"Orion, no!" Anya shouted. In the slow-motion world of my hyperdrive state her voice sounded like the long reverberating peal of a distant bell.

I turned toward her as the Golden One backed away from me.

"Please, Orion!" Anya begged. "Please!"

I stopped, staring at her lovely tormented face. In those fathomless silver-gray eyes I saw no fear of me at all. I knew I had to kill her, kill them all. I loved her still, yet the memory of her betrayal burned my soul like a branding iron. Had that love been built into me, too, like my other instincts? Was it her way to control me?

I stood in the middle of a triangle, pulled three different ways at once. The Golden One first; death to my creator, the one who made me to endure pain and sorrow that he would not face himself. My hands stretched again for his throat, even while he backpedaled in dreamlike slow motion. The other Creators were scattering, although the square was completely blocked now by the energy screen that Set had turned into a black impassable barrier.

Anya was reaching toward me, her simple words enough to freeze me in my tracks. Yet within me Set was urging me on with all the whips and scourges at his power.

Love. Hate. Obedience. Revenge. I was being torn apart by the forces that they wielded over me. Time hung suspended. The Golden One, his face a rictus of fury and fear, had focused his mind on me like a powerful laser beam, exerting every joule of energy he could command to bend me to his will. The more his mighty power blazed at me, the more Set poured his ferocious energy into me, draining the generators that powered the city, driving me to overcome the Golden One's conditioning, pushing me to grasp his throat in my hands and crush it.

Between them they were tearing me apart. It was like being riddled in a crossfire between two maddened armies, like being stretched into a bloody ribbon of flayed flesh on a sadistic torturer's rack.

Anya stood to one side of me, her eyes pleading, her lips open in a cry that I could no longer hear.

Obey me! commanded the Golden One inside my head.

Obey me! Set thundered at me silently.

Each of them was pouring more and more of his energy into me, like a pair of enormous lasers focused on a helpless naked target.

"Use their energy!" Anya's voice reached me. "Absorb their energy and use it for *yourself!*"

From the deepest recesses of my soul came an echoing response, a newly awakened voice, tortured, tormented, filled with anguish. What about me? it cried. What about Orion? Me, myself. Must I be a weapon of deliberate genocide? Must I forever be a toy, a puppet manipulated by my creator or by his ultimate enemy? When will Orion be free, be totally and completely human?

"NEVER!" I roared.

I could feel Set's surprise and the Golden One's shock. I could sense Anya breathlessly watching to see what I would do.

All that energy pouring into me. All that power: the overwhelming brilliance of the Golden One, the hell-hot fury of Set. All focused on me. While Anya watched, bright-eyed.

"Never!" I shouted again. "I will never obey either one of you again! I free myself of you both! Now!"

I spread my arms and felt as if binding chains had snapped and been thrown off.

"I'm free of you both!" I snarled at them: the Golden

One standing stunned before me, Set raging within my own skull. "You can both go to hell!"

The Golden One's mouth hung open. Anya's expectant expression began to turn into a smile and she started to step toward me.

But Set's furious voice within me seethed, "No, traitorous ape. Only you shall go to hell."

Chapter 30

Abruptly I was spinning, falling, flailing through empty space, stars whirling around me dizzyingly. The square, the city, the earth were gone. I was alone in the fierce cold of the void between worlds.

Not totally alone. I could feel Set's furious hatred raging, even though he no longer controlled me from within.

I laughed soundlessly in the black vacuum. "You can punish my body," I told Set mentally, "but you no longer control it. You can send me to your hell but you can't make me do your work."

I sensed him howling with wrath. The stars themselves seemed to shudder with the violence of his anger.

"Orion!" I heard Anya's mind calling to me, like a silver bell in the wilderness, like a cool clear stream on a hot summer's day.

I opened my mind to her. Everything that I had experienced, all my knowledge of Set and his plans, I transmitted to her in the flash of a microsecond. I felt her mind take in the new information, saw in my own inner eye the shocked expression on her face as she realized how narrowly she and the other Creators had escaped final death.

"You saved us!"

"Saved you," I corrected. "I don't care about the others."

"Yet I . . . you thought that I had betrayed you."

"You did betray me."

"And still you saved me?"

"I love you," I replied simply. It was the truth. I loved her completely and eternally. I knew now that it was my own heart's choice, not some reflex built into me by the Golden One, not some control that Anya wielded over my mind. I was free of all of them and I knew that I loved her no matter what she had done.

"Orion, we're trying to reach you, to bring you back."

"Trying to save me?"

"Yes!"

I almost laughed there in the absolute cold of deep space. The stars were still pinwheeling around me, as if I were in the center of an immense kaleidoscope. But I saw now that one particular star was not spinning across the blackness of the void. It remained rock still, the exact center of my whirling universe. That blood red star called Sheol. It seethed and boiled and reached out for me.

Of course. Set's hell. He was plunging me into the center of his dying star, destroying me so completely that not even the atoms of my body would remain intact.

Anya realized what he was doing as immediately as I did.

"We're working to pull you back," she told me, her voice frantic.

"No!" I commanded. "Send me straight into the star. Pour all the energy the Creators can command into me and let me plunge into Sheol's rotting heart."

In that awful endless moment, suspended in the infinite void between worlds while time itself hung suspended, I realized what I must do. I made my choice, freely, of my own will.

For my link with Anya was two-way. What she knew, I knew. I saw that she did love me as truly as a goddess can love a mortal. And more. I saw how I could destroy Set and his entire world, his very star, and end his threat to her and the other Creators. I didn't care particularly about them, and I still loathed the self-styled Golden One. But I would end Set's threat to Anya once and for all, no matter what it cost.

She saw what I wanted to do. "No! You'll be destroyed! We won't be able to recover you!"

"What difference does that make? *Do it!*"

Love and hate. The twin driving forces of our manic passionate hot-blooded species. I loved Anya. Despite her betrayal I loved her. I knew it was impossible, that despite the few snatches of happiness we had stolen there was no way that we could be together forever. Better to make an end of it, to give up this life of pain and suffering, to give her the gift of life with my final death.

And I hated Set. He had humiliated me, tortured my body and my mind, reduced me to a slavish automaton. As a man, as a human being, I hated him with all the roaring fury my kind is capable of. Through the eons, across the gulfs between our worlds and our species, for all of spacetime I hated him. My death would demolish his hopes forever, and in my blood-hot rage I knew that death was a small price to pay if it meant death to *him* and all his kind.

With an effort of my own free will I stopped my body's spinning and arrowed straight toward simmering red Sheol. Not only will I die, I thought. Not only will Set and his loathsome kindred die. His world will die. His star will die as well. I will destroy all of them.

Too late Set realized he had lost control of my body. I felt his shocked surprise, his desperate panic.

"Everything you have told me has been a lie," I said to him mentally. "Now I tell you one eternal truth. Your world ends. Now."

All the energies that the Creators could generate from thousands of stars through all the ages of the continuum were being trained on me. My body became the focal point of such power as to tear worlds apart, annihilate whole stars, rip open the very fabric of spacetime itself.

I sped toward the seething mass of blood red Sheol, no longer a human body but a spear of blinding white-hot energy from across the continuum aiming at the decaying heart of the dying star. Tendrils of fiery plasma snaked up toward me. Arches of glowing ionized gas appeared and streamed above the star's surface like bridges of living, burning souls. Disembodied, I still saw the churning surface of the star, bubbling and frothing like some immense witch's caldron. Magnetic fields strong enough to twist solid steel into taffy ribbons clutched at me. Vicious flares heaved fountains of lethal radiation as if Sheol were trying to protect itself from me.

To no avail.

I plunged into that maelstrom of tortured plasma, seeking its dense core where atomic nuclei were fusing together to create the titanic energy that powered this star. With grim pleasure I realized that Sheol was truly dying already, its nuclear fires simmering, faltering, making the entire star shudder as it wavered between stability and explosion.

"I will help you to die," I said to the star. "I will put an end to your agony."

Through layer after layer of thickening plasma I dove, straight to Sheol's heart, where the subatomic particles were packed more densely than any metal could ever be.

Down and down into the depths of hell where not even atoms could exist and remain whole, deeper still I beat my way past wave after wave of pure gamma energy and pulses of neutrinos, down to the hardening core of the star where heavy nuclei were creating temperatures and pressures that they themselves could no longer withstand.

There I released all the energy that had been pent up in me, like driving a knife into the heart of an ancient, dreaded enemy. Like putting to rest a soul tormented by endless cancerous suffering.

Sheol exploded. And I died.

Chapter 31

I t was at that final moment of utter devastation, with the star exploding from the energy that I had directed into its heart, that I realized how much more the Creators knew than I did.

I died. In that maelstrom of unimaginable violence I was torn apart, the very atoms of what was once my body ripped asunder, their nuclei blasted into strange ephemeral particles that flared for the tiniest fraction of a second and then reverted ghostlike into pure energy.

Yet my consciousness remained. I felt all the pains of hell as Sheol exploded not merely once, but again and again.

Time collapsed around me. I hung in a spacetime stasis, bodiless yet aware, while the planets spun around the Sun with such dizzying speed they became blurs, streaks, near circles of colored lights, brilliant pinwheels whirling madly as they reflected the golden glory of the central sun.

I watched millions of years unfold before my godlike vision. Without a corporeal body, without eyes, the core of my being, the essential pattern of intelligence that is *me* inspected minutely the results of Sheol's devastation.

With some surprise I realized that I had not completely destroyed the star. It was too small to explode into a supernova, the kind of titanic star-wrecking cataclysm that leaves nothing afterward except a tiny pulsar, a fifty-mile-wide sphere of neutrons. No, Sheol's explosion had been the milder kind of disaster that Earthly astronomers would one day call a nova.

Disaster enough.

The first explosion blew off the outer layers of the star. Sheol flared with a sudden brilliance that could be seen a thousand light-years away. The star's outer envelope of gas blew away into space, engulfing its single planet Shaydan in a hot embrace of death.

On that bleak and dusty world the sky turned so bright that it burned everything combustible on the surface of the planet. Trees, brush, grasses, animals all burst into fire. But the flames were quickly snuffed out as the entire atmosphere of Shaydan evaporated, blown off into space by the sudden intense heat. What little water there was on the planet's surface was boiled away immediately.

The burning heat reached into the underground corridors that the Shaydanians had built beneath their cities. Millions of the reptilians died in agony, their lungs scorched and charred. Within seconds all the air was sucked away and those few who escaped the heat suffocated, lungs bursting, eyes exploding out of their heads. The oldest, biggest patriarchs died in hissing, screeching agony. As did the youngest, smallest of their clones.

Rocks melted on the surface of Shaydan. Mountains flowed into hot lava, then quickly cooled into vast seas of glass. The planet itself groaned and shuddered under the stresses of Sheol's eruption. All life was cleansed from its rocky, dusty surface. The underground cities of Shaydan held only charred corpses, perfectly preserved for the ages by the hard vacuum that had killed even the tiniest microbes on the planet.

And that was only the first explosion of Sheol.

Thousands of years passed in an eyeblink. Millions flew by in the span of a heartbeat. Not that I had physical eyes or heart, but the eons swept by like an incredibly rapid stop-motion film as I watched from my godlike perch in spacetime.

Sheol exploded again. And again. The Creators were not content to allow the star to remain. Bolts of energy streaked in from deep interstellar space to reach into the heart of Sheol and tear at it like a vulture eating at the innards of its chained victim.

Each explosion released a pulse of gravitational energy that cracked the planet Shaydan the way a sledgehammer cracks a rock. I saw quakes rack that dead airless world from pole to pole, gigantic fissures split its surface from one end to another.

Finally Shaydan broke apart. As Sheol exploded yet again the planet split asunder in the total silence of deep space—just as its reptilian inhabitants had always been silent, I thought.

Suddenly the solar system was filled with projectiles whizzing about like bullets. Some of them were the size of small planets, some the size of mountains. I watched, fascinated, horrified, as these fragments ran into one another, exploding, shattering, bouncing away only to smash together once more. And they crashed into the other planets as well, pounding red Mars and blue Earth and its pale battered moon.

One oblong mass of rock blasted through the thin crust of Mars, its titanic explosion liquefying the underlying mantle, churning up oceans of hot lava that streamed across that dead world's face, igniting massive volcanoes that spewed dust and fire and smaller rocks that littered half the surface of the planet. Rivers of molten lava dug deep trenches across thousands of miles. Volcanic eruptions vomited lava and pumice higher than the thin Martian atmosphere.

I turned my attention to Earth.

The explosions of Sheol by themselves made little impact on the earth. With each nova pulse of the dying star the night skies of Earth glowed with auroras from pole to equator as subatomic particles from Sheol's exploding plasma envelope hit the planet's protective magnetic field and excited the ionosphere. The gravitational pulses that eventually wrecked Shaydan had no discernable effect on Earth; the nearly four hundred million miles' distance between Sheol and Earth weakened the gravitational waves to negligible proportions.

But the fragments of Shaydan, the remains of that dead and shattered world, almost killed all life on Earth.

A million-year rain of fire sent thousands of stone and metal fragments from Shaydan plunging into Earth's skies. Most were mere pebbles that burned up high in the atmosphere, brief meteors that eventually sifted down to Earth's surface as invisible motes of dust. But time and again larger remnants of Shaydan would be caught by Earth's gravity well and pulled down to the planet's surface in fiery plunges that lit whole continents with their roaring, thundering passages.

Time and again pieces of rock and metal would punch through Earth's tortured air, howling like all the fiends of hell, to pound the surface with tremendous explosions. Like billions of hydrogen bombs all exploding at once, each of these giant meteors blasted the planet hard enough to rock it on its axis.

Where they hit dry ground, they spewed up continent-sized clouds of dust that rose beyond the stratosphere and then spread darkness across half the world, blocking out sunlight for weeks.

Where they hit the sea, they rammed through the thin layer of crustal rocks underlying the oceans and broke into the molten-hot mantle beneath. Centuries-long geysers of steam rose from such impact sites, clouding over the sunlight even more than the dust clouds of the ground impacts.

Temperatures plummeted all around the world. At the once-temperate poles, salt water froze into ice. Sea levels dropped worldwide and large shallow inland seas dried up altogether. The shallow-water creatures who had lived in and around those seas perished; delicate algae and immense duckbills alike died away, deprived of their habitats.

More of Shaydan's fragments pounded down on Earth, breaking through the crustal rocks, triggering massive earthquakes as fissures the length of the planet widened, chains of new volcanoes thundered, and whole continents split apart. I saw the birth of the Atlantic Ocean and watched it spread, shouldering Eurasia and Africa apart from the Americas.

Mountains rose from flatlands, continental blocks of land shifted and tilted, weather patterns were completely altered. High plateaus rose up to replace floodplains and swamps and more species of plants and animals were wiped out forever, totally destroyed by the incessant pounding the planet was suffering through.

The climate grew cooler still as new mountain chains blocked old airflows and dry land replaced swamps and inland seas. Ocean currents shifted as new tectonic plates were created out of the fissures that cracked half the planet and old plates were pulled back into the hot embrace of the planetary mantle with shuddering fitful earthquakes that shattered still more habitats of life.

If I had possessed eyes, I would have wept. Thousands upon thousands of species were dying, ruthlessly wiped out of existence because of me, because of what I had done. By destroying Sheol, by shattering Shaydan, I was killing creatures large and small, plant and animal, predator and prey, all across the face of the earth.

Whole families of microscopic plankton were annihilated from pole to pole, entire species of green plants driven into extinction. The graceful shelled ammonites, which had withstood Set's deliberate devastation of Earth more than a hundred million years earlier, succumbed and disappeared from the rolls of life.

And the dinosaurs. Every last one of them. Gigantic fierce Tyrannosaurus and gentle duckbill, massive Triceratops and birdlike Stenonychosaurus—all gone, totally, forever gone.

I did not mean to kill them. Yet I felt a cosmic guilt. My rage against Set and his kind had resulted in all this suffering, all this death. My personal revenge had been won at the price of scrubbing the earth nearly clean of life.

I looked again at the new earth. Ice caps glittered at its poles. The rough outlines of the continents looked familiar now, although they were still not spaced across the globe in the way I remembered. The Atlantic was still widening, red-tipped volcanoes glowing down the length of the fissure that extended from Iceland to the Antarctic. North and South America were not yet connected, and the basin that would one day be the Mediterranean was a dry and grassy plain.

I saw a forest of leafy trees standing straight and tall against the morning sun. The sky was clear. The bombardment of Shaydan's fragments had ended at last.

A gentle stream flowed through the woods. Grass grew on the ground right down to its banks. Flowers nodded brightly red and yellow and orange in the breeze while bees busily attended them. A turtle slid off a log and splashed into the stream, startling a nearby frog who hopped into a waterside thicket.

Birds soared by in fine feathery plumage. And up on a high branch sat a tiny furred ratlike animal, its beady black eyes glittering, its nose twitching worriedly.

This is all that's left of life on Earth, I thought to myself. After the catastrophe that I caused, the planet has to make a new beginning.

I realized that just as Set had scoured the Earth to make room for his own kind of reptilian life, I had inadvertently put the planet through another holocaust that would eventually lead to my kind of life. That ratlike creature was a mammal, my ancestor, the ancestor of all humankind, the progenitor of the Creators themselves.

Once again I realized that I had been used by the Creators. I had given my body, my life, not merely to destroy Shaydan but to scrub the Earth clean and prepare it for the rise of the mammals and the human race.

"Just as I was going to do."

It was Set's voice speaking in my mind.

"I am not dead, Orion. I live here on Earth with my servants and slaves—thanks to you."

BOOK IV

EARTH

Though much is taken, much abides; and though
We are not now that strength which in old days
Moved earth and heaven, that which we are, we are—
One equal temper of heroic hearts,
Made weak by time and fate, but strong in will
To strive, to seek, to find, and not to yield.

Chapter 32

Set lived.

That single thought burned through my consciousness like a hot branding iron searing my flesh. He had survived the destruction of his race, of his planet, of his star. He still lived. On Earth.

I had destroyed Sheol and Shaydan, wiped out most of the life-forms on Earth. In vain. I had failed to kill Set.

"I will find you," I said silently. Bodiless, with nothing but my essential awareness, I threw out the challenge to my deadly enemy. "I will find you and destroy you for all time."

"Come and try," came Set's immediate answer. "I look forward to meeting you for the final time."

His consciousness shone like a beacon against the black void of spacetime. I knew where and when he was. Concentrating every bit of willpower I possessed, I focused on Set. I willed myself through the tangled skein of the continuum to the place and time where he existed.

A flash of absolute cold, a moment of utter darkness and cryogenic chill, then I opened my eyes and took in a deep breath of life.

I was lying on my back, my naked body resting on warm soft earth. Tall trees rose all around me and the soft breeze brought scents of flowers and pine. I heard the melodious trill of a bird. My hands clutched at the ground and I pulled sweet-smelling grass to my face.

Yes. Paradise once again.

I sat up and looked around. The ground sloped gently before me. A brown bear shambled in the distance, trailed by two balls of fur that were her cubs. She stopped and raised her head, sniffing the air. If my scent alarmed her, she gave no notice. She just resumed her slow pace away from me, the cubs trotting along behind.

I am Orion the Hunter, reborn. Naked and alone, my mission is to find the monster Set and kill him. Kill him as he intends to kill me. Destroy him and his kind forever as he intends to destroy my kind, the human race, forever.

Smiling grimly to myself, I got to my feet and started walking slowly down the gentle slope, through the tall straight trees that dappled the afternoon sunshine with their swaying leafy branches. If this truly was part of the forest of Paradise, then Set would be at his fortress by the Nile.

The sun was too high in the sky to judge directions, so I merely followed the first stream I came to, figuring that it would eventually lead to the Nile. I knew I had a long walk ahead of me, but I had learned from Set that time means little to one who can catapult himself through the continuum at will. Patience, I counseled myself. Patience.

For days on end I walked alone, seeing neither another human being nor any of Set's reptilians. This was a sparsely populated time, I recalled. There were probably fewer than a million humans living in the early Neolithic; their first great population explosion would not take place until they developed agriculture. How many of his own kind had Set been able to bring from Shaydan, I asked myself? Hundreds? Thousands?

I knew he had transported dinosaurs from the Mesozoic Age to this time and place: the giant lizards and fighting dragons I had met earlier were sauropods and carnosaurs from the Cretaceous.

The forest of Paradise was far from empty, however. The woods teemed with life, from tiny burrowing mice to growling, roaring lions. Using nothing but stones and wood, I quickly fashioned myself a serviceable spear and hand ax. By the second day I had a raw pelt of deerskin to wear as a loincloth. By the second week I had added a vest and leg wrappings tied with beef gut.

I felt completely alone, of course. Yet I did not mind the solitude. It was a relief, a welcome respite from the turmoil I had been through and the dangers I knew lay ahead of me. I did not try to contact the Creators, remembering that such mental signals served as beacons that allowed Set to pinpoint my location. I wanted to remain hidden from him as much as I could. For the time being.

He knew I was here. Day after day I saw long-winged pterosaurs gliding high in the bright blue skies. As long as I remained in the forest I was safe from their prying eyes, I reasoned. They could not see me through the leafy canopy of the trees.

I wondered where the Creators were, if they knew what I was up to. Or were they scattering across the galaxy in this spacetime, still fleeing Set after Anya's capitulation to him?

I thought of Anya, of how she had betrayed me at one point in time yet swore she loved me at another. Was she watching over me now or running for her life? I had no way of knowing and in truth I did not care. All that would be settled later, after I had dealt with Set. If I survived, if I succeeded in killing him once and for all, then I could confront Anya and the other Creators. Until then I was on my own, and that's the way I wanted it.

Try as I might, I could not understand how the Creators could be running for their lives in one era and yet living peacefully in their mausoleum of a city in the distant future. Nor how Set's home world could be utterly destroyed and yet he alive and burning for revenge against me here in the Neolithic.

"How could you understand?" I once again heard the mocking voice of the Golden One in my memory. "I never built such understanding into you. Don't even try, Orion. You were created to be my hunter, my warrior, not a spacetime philosopher."

Limited. Maimed from the instant of my conception. Yet I ached for understanding. I recalled the Golden One telling me that the spacetime continuum is filled with currents and tides that shift constantly and can even be manipulated by conscious effort.

I gazed down the stream I had been following for many weeks. It was a fair-sized river now, flowing smoothly and silently toward some distant rendezvous with the Nile. To me, time was like a river, with the past upstream and the future downstream. A river that flowed in one direction, so that cause always came before effect.

Yet I knew from what the Creators had told me that time was actually more like an ocean connecting all points of the spacetime continuum. You could sail across that wide ocean in any direction, subject to its own inherent tides and currents. Cause did not necessarily precede effect always, although to a time-bound creature such as myself who senses time linearly, it always seems that way.

Each night I scanned the heavens. Sheol was still in the sky, but it looked sickly, dull. Except one night when it flared so brightly it cast bold shadows on the ground. It still shone bright enough to be seen at high noon the following day. Then it faded again.

The Sun's companion star was still exploding, blowing off whole layers of plasma, peeling itself like an onion until there would be nothing remaining except a central core of gases too cool to produce the fusion reactions that make a star shine. The Creators were still directing its destruction from the safety of the far future.

The land around me began to look familiar. I had walked this ground before. For much of a morning I followed the riverbank, recognizing a sturdy old beech tree that slanted out over the placid stream. I spotted a boulder half overgrown with tall fronds of grass and berry bushes. The charred remains of a campfire blackened the ground in front of it. Anya and I had camped here.

Stretching to my fullest height, I felt the breeze, inhaled the scent of flowers and pine trees. The soft blue sky was marred by a thin gray cloud wafting on the wind. I smelled the faint, distant charred odor of fire. Kraal's village was no more than a couple of days from here, I realized.

I turned my steps away from the river, aiming for the village of Kraal and Reeva, the two who had betrayed me.

My usual procedure was to hunt down some game along toward sunset, when the animals came to the river to drink. Although the river was far behind me by the time the day's shadows were lengthening, I found a pond, a natural water hole, and hunkered down in a clump of bushes next to a tough old hickory to wait for my dinner to appear. The wind was in my face, so not even the most sensitive doe could scent me. I remained quite still, an immobile part of the landscape, and waited.

Hundreds of birds were singing and calling in the branches above me in the final moments of the day as the first animals cautiously approached the water hole. Several squirrels appeared, their tails twitching nervously. Then they were joined by other little furry things, woodchucks or something of that kind.

Eventually deer came for their evening drink, stepping delicately, stopping to sniff the air and search the purpling shadows with their big liquid eyes. I tightened my grip on my spear but remained hidden and unmoving, not so much out of compassion for them as because they were on the opposite side of the pond and too fleet afoot for me to reach them.

I heard a grunting sound behind me, almost a growl. Turning only my head, I saw the bushes shaking. Then a heavy-sided brown boar waddled toward me, tusks the size of carving knives. He took no notice of me whatsoever except to grunt and grumble as he passed by and shambled to the water's edge.

He was not afraid of humans. Probably he had never seen one before. He would never see another.

The boar bent his head and began noisily slurping at the water. In one fluid motion I rose to my feet and raised my spear high above my head. Using both hands, I rammed its fire-hardened point into the boar's back just behind his shoulder blade. I felt it penetrate his tough hide and slide wetly through lung and heart.

The boar collapsed without a sound. The deer on the far side of the pond, startled by my sudden movement, leaped away a few yards but then soon returned to the water's edge.

I congratulated myself on an easy kill as I started the grisly business of skinning the boar and slicing off the best meat with my stone tools.

I congratulated myself too soon.

The first sign of danger was when the deer suddenly looked up, then bounded off into the woods. I took no notice of it. I was kneeling over my kill, too busy hacking away at the boar's carcass in anticipation of a pork dinner.

Then I heard a coughing growl behind me that could only come from the deep chest of a lion. Turning slowly, I saw a shaggy-maned saber-toothed cat staring at me with glowing golden eyes, saliva drooling from one corner of a mouth armed with twin curving gleaming daggers.

He wanted my kill. Like a latter-day mafioso he had let me do the work, and now he intended to help himself to the profits.

I glanced into the shadowy bushes, trying to determine if this male was alone or if there were females lying in wait to spring at me. He seemed alone. Looking more sharply at him, I saw that his ribs poked through his tawny pelt. He took a limping step toward me.

He was either sick or hurt or too old to hunt for himself. This lion had been reduced to scavenging kills made by others, bluffing them away.

Sick though he may be, however, he still had the claws and teeth that could kill. My senses went into hyperdrive as I realized that my spear rested on the ground slightly more than an arm's reach away.

If I got up and walked away, chances were the saber-tooth would take the boar's carcass and leave me alone. But if he decided to attack me, turning my back to him was a foolish thing to do. Perhaps it would invite his attack.

The beast took another step toward me and growled again. The limp was noticeable; his left rear leg was hurt.

I had no intention of letting this rogue take my meal away from me. If he could bluff, so could I. Slowly, as we faced each other with unblinking eyes, I reached for my spear. As my outstretched fingers touched the smoothed wood, the saber-tooth decided that he would have to do more than growl.

He sprang at me. I grabbed the spear as I flattened myself on the ground and rolled away from him. Hurt though he may have been, the lion landed on all fours atop the boar's carcass and instantly whirled around to pounce on me.

I butted the spear against the ground and aimed its

point at its throat. His own leap spitted him on the spear point, his own weight forced him down onto its shaft. Blood spurted and the saber-tooth gave a strangled gurgling roar, clawing at me with his forepaws. One swipe raked my chest before I could drop the spear and back away.

The beast screamed and thrashed, trying to dislodge the spear from its throat. I scuttled away, no weapons except my bare hands, unable to do anything but watch the saber-tooth rolling on the ground, pawing at the spear's wooden shaft while his life's blood gushed onto the ground.

It was an awful way to die. Insanely, I sprang to my feet and ran to the struggling beast. I pulled at the spear with all my might, yanking it out of the bubbling wound in his throat. We both roared with a combination of blood fury and savage love as I plunged the spear into his heart.

I watched the light in his tawny eyes glimmer and die, leaning on the spear, half-ashamed of myself, half-exultant. I had ended the lion's life. I had ended his suffering.

But as I looked down on his once-noble carcass I knew that jackals and other scavengers would soon be tearing at his rotting flesh. There is no dignity in death, I told myself grimly. Only the living can have dignity.

Chapter 33

So it was that I wore a saber-tooth's pelt over my head and shoulders when I approached the village of Kraal.

I followed the smoke cloud that stained the otherwise pristine sky, thinking at first that the village must have grown much larger than it had been when I had last seen it. By the second day I began to realize that the drifting gray cloud was too big, too persistent, to be from cooking fires. I began to fear the worst.

By noon I could smell death in the air: the greasy, charred odor of burned flesh. I saw birds circling high in the distance. Not pterosaurs; vultures.

It was midafternoon when I pushed through the thorny underbrush and saw Kraal's village. It had been burned quite thoroughly, every hut reduced to smoldering ashes, the ground blackened, a heap of charred bodies in the middle of the village burned beyond recognition. The vultures circled above. They had their own kind of patience. They were waiting for the ground to cool and the dead to stop smoking before they landed to begin their feast.

Kneeling, I examined the three-clawed prints of dinosaurs and Shaydanians that were all around the village. They had left a clear trail heading off in the northeasterly direction of Set's fortress by the Nile. There were human footprints among them. Not everyone in the village had been slaughtered.

I straightened up and turned toward the northeast. So this was the reward Kraal and Reeva had earned for their collaboration with Set. The monster had razed their village and killed most of the inhabitants. Those that had not been slaughtered had been marched off into slavery.

I found myself hoping that Kraal and Reeva were still among the living. I wanted to find them, wanted them to see me. I wanted to see how much they enjoyed dealing with the devil.

As I trekked toward Set's fortress I wondered what had befallen Chron and Vorn and the other slaves that I had freed. Were they dead or back in slavery?

For the rest of that day and most of the next I followed the broad trail that the dinosaurs had trampled through the underbrush. At first I thought that I might catch up with them and their human captives, but I soon put that idea out of my mind. What good would it do to try to free them? It would merely alert Set to my presence, confirm to him that I had arrived here. I wanted as much surprise on my side as possible; it was just about the only weapon I would have when I finally went against him.

Toward sundown on the second day after the village I noticed a set of human footprints that diverged from the main trail. The dinosaurs had been leading their prisoners directly northeast, toward Set's fortress; their trail through the forest as straight as a Roman road or the flight of an arrow.

But at least two humans had run off into the underbrush, trying to escape them. I turned off the dinosaur trail and started after them. Less than ten minutes later I saw that a single dinosaur's tracks joined theirs; whoever was directing the raiders had sent one fighting dragon after the escapees.

The sun was setting behind a range of low hills when I saw them. In a clearing among the trees a man cowered on his knees while a woman holding an infant in her arms trembled behind him. One of Set's clones stood before them, not much taller than the woman, his scales the salmon pink of a barely adult Shaydanian. Off to the edge of the clearing hunched a two-legged dragon, his fierce head nearly as tall as the young trees, his eyes glittering with hunger.

I saw that the Shaydanian was about to kill the man. He grasped him by the throat, drawing blood with his claws.

I shouted, "Leave him alone!" And raised my spear over my head.

The Shaydanian turned, hissing surprise, as I hurled the spear with all my strength. It struck him in the chest, knocking him over backward. He fell practically on top of the startled little family of humans.

The dragon turned toward me also. I focused on it and for a dizzying instant saw the scene through its slitted eyes: the human male still on his knees, gaping at the dead reptilian; the female looking shocked, clutching the baby to her breast; and the tall broad-shouldered Orion standing a dozen yards away, hands empty, weaponless.

I willed the dragon to go off and rejoin the others. I gave it the mental picture of chasing down goats and cows and even bears. It hissed like a teakettle and raised itself to its full height on its two powerful legs. Its head bobbed back and forth between the little family and me, as if uncertain of what to do. We certainly made an easy meal for it. I concentrated as hard as I could on directing it away from us. Finally it pranced off through the trees.

I let loose a breath I had been holding for what seemed like hours. The man climbed painfully to his feet. I saw that his back was crisscrossed with claw slashes oozing blood. I started toward the trio of humans and the dead Shaydanian to retrieve my spear.

I recognized Kraal and Reeva the same instant they realized who I was.

"Orion!" he gasped, dropping back to his knees.

Reeva's eyes widened and she clasped the baby even closer to her. I saw that she was pregnant again.

I said nothing as I walked up to the dead reptilian and yanked my spear from its scaled hide.

"Spare her, Orion," Kraal begged, still kneeling. "Take your revenge on me, but spare Reeva and the boy."

"Where is my knife?" There was much that I wanted to say to this weak, sniveling traitor. Those were the only words that came out, though.

He fumbled under the filthy pelt that covered his middle and handed me the knife, its sheath and strap, with shaking hands.

"You must be a god," Kraal said, lowering his face to the ground at my feet. "Only a god could kill those monsters. Only a god could wear the skin of a lion."

"God or man, you betrayed me."

"And what have you done for us?" Reeva snapped, her eyes flashing fire. "Since we have known you we've had nothing but death and destruction."

"You were a slave when I first saw you. I made you free."

"Free to be hunted by Set and his devils! Free to be killed and tortured and see our villages burned to the ground!"

"You decided to serve Set. That is your reward. You betrayed not merely me, you betrayed all of your own people. And Set betrayed you. That is justice."

"What will you do with us?" Kraal asked, still groveling.

I reached down and yanked him to his feet. "I will do battle with Set. I will try to kill him and all his kind so that you can inherit this land and live in freedom."

His jaw dropped open. Reeva, suspicious, asked, "Why would you do that for us?"

I made a small smile for her. "I don't want that little boy to grow up in slavery. I don't want any human being to be the slave of that inhuman monster."

I camped with them that night. It was clear that they were afraid of me, thoroughly mystified about my motives in allowing them to live and trying to battle against the seemingly all-powerful Set. The baby's name, they told me eventually, was Kaan.

As I had feared, Set was methodically, determinedly wiping out every tribe of humans he could find. Shame-faced, stammering, Kraal told me that at first Set's minions treated them well as he and Reeva helped the demons to round up entire villages of people and march them off into slavery. Chron, Vorn, and all the others I had known had been taken away in that manner.

"But when the red star began to flash and shake in the sky, Set became very angry. His demons started to slaughter whole villages and burn them to the ground. At last they surrounded our village with dragons and killed almost everyone. Then they burned the village and took us away with them into slavery."

I nodded in the evening shadows. "And you tried to escape."

"Reeva ran away from them and I followed her," Kraal told me. "We ran as fast as we could but still one of the devils found us with his dragon. And then you appeared, like a god, to save us."

Through all this Reeva said nothing, though I could

feel her eyes on me.

"Set is evil," I said to Kraal. "He intends to kill every one of us. Some he will use as slaves, but death is the final reward he has waiting for us all."

"You intend to fight him?" Kraal asked.

"Yes."

"Alone?" asked Reeva. The tone of her question made me realize that she feared I would force them to help me.

"Alone," I replied.

"And the priestess? Anya? Where is she? Will she not help you?"

"No, she can't help me," I said. "I must face Set by myself."

"Then he will kill you," Reeva said, matter-of-factly. "He will kill us all."

"Perhaps," I admitted. "But not without a battle."

In the morning I wished them well, told them to live as best as they could.

"Someday," I said, "when young Kaan is big enough to walk and speak, when the new baby you are carrying is weaned, you will meet other people like yourselves and know that Set has been destroyed. Then you will at last be free."

"What if Set kills you, instead?" Reeva asked.

"Then one day much sooner his demons and dragons will find you and kill you."

I left them with that fearful thought and started off again toward the northeast.

Day after day I walked alone through the forest of Paradise toward my rendezvous with Set. I passed the hollowed rock cliff where I had invented the god who speaks. I passed two other villages, as burned and dead as Kraal's. I saw no other human being anywhere in Paradise.

Set's demons had visited all the villages, burning and killing, carrying off a few people to serve as slaves, slaughtering all the rest. He was wiping this world clean of humanity, except for a few slaves. He was making the Earth the home of his own reptilian kind.

I reached the edge of the forest at last and looked out from between the trees to the broad undulating plain of grass that stood between me and Set's fortress.

Pterosaurs glided through the sunny sky high above. On the horizon I saw the lumpy dark shape of a sauropod. Set had his scouts out looking for me. He knew I was coming after him and he was waiting for me, alert and ready.

I sat myself on the ground, my back against the rough bark of a massive maple, thinking hard about my next move.

It was lunacy to try to reach Set's fortress by myself, armed with nothing more than a wooden spear and a few stone implements. I had to have help. That meant that I had to return to the Creators.

For hours I resisted the idea. I had no desire to go back to them. I wanted to be free of them for all time. Or at the least, I wanted to meet them as an equal, a man who had defeated their most dangerous enemy with his own strength and wits, not a maimed toy that did not work correctly and was in constant need of help.

But there was no alternative. I could not face Set alone and unarmed. I needed their help.

Yet I knew that once I tried to make contact with the Creators, Set would home in on my mental beacon like a serpent gliding through the darkness is guided by its prey's body heat. If I tried to make contact with the Creators and failed, Set's demons would be upon me within hours.

That meant I could not merely seek out contact with the Creators and hope that they would bring me across spacetime to them. I had to make the leap myself, with my own power.

Night was falling. Crickets chirruped and winged insects whined through the shadows. I climbed up the maple's trunk and flattened myself prone on one of its sturdy branches. Somehow I felt safer up in the tree than on the ground.

My monkey heritage, Set would have called it. Yet I truly did feel safer.

Closing my eyes, I tried to recall all the times I had been shifted through the continuum from one point in spacetime to another. I recalled the pain of death, repeated over and over. Concentrating, forcing myself to see through that pain, beyond it, I sought the memory of translating myself across the continuum.

I had done it before, although I was not certain that one of the Creators had not helped me without my being aware of it. Now I wanted to do it completely on my own. Could I?

The secret was to tap enough energy to create a warp in spacetime. Energy is subject to the control of a conscious mind just as matter is. And the universe teems with energy. Stars radiate their energy throughout spacetime, drenching the continuum with their bounty. Even as I lay sprawled on this tree branch in the dark of night, countless trillions of neutrinos and cosmic particles were flowing through my body, filling the night, swarming through the world around me.

I used that energy. Focusing it with my mind the way a lens focuses light, I bent that energy to my will. Once again I felt that moment of cryogenic cold, that instant of nothingness that marked the transition across the awful gulfs of the continuum.

I opened my eyes.

The city of the Creators stood all around me, magnificent temples and monuments from all the ages of humankind. Empty and silent, abandoned.

The energy dome shimmered above, tingeing the clear blue sky with a slight golden cast. Elsewhere on this tranquil Earth human beings very much like me lived their normal lives of joy and sorrow, work and love. But the Creators had fled.

For hours I walked through their city, their monument to themselves. Marble and bronze, gold and stainless steel, glass and glossy wood. To what avail? This world of theirs went along without them, but for how long? How long would the continuum maintain its stability with Set still alive and the Creators scattered among the stars? For how long could the human race exist with its implacable enemy still working to destroy all humanity?

I found myself in the main square once again, facing the Parthenon and its heroic statue of Athena. My Anya's face looked down at me, a Greek battle helmet tilted back on her head, a great spear gripped in one slender hand.

I lifted my arms to the thirty-foot-tall statue rising before me.

"How can I win, all alone?" I asked the unfeeling marble. "What can I do, by myself?"

The statue stirred. Its marble seemed to glow from within and take on the tones of living flesh. Its painted eyes became live, grave gray eyes that looked down on me solemnly. Its lips moved and the melodious voice I knew so well spoke to me.

"You are not alone, my love."

"Anya!"

"I am with you always, even if I cannot help you directly."

The memory of her abandonment welled up in me. "You deserted me once."

The living statue's face almost seemed to cry. "I am ashamed of what I did, Orion."

I heard myself reply, "You had no alternative. I know that. I understand it. My life was unimportant compared to the survival of the Creators. Still, it hurts worse than Set's fires."

Anya answered, "No such noble motives moved me. I

was filled with the terror of death. Like any mortal human, I fled with my life and left the man I love most in all the universes to the mercies of the cruelest of the cruel."

"I would have done the same," I said.

She smiled sadly. "No, Orion. You would have died protecting me. You have given your life many times, but even faced with final extinction you would have tried to shield me with your own life."

I had no response to that.

"I took on human form as a whim, at first," Anya confessed. "I found it exciting to share a life with you, to feel the blood thundering through my body, to love and laugh and fight—even to bleed. But always I knew that I could escape if it became necessary. I never faced the ultimate test, true death. When Set held me in his power, when I knew that I would die forever, that I would cease to be, I felt real fear for the first time. I panicked and ran. I abandoned you to save myself."

"I thought I hated you for that," I told her. "And yet I love you still."

"I am not worthy of your love, Orion."

Smiling, I replied, "Yet you have my love, Anya. Now and forever. Throughout all time, all space, all the universes of the continuum, I love you."

It was true. I loved her and forgave her completely. I did this of my own will; no one was manipulating me. This was not a response that the Golden One had built into my conditioning. I truly loved Anya, despite what she had done. Perhaps, in a strange way, I loved her in part *because* she had experienced the ultimate fear that all humans must face. None of the other Creators had shown the courage even to try.

"And I love you, my darling," she said, her voice growing faint.

"But where are you?"

"The Creators have fled. When they saw that Set could

attack them here, in our own sanctuary, they abandoned the Earth altogether and fled for their lives."

"Will you return to me?" I asked.

"The other Creators fear Set so much! They thought that destroying Sheol would put an end to him, but now they realize he is firmly entrenched on Earth. Only you can stop him, Orion. The Creators are depending entirely on you."

"But I can't do it alone!" I called to her diminishing voice. I could feel her presence fading, dwindling, the statue losing its living warmth, returning to pure marble.

"You must use your own resources, Orion," Anya's voice whispered to me. "The Creators are too afraid to face him themselves."

"Will *you* return to me?" I repeated.

"I will try." Fainter still.

"I need you!"

"When you need me most, I will be there for you, Orion." Her voice was softer than the sighing of an owl's wing. "When you need me most, my love."

Chapter 34

I was alone in the empty main square again, staring at the cold marble statue of Athena.

Alone. The Creators expected me to face Set and his minions without them, without even their help.

Feeling drained, exhausted, I went to the marble steps of the Parthenon and sat down, my head sunk in my hands. From across the square the giant golden Buddha smiled placidly at me.

For the first time in all my lives I was facing a situation where my strength by itself was of practically no value. I had to use my mind, the powers of thought, to find a way to defeat Set. He overpowered me physically, that I knew from painful experience. He had an army of Shaydanians at his clawed fingertips and legions of dinosaurs under his control.

I had my body and my wits. Nothing more.

The Buddha statue seemed to be watching me, its smile friendly and benign.

"It's all well and good for you to preach desirelessness," I grumbled aloud to the gold-leafed wood. "But I have desires. I have needs. And what I need most is an army—"

My voice stopped in midsentence.

I knew where there was an army. A victorious army that had swept from the Gobi Desert to the banks of the Danube River. The army of Subotai, greatest of the Mongol generals who conquered most of the world for Genghis Khan.

Rising to my feet, I mentally gathered the energy to project myself into the thirteenth century of the Christian era, to the time when the Mongol Empire stretched from the coast of China to the plain of Hungary. I had been there before. I had assassinated their high khan, Ogotai, the son of Genghis Khan. A man who had befriended me.

The city of the Creators disappeared as I passed through the cryogenic cold of a transition through spacetime. For an instant I was bodiless in the utterly black void of the continuum. Then I was standing on a cold windswept prairie, heavy gray storm clouds thickening overhead. There was not a tree in sight, but in the distance I could make out the ragged silhouette of a walled city against the darkening clouds.

I headed for the city. It began to rain, a cold driving rain mixed with wet sleet. I pulled my lion pelt around my torso and shut down the peripheral circulation in my capillaries as much as I dared to keep my body heat inside me. Head down, shoulders forward, I bulled my way through the icy rain as the ground beneath my feet turned to slick gooey mud.

The city was not burning, which meant either that Subotai's army was besieging it or had already captured it. I thought the latter because I saw no signs of a camp, no great horse corrals or mounted warriors on picket patrols.

It was fully dark by the time I reached the city gate. The wall was nothing more than a rough palisade of pointed logs dug into what was fast becoming a sea of mud. The gate was a crude affair of planks with spaces between them for shooting arrows through.

It was open. A good sign. No fighting was going on or expected.

A half-dozen Mongol warriors stood in the shelter of the gate's overhanging parapet, a small fire crackling fitfully beneath a makeshift board that only partially protected it from the pelting rain.

The Mongols were wiry, battle-scarred veterans. Yet without their ponies they looked small, almost as small as children. Deadly children, though. Each of them wore a chain-mail vest and a conical steel helmet. They carried curved sabers and daggers at their belts. I saw their inevitable bows and quivers full of arrows resting against the planks of the half-open gate.

One of them stepped out to challenge me.

"Halt!" he commanded. "Who are you and what's your business here?"

"I am Orion, a friend of the lord Subotai. I have come from Karakorum with a message from the High Khan."

The tough warrior's eyes narrowed. "The nobles have elected a new High Khan to replace Ogotai?"

I shook my head. "Not yet. Kubilai and the others are gathering at Karakorum to make their choice. My message concerns other matters."

He eyed my dripping lion's pelt and I realized he had never seen a saber-tooth before. But he showed no other sign of curiosity as he demanded, "What proof have you of your words?"

I made myself smile. "Send a messenger to Subotai and tell him that Orion is here to see him. Describe me to him and he will be glad to see me."

He looked me up and down. Among the Mongols my

size was little short of phenomenal. And Subotai knew of my abilities as a fighter. I hoped that no word had reached him from Karakorum that I had murdered the High Khan Ogotai.

The warrior dispatched one of his men to carry my message to Subotai, then grudgingly allowed me to share the meager warmth of their fire, out of the cold rain.

"That's a fine pelt you are wearing," said one of the other guards.

"I killed the beast a long time ago," I replied.

They told me that this city was the capital of the Muscovites. I remembered that Subotai had been eager to learn all that I could tell him about the black-earth region of the Ukraine, and the steppes of Russia that led into the plains of Poland and, beyond the Carpathian mountains, into Hungary and the heartland of Europe.

By the time the messenger returned, my back felt as if it were coated with ice even though my face and hands were reasonably warm. A pair of other warriors came with the messenger, decked in shining armor cuirasses and polished helmets, jewels in their sword hilts. With hardly a word they took me through the mud streets of the city of the Muscovites to the quarters of Subotai.

He was not much different from the man I had met in an earlier lifetime. As small and wiry as any of his warriors, Subotai's hair and beard were iron gray, his eyes jet black. Those eyes were lively, intelligent, curious about this great world that stretched so far in every direction.

He had taken a church for his personal quarters, probably because the wooden structure was the largest building in the city and afforded the grandest room for audiences and nightly drinking bouts. I walked the length of the nave toward Subotai; the floor of the church had been cleared of pews, if any had ever been there. Stiffly pious pictures of Byzantine saints gazed down morosely at the pile of pillows where the altar had once been. Subotai reclined there with a few trusted companions and a dozen or so slim young local women who served food and wine.

Behind him the church's apse was rich with gold bas reliefs gleaming in the candlelight. Some of the gold had already been stripped from the wall; I knew the Mongols would soon melt down the rest. Set into the arch high above was a mosaic of mournful Christ, his wounded hands raised in blessing. It startled me to see that its face was almost an exact portrait of the Creator I called Zeus.

Armed warriors lazed along the side walls of the converted church, drinking and talking among themselves. I was not fooled by their seeming indolence. In an instant they would cut off the head of any man who made the slightest threatening gesture. Or any woman. At a word from Subotai they would gleefully reward a liar or anyone else who displeased their general by pouring molten silver into his ears and eyes.

Yet these Mongols knew the virtues of loyalty and honesty better than most so-called civilized peoples. And there was no question about their bravery. If ordered to, they would storm the strongest fortification in human-wave attacks that would either carry through to victory or leave every one of them dead.

Subotai was drinking from a golden chalice encrusted with gemstones. The lieutenants reclining beside him held cups of silver and alabaster. It never ceased to amaze me: no matter how poor or rude a tribe might be, their priests always had gold and silver, their churches were always the best prizes for looters.

"Orion!" Subotai shouted, leaping to his feet. "Man of the west!"

He seemed genuinely glad to see me. Despite his gray hair he was as agile and eager as a youth.

"My lord Subotai." I stopped a few paces before him and made an appropriately low bow. I was glad to see him, too. When I had known him earlier, he had vibrated with a restless energy that had carried him and his armies to the ends of the earth. I was happy to see that such energy still animated him. He would need it if he agreed to do what I was going to ask of him.

He extended his hand to me and I grasped his wrist as he grasped mine.

"It is good to see you again, man of the west."

Looking down at him, I said solemnly, "I bring you a gift, my lord."

I took the soggy pelt of the saber-tooth from my shoulders and held it out to him. The head had been thrown back so that he could not see the lion's gleaming fangs until that moment. He goggled at it.

"Where did you find a beast such as this?"

I could not help grinning. "I know of places where many strange and wonderful beasts exist."

He grinned back at me and led me to the piles of pillows where he had been reclining. "Tell me the news from Karakorum."

As he gestured for me to sit on the pillows at his right hand I inwardly breathed a sigh of relief. Subotai would have never clasped my arm if he intended to kill me. He was incapable of treachery against a friend. Neither he nor anyone else knew, apparently, that I had assassinated his High Khan, Ogotai, a man who had been my friend in a different life.

While a beautiful young blonde handed me a cup of gold and an equally lovely girl poured spiced wine into it, I told him simply that Ogotai had died in his sleep and that I had seen him that very night.

"He seemed content and pleased that the Mongol Empire ruled almost all the known world in peace. I think he was happy that no enemies stood against the Mongols."

Subotai nodded, but his face turned grave. "Soon, Orion, the unthinkable may happen. Mongol may turn against Mongol. The old tribal wars of the Gobi may erupt again, but this time huge armies will battle one another from one end of the world to the other."

"How can that be?" I asked, truly shocked. "The Yassa forbids such bloodletting among Mongols."

"I know," replied Subotai sadly. "But not even the law of the Yassa can stop the strife that is to come, I fear."

As we reclined there on the silken pillows beneath the sorrowful eyes of Byzantine saints looking down upon us from their gilded unchanging heaven, Subotai explained to me what was happening among the Mongol generals.

Simply put, they had virtually run out of lands to conquer. Genghis Khan, the leader they revered so highly that no Mongol would speak his name, had set the tribes of the Gobi on the path to world conquest. With all of China, all of Asia to battle, the warriors of the Gobi stopped their incessant tribal conflicts and set out to conquer the world. Now that world had been conquered, except for dreary dank outlands such as Europe and the subcontinent of India where the heat killed men and horses alike.

"The election of the new High Khan will bring divisions among the Mongols," Subotai predicted gloomily. "It will be an excuse to go back to the old ways of fighting among ourselves."

I understood. The empire of Alexander the Great had broken up in the same manner, general battling general to hold the territory already possessed or to steal territory from a former comrade in arms.

"What will you do, my lord Subotai?" I asked.

He drained his chalice and put it down beside him. Immediately one of the slaves filled it to the brim.

"I will not break the laws of the Yassa," he said. "I will not spill the blood of other Mongols."

"Not willingly," said one of the men sitting around us.

Subotai nodded, his mouth set in a tight grim line. "I will lead my warriors westward, Orion, past the river they call Danube. It is a difficult land, cold and filled with dismal forests. But it is better than fighting amongst ourselves."

If Subotai intended to march into Europe, he would devastate the civilization there that was just beginning to throw off the shackles of ignorance and barbarism that had followed the collapse of the Roman Empire. In another few centuries the Renaissance would begin, with all that it would eventually mean for human knowledge and freedom. But not if the Mongols laid waste to all of Europe, from Muscovy to the English Channel.

"My lord Subotai," I said slowly, "once you asked me to tell you all I knew of this land where you now camp, and of the lands further west."

Some of his old vigor returned to his eyes. "Yes! And now that you have returned to me, I am more eager than ever to learn about the Germans and Franks and the other powers of the lands to the west."

"I will tell you all I know, but as you already understand, their lands are cold and heavily forested, not good territory for a Mongol warrior."

He made a deep sigh. "But what other lands are there for my men?"

His question brought a smile to my lips. "I know a place, my lord, where open grassland stretches for as far as a man can ride in a whole year. A place of great cats with sabers for teeth and other beasts, even more ferocious."

Subotai's eyes widened and the warriors around him stirred.

"There are few people in this land, so few that you could ride for weeks without seeing anyone."

"We would not have to fight?"

"You *will* have to fight," I said. "The land is ruled not by men, but by monsters such as no man has ever seen before."

"Monsters?" blurted one of the warriors. "What kind of monsters?"

"Have you seen them yourself?"

"Are you spinning tales to try to frighten us, man of the west?"

Subotai hushed them with an impatient gesture.

I replied, "I have been there, my lords, and seen this land and the monsters who rule it. They are fierce and powerful and hideous."

I spent the next hour describing Set and his Shaydanian clones, and the dinosaurs that he had brought from the Mesozoic.

"What you speak of," said Subotai at last, "sounds much like the djinn of the Persians or the tsan goblins that the people of the high mountains fear."

"They are to be feared, that is true enough," I said. "And they have great powers. But they are neither ghosts nor goblins. They are as mortal as you or I. I myself have killed them with little more than a spear or a knife."

Subotai sank back on his silken cushions, deep in thought. The others drank and held out their goblets for more wine. I drank, too. And waited.

Finally Subotai asked me, "Can you lead us to this land?"

"Yes, my lord Subotai."

"I would see these monsters for myself."

"I can take you there."

"How soon? How long a journey is it?"

Suddenly I realized that I was talking myself into a double-edged trap. To bring Subotai or any of the Mongols back to the Neolithic, I would have to reveal to them powers that would convince them that I was a sorcerer. The Mongols did not deal kindly with sorcerers: usually they put them to the sword, or killed them more slowly.

And once in the Neolithic they might very well take one look at Set's reptilians and decide that they were supernatural creatures. Although the Mongols feared no human, the sight of the Shaydanians might terrify them.

"My lord Subotai," I answered carefully, "the land I speak of cannot be reached on horseback. I can take you there tomorrow morning, if you desire it, but the journey will seem very strange to you."

He cast me a sidelong glance. "Speak more plainly, Orion."

The others hunched forward, more curiosity on their faces than fear.

"You know that I come from a far land," I said.

"From beyond the sea that stretches to the sky," Subotai said, recalling what I had told him years before.

"Yes," I agreed. "In my land people travel in very strange ways. They do not need horses. They can go across far mountains and seas in the blink of an eye."

"Witchcraft!" snapped one of the warriors.

"No," I said. "Merely a swifter way to travel."

"Like the magic carpets that the storytellers of Baghdad speak of?" asked Subotai.

I grabbed at that idea. "Indeed, my lord, very much like that."

His brows rose a centimeter. "I had always thought such tales to be nothing more than children's nonsense."

Bowing my head slightly to show some humility, I replied, "Children's nonsense sometimes becomes reality, my lord. You yourself have accomplished deeds that would have seemed impossible to your grandfathers."

He made that sighing noise again, almost a snort. The others remained silent.

"Very well," said Subotai. "Tomorrow morning you will take me to this strange land you describe. Me, and my personal guard."

"How many men will that be?" I asked.

Subotai smiled. "A thousand. With their horses and weapons."

The warrior sitting next to Subotai on his left said without humor, "You will need a large carpet, Orion."

The others burst into laughter. Subotai grinned, then looking at the surprise on my face, began to roar. The joke was on me. The others lolled back on the cushions and howled until tears ran down their cheeks. I laughed, too. Mongols do not laugh at sorcerers and witchcraft. As long as they were guffawing they were not afraid of me. As long as they did not fear me they would not try to knife me in my back.

Chapter 35

One of Subotai's tough, battle-scarred veterans led me to a stall in the loft of the church where a few blankets and pillows had been put together to make a serviceable bed. I slept soundly, without dreams.

The sun shone weakly through tattered scudding gray clouds the next morning. The rain had stopped but the streets of Kiev were rivers of gooey gray-brown mud.

Subotai's quartermaster had apparently spent the night hunting up equipment taken as spoils from the Muscovites big enough for me to wear. Obviously nothing made for the Mongols themselves would fit me.

I came down to the nave of the converted church decked in a chain-mail shirt, leather trousers, and boots that felt a little too snug but warm. A curved scimitar of Damascus steel hung at my side, its hilt sparkling with precious gems. The faithful old iron dagger that Odysseus had given me was now tucked into my belt.

A red-haired slave led me out into the watery sunlight,

where a pair of Mongol warriors waited on their ponies. They held a third horse, slightly bigger than the other two, for me. Without a word we rode through the muddy streets and past the gate that I had entered the night before.

Out beyond the city wall waited Subotai's personal guard, a thousand hardened warriors who had beaten every army hurled against them from the Great Wall of China to the shores of the Danube River. Mounted on tough little ponies, grouped in precise military formations of tens and hundreds, each warrior was accompanied by two or three more horses and all the equipment he would need for battle.

At the head of the formation Subotai's magnificent white stallion pranced as impatiently as the great general himself must have felt.

"Orion!" he called as I approached. "We are ready to move."

It was a command and a challenge. I knew I had to translate the entire mass of them through spacetime, but I feared to attempt doing it as abruptly as I myself moved through the continuum.

So, playacting a bit, I squinted up at the weak sun, turned slightly in my creaking saddle, and pointed roughly northward.

"That is the way, my lord Subotai."

He gave a guttural order to the warrior riding next to him and the entire formation wheeled around and followed us at a slow pace.

I led them into the dismal dark woods that began a bare half mile from the city's walls. Concentrating with an intensity I had never known before, I uttered a silent plea for help to Anya as I tried to focus all the energy I could tap for the translation through spacetime.

The woods grew misty. A soft gray billowing fog rose from the ground and wrapped us in its chill tendrils. Our mounts trotted ahead slowly, Subotai at my side, his bodyguards behind me, close enough to slice me to ribbons at the slightest provocation. The fog grew thicker, blanketing sound as well as sight. I could hear the muffled tread of the horse's hooves in the muddy ground, an occasional snort, the jangle of a sword hilt against a steel buckle.

I ignored all distractions. I even ignored Subotai himself as I gathered my mental strength and forced the entire group of us across the continuum. I felt the familiar moment of utter cold, but it was over almost before it began.

I realized that I had squeezed my eyes shut. Opening them, I saw that we were still in a forest. But the mist was dissolving, evaporating. The ground beneath us was firm and dry. The sunlight filtering through the tall leafy trees was strong and bright.

We were now in the forest of Paradise, I realized, riding north by east toward the edge of the woods. The time was the early Neolithic. This was the place and the time where Set had determined to make his stand: to wipe out the human race while it was still small and weak, to wreak vengeance upon me and the Creators for destroying his home world, to seize the planet Earth and make it his own forever.

I glanced at Subotai. He rode his pony quietly, his face impassive. But his eyes were darting everywhere. He knew we were no longer in the chill, dank land of the Muscovites. The sun was warm, even under the magnificent trees. He was noting every tree, every rock, every tiny animal that darted through the underbrush. He was building up a map inside his head as we rode through this land that was completely new to him.

At last he asked me, "You say there are no other men here?"

"There are a few scattered tribes, my lord. But they are

small and weak. They possess no weapons except crude wooden spears and bows that have not the range of the Mongol bow."

"And few women, also?"

"Very few, I fear."

He grunted. "And the monsters? How are they armed?"

"They use giant lizards to do their fighting for them—dragons bigger than ten horses, with sharp claws and ferocious teeth."

"Animals," Subotai muttered.

I corrected, "Animals that are controlled by the minds of their masters, so that they fight with intelligence and courage."

He fell silent at that.

For most of the day we rode through the forest, the Mongol warriors behind us filtering through the trees as silently as wraiths. There was no pause for a meal, we chewed dried meat and drank water from our canteens while in the saddle.

It was nearly sundown when we reached the edge of the forest and saw the endless expanse of grass stretching out beyond the horizon.

Subotai actually grinned. He nosed his pony out from under the trees and rode a hundred yards or so onto the grassy plain.

"How far does this land extend?" he called back to me.

Making a quick mental calculation, I shouted back, "About the same as the distance between Baghdad and Karakorum!"

He gave a wild shout and spurred his mount into a gallop. His bodyguards, startled, went yowling and charging after him, leaving me sitting in my saddle, staring at the unusual sight of Mongols whooping like boys wild with joyful exhilaration.

Then I saw a pterosaur gliding against the bright blue sky, high above.

"I welcome your return, Orion." Set's cold voice rang inside my head. "You have brought more noisy monkeys to annoy me, I see. Good. Slaughtering them will please me very much."

I clamped down on my thoughts. The less Set knew about who these men were, the better. I had to fight him in the time and place of his choosing, but whatever element of surprise I could hold on to was vital to me.

Subotai returned at a trot after nearly half an hour of hard joyriding, his normally doughty face split by a wide grin.

"You have done well, Orion. This land is like the Gobi in springtime."

"It is like this all year round," I said. In a few thousand years it would become the most arid desert on Earth, as the ice sheets covering Europe in this era retreated and the nourishing rains moved north with them. But for now, for as long as Subotai and his sons and his sons' sons lived, the grass would be green and abundant.

"We must bring the rest of the army here, and our families with their yurts and herds," Subotai said enthusiastically. "Then we can deal with these demons and dragons of yours."

I was about to agree when I spotted the lumpy brown shape of a four-legged sauropod on the horizon.

Pointing, I said, "There is one of the beasts. It is not a fighting dragon, but it can be dangerous."

Subotai immediately spurred his horse into a charge toward the sauropod. A dozen of his guard charged out after him. I urged my mount into a gallop, too, and we all dashed for the hump-backed brown and dun dinosaur as it plodded slowly away from us. I felt the wind in my face and the straining muscles of my pony beneath me; it was exhilarating.

As we neared the sauropod, its head turned on its long, snaky neck to look at us. I realized that Set was using the beast as a scout, examining us through the reptile's eyes. I could sense him hissing with his equivalent of amused laughter.

The animal lumbered off toward a small rise in the land, little more than a grassy knoll where some thick berry bushes grew.

"Be careful!" I shouted to Subotai over the pounding of our horses' hooves. "There may be others."

He was already unlimbering the compact double-curved bow that had been slung across his back, his horse's reins clamped in his grinning teeth. The other Mongols were also fitting arrows to their bows without slowing their charge in the slightest.

I got the strong mental impression of Shaydanians hiding in those bushes and behind the knoll. Mounted on dragons. I kicked my horse into a harder gallop and tried to catch up with the impetuous Subotai.

The sauropod reached the rise of the knoll and, instead of climbing it or going around it, turned to face us. It made a screeching, whistling hoot and raised itself up on its hind legs, its head rearing more than forty feet above us, the talons of its forefeet glinting viciously in the sunlight.

Subotai let loose an arrow that struck the beast squarely in its exposed chest. It screamed and lunged toward him. Subotai's horse panicked and reared up. A lesser man would have been thrown from his saddle, but Subotai, practically born on horseback, held his seat.

A dozen more arrows flew at the monster, striking its chest, belly, neck. I was close enough to hear the solid chunking thud each missile made as it penetrated the reptile's scales. My sword was in my hand and I drove my horse to Subotai's side, ready to protect him as he regained control of his mount.

Then the trap was sprung. From both sides of the knoll

half a dozen fighting dragons sprang, with Shaydanians mounted on their backs, guiding them. All the horses panicked at the sight of these fierce, terrifying carnosaurs dashing toward them. Several of the men were thrown. My own horse bucked and reared, wanting desperately to get away from the sharp teeth and claws of these ferocious monsters.

I controlled my mount mentally, blocking out the vision of the dreadful devils as I drove it headlong into the nearest of the carnosaurs. My one thought was to protect Subotai. Already dragons were crunching some of the downed men in their voracious jaws, their screams rising over the dragons' hissing snarls.

From behind me I heard an enormous deep roar, like a giant enraged lion, and the ground-shaking thunder of thousands of horses' hooves. Subotai's entire guard was charging out of the woods toward the beasts that threatened their lord.

My senses went into hyperdrive as I charged my poor terrified pony straight toward the claws of the nearest carnosaur. I saw bubbles of saliva between its saber-sharp teeth, saw its slitted reptilian eyes turn away from Subotai toward me, saw the Shaydanian mounted on its back focusing his attention on me also.

The carnosaur swung one mighty clawed hand at me. I slid off my saddle and dropped to the ground, sword firmly in my hand. The carnosaur's claws lifted my pony entirely off the ground, gouging huge spurting furrows along its flank, and threw it screaming through the air.

I saw all this happen in slow motion, as if watching a dream. Before the dinosaur finished its clawing kill of my pony I ducked low and leaped between its hind legs, ramming my scimitar into its groin with every bit of strength in me.

Then I saw the Shaydanian topple from the screeching carnosaur's back, an arrow in his chest. Before he hit the ground I glanced over my shoulder to see Subotai already nocking another arrow, reins still in his teeth, lips pulled back in what might have been a grin or a grimace.

The carnosaur started to topple upon me and I had to skip quickly away as it floundered to the ground with a bone-shaking thump. My sword was still buried in its groin, so I dashed to the crushed bloody remains of one of the Mongols and picked up the bow he had dropped in the final instant of his life.

By now the rest of Subotai's thousand were in arrow's range and all the carnosaurs were under relentless attack. The Mongols are brave, but not foolhardy. Their first goal was to rescue their leader, Subotai. Once they saw that he was out of trouble they hung back away from the enemy and attacked with arrows.

Quickly, methodically they picked off the Shaydanians mounted atop the dragons. The carnosaurs themselves were another matter. Too big to be more than annoyed by the Mongols' arrows, they dashed at their tormentors, who galloped off a safe distance before returning to the attack. It was like a bullfight, with the huge monsters being bled until their strength and courage lay pooling on the grass.

As they fired at the milling, screeching carnosaurs I jumped atop one of the riderless horses and followed Subotai as he rejoined his men. He had never let go his grip on his bow, and he was firing at the beasts even as he rode away from them, turning in his saddle to let an arrow fly while his pony galloped toward the rest of the warriors.

The poor outnumbered beasts tried to escape but the Mongols showed no more mercy than fear. They pursued the carnosaurs, pumping more arrows into them until the animals slowed, gasping and hissing, and turned to face their tormentors.

Then came the coup de grace: Mongol lancers charged the weakened, slowed carnosaurs on their sinewy little ponies, a dozen scarred dark-skinned St. Georges spitting a dozen very real hissing, writhing dragons on their spears.

I rode back to retrieve my sword as Subotai trotted back to the carcasses by the knoll and got off his pony to examine the bodies of the slain Shaydanians.

"They do look like the tsan goblins that the men of the high mountains speak of," he said.

I looked down at the dead body of one of Set's clones. Its reptile's eyes were open, staring coldly. Its reddish scales were smeared with blood where three arrows protruded from its flesh. Its clawed hands and feet were stilled forever, yet they still looked dangerous, frightening.

"They are not human," I said, "but they are mortal. They die just as a man does, and their blood is as red as ours."

Subotai looked at me, then past me to where his men were laying out the bodies of the slain Mongols side by side.

"Five killed," he muttered. "How many of these dragons does the enemy possess?"

"Hundreds, at least," I said, watching the Mongol warriors as they tore branches from the bushes around the knoll and began to build a makeshift funeral pyre.

Thinking of Set's core tap that gave him the energy to leap backward in time, I added, "He can probably get more to make up his losses in battle."

Subotai nodded. "And his city is fortified."

"Yes. The walls are higher than five men standing on each other's shoulders."

"This skirmish," said Subotai, "was merely the enemy commander's attempt to determine how many men we have, and what kind of fighters we are. When none of his scouts return home, he will know the second, but not the first."

I bowed my head. He had military wisdom, but he could not realize that Set had witnessed this fight, seeing us through the eyes of his clones.

"You must go back and bring the rest of the army here," Subotai decided. "And do it quickly, Orion, before the enemy realizes that we are only a thousand men—minus five."

"I will do it this night, my lord Subotai."

"Good," he grunted.

I was about to turn away when he reached up and clasped me on the shoulder. "I saw you charge into that beast when my mount was bucking. You protected me when I was most vulnerable. That took courage, friend Orion."

"It seemed the wisest thing to do, my lord."

He smiled. This gray-bearded Mongol general, his hair braided, his face still shining with the sweat of battle, this man who had conquered cities and slain thousands, smiled up at me as a father might.

"Such wisdom—and courage—deserve a reward. What would you have of me, man of the west?"

"You have already rewarded me, my lord."

His dark eyes widened slightly. "Already? How so?"

"You have called me friend. That is reward enough for me."

He chuckled softly, nodded, and took me to the tent his men had pitched for him. As the sun went down we shared a meal of dried meat and fermented mare's milk, then stood side by side as the funeral pyre was lit and the bodies of the slain Mongols properly sent on their way to heaven.

I held my face immobile, knowing that the abode of the gods was nothing more than a beautiful dead city in the far future, a city that the gods had abandoned in fear for their lives. There were no gods to protect or defend us, I knew. We had no one to rely on except ourselves.

"Now," Subotai said to me as the last embers of the pyre glowed against the night's darkness, "bring me the rest of my army."

I bowed and walked off a way from the camp. Moving the entire army and all their families and camp followers would not be easy. Perhaps I could not do it without aid from Anya or the other Creators. But I would try.

I closed my eyes and willed myself back to the bleak city of wooden huts and mud hovels. Nothing happened.

I concentrated harder. Still no result.

Throwing my head back, I stared up at the stars. Sheol glimmered weakly, a poor dulled reflection of its former strength. And I realized that Set had blocked my way through the continuum, just as he blocked Anya when we had first come to this time and place.

He had trapped me here, with Subotai and barely a thousand warriors.

I heard his hissing laughter in my mind. I had led Subotai into a trap. Set intended to keep us here and slaughter us down to the last man.

Chapter 36

I could not face Subotai. He had followed me on faith, believing that I would lead him to a land where he and his people could live in peace once they had conquered the aliens who controlled the area. He had trusted me and called me friend. How could I tell him that I had led him into a deadly trap?

This was my doing, my fault. I could not look upon the battle-hardened face of my Mongol general again until I had corrected the situation. Or died trying.

I had learned one thing of supreme importance from Set. Energy is the key to all powers. Cut off the source of his energy and your enemy becomes helpless. Set's source of energy was the core tap that reached down to the molten heart of Earth. I had to reach it and somehow destroy it.

The tap was deep inside Set's fortress, which lay more than a day's march from where Subotai's troops had camped for the night. I had to get there, and quickly, before

Set unleashed an attack upon Subotai that would slaughter all the Mongols.

But I was cut off from *my* energy source. Set had put a barrier between me and the heavens that prevented me from utilizing the energy streaming in from the sun and stars. Was this shield merely a bubble that covered the immediate region around me, or had he wrapped the entire planet in a shimmering curtain that blocked the energy streaming earthward from the stars?

It made no difference. The fact was that I was cut off from the energies that would allow me to fight Set. There was only one thing to do: reach his own core tap and either destroy it or use it against him.

There was no way that I could accomplish anything in this one night. I took a horse from the Mongols' makeshift corral and rode toward the northeast and Set's fortress. I only hoped that I could reach it before the devil launched an annihilating attack upon Subotai.

The sun rose dim and hazy, a weak pale phantom of its usual glory. Set's shield was incredibly strong, I realized. Pterosaurs were already crisscrossing the watery gray sky. They could not miss seeing me riding alone across the wide plain of grass.

I wondered what Subotai was thinking of me. Probably he was not alarmed yet, thinking that I had returned to Muscovy and was making preparations for bringing the rest of his army to him. I hated to think that he would believe I had betrayed him. I did not fear his anger or punishment, but I felt miserable at the thought that he might feel I had broken his trust.

Despite the wan appearance of the sun, the day became quite hot. Set's shield was selective, allowing the longer wavelengths of sunlight to reach the ground and heat it. I knew that if I had the proper instruments with me, they would show that none of the higher-energy wavelengths were penetrating the shield. Nor were any energetic cosmic particles getting through, I was certain.

Late in the afternoon a trio of Shaydanians mounted on fighting dragons appeared out of the shimmering heat haze, heading directly for me. The pterosaurs had done their job. I was to be killed or captured and brought before Set once again.

For the first time since I had known them, these Shaydanians bore weapons. They each carried oddly convoluted lengths of bright metal strapped across their backs. Once they spotted me they unslung the devices and, clutching them in both hands like rifles, urged their two-legged carnosaurs into a trotting pace.

I slid off my mount and shooed it away from me. I had already sacrificed one pony to the carnosaurs. That was enough. Idly I thought that I must be acquiring some of the Mongols' reverence for horses.

As the carnosaur-mounted devils approached me I focused my consciousness on the nearest of the three, reaching into his mind for a brief moment. The rifles, with their bulbous metallic blisters and needle-slim muzzles, projected streams of fire, like a small flamethrower. Set realized that he could no longer rely on fangs and claws to deal with the Mongols; he needed weapons. What more terrifying weapon than a flamethrower, especially coming from a reptilian that already had the Mongols worried that they were facing supernatural demons?

I saw something else in the Shaydanian's mind during that fleeting instant: they were not under orders to take me alive. Set had no intention of taking further chances with me. These three clones of his were going to kill me, here and now.

My senses shifted into hyperdrive immediately and the scene slowed as if time were stretching like a piece of warm taffy. The three Shaydanians lifted their rifles to their shoulders, aiming at me through diamond-shaped crystal sights. I saw their taloned fingers tightening on the curved triggers.

As they aimed at me their attention was shifted momentarily from guiding their mounts. The fierce two-legged carnosaurs, directed mentally by their riders, continued to trot toward me. But their tiny brains were not under the firm control of the Shaydanians, for one fleeting moment.

Desperately I sent a lance of red-hot mental energy into those three dinosaurs' brains. They screeched and reared to their full height, throwing two of the Shaydanians to the ground and forcing the third to drop his rifle and clutch at his mount's hide with both clawed hands.

All this I saw in slow motion. Even as the two thrown Shaydanians were falling toward the ground, I ran and dove full-length for the rifle that was spiraling through midair. I grabbed it before it touched the grass. As my fingers tightened around it I heard the thumps of the two riders hitting the ground hard.

The dinosaurs were still hissing, the two freed of their riders galloping off away from us. The third, though, was under his rider's control once again and heading straight for me.

I rolled away from a stamping clawed foot that would have crushed me under the carnosaur's weight and fired from the hip at its rider. The stream of flame sliced him in two across midtorso. As his severed body slipped bloodily from the dinosaur's back, the beast wheeled and came at me, massive head bent low, cavernous mouth gaping, lined with saw-edged teeth the size of my scimitar.

I pulled the rifle's trigger as hard as I could while dodging sideways. The stream poured flame down its gullet and slashed down the length of its thick neck. It hit the ground with a tremendous thud, literally shaking the earth, bellowing like a runaway steam locomotive to the very last.

I looked up. The two other Shaydanians were scrambling for the rifles they had dropped. I fired at the nearer of them and he toppled over dead. But when I turned to the third of them, my rifle did not respond. It was empty, its fuel depleted.

The Shaydanian had reached his own rifle and was picking it up from the grass. I threw my useless weapon at him and charged after it, drawing my scimitar from its scabbard. The rifle hit him like a club, knocking him down again on his rump. Before he could train his own rifle on me I was close enough to kick it out of his hands.

He glowered at me through his red slitted reptilian eyes and scrambled to his feet. Hissing, he advanced on me, clawed hands reaching out. I slashed at him with the scimitar once. He raised an arm to block the blow, but I swung the blade under and then lunged at him. The point penetrated the scales of his chest and went completely through him. With a final hiss of death agony he collapsed and, sliding off my blade, fell to the bloodstained ground.

Immediately I projected a mental image at Set. I sent him a scene that showed two of his clones lying dead on the bloody grass but the third standing over my own burned corpse. With every ounce of cunning in me, I presented myself mentally as one of Set's clones, and the body at my feet as my own.

"You have done well, my son," came Set's mental voice. "Return now with the corpse so that I may examine it."

I mentally called one of the carnosaurs back to me and mounted it for the trip back to the fortress by the Nile. Had Set truly believed the false message I had sent him? Or was he merely drawing me to his fortress so he could dispose of me more easily?

There was only one way to find out. I headed the dinosaur toward the fortress, concentrating every moment on my phony image so that even the pterosaurs scouting high overhead would "see" what I wanted them to, and report it back to Set.

It was nightfall by the time I reached the garden by the Nile. The fortress was a short ride away. I would reach it in darkness, which suited me well. I knew there was no chance of my keeping up my deception once inside Set's walls—if Set had been deceived at all.

The sky was utterly black and starless, as dark as the deepest pit of hell as I rode the carnosaur up to the curving fortress wall. The faint phosphorescent glow of the wall itself was the only hint of light in that night made frighteningly black by Set's energy shield. Not an insect buzzed, not a frog peeped or an owl hooted. The murky shadows were as silent as Set's reptilians themselves. The night was eerily, unnaturally still, as if Set was mentally controlling even the wind and the flow of the Nile.

Climbing from the back of my mount to the top of its thickly boned head, I reached as high as I could along the wall. My hands fell short of its top, but the surface of the wall was not perfectly smooth. Like the shell of an egg, there was a slight, almost microscopic roughness to it. Not much, but perhaps enough to climb with. And the wall curved inward. Yanking off my Muscovite boots, I clambered barefoot along the slippery curved surface while directing the dinosaur to go on the gate alone.

Several times my precarious footing on the eggsmooth wall faltered and I almost slid back down to the ground. I had to consciously prevent my hands and feet from sweating and becoming slippery. At last, after what seemed like an hour of painfully slow climbing, I reached the top of the wall and slid myself flat on my belly across its edge.

I could feel the energy humming from deep within the fortress. It made the wall vibrate. The eggshell-like material was warm, not from the day's sunshine but from the energy pulsating from below. Now my task was to reach the source of that energy, the core tap at the heart of this fortress.

I quickly realized I was not alone on the wall's narrow top. Peering into the darkness, I saw nothing ahead of me. Turning around to look behind, my guts twisted in sudden fear. One of those enormous dead-white snakes was slithering toward me, its beady eyes glowering red hatred, its jaws already open, its fangs already dripping venom.

"Did you think you could trick me, foolish ape?" Set's voice in my head sent a shiver through me. "Did you really believe that your monkey's mind could be superior to mine? Welcome to my fortress, Orion. For the final time!"

If ever my body went into hyperdrive, it was at that instant. I rolled over on my back and kicked my legs over my feet like an acrobat to end up standing on the balls of my feet even as the huge snake sprang at me.

Its first strike fell short because I was no longer where it had expected me to be. But it immediately drew itself together, coiling for another strike as I drew my scimitar from its scabbard. The snake's immense body was thicker than my arm and at least twenty feet long. It hissed and reared back in slow motion, then struck at me again.

This time I was ready. With a two-handed swing I slashed its head from its body and saw it go sailing off slowly into the darkness below. Its decapitated body hit me in the chest, smearing blood on me and staggering me backward several steps. For long moments the headless serpent writhed and twitched while my senses returned to normal and my breathing slowed down.

"How many can you fight, simian?" Set taunted me. "I have an unending source of creatures to do my bidding. How long will your strength last against my legions?"

For a second or two I stood there in the darkness, seeing nothing but the faint glow of the phosphorescent wall's top curving off into the gloom like a softly lighted highway. More snakes were on their way, I knew. And squads of Shaydanians armed with flame rifles or more. All under Set's mental control.

I searched my memory to ascertain exactly where along the wall I stood in relation to the gate. Then I dashed off in the other direction.

I heard bodies stirring in the circular courtyard below. Probably Set's clones rousing themselves to come after me. He had fighting dragons penned down there, too. And sauropods. And human slaves.

All under his control. But could he control them all at the same time?

I reached the spot where I remembered the pterosaurs' roost to be and leaped down into the darkness. Sure enough, I landed only a few feet below in the midst of the sleeping winged lizards. They hissed and squawked and flapped their huge clawed wings as I swung my sword wildly among them, driving them into the air.

With one hand I grabbed the clawed feet of a pterosaur as it launched itself off their roosting platform. I was far too heavy for it to support and we sank, the beast screaming and flapping madly, to the hard-packed earth below. I let go of my animate parachute once I saw the ground below me. I hit with a jarring thump and rolled over; the pterosaur disappeared into the shadows, flapping and wailing like a banshee.

Confusion. I had lost the element of surprise; indeed, I had never had it. But I could cause confusion there in the courtyard. Let's see how firm Set's control is over all his menagerie, I said to myself.

The carnosaurs and sauropods were stomping and hissing in their pens, as if angry at being awakened by the squawking of the pterosaurs. Good! In the dimness of the unlit courtyard I dashed for the carnosaur pens, throwing a mental projection of pain at them as I raced through the shadows.

Their answering screeches was music to my ears. A Shaydanian suddenly appeared out of the darkness before me, flamethrower in his hands. I swung my scimitar overhand, crunching through collarbone and ribs, slicing him open from neck to gut. With my left hand I grabbed his rifle as he fell.

Sheathing my bloody sword, I turned and fired a bolt of flame at the carnosaurs' pens. That panicked them and they smashed through the railings, screeching wildly. A similar blast of flame turned the normally placid sauropods into a maddened herd of thundering brutes that likewise broke free of their enclosures and stampeded across the courtyard.

Total confusion swept the courtyard. Chaos reigned as the Shaydanians stopped trying to find me in their sudden rush to get out of the paths of the frightened dinosaurs that were dashing every which way.

I ran to the barred inner gate where the human slaves were kept and kicked it open. It was totally dark in there, and with the screeching and roaring from the courtyard I would not have been able to hear a brass band playing. I took a step inside and tottered on empty air, tried to recover, and found myself staggering ludicrously down a steep set of stairs into total darkness.

Chapter 37

I fell against a warm body that screamed in the pitch black and flinched away from me.

Human voices muttered in the darkness, some fearful, most groggy with sleep. The place smelled with the fetid stench of sweat and excrement. I nearly gagged, but pulled myself to my feet amid the jostling of other bodies pressed too close together.

"Come with me!" I commanded over the dimmed noise from the courtyard. "Follow me to freedom!"

Someone struck a spark and a tiny lamp flickered to life. I saw that I was in a vast room, far too large for the pitiful lamp to fully illuminate. Crowds of emaciated, grimy, frightened faces peered at me, their eyes red, cheeks hollow, bare skin mottled by the bites of lice and lashes of whips. Jammed together like dumb beasts in some inhuman charnel house, hundreds of men and women blinked unbelievingly at my words. I had no way to tell how many more stood in the dark shadows beyond the lamp's feeble reach.

"Come on!" I shouted. "We're going to get out of here!" And I tossed the flame rifle to the man nearest me. He staggered back a bit, then stared wonderingly at the weapon in his hands.

"Orion!" a young voice shouted. Someone pushed his way through the shadows, jostling the crowd as he struggled toward me. "Orion, it's me! Chron!"

I barely recognized him. He had aged ten years. His body was emaciated, his skin pale and sickly, his eyes sunk deeply into a face that was far too old for his years.

"Chron," I said.

There were tears in his red-rimmed eyes. "I knew you would come. I knew they couldn't kill you."

"It's time to kill the devils!" I snarled. "Let's go!"

I started up the steps, Chron right behind me. Some of them followed us. How many, I neither knew nor cared. Just as I reached the top of the stairs a Shaydanian appeared at the doorway. I thrust my sword through his belly before he had a chance to react. I handed his rifle to Chron. Now we had two.

We burst out into the courtyard where the dinosaurs were milling around, literally shaking the ground with the stamping of their heavy feet. One of the men behind me fired a burst of flame at a Shaydanian. Another bolt of flame seared past me and splashed against the wall. I broadcast mentally to the carnosaurs the image of devouring the Shaydanians, but they seemed more interested in the immense sauropods—their natural prey.

The Shaydanians did not seem to realize that their human slaves were making a break for freedom. Some of them, at least. Glancing over my shoulder, I saw that only a few dozen had followed up the stone steps. The rest must have stayed cowering in their dungeon.

Focusing all my mental energy on one carnosaur, I

drew it to me, snorting as it trotted on its two powerful hind legs. I jumped onto its back and charged into the Shaydanians who were boiling out of a wide double door set into the curving wall.

They fired their rifles at my mount. Screaming with pain and fury, the carnosaur smashed into the grouped Shaydanians, clawing them with his hind feet, crushing the life from them with his terrifying jaws. I slid from the dinosaur's back while it wreaked havoc among Set's clones and picked up four fallen flame rifles.

Racing back to where the humans huddled close to the wall, gaping at the wild melee with round eyes, I handed out the rifles.

Shouting, "Head for the outer gate! Make your way to freedom!" I looked about for another carnosaur to commandeer.

The courtyard was in absolute chaos. Carnosaurs were clawing and snapping at the sauropods, which defended themselves with lashing tails and their own considerable claws. Here a sauropod reared up on its hind legs and ripped a carnosaur with both its forefeet, driven by nearly two tons of bone and sinew. There a carnosaur stood with one massive hind leg firmly clamped on a sauropod's fallen neck, bending down to tear out huge chunks of living flesh with its saw-edged teeth. Screaming and howling tore the night apart, tremendous bodies ran thundering across the courtyard, slamming into its curving wall so hard I thought they would knock it down.

More Shaydanians were pouring out of several doorways now, firing their flame rifles at the enraged dinosaurs. The small band of humans had edged halfway around the wall and were almost at the gate before any of Set's clones realized they were making a break for freedom.

I saw a squad of twenty Shaydanians slinking along the inner perimeter of the wall toward the gate from the opposite side. They could not cut across the courtyard without being trampled by the terrified sauropods or attacked by the ravening carnosaurs.

But I could. I dashed toward the gate, dodging between those mighty brutes, trusting to my speeded-up senses to take me safely through the mad melee. Scimitar in hand, I ran to help the humans I was trying to free.

"Foolish ape," I heard Set snarling at me. "Even if I cannot control all my servants at once, I can control these few well enough to destroy you."

The leader of the Shaydanians stopped his squad with an upraised hand and pointed toward me. As they leveled their rifles at me I desperately dodged behind the massive legs of a sauropod, feeling like a tiny mouse among a herd of madly charging elephants.

I tried to seize control of the sauropod's mind, but Set was there before me. The great beast's bony little head swung around on its long neck and it glowered at me with Set's eyes.

"I will kill you," he seethed in my mind. Somewhere deep inside this fortress Set directed his troops against me, remorseless, untiring. Perhaps he could not control each of his beasts and clones at the same time. But he could concentrate his control wherever he wanted to. Once he had killed me he could restore order to his domain.

The huge beast tried to stomp me beneath its ponderous feet and I had to jump back away from it. A bolt of flame sizzled past, close enough to singe the hair on my arm. I ducked back behind the enormous sauropod as it turned circling to find me and crush me to death. The Shaydanians were firing at me, tongues of flame lancing through the shadows.

They hit the dinosaur instead and it hooted madly with pain. Then I saw one of the humans fire his rifle into the Shaydanians. It was Chron, risking himself to protect me. I felt Set's grip on the sauropod loosen momentarily as he turned his attention to his squad of clones. Ruthlessly grabbed at the beast's dim mind and forced it to charge into the squad even as it began firing back at Chron.

The massive dinosaur lunged at the source of its pain. I felt Set wrenching control of the animal away from me, but too late. Its enormous bulk was too much to turn or even slow down quickly enough. The clones saw nearly two tons of flesh hurtling at them and tried to scatter while they fired their blazing weapons at the beast.

It smashed into the wall in a final fury of pain, screaming like a newborn as half a dozen tongues of flame roasted it from both sides.

I dashed in right behind the sauropod and slashed the life from the first Shaydanian I could reach. The rebelling slaves cut down the part of the squad that had separated to their side of the fallen sauropod. I attacked the other half with my scimitar.

Even in hyperdrive I could not kill them all unscathed. My sword was a blurred gleaming scythe of death, but by the time all the Shaydanians were dead I had taken burn wounds on my legs and chest.

I slumped against the wall and slid down to a sitting position, my chest oozing blood like a rare steak, my legs charred and smoking. Automatically I clamped down on the messages of pain my nerves were screaming at my brain. I deliberately tightened all the blood vessels in the lower part of my body to prevent myself from going into shock.

Inside my head I heard Set's hissing laughter and knew that it was only a matter of moments before he sent more of his clones to finish me off.

The dinosaurs were still shaking the courtyard with their thunderously wild thrashings. The ground shook perceptibly.

More than perceptibly, I realized. The ground was trembling, vibrating as if an earthquake had begun.

"This is the moment I have been waiting for, my love.

Now I strike at the devil's heart!"

It was Anya's voice in my mind.

The earth was quaking, heaving. The circular wall of the courtyard was swaying sinuously like a sheet of cloth caught in a high wind. All the dinosaurs seemed to stop their fighting at once, as if on cue or someone's direction, and made a furious charge for the main gate, the only gate that led out into the open.

I saw the human slaves stand aside near the gate, petrified with terror, as the dinosaurs surged to the gate and smashed it open like cracking an eggshell and poured out into the open countryside.

For an instant all was still. The courtyard was littered with the massive bodies of dead dinosaurs and the red corpses of Set's clones. Then the humans started running through the smashed-open gate to freedom. Most of them. A few dashed back to the dungeon where the others still lay cowering. Within moments the rest of them began to come out of the darkness of their captivity and run, haltingly, for the world outside the wall.

Young Chron ran toward me but I waved him away.

"Get out," I shouted to him. "Get out to the open country where you'll be safe."

"But you—"

"Go! Now! I'll be all right."

He hesitated, then reluctantly turned toward the gate and followed the others out toward safety.

Through all this the ground trembled, then stopped, trembled again and stopped again. Finally the courtyard was empty of every living creature except me. The ground stopped shaking. Silence returned. And the stars shone down out of a cloudless sky.

"Anya," I called aloud. "Are you here?"

"I will be soon, my love. Soon."

I understood what she had done. While the other Creators had assumed their natural form as spheres of pure energy and scattered out among the stars, Anya had hidden herself deep within the earth, waiting.

I wondered if time passed at the same rate for a goddess as it did for a man. She had projected herself back to this point in spacetime to wait for Set's command of his core tap to falter enough for her to seize control of it. My makeshift attack up here in the courtyard had given her the chance. While Set was concentrating on dealing with me, Anya took control of the energy bubbling up from the earth's molten core.

Set himself had shown me how even the Creators could be destroyed once their source of energy was denied them. Anya had taken that lesson and turned it on the devil himself. She had taken over the core tap and was now in the process of dismantling it. His screen that blotted out starlight was already gone.

The ground shook again, harder than before. I could hear the rumbling deep beneath me, like the muttering of some titanic beast. The courtyard was undulating, solid earth surging up and down like the waves of the sea. The circular wall swayed drunkenly. A section of it broke apart and came crashing to the ground.

Still I sat there, trying not to bleed to death, unsure of whether or not I could get to my feet even if I tried. The ground beneath me shuddered even more. The wall at my back quivered and groaned.

And then the middle of the courtyard erupted in a fireball that blinded me, it was so bright. Squinting so hard that tears coursed down my cheeks, I blurrily made out a fountain of red-hot lava erupting from the bowels of the earth, pulsing out waves of heat that seared my face even though I was a good hundred yards away.

"The core tap is destroyed, my love," said Anya's voice. "I can join you now."

"Not before I do," came Set's implacably hate-filled voice.

And out of that bubbling fountain of molten hot lava boiling up from the earth's core stepped the huge red form of Set, looking like evil incarnate, a horned demon whose reptilian eyes glittered with fury and hatred for me.

I grasped the scimitar at my side and tried to push myself up to a standing position. No use. I was too weak to stand, I had lost too much blood.

Set's taloned feet paced closer to me, closer, until he loomed above me, silhouetted against the darkness by the glowing red-hot lava of the molten fountain in the center of the courtyard.

"You have destroyed my world, Orion," his words burned through my mind. "But you have not destroyed *me*. I will destroy you."

He reached down and clenched his clawed fingers around my throat. Lifting me completely off my feet, he began to choke the life out of me. His claws cut into my flesh, my blood flowed over his hands and arms.

I slashed at him with the scimitar, but I was too weak to harm him. His mighty arms protected his chest against my feeble swipes, and his scaly armor was proof against my blade's edge.

Turning with me dangling between his crushing hands, Set paced slowly back to the fountain of fire. My vision was blurring, I could not breathe. The world was going dark.

"You will roast in the flames of agony for all eternity, Orion. I still have enough control over the forces of spacetime to give you the most painful death of all. Burn in hell, Orion! Forever!"

He raised me high above the boiling fountain of lava. I could feel my flesh roasting, bubbling, the pain burning to the core of my mind.

I still held the curved sword in my right hand. Raising it with the last of my strength, I plunged its point into Set's eye and rammed it deep into his brain as hard as I could. I felt the blade grating on the bone of his eye socket, heard him howl with agony and rage.

He tottered but did not ease his grip on my throat. The hot lava seethed against my skin, all I could see was red burning molten lava and Set's even redder face, lips pulled back in a hate-filled snarl, the curved blade of the scimitar sticking out from his eye socket, blood streaming across the glittering red scales of his cheek.

And then a flash of silver blazed before my clouding eyes. Set screamed again and I felt myself whirling through the air. Suddenly the lava was no longer broiling my skin. A gleaming silver globe hovered in midair, a jagged blue-white lightning bolt crackling from its glowing spherical surface, writhing and hissing like an electrical snake clamped to the broad back of Set's scaly body.

A golden globe appeared, and then a pure white one. And one of deepest ruby red, all of them firing twisting, sputtering shafts of electricity into Set's body. He dropped me, screeching and hissing, his tail lashing wildly, his hands clutching at empty air. He staggered backward toward the fountain of lava, his body wrenching and thrashing as his screams pierced through me like hot knives.

More globes appeared, copper and emerald green, bronze and gleaming brass, each of them adding its lightning blast to Set's tortured form, pushing him bodily into the seething fountain of fiery lava.

With a final shriek of agony and despair Set plunged into the bubbling molten metal, the red scales of his body disappearing in the blazing, searing fountain of hell that he himself had created.

Chapter 38

I lay on my burning back, more dead than alive.

The globes of energy hovered around me and took on human forms: Anya, Zeus, red-haired Ares, beautiful Aphrodite, dark-eyed Hera. And the Golden One, of course, looking as smug as ever.

He stepped forward, smiling, his golden mane glowing against the night, a long cloak of gold and white wrapped around his muscular body.

"We've done well," he said cheerfully. "That devil will never bother us again."

"Orion has done well," Anya countered, kneeling beside me on the blood-soaked ground of the courtyard. I felt dizzy, weak. I was consciously suppressing the pain from my burns, yet I knew that my wounds were deep, perhaps fatal. But once she touched my grimy brow with her cool fingers I felt new strength flowing into me.

"Oh, he played his part. It all went according to my plan."

Zeus cocked an eyebrow. "Come now, Aten, if it hadn't been for Orion, we would never have been able to penetrate Set's defenses."

With some vehemence in her voice, Anya added, "Orion distracted the monster long enough for me to take control of his energy source and destroy it."

I looked around the shattered courtyard. Dead carcasses of sauropods and carnosaurs lay like small hills. Bodies of slain Shaydanians sprawled among them. The curving fortress wall was half smashed down. The searing fountain of lava had disappeared.

"It was a time stasis," Anya said to me softly. "Set intended to plunge you into that fountain of hell and leave you in it forever."

"Instead . . ." My voice was a strangled dry croak.

"Instead we pushed him into his own hell," she said. "While you distracted him, we were able to shut off his energy source and return from our hiding places to attack him."

"He's dead."

"He is in stasis," said Zeus. "Roasting for eternity."

Alarmed, I propped myself up on one elbow. "Then he could be released?"

Aten made a sneering smile. "None of *us* will release him! Would you, Orion?"

I shook my woozy head, muttering. "It would have been better to kill him."

"Not so easily done, my love. Be satisfied that we have won."

"Lots of the dinosaurs got loose," I remembered.

"Good hunting for your Mongol friends," said Aten. He pulled his cloak tighter about him. It began to shimmer.

"Wait!" I called.

The Creators looked down at me, their faces curious or annoyed.

"What about Subotai? He is here with only his personal guard, less than a thousand men."

"Quite enough, I should think," said Zeus.

"I promised him that I would bring his entire army here. That means all his people, their women, their flocks and herds, their yurts and all their belongings."

"Why bother?" asked Aten scornfully. "The barbarian general accomplished nothing. He's useless to us."

Struggling up to a sitting position, I answered, "He is my friend. I promised him."

"Ridiculous." Aten sneered.

"That's not for you to decide alone," Anya snapped.

"I'm afraid I agree with Aten," said Zeus. "It would serve no useful purpose."

"It's difficult enough trying to keep the continuum from unraveling," said sharp-featured Hermes. "Why make a change that we don't have to make?"

"I'll do it myself," I said.

They all stared at me.

"You?" Aten laughed. "A toy that I created, acting like a god?"

"Which of you brought Subotai and his thousand men to this time and place?" I demanded.

They glanced around at one another, finally focusing all their glances on Anya.

She shook her head, smiling. "Not I. I was hiding deep underground, waiting for the moment to strike at Set's core tap. The rest of you were scattered among the stars."

"You can't mean that Orion did it himself!" Aten almost shouted.

Anya nodded. "He must have. None of us did."

"I did it myself," I said.

Zeus smiled without humor. "Orion, you are learning the powers of a god."

"There are no gods," I replied grimly. "Only beings such as yourselves—and Set."

They stirred uneasily.

"If Orion wants to bring Subotai's people here, I say he has earned that right," Anya said firmly.

No one contradicted her.

I closed my eyes, grateful for her in so many ways that I could not even begin to count them. In that one fleeting instant I saw history unreeling before me like a spool of film spinning at blurring speed.

I saw Subotai's people settling across this broad grassy savannah that stretched from the Red Sea to the Atlantic.

I saw Mongol warriors spitting carnosaurs on their lances, brown-skinned men in stained leathers and steel helmets, riding tough little Gobi ponies, who would give rise in later generations to splendid tales of knights in shining armor slaying fire-breathing dragons to save enchanted princesses.

I saw those Mongols learning agriculture from the natives of Paradise, intermarrying with them generation after generation as the glaciers retreated northward from Europe, taking the rains with them and turning the broad grasslands into the parched desert called Sahara.

I saw the great-great-grandchildren of Subotai's army moving to the Nile valley, leaving the withering savannah, inventing irrigation and civilization. That made me smile: the so-called barbarian Mongols fathering the earliest civilization on Earth.

And I saw tortured Sheol breathe its final burst of flame and collapse at last into a gaudy ovoid of a planet, spinning madly, striped in brilliant colors, still heated from within by the energy of its final collapse, circled by dozens of fragments of the shattered Shaydan. I knew Zeus would be pleased to have the planet named after him.

And I saw, with a sinking heart, that all the slaughter I had done, the destruction of Sheol and the planet Shaydan, the time of great dying that I had rained upon the earth, the extinction of the dinosaurs and countless other forms of life—all this had been part of the Golden One's plan.

I heard his haughty laughter as I watched once again the reign of death that I had inflicted upon the earth.

"I am evolution, Orion," he boasted. "I am the force of nature."

"All that killing," I heard myself sob.

"It was necessary. My plans span eons, Orion. The dinosaurs were just as great an obstacle to me as they were to Set. They had to be removed, or else I could never have brought the human race into being. *You* wiped them out, Orion. For me! You think you are almost a god, but you are still *my* creature, Orion, my toy. Mine to use as I see fit."

Epilogue

In the timeless city beneath the golden energy dome Anya healed me of my wounds, both physical and spiritual. The other Creators left us alone in that empty mausoleum of a city, alone among the temples and monuments that the Creators had built for themselves.

My burns healed quickly. The gulf between us caused by her seeming betrayal, less so. I realized that Anya had to make me think she had abandoned me, otherwise Set would have seen her trap when he probed my mind. Yet the pain was still there, the awful memory of feeling deserted. As the days quietly passed and the nights, the love we felt for each other slowly began to bridge even that gap.

Anya and I stood on the outskirts of the city before the massive bulk of the enormous pyramid of Khufu, its dazzling white coat of polished limestone gleaming gloriously in the morning light, the great Eye of Amon just starting to form as the sun moved across the sky toward the position that created the shadow sculpture.

I felt restless. Even though we had the entire empty city to ourselves, I could not overcome the uncomfortable feeling that we were not truly alone. The other Creators might be scattered across the universes, striving to maintain the spacetime continuum that they themselves had unwittingly unraveled, yet I had the prickly sensation in the back of my neck that told me we were being watched.

"You are not happy here," Anya said as we walked unhurriedly around the base of the huge, massive pyramid.

I had to admit she was right. "It was better when we were back in the forest of Paradise."

"Yes," she agreed. "I liked it there, too, even though I didn't appreciate it at the time."

"We could go back there."

She smiled at me. "Is that what you wish?"

Before I could answer, a shimmering sphere of glowing gold appeared before us, hovering a few inches above the polished stone slabs that made up the walkway around the pyramid's base. The globe touched lightly on the paving, then contracted to form the human shape of Aten, dressed in a splendid military tunic of metallic gold with a high choker collar and epaulets bearing a sunburst insignia.

"Surely you're not thinking of retiring, Orion," he said, his tone just a shade less mocking than usual, his smile radiating more scorn than warmth.

Turning to Anya, he added, "And you, dearest companion, have responsibilities that cannot be avoided."

Anya moved closer to me. "I am not your 'dearest companion,' Aten. And if Orion and I want to spend some time alone in a different era, what is that to you?"

"There is work to be done," he said, the smile fading, his tone more serious.

He was jealous of me, I realized. Jealous of the love that Anya and I shared.

Then the old smug cynicism came back into his face. He cocked a golden eyebrow at me. "Jealous?" he read my thoughts. "How can a god be jealous of a creature? Don't be ridiculous, Orion."

"Haven't I done enough for you?" I growled. "Haven't I earned a rest?"

"No. And no. My fellow Creators tell me that you have grown much like us in your powers and wisdom. They congratulate me on producing such a useful . . . creature."

He was going to say "toy" until he noticed my fists clenching.

"Well, Orion," he went on, "if you are going to assume godlike powers, then you must be prepared to shoulder godlike responsibilities, just like the rest of us."

"You told me that I was your creature, a tool to be used as you see fit."

He shrugged, glancing at Anya. "It comes out to the same thing. Either you bear responsibilities like the rest of us or you obey my commands. Take your choice."

Anya put her hand on my shoulder. "You have the right to refuse him, my love. You have earned that right."

Smirking, Aten replied, "Perhaps so. But *you*, goddess, cannot evade your responsibilities. No more than I can."

"The continuum can struggle along without me for a while," she said, almost as haughty as Aten himself.

"No, it can't." Suddenly he was utterly serious. "The crisis is real and urgent. The conflict has spread across the stars and threatens the entire galaxy now."

Anya paled. She turned her fathomless silver-gray eyes to me, and I saw real pain in them.

I knew that we could escape to Paradise if we wanted to. To those who can control time, what matter days or years or even centuries spent in one era or another? We could always return to this exact point in spacetime, this individual nexus in the continuum. The crisis that Aten feared would still be waiting for us.

Yet how could we be happy, knowing that our time in Paradise was limited? Even if we remained there for a thousand years, the task awaiting us would loom in our minds like the edge of a cliff, like a sword hanging over our heads.

Before Anya could reply I said, "Paradise will have to wait, won't it?"

She nodded sadly. "Yes, my love. Paradise will have to wait."

Acknowledgments

The epigraphs that begin each section of this novel are from the *Rubaiyat of Omar Khayyam;* "The City in the Sea" by Edgar Allan Poe; *Paradise Lost* by John Milton; and "Ulysses" by Alfred, Lord Tennyson.

The legend of the Light-Stealer and the Punisher is adapted from ideas originally developed by Isaac Asimov in his essay, "Planet of the Double Sun," and is used here with his kind and generous permission.

Afterword

The story of Orion began in my mind many years ago
when I first contemplated the concept that the myths
and legends of ancient times must have been based
on actual persons and events, at least in part.

Gilgamesh, Prometheus, the Phoenix that perishes in
flames yet rises anew from the ashes—how much of these
tales are fanciful elaborations and how much of them are
real? We will never know, of course. The dusty debris of
history has covered up the original events—whether they
were actual adventures of living men and women or the
total invention of some clever moralist.

Be that as it may, the true significance of a myth or
legend lies not in its actuality but in its ability to instruct
and inspire listeners (or readers). Over the course of time
since the development of speech countless human beings
have lived through uncountable adventures. Only a precious few have served as the nuclei for the myths that have
moved all the generations that followed.

As Joseph Campbell and others have pointed out, some myths are universal to all human tribes. They have such a powerful statement to make that every known human society has adapted a variation of the same myth. For example, every culture has a Prometheus myth that tells how a god gave fire to a freezing, starving humankind and how, with fire, humans became almost godlike in their power while their benefactor was punished by his fellow gods.

As I wrote the continuing tale of Orion I found that the story moved between mythology and history, between legend and archeology. In this present volume, the saga moves into realms of natural history, both biological and astronomical.

Underlying all of that, however, is the deeper current of the novels, a level that I had no inkling of when I first began to write of Orion's fantastic adventures. That level is, of course, the relationship of humankind to its gods.

The original novel, *Orion*, was driven by my curiosity about the Neanderthals. Paleontologists have found that there were two fully intelligent species of Homo sapiens on Earth some fifty thousand years ago: the Neanderthals and ourselves. The Neanderthals disappeared, and their disappearance is the subject of that first novel about Orion.

In writing it, however, the deeper theme arose from my subconscious. Given a far-future version of humankind, distant descendants of ours with vastly superior knowledge and technology at their disposal, they could invent the means to travel back through time and create the human race.

They would seem to their creatures as gods. What is more, given that possibility, we no longer need the supernatural gods that populate our religions. We have met our Creator, as Pogo would say, and he is us!

How apt and fitting. Many philosophers and modern-day psychologists have theorized that our gods are the creation of the human mind, an attempt to impose order and justice on a seemingly indifferent universe. Turn the concept full circle and we have human descendants from the distant future creating the human race itself. The gods that people worship have always seemed to have the same foibles and vanities that you and I have. The patriarchal God of the Old Testament appears to me very much like a spoiled, petulant nine-year-old boy. Perhaps that is because the gods are just as human as we.

All it takes is time travel.

Thus we have Orion, a human being purposely built by such a Creator to serve and obey, a hunter who was created to find and kill the enemies of his Creator. In time he begins to realize that the so-called gods are as human and fallible as he is himself. In time he begins to learn how to be a god himself. Or tries to.

Orion, then, is humankind's representative, attempting to understand what the gods demand of him. Each step forward in his understanding brings him a step closer to godhood—a progress that some of the "gods" approve of, while others do not.

So much for the underlying tensions that drive the saga of Orion. Now for the particulars of this novel.

Among the myths that every human culture seems to share there is the myth of supernatural beings who are entirely evil: devils, demons, the Satan and Beelzebub that Dante and Milton wrote of. Their descriptions have always seemed decidedly reptilian to me.

To create a satanic reptile for this novel meant that I had to deal with the possibility of a species of reptile that is fully as intelligent as H. sapiens. No, actually my Set—to give him his ancient Egyptian name—would have to be as intelligent as my fictitious Creators, the godlike human descendants from our future.

For years I have been intrigued by the possibility of

reptilian intelligence. Intelligent lizards are an old standby of science fiction, including my very first published novel of thirty years ago. Yet it always seemed unlikely to me that reptiles could be intelligent, regardless of their utility as "alien" creatures for science-fiction tales.

In the past decade several paleontologists have suggested that if the dinosaurs had not been extinguished in the great wave of extinctions that swept the earth some sixty-five million years ago, they might ultimately have given rise to an intelligent species. Dale A. Russell, of the Canadian National Museum of Natural Sciences at Ottawa, is the leading champion of this idea. He proposes that a small Cretaceous bipedal carnosaur, *Stenonychosaurus inequalus*, might have evolved into a big-brained, erect-walking intelligent reptile, given time.

Yet it seemed to me that time and brain size were not the only requirements for the development of intelligence. Intelligence requires interaction among individuals, communication. Had Albert Einstein been left in a wilderness at birth and never met another human being, he would never have developed the ability to speak, let alone do physics.

Most modern reptile species lay their eggs and never return to them, leaving the hatchlings to fend for themselves. So did most of the dinosaurs, although at least one species of duckbilled dinosaurs apparently cared for their young. For this novel I proposed that the reptilians that evolved on the fictitious planet Shaydan orbiting the equally fictitious star Sheol evolved intelligence through motherly care and a form of telepathy.

The telepathy is something of a cheat, I admit. But think of your own childhood experiences. Did not your mother have moments of startling telepathic powers?

The astronomical setting for this novel is accurate—up to a point. It is entirely possible to "rebuild" the solar system with a small unstable dwarf star at the same distance from the sun that the planet Jupiter is now. The gravitational perturbations on the earth and the other inner planets of our solar system would be negligible. The sun's companion star could have one or more planets orbiting around it, just as the planet Jupiter now possesses sixteen or more moons.

Ask any astronomer, though, and he or she will tell you that there is no way Jupiter could be the remnant of a star that exploded. No natural way, is what they implicitly are saying. For the novelist, however, it is possible to use deliberate changes caused by forces other than blind nature. In this novel the dwarf star Sheol evolves into our familiar planet Jupiter through the determined efforts of Orion and the Creators.

The breakup of Sheol's one planet causes a rain of meteors on Earth that triggers the Time of Great Dying, the titanic wave of extinctions that wiped out not merely the dinosaurs but thousands of other species of land, sea, and air some sixty-five millions years ago. The end of the Cretaceous saw the slate of life on Earth wiped almost clean.

The nearly emptied world that existed after the great Cretaceous calamity contained abundant empty ecological niches that new forms of life could move into. The age of mammals began, leading ultimately to the earliest hominids.

A great cataclysm did indeed shake the earth some sixty-five million years ago. It *caused* the end of the Cretaceous Period, just as a similar disaster some two hundred fifty million years ago caused the end of the Permian Period and led to the rise of the dinosaurs.

The dinosaurs began in a planetwide catastrophe that scrubbed away more than half the species then occupying the earth. They died in a paroxysm of similar proportions. The available evidence strongly points to a bombardment of meteors and/or comets that was either accompanied by or actually triggered tectonic shifts of the landmasses that altered sea levels and climate all around the globe.

Stephen Jay Gould and his fellow biologists tell us that these disasters were works of blind nature, brief moments in the grand flow of the eons that forced evolution into new pathways. To the novelist, however, it is irresistibly tempting to assign these evolutionary forces to purposeful characters. It makes for a much more interesting story. It allows us to contemplate the works of nature in moral terms. It turns the blindly uncaring forces of nature into *choices* made by thinking, feeling characters who know the differences between good and evil.

For myself, I think there is probably much more to the Time of Great Dying than a cataclysmic rain of fire from the heavens, dramatic though that may be. As the Cretaceous was nearing its end a new form of life arose on Earth: a life-form so ubiquitous and lowly that we seldom give it much thought unless we are forced to deal with it directly. That life-form is grass.

Grasses are one of the most successful forms of life on Earth. All the cereal grains that feed humankind are types of grasses, for example. They first appeared on Earth in the late Cretaceous and shouldered earlier forms of vegetation out of existence.

Did grass kill the dinosaurs? Animals that feed on grasses today are equipped with very specialized teeth and digestive systems to crop and metabolize a food that contains a high percentage of tough silica. Could the herbivorous dinosaurs handle the grasses that replaced the earlier vegetation? If they could not and starved, the carnivorous dinosaurs that preyed on the herbivores would have died off, too.

This is mere speculation, however. And it does not explain why so many other life-forms—from plankton to plesiosaurs—died off at the same time. Yet it is instructive to consider that the so-called Time of Great Dying was also a period of birth for new life-forms, the grasses in particular.

So much for what we know of paleontology, and what we speculate. This book is a novel, a work of fiction, and of science fiction at that.

The basic scientific underpinning for this tale is as sound as careful research can make it, although I have taken liberties with agreed-upon scientific canon where I felt it necessary for the sake of the story. As I have throughout all of Orion's adventures, I have endeavored to use the stuff of myth and legend as a means to explore the human soul; more particularly, to explore the relationship of humankind and its gods.

With an exploding star and a shattered planet we link astronomical events with death and birth on Earth. Intelligent reptiles give rise to the legends of devils that haunt the dark hours of every human culture. Dinosaurs that somehow survived into prehistoric human times lead to our legends of dragons.

And a single human being, created to obey the whims of the gods, strives not merely to survive but to understand, not blindly to obey but to learn how to be a god himself.

These are the ingredients of science fiction. The science must be accurate, yet the author must be free to invent new possibilities—as long as no one can show that they are totally impossible in the real world. The characters must be believable, no matter how fantastic their adventures. They must feel and love and bleed even as you and I do, otherwise we do not have a story to read, we have a treatise.

This is what I am trying to do with these tales of Orion. His story is not completed yet.

Ben Bova
West Hartford, Connecticut

THE DRAGON REBORN

Sequel to *The Great Hunt*

Book Three of *The Wheel of Time*

by

Robert Jordan

Praise for *Eye of the World*

"A powerful vision of good and evil...fascinating people moving through a rich and interesting world."   —Orson Scott Card

"Richly detailed...fully realized, complex adventure."
    —*Library Journal*

"A combination of Robin Hood and Stephen King that is hard to resist...Jordan makes the reader care about these characters as though they were old friends."   —*Milwaukee Sentinel*

Praise for *The Great Hunt*

"Jordan can spin as rich a world and as event-filled a tale as [Tolkien]...will not be easy to put down."   —*ALA Booklist*

"Worth re-reading a time or two."   —*Locus*

"This is good stuff...Splendidly characterized and cleverly plotted...The Great Hunt is a good book which will always be a good book. I shall certainly [line up] for the third volume."
    —*Interzone*

The Dragon Reborn

coming in hardcover in August, 1991

THE BEST OF BEN BOVA

☐ ☐	53217-1	THE ASTRAL MIRROR	$2.95 Canada $3.50
☐ ☐	51300-2	BATTLE STATION	$3.95 Canada $4.95
☐ ☐	53245-7	COLONY	$3.95 Canada $4.95
☐ ☐	50319-8	CYBERBOOKS	$4.50 Canada $5.50
☐ ☐	53212-0	ESCAPE PLUS	$2.95 Canada $3.50
☐ ☐	53243-0	THE KINSMAN SAGA	$4.95 Canada $5.95
☐ ☐	53225-2	THE MULTIPLE MAN	$2.95 Canada $3.95
☐ ☐	53210-4	OUT OF THE SUN	$2.95 Canada $3.50
☐ ☐	50238-8	PEACEKEEPERS	$4.95 Canada $5.95
☐ ☐	53205-8	PRIVATEERS	$3.95 Canada $4.95

Buy them at your local bookstore or use this handy coupon:
Clip and mail this page with your order.

Publishers Book and Audio Mailing Service
P.O. Box 120159, Staten Island, NY 10312-0004

Please send me the book(s) I have checked above. I am enclosing $ _____
(please add $1.25 for the first book, and $.25 for each additional book to cover postage and handling.
Send check or money order only—no CODs).

Name _____
Address _____
City _____ State/Zip _____
Please allow six weeks for delivery. Prices subject to change without notice.